Praise

"One of the most original practitioners writing
any kind of fiction."
—*The Sunday Times* (London)

The Machiavelli Covenant

"A major production."
—*The New York Times*

"More than a thriller, *The Machiavelli Covenant*
is superb suspense, suberbly written . . .
Folsom's best so far."
—Stephen Coonts,
New York Times bestselling author of
Final Flight

"Folsom writes white-hot page-turners, guaranteed
to singe your fingers and fry your hair."
—Douglas Preston,
New York Times bestselling author of *Impact*

The Exile

"Folsom can flat-out write an action scene."
—*Kirkus Reviews*

"Hold on tight—from the first scene Folsom
spins a tale of page-turning suspense."
—W. E. B. Griffin

Days of Confession

"Fast . . . Tense . . . A gripping thriller."
—*The Denver Post*

"As thrilling and as action-packed as
The Day After Tomorrow."
—*Fort Worth Daily Sun*

"A real page-turner . . . Unexpected twists
and turns abound."
—BPI Entertainmet Newswire

"Folsom is an enthusiastic storyteller with a talent
for vivid characterization on a big canvas."
—*Chicago Times*

The Day After Tomorrow

"A heart-thumping, stay-up-late novel . . . Wild,
unputdownable . . . Brilliant."
—*Los Angeles Times Book Review*

"A chilling jigsaw puzzle . . . This thriller doesn't
leap out of the starting gate—it's catapulted!"
—*The Cleveland Plain Dealer*

"Big, juicy . . . Delivers a lot of bang for the buck."
—*Chicago Tribune*

"A thriller that doesn't quit."
—*Cosmopolitan*

THE
HADRIAN
MEMORANDUM

—⧟—

BOOKS BY ALLAN FOLSOM

• • •

The Day After Tomorrow
Day of Confession
*The Exile**
*The Machiavelli Covenant**
*The Hadrian Memorandum**

*Denotes a Tom Doherty Associates book

THE
HADRIAN
MEMORANDUM

ALLAN FOLSOM

A TOM DOHERTY ASSOCIATES BOOK • NEW YORK

NOTE: If you purchased this book without a cover, you should be aware that this book is stolen property. It was reported as "unsold and destroyed" to the publisher, and neither the author nor the publisher has received any payment for this "stripped book."

This is a work of fiction. All of the characters, organizations, and events portrayed in this novel are either products of the author's imagination or are used fictitiously.

THE HADRIAN MEMORANDUM

Copyright © 2009 by Allan Folsom

All rights reserved.

A Tor Book
Published by Tom Doherty Associates, LLC
175 Fifth Avenue
New York, NY 10010

www.tor-forge.com

Tor® is a registered trademark of Tom Doherty Associates, LLC.

ISBN 978-0-7653-6133-2

First Edition: October 2009
First Mass Market Edition: December 2010

Printed in the United States of America

0 9 8 7 6 5 4 3 2 1

AUTHOR'S NOTE

The Hadrian Memorandum was completed before the massive BP oil disaster in the Gulf of Mexico. Tragically, it makes our story even more poignant and immediate than it was at the time of writing and underscores our responsibility as inhabitants and caretakers of this planet to rapidly find a workable substitute for fossil fuels and end our unprecedented reliance upon them.

Allan Folsom
Santa Barbara, California

For Karen and Riley,
and in memory of Julian Ludwig and Kris Kristy

THE
HADRIAN
MEMORANDUM

1

Nicholas Marten knew they were being watched. But by whom or how many, there was no way to tell. He glanced at Father Willy Dorhn, his walking companion, as if for an answer, but the tall, razor-thin, seventy-eight-year-old German-born priest said nothing. They kept on, ducking through overgrowth, crossing narrow, fast-running streams, following a dense, nearly invisible trail that snaked through the rain forest.

Now the track turned upward and they climbed higher. It was hot, easily a hundred degrees, maybe more. The humidity made it seem worse. Marten wiped sweat from his neck and forehead, then swatted at the cloud of mosquitoes that had haunted them from the start. Every piece of clothing stuck to him. The stench of plant life was overwhelming, like an intense perfume from which there was no escape. The sharp cries of tropical birds rang through the leafy, sun-blocking canopy above, far louder and more shrill than he imagined any natural sound could be. Still Father Willy, Willy as he'd asked to be called, said nothing, just continued on, walking a trail he plainly knew so well from his half century on the island that his feet seemed to make all the decisions.

Finally he spoke. "I don't know you at all, Mr. Marten," he said without looking at him. Spanish was the official language of Equatorial Guinea, but he used English when talking to Marten. "Soon I will have to decide if I can trust you. I hope you understand."

"I understand," Marten said, and they hiked on. Minutes passed, and then he heard a low, rumbling sound he couldn't place. Little by little it intensified, drowning out the sounds of the birds and becoming very nearly a roar. Then he knew. Waterfalls! In the next seconds they rounded a bend in the trail and stopped before a cascade of falls that thundered past them in a rising mist to disappear into the jungle a thousand feet below. Willy stared at the spectacle for a long moment, then slowly turned to Marten.

"My brother told me you were coming, to expect you," he said over the roar of the water. "Yet he has never met you. Never talked with you. So whether you are the man he told me about or someone else who has taken his place, I have no way to know."

"All I can tell you," Marten said, "is that I was asked to come to see you. To listen to what you have to say and then to go home. I know very little more than that, except that you think there is trouble here."

The priest studied Marten carefully, still unsure of him. "Where is this 'home'?"

"A city in the north of England."

"You are American."

"Was. I'm an expat. I carry a British passport."

"You are a reporter."

"A landscape architect."

"Then why you?"

"A friend who indirectly knows your brother asked me to come."

"What friend?"

"Another American."

"He is a reporter."

"No, a politician."

Willy's eyes found Marten's and held there. "Whoever you are, I will have to trust you, because I fear my time is increasingly short. Besides, there is no one else."

"You can trust me," Marten said, and then looked around. They seemed wholly alone, yet he still had the sense they were being watched.

"They have gone," Willy said quietly. "Fang tribesmen. Good friends. They followed us for a time until I assured them I was alright. They will make certain no one else comes." Abruptly he reached inside his priest's frock and took out a letter-sized envelope. He flicked it open, slid out several folded pages and held them unopened in his hand. "What do you know of Equatorial Guinea?"

"Not much. Just what I read on the plane. It's a small, very poor country run by a dictator-president named Francisco Tiombe. In the last decade oil was discovered and—"

"Francisco Tiombe," Willy cut him off angrily, "is the head of a brutal, ruthless family who consider themselves royal but are not. Tiombe killed the former president, his own cousin, in order to gain power and reap the riches from oil leases. And rich he is, enormously rich. He recently bought a mansion in California for forty million U.S. dollars, and that is only one of a half dozen he has around the world. The trouble is he has chosen not to share that wealth with the masses who remain poorer than poor." Willy's passion grew deeper.

"They have nothing, Mr. Marten. The few jobs, when they can find them, are pennies-a-day labor and selling what little food they can grow or fish they can catch. Safe drinking water is like gold and is sold as if it were. Electricity, in the villages that have it, goes on, then off. Mostly it is off. Medical facilities are laughable. Schools barely exist. For any kind of decent life at all, there is no hope." Willy's eyes bore into Marten. "People are angry. Violence has flared often and is getting worse. Government troops react to it with savage, repeated, unspeakable cruelty. So far it has been limited to the mainland and nothing has yet happened in Bioko, but fear is in the air everywhere and people are certain it will soon spread here. At the same time, there has been a large influx of oil workers. Most are from an American company called AG Striker. It is as if something big is happening or is about to happen, but no one knows what it is. Because of the violence, Striker has brought in mercenary soldiers from a private military company known as SimCo to protect its people and facilities."

Suddenly Willy held up the pages he'd taken from

the envelope and one by one opened them. They were color photographs printed on computer paper with an electronic date stamp in the lower right-hand corner. The first showed the main entry to a large oil exploration work area. The grounds were enclosed by a high chain-link fence topped with razor wire. Armed, uniformed men stood guard at the entry gate.

"These are local men, lucky enough to have been hired and trained to guard the compound by the mercenaries. If you look carefully"—Willy slid a thin forefinger across the photograph to pinpoint two muscular Caucasian men with buzz-cut hair, wearing tight black T-shirts, camouflage pants, and wraparound sunglasses standing in the background—"these are two of the SimCo men who trained them. Here is a computer-enhanced closer look at them." Willy showed Marten the second page.

The two men were seen clearly. The first was big and brawny and had singularly flat ears that barely stuck out from his head. The second was thin and wiry and noticeably taller.

"I have been an amateur photographer for more than seventy years. In that time I have eagerly stayed abreast of the most current technology. My camera is digital. When the electricity comes I transfer the images to my computer and make prints like these. I have taught many in the local community about photography."

"I don't understand."

"One night a young native boy asked to borrow

my camera. He had done it before, and so I let him take it again. Then I became curious about what he was doing and asked him. 'Big bird in jungle,' he said, 'come very early almost every day to different places. Tomorrow I know where it come.' What kind of big bird? I asked. He said, 'Come and see,' and I went with him."

Now Willy opened the third folded page. It was a photograph of a jungle-green, unmarked helicopter set down in a forest clearing at daybreak. Several men were in the doorway helping unload crates to a half-dozen natives who, in turn, were loading them into an old open-bed truck.

Willy showed Marten the next photograph. A close-up of two of the men in the helicopter doorway.

"Same men guarding the oil interests," Marten said.

"Yes."

Willy's fingers slid open the next photograph: an enhanced close-up of the truck revealing supplies that had been opened for inspection. Clearly seen was a case of assault rifles, another with ammunition, another with a dozen or more three- to four-foot-long tubular pieces that looked like handheld rocket grenade launchers, and several cases of what appeared to be the rockets themselves. In the upper right-hand corner, another man, a third Caucasian in black T-shirt and camouflage fatigues, was clearly seen. He was tall with short hair and chiseled features and was a good ten years older than the first two.

"The guns are AK-47s. The natives are Fang and Bubi tribesmen involved in a growing, organized insurrection against the government. Already more than six hundred people have been killed, mostly natives but also a small number of oil people."

"You mean the same men hired to protect the oil workers are arming a revolt against them?" Marten was astonished.

"So it seems."

"Why?"

"It's not for me to say, Mr. Marten. But I would assume it is the reason you have come. To find out." Suddenly Willy took a cigarette lighter from his jacket. "I gave up smoking thirty-two years, four months, and seven days ago. The lighter still gives me comfort." Abruptly his thumb slid over the top of it. There was a click and flame burst from its snout. Seconds later the paper photographs flared up. As quickly Willy dropped them on the ground and watched them turn to ash, then he looked to Marten.

"It's time we go back. I have evening services." Abruptly he turned and led Nicholas Marten back down the trail the way they had come.

Some twenty minutes later they neared the end of it. They could see the dirt road they had walked up from the village and the steeple of Willy's small wooden church reaching over the tree line. Overhead, a monkey swung from tree limb to tree limb. Another followed. Then both stopped and looked down at the men below, chattering wildly as they did. Tropical birds screeched in reply, and for a moment the entire rain forest seemed to come alive at fever pitch. As quickly it stopped. A few seconds later heavy rain began to fall. Another thirty and it became a torrential downpour.

Then they were at trail's end turning onto the road that had now turned to mud. For the first time since they left the cascade of falls Willy spoke.

"I trusted you, Mr. Marten, because I had to. I could not give you the photographs because there is no way to know who you might run into when we part. Hopefully, you have clear memories of what you have seen and what I have told you. Take that information with you and leave Bioko as quickly as you can. My brother is in Berlin. He is a very capable man. I hope that by the time you reach him neither he nor your American politician friend will have need for you to tell them any of this. Tell them anyway. Perhaps something can be done before it is too late. Purposeful war is being made here, Mr. Marten, for reasons I don't know. There will be more of it, and with it will come terrible bloodshed and immense suffering. Of that I am certain."

"Padre! Padre!" The voices of alarmed children suddenly rang out of nowhere. The men looked up to see two tribal boys, maybe ten or twelve years old, running toward them down the mud-slick road.

"Padre! Padre!" They cried out again in unison. "Padre! Padre!" At the same time the sharp crackle of automatic-weapons fire erupted from the direction of the village behind them.

"Oh Lord, no!" Willy spat loudly and started toward the children as rapidly as his aging body would take him. In the next instant an open-bed army truck filled with heavily armed troops came around a bend. A second truck was right behind it. Marten started after him on the dead run. Father Willy must have sensed what he was doing because he suddenly turned and looked back, his eyes wide with fear.

"No!" he yelled. "Go back! Tell them what you have seen! Run! Into the jungle! Run for your life!"

2

Marten hesitated, then turned and ran, rushing madly through the tropical downpour and back up the trail he and Willy had come down only moments earlier. Seconds later he pulled off it and ducked into an undergrowth of huge ferns to look back.

What he saw sickened him. The first army truck slid to a stop just as Father Willy reached the young boys. Immediately soldiers jumped from it. As they did, Willy stepped in front of the boys, trying to protect them. In answer, a rifle butt was slammed against his head. The boys screamed as he fell and tried to fight the soldiers. Simultaneous rifle butts hit the first boy in the face. Two more hit the second; one in the face, the other at the back of his head as he fell. Then the motionless figures of all three were picked up and thrown facedown onto the truck bed. At the same time, the other army truck swerved around the first, raced toward the place where Marten and Father Willy had parted, and stopped. Immediately twenty or more soldiers leapt from it and started fast up the trail toward the place where Marten hid.

"Christ!" he breathed and pushed wildly from his hiding place, running back up the jungle path three hundred yards ahead of them at best. In seconds he realized he was leaving tracks in the mud. He looked left, then right, then picked a spot, and plunged off the trail into heavy undergrowth, his sudden move startling monkeys and tropical birds and sending them into a screaming fit in the trees above.

He ran on. Thirty feet, forty, fifty. Suddenly he stopped short. There was nothing before him but impenetrable rain forest, all of it thick as a carpet. He turned around. There was nowhere to go but back the way he had come.

He'd covered less than half the distance to the main trail when he heard them coming. They were moving hard and fast and jabbering in Spanish.

Abruptly their talking stopped and the sounds of them moving died out. The monkeys and birds stopped, too. So did Marten. Except for the rain, the jungle was silent. He held his breath. They were close and listening. He inched backward, his eyes locked on the foliage in front of him, feeling his way over the sodden ground. Then he heard someone shout, and the place where he had turned off the trail exploded with rushing men. They had found his track.

Marten whirled and raced through the tangle of

growth in front of him. The rain came down harder, all but drowning out the shouts of his pursuers. He clambered over a rotting log, jerked apart a curtain of low-hanging vines, and slipped through it. The pounding of his heart roared over everything else. He didn't have a chance and he knew it. God help him when they got him.

The rain and mud made footing next to impossible. He slid and started to fall, then recovered and looked back. He could see the first group clearly. There were three of them. Forty feet behind him at best. Big, powerful black men in jungle camouflage uniforms. Razor-sharp machetes flailing the thick growth before them. Then the lead man saw him and they locked eyes.

"There he is!" he yelled in Spanish, and they surged forward.

Those eyes—homicidal and utterly merciless—and the determination behind them were the most frightening thing Marten had ever seen. In that instant he knew that if they caught him he wouldn't just be killed, he'd be butchered on the spot.

He ran on, the jungle as thick as a web around him, as if the rain forest itself had joined the enemy. Behind him came more shouts and then more still. They were closing in, and fast.

"My God," he breathed. "My God!"

His lungs were on fire; his legs had nothing left. He was starting to turn, to look back, more out of instinct than anything else, when suddenly the ground gave way beneath him. In a blink he was plummeting down a steep embankment. Trees, ferns, vines, foliage of every kind flew past. He tried to dig in his heels, to get some kind of purchase that would slow him. At the same time, he reached out, frantically trying to grab hold of anything that would break his fall. Nothing did. The rain-soaked soil was so slick it might well have been ice. He went faster. Then faster still.

Suddenly his right arm circled a vine, and he pulled it in tight. There was a wrenching jolt and he stopped, face up against the sky. For the briefest moment he clung there, the tropical rain washing over him. Then he let out a huge breath and looked down. His legs stretched out over nothing. He had come that close to going over the edge and plunging into whatever was below. He flashed on the cascade of falls he'd seen when he'd been with Father Willy less than an hour before. Remembered looking down and seeing them disappear into the jungle floor a thousand feet beneath. If that was the terrain here, he had come within inches of his death.

Suddenly his chest heaved and he made some kind of animal cry, half sheer horror and half release. From somewhere far above he heard the voices of the soldiers. They were rough and raw and urgent. He had no idea how far he had fallen or if there was a way they could work around and come at him from the side or if they had ropes and would just rappel down to where he was.

He looked to his left and saw another vine. Beyond it was another. If he could use them to move across the face of the cliff or steep hillock or whatever it was, maybe he could find solid footing on the other side. If so, he might work his way into the jungle and hide there until darkness came. Something, he estimated, that would occur in no more than two hours.

He took a deep breath and grasped the vine tightly. Another breath and he swung toward the one just beyond it. He reached it and grabbed hold, then carefully tested its strength. Satisfied, he let go of the first vine. He repeated the procedure once and then again. Now he could see his destination, the edge of the ravine into which he had fallen. The rain came down harder. If the soldiers were still up there, he had no way to know.

Another breath and he swung again, almost reaching the far side before the momentum pulled him back. He tested the vine and swung once more. Closer this time, but not quite. Another swing and he almost had it, his fingers brushing the shrubbery that lined the edge before his momentum carried him back.

"Easy," he breathed and swung again. This time he went a little further. The shrubs were right there. He reached out, grabbed hold of the closest plant, and—suddenly there was a sickening jolt as the vine pulled free of the soil above. For a moment he hung in midair; then came a shower of rocks and mud and he plunged backward into nothing.

He heard himself scream as he fell. For a second he thought he saw water, a fast-rushing stream cutting through the jungle far beneath him. He kept falling and falling. Then he hit something hard and everything went black.

3

Seconds or minutes or days passed before Marten opened his eyes and looked up. He was alive, he thought, and wet and moving. The night sky above, what little he could see of it through the thick canopy of trees, was bright and starlit. Then he realized that he was in a river of some kind and the current was carrying him downstream.

It was then he remembered Father Willy and the photographs and the soldiers, his mad escape through the jungle, the vine and its pulling free, his terrifying fall. The thing he had hit hard, that had knocked him unconscious, had been the river; water, so delicate while drinking or bathing, so like concrete when your body hits it at high speed and from a distance. And now, so obstinate when you tried to navigate through it. What he had to do was to swim to one shore or another, then take stock and see if he was really alive or if this was all some kind of dream after death and the place he was trying to navigate was the netherworld.

• Thursday, June 3. 12:12 A.M.

Marten read the illuminated face of his watch. Somehow he had reached the riverbank and crawled up it in the dark. How far he had come he didn't know. His only reference was the sound of rushing water not far away. For a long time he lay there doing little more than breathing. Then slowly, deliberately, he moved his right arm and then his left. Then one leg and then the other. Each move had hurt, but as far as he could tell nothing was broken. Now he took stock of the rest. There was a long raw scrape on his right leg that ran from just below his knee to his ankle. His left elbow and forearm were raw as well, the same as his forehead at the hairline. His lightweight tropical shirt and trousers were both torn but serviceable; his travel pouch that held his passport and small travel wallet around his neck was still there. His hiking boots, while soaked through, were still on his feet.

He sat up and listened, wondering if the soldiers had been able to follow him. If they were out there now in the dark, closing in through the thick growth of the jungle that lined the riverbank. He heard nothing but the distant chatter of a night bird. Again he looked up through the trees. As before, he saw starlit sky. Then the thought came that he had no idea where he was or which way the river flowed, east or west, north or south.

Bioko, he knew, was an island in the Gulf of Guinea. That meant that whatever waterway he had been swept along would eventually run into another, larger channel that would lead to another and then to the sea itself. If he could follow it and reach the shore he might find a village that had a boat he could hire that would take him north to the capital city of Malabo and the Hotel Malabo, where he'd left his things and where he might learn the fate of Father Willy, and then, as quickly as possible, get on a flight back to Europe.

Marten pushed himself to his feet and walked

twenty or so yards back to the river's edge. Judging the direction of the current, he moved off in the dark, hugging the riverbank and following it toward what he hoped would be the sea.

4

• SimCo Headquarters. Malabo. 12:23 A.M.

The always punctual Conor White sat in the small darkened office near the front of the large motor home that served as both his temporary company headquarters and, in the rear, his private living area. His computer screen aglow in front of him, he waited for twelve twenty-five, the time his party in Virginia would be ready to receive the secure e-mail he was about to send.

• 12:24 A.M.

White tapped his fingers in anticipation. They'd lost power earlier in the evening because of the storm that had twisted over the island, coming on land in the south and then retreating back to sea only to slam into the north several hours later. Immediately the SimCo compound's backup generator had kicked in. Then the power had come back on and the generator had been shut down. None of this was new to Conor White, president and CEO of SimCo, the man in charge of the private security company's four-hundred-man armed force in Equatorial Guinea and its seventy-man contingent in Iraq. At forty-five, the powerfully built, six-foot-four White, with his chiseled good looks and dark razor-cut hair, could still be a model for the modern professional mercenary soldier. A former colonel in the British army's SAS—the Special Air Service Regiment—he'd formed his first private military security firm, Argosy International, eight years earlier in the Netherlands, selling it as a "military security company" that provided what he referred to as "operational support to legitimate governments and companies around the world." Since then he'd built Argosy into a thousand-employee firm with satellite bases in five different countries.

Then, a little more than a year earlier, at the urging of Josiah Wirth, chairman and chief executive of the Texas-based oil and energy company AG Striker, and Loyal Truex, former U.S. Army Ranger and founder and head of Hadrian Worldwide Protective Services Company, the world's largest private military organization, he'd abruptly sold his interest in Argosy. Shortly afterward he formed the Bristol, England–based SimCo LLC, a smaller, far more agile military security company where the emphasis was narrowed to "providing protective security services to major companies doing business in underdeveloped regions of the globe." Less than a month later, SimCo signed a long-term contract with Striker to provide those same services for the AG Striker Company in Equatorial Guinea. Ten days after that, White signed a separate contract for SimCo to provide operational support to Hadrian in Iraq, where it had long been Striker's chief private defense contractor under an agreement between Striker and the U.S. Department of Defense.

It was to Hadrian's Loyal Truex that Conor White waited to send his urgent and necessarily secure postmidnight e-mail. Another man might have been nervous about what he had to report; he wasn't. As far as he was concerned he was in the middle of a war, and war was not only deadly but often troublesome and, these days especially, highly unpredictable. Moreover, he had been and still was a highly trained professional soldier. He acted accordingly.

• 12:25 A.M.

He pressed the pound sign on the keyboard. Immediately a message flashed on the screen in front of him: YOUR LXT DIGITAL IS ACTIVATED. PLEASE ENTER YOUR PERSONAL CODE.

White's fingers reached out, and he entered the code. Instantly the words LOCK FUNCTION appeared on his screen. It meant the transmission line from Conor White, SimCo/Malabo, Equatorial Guinea, to LoyalTruex, Hadrian/Manassas, Virginia, was secure.

Immediately he typed in the following: We've got a potential bad one. There are photographs of our guys unloading arms to the rebels.

Two seconds passed, then Truex replied.
Photographs?

CONOR WHITE: Yeah. Clear as day. No doubt about who our guys are if somebody wanted to examine it. I'm included with the other ops. I've seen several of the pics myself, computer-printed hard copies. They were taken last week. All have date codes.

LOYAL TRUEX: *Have the photos been distributed?*

CW: Not that we know. The copies I saw were brought to our guys in the field by a local native who wanted to sell them.

LT: *Who took them?*

CW: Old German priest in Bioko. The army got him, he's in a coma. His place was searched. His printer found and destroyed. Digital camera found, too. Only camera he had. No photographs, no extra prints discovered. The memory card was new. The old one with the photos is missing.

LT: *What if he e-mailed the pictures somewhere?*

CW: There is no Internet connection in Bioko South, where he lived. To send them he would have had to use an E.G. government, Striker, or SimCo facility in Malabo, only places that have IT connections. He didn't.

LT: *Camera cell phone transmission?*

CW: His only cell phone was old. Had no camera technology. Cell transmission from Bioko South is unreliable anyway.

LT: *He could have faxed the printer copies.*

CW: Fax machine was found in his office, broken. Two more in the village. Both checked for recent communication. None in six months for one, three months for the other. Both destroyed. Owners now deceased. Ongoing check for more machines in surrounding villages. More—local telephone company records accessed. So far no fax or cell-photo transmissions to anywhere other than E.G. in last six weeks. Locals under us checking number by number now. Sense nothing sent, area still too primitive.

LT: *What about regular mail service? He could have mailed them.*

CW: Mail service from the south is erratic at best. Pickups would have gone to central post office in Malabo. Only possible tracking was if he sent them via registered mail. There is no record that he did. If he did send them via regular mail, they would be impossible to trace.

LT: *CRITICAL—retrieve and destroy photographic evidence of any kind. Paper, electronic, etc. MOST IMPORTANT—locate, retrieve, and destroy the camera's ORIGINAL MEMORY CARD. Locate and destroy any local computer or printer that might have copies on the hard drive or memory. FURTHER: Find and challenge ANYONE who might have seen the photos. Find out what they know/who they might have talked to and act accordingly. If any of this gets out it could shift the Ryder Commission spotlight directly to E.G., then swing it right back to Iraq. DO WHAT NEEDS TO BE DONE AND DO IT FAST. PAY WHATEVER IT COSTS. LEAVE NO TRAIL. We can't have any of this go public.*

CW: Wilco. As stated, retrieval process already under way.

LT: *Keep me posted.*

With that Loyal Truex signed off, leaving Conor White alone to breathe and reflect in the darkened cabin of his SimCo motor home.

"Right," he said finally, his accent clearly upper-class British boarding school.

He'd known Loyal Truex since the First Gulf War when British SAS and U.S. Army Ranger advance teams went deep behind enemy lines to gather intelligence on Soviet Scud mobile missile launchers. They'd spent three nights and four days crammed into a tiny cave within a camel's breath of a large contingent of Saddam Hussein's Republican Guard, where the slightest mistake or lack of discipline by either of them would have cost them their lives. Since Hadrian's foray into Iraq just after the beginning of the Second Gulf War he'd worked both with Truex and for him, and more than once in the field. As a result he not only respected Truex's leadership abilities and the logic behind his thinking, he wholly understood the orders he had just been given: *Find and challenge* anyone *who might have seen the photos. Do what needs to be done. Pay whatever it costs. Leave no trail.* Translated it meant: Locate all possible recipients of the photographs; confront them with a show of force; break down any resistance; retrieve the photographs; afterward, kill if necessary.

Conor White shut off the computer. The job was big and ugly and complex. But it was doable. "Right," he said again, then stood up and made his way toward his sleeping quarters in the rear.

5

Daybreak.

Nicholas Marten stirred from a deep sleep as something small scurried across his face. In reflex action, he reached up and brushed away whatever it was. He started to doze off again when he felt a similar scurrying across the top of his head. He brushed it off, then suddenly was fully awake. He looked down. Hundreds of small red and gray crabs were crawling over him. His arms, his legs, his torso, everywhere. He cried out and jumped up, slapping at anything on his body that moved. Quickly he backed away, watching the crabs scurry in every direction. As he did he touched a wall of some kind. He whirled around. All he saw was strong wooden staves, running from the sandy mud at his feet to crown a foot or more above his head. For an instant he thought it was a crude jail, its bars made of wood. Then he felt water rush in against his feet and a moment later pull back. Instantly he looked around, expecting to see the grinning faces of his captors. Instead he saw more wooden bars and then more outside of where he was. Then he understood. The bars were tree roots. He was in a sandy marsh infested with mangrove trees. The water pushing in and then out at his feet was the incoming tide. The crabs had simply been looking for higher ground to escape the rising water, and he had been their most available avenue.

Where he was now was as much a mystery as where the river had deposited him in the middle of the night. How he had found his way from the river to this thicket of mangroves in the dark—walked, crawled, swam—he had no idea. What he did know was that the river had been fresh water, and the water here was salt. It meant, with the wash of incoming tide, he was somewhere close to the sea.

He moved out from his jail-like habitat to find more of the same. Mangrove trees, he knew, grew where few, if any, other trees would survive, in areas inundated by saltwater. It was the high roots themselves that extruded the salt, which later would be secreted through cells on their leaves. But while it was the roots that protected the plant from the salt, right here and now those same roots were the problem because Marten was surrounded by them in every direction. Whichever way he chose to go, if it was wrong, he would go deeper into the swamp and maybe never find his way out. On the other hand, the tide was coming in and he could see high-water marks where the roots crowned above him, meaning that soon he would have no place to go but up into the trees themselves. He and thousands of crabs and snakes or anything else trying to escape rising water.

Again he watched the flow of the incoming tide, the way it carried in from the left across his feet and then washed back out. The tide was coming in from the sea and washing out to the sea. If he were to reach it, that was the direction he should go. Just how far it was or how long it would take to get there, he had no way of knowing.

Abruptly he turned and followed the tide. Crouching, ducking, twisting, sometimes crawling, he fought his way through mud and crabs and mangroves for ten minutes and then fifteen and then fifteen more. In that time the water rose from ankle level to just below his knees. In the early light he saw nothing but mangroves and the crabs that had climbed their roots.

Then something hard bumped into him. And he turned to see a large piece of floating driftwood, part of a dead tree. Like everything else it was covered with crabs. He started to push it away, then suddenly froze in horror. Entrapped in its branches were the bodies of a native woman and three young children, the oldest five at the most. All four had had their throats cut, and the crabs were hungrily scuttling in and out of the wounds carrying off what pieces of human loot they could.

A surge of tide pushed the log against Marten once more. Quickly he shoved it aside and moved on. The woman was dead, the children were dead, there was nothing he could do except say a prayer for them and wonder if they had been from Father Willy's village and if he had known them. God, he thought, what are these people doing to each other? And are the SimCo mercenaries making it worse?

Little by little the sky grew brighter, making the canopy of mangroves seem even thicker than before. It was already hot, and the air was a shroud of humidity. Mosquitoes began to swarm, and Marten swatted at them as he went. He was thirsty and hungry and increasingly apprehensive. For all he knew he might have only begun to cross the swamp. It could stretch on for miles before it reached the sea. He began to wonder if he was a fool to try to cross it. How long would it be before his legs gave out or he lost his bearings and turned back the way he had just come? Or stumbled into quicksand, which he knew could be anywhere?

He stopped and looked back. Retracing his steps could be as treacherous as moving on. Even if he made it back to the river he would only have to find another way out. That was if he didn't run into soldiers first. No, it was best to trust his instincts and keep on the way he was, following the incoming tide.

Ten minutes more and the first sun of the day cut a swath across the trees above him. Another ten and it hit him squarely in the face. In that moment he knew he was looking due east. It meant he was headed toward Bioko's eastern shore. A half hour later he stopped and shaded his eyes. When he did, the breath went out of him. Through the trees he could see the ocean, its low breakers rolling in beneath a cloudless sky.

"Yes! Yes!" He let out an explosive cry of joy and relief.

Wet, bone weary, hungry, battered, torn, and thirsty, whatever he had done, however he had done it, however far he had come, he had crossed the never-ending prison of mangroves and made it out of the swamp. At that moment nothing in his life had ever seemed more wondrous than the sight of the sandy beach and the rolling sea before him.

For a while he simply sat and rested. Finally he stood and looked left, toward the north. A half mile or so up he could see the rusting hull of what once must have been a coastal freighter buried in the sand. All that was left now was the stern and a piece of bow, connected by what remained of its midsection. Beyond it stretched miles of beach. Nowhere did he see a sign of humanity. No village, no fishermen, no boats at anchor. No person or thing that might provide water and food or help him get to Malabo at the northernmost tip of Bioko. All that had happened, it seemed, was that he had traded the endless maze of the mangroves for miles of uninhabited, desolate beach. It made his fate nearly the same as before. All he could do was put one foot in front of the other and move on.

He looked at his watch.

7:48 A.M.

A glance at the cloudless sky, a deep breath, and he stepped off.

6

"Look!" Twenty-four year-old Luis Santiago cried out in Spanish. He was staring off through the high grass and toward the ocean. Immediately his companions, Gilberto, Rosa, and Ernesto, rushed to join him.

"Marita!" Rosa called over her shoulder to the group's leader, a young Spanish doctor hunched over the hood of one of two aging, mud-splattered Toyota Land Cruisers looking over a map with two uniformed native guides.

"What is it?" she called back in Spanish.

"A man on the beach!"

Marita turned to look.

"There." Luis pointed toward the sand.

Marita Lozano shaded her eyes. At first she didn't see him, and then she did: a lone man in the distance staggering along the beach near the water's edge. They were at the side of a mud-rutted dirt road a good fifty yards from the shoreline and probably not visible through the tall grass from where the man walked. He was moving slowly and more than once stopped to look around as if he were trying to get his bearings. Then he moved on, his gait unsure, his balance unsteady. Finally he stumbled and fell and then lay still.

"Quickly!" Marita shouted. "Quickly! Quickly!"

The group rushed forward.

Nicholas Marten was in and out of a dream. He thought he saw the face of a beautiful young woman staring down at him. Then she was replaced by a young man with a canteen trying to hold him up and give him water. Then he saw two sturdy black men dressed in uniforms trying to help him to his feet. After that everything faded and he was in England, arriving midday and by rental car at some grand country manor—the Fifield estate near the city of Oxford. The blue sky was mottled with white puffy clouds, the surrounding trees and rolling lawns of Fifield, a bright early-summer green.

Soon he was past a phalanx of men in dark suits and sunglasses, and quickly afterward smiling, shaking hands, and then bear-hugging a tall, elegant, silver-haired man he affectionately called "Cousin Jack"; the same man who, with like affection, called him "Cousin Harold." The same man who knew what few others anywhere in the world did, that at one time not many years earlier he had been a Los Angeles Police Department homicide detective named John Barron, a member of an elite squad that had disintegrated in a complex circumstance of murder and horror. Faced with the threat of lethal reprisals from dark forces inside the LAPD, he had changed his name to Nicholas Marten and fled with his sister to a new life in Europe: his sister as governess to a wealthy family in Switzerland; he at first as a student of landscape architecture at the University of Manchester in northern England, and then as a professional landscape architect and full-time employee of the respected firm of Fitzsimmons and Justice in that same city.

In short order Marten and "Cousin Jack" were seated alone in the manor's orangerie and being served lunch: Scottish salmon, Irish potatoes, French beans, Italian white wine, and Spanish mineral water, thereby spreading culinary goodwill over a number of countries.

Even in his dream Marten smiled. "Cousin Jack" was no ordinary cousin, nor was he a relative at all. He was a man he'd been as close to as one human could be to another; a man who had saved his life and whose life he had saved during a near-weeklong hellish journey in Spain some sixteen months before. He was also a man he'd never really expected to see again. "Cousin Jack" was John Henry Harris, the president of the United States.

Earlier that same morning Marten had left his home in Manchester and taken a flight to London, then driven a rental car into the countryside. President Harris was in England to meet with the British prime minister but had set aside time to meet privately with his old friend. The encounter, as Marten well knew, was not without purpose. Their Spanish adventure, in Barcelona and then at the monastery at Montserrat, had been perilous at best, and so his summons to meet "Cousin Jack" alone at Fifield, a beautiful but isolated estate, gave him good cause for unease.

"You want to know what this is about?" the

president asked when the pleasantries and reminiscences were over.

"Yes." Marten smiled carefully. "I want to know what this is about."

"You've heard of the German novelist Theo Haas."

"The Nobel Prize winner? Of course. I've read him and read about him. He's a brilliant, cantankerous, eighty-year-old troublemaker."

"Yes," the president said, smiling, "he is. That aside, he was in Washington three days ago and met with one of his most ardent fans, Representative Joe Ryder of New York. Ryder is the chairman of the House Oversight and Government Reform Committee, which is the main investigative committee in the U.S. House of Representatives."

"I know." Marten smiled as well. "The Internet works in Manchester the same as most everywhere else. I keep an eye on the national news. I haven't forgotten where I was brought up."

"Then you would also know that Ryder is focused on the billions of dollars we are spending in Iraq. He's particularly interested in the cost overruns by a Texas-based oil field management and exploration company called AG Striker and a chief Striker subcontractor, a private military security firm called Hadrian. Both are working under long-term State Department contracts and have been paid hundreds of millions of U.S. taxpayer dollars for their services, a lot of it in vague, unsubstantiated cross-billings. Ryder's job to is clarify those expenditures, but he can't because the agreements are 'classified.' "

"Not to you."

"No, not if I press it." The president put down his fork and took a sip of mineral water. "The public expects its president to be informed, but I have to be careful not to stir up a hornet's nest if it's not warranted."

Marten stared at him. "What are you getting at?"

"In his meeting with Congressman Ryder, Theo Haas suggested that something might be going on between AG Striker and Hadrian that is apart from the situation in Iraq. He was referring to a Striker oil operation in Equatorial Guinea." President Harris reached into his jacket and took out a folded piece of paper.

"Joe Ryder gave me this." He handed it to Marten. "It's a copy of a letter Haas received from his brother, Father Willy Dorhn, a German priest who lives on the island of Bioko, which is part of Equatorial Guinea. In the letter Father Willy describes the changes he has seen in the country over the past few months. His main reference is to a rapidly escalating and violent civil unrest on the mainland, the brutal reaction to it by the regime in power, and the fear that it will soon spread to Bioko. At the same time, more and more people from Striker Oil are arriving there, and a private British military security contractor called SimCo has been brought in to protect them." The president stopped. "Read it yourself."

Marten studied him, then took a sip of water and looked at the letter. He read it and handed it back.

"What does this have to do with me?"

President Harris looked at him directly. "After Haas received his brother's letter, he did some homework and learned that SimCo has been in existence for just over a year. In that time it signed two long-term contracts, one to provide Striker with security services in Equatorial Guinea and another to do the same as a subcontractor to Hadrian in Iraq."

"You're suggesting there's some kind of arrangement between Striker and Hadrian that involves SimCo in both Iraq and Equatorial Guinea."

The president nodded. "That's what Hass thought. He apologized to Ryder for having the mind-set of a novelist and then told him he was fully aware of Ryder's interest in the Striker/Hadrian situation in Iraq. 'Is it not possible, my friend,' he told him, 'that United States taxpayers may be secretly footing the bill for what is happening in Equatorial Guinea as well?' "

"You mean SimCo is a front for Hadrian in Equatorial Guinea."

"Perhaps."

"It's not illegal."

"Unless it's being done, as Haas suggests, to have the U.S. taxpayers unknowingly fund it, the money coming from the Striker/Hadrian/State Department contracts in Iraq."

"Striker's a very successful oil company with apparently enough trouble in Iraq. Why would they do something like that and expose themselves even more?"

"Don't know that they did. But I'd like to find out," the president took a bite of the salmon, washed it down with mineral water, and then looked back to Marten. "There may be nothing to it at all. Everything might be wholly legal. On the other hand, things in Equatorial Guinea are happening quickly and with a lot of bloodshed, and if Striker and Hadrian are somehow trying to make a profit from it with taxpayer money we need to know. At this stage there's not enough to alert the CIA or anyone else. Moreover, if we did, we would risk tipping our hand to Striker and Hadrian, because they have very good friends in both the Agency and in the Pentagon. On top of that, an intelligence inquiry, even a quiet one, might very well be leaked to the media, and then we would have to deal with that."

Marten stared at the president. "I hope you're not thinking what I think you're thinking."

"Joe Ryder suggested we send an 'independent contractor' of our own down there to quietly look around and see what's going on. Somebody who knows what he's doing and can have some straight talk with Father Dorhn, then report back with what he thinks is happening, if anything."

Marten put up his hands in protest. "Mr. President, I'm honored at the suggestion, but I've got five very demanding accounts breathing down my neck."

"Father Dorhn has been in Equatorial Guinea for fifty years." The president ignored his objection and speared a neatly sliced piece of Irish potato. "If anyone knows what's going on there he does, and from his letter he seems to know quite a lot."

"Either that," Marten pushed back, "or Theo Haas is just worried about him and wants someone to do something about it. Or maybe, as he said, he just has the mind-set of a novelist and is trying to create a story where there is none. He doesn't have his rascally reputation for no reason."

President Harris grinned. "My sense is that you're right. Probably what you'll end up with is a week's all-expenses-paid vacation at an island paradise."

Marten put down his fork and stared at the president. "Aw, come on, cousin, you can find somebody else."

"As competent and trustworthy as you?"

"There are hundreds, probably thousands of people as competent and trustworthy as me. Probably even more competent and trustworthy."

The president looked up and let his eyes find Marten's. "Perhaps, my dear friend, but I don't know them."

7

• Bioko. 12:20 P.M.

Marten felt harsh sunlight cross his face. A second later there was a jarring bump, and his body flew upward only to be caught in a restraint of some kind and forced back down. Abruptly he awoke and through the fog of a deep, exhausted sleep saw that the cuts and scrapes on his right leg and left arm had been bandaged. Immediately there was another jolt, and his head cleared enough to realize that he was in a moving vehicle. Startled, he looked up and found staring at him perhaps the most captivatingly beautiful woman he had ever seen. With medium-length dark hair tucked behind her ears, a little turned-up nose, and dazzling green eyes, she was petite, sexy, and impish in a way that was wholly natural.

"This road is filled with potholes," she said in accented English. "You have been sleeping. You were quite tired."

Marten tried to shake off the lingering stupor and looked around. They were in the backseat of a battered, mud-splattered Toyota Land Cruiser that was traveling rapidly over a rutted dirt road. Two young, uniformed black men rode in front, one driving, the other sitting next to him. Marten looked over his shoulder. A second Land Cruiser was following close behind. It was dirty and plastered with mud as well. To the right, he could see open swampland dappled with splotches of bright sun that cut through an overcast sky. To the left, steep hills rose up sharply to disappear in a thick blanket of low-hanging mist.

"My name is Marita Lozano." The young woman smiled. "I am a physician. My companions in the car behind are medical students. We have come to Bioko from Madrid to give AIDS education to the people in the southern part of the island. As you probably know, a civil war has broken out here. The army ordered to us to return to Malabo immediately."

"The army?" Marten was suddenly alarmed.

"They stopped our cars a short time ago and told us to follow them."

Marten looked past the uniformed men in front and through the dirty, mud-streaked windshield to see an Equatorial Guinea army Humvee of sorts kicking up mud and gravel some thirty yards ahead of them. Uniformed soldiers were seated inside, while another, standing, manned a roof-mounted machine gun.

Marten looked back to Marita. "Did they see me?"

"Yes." She nodded. "They seemed to think you were one of us, and I let them. I simply said you were tired and were sleeping."

"They didn't ask for identification?"

"Only mine. Our guides told them who we were and what we were doing here." She smiled gently and with it came the perky impishness he'd seen before. "I knew you had been caught up in the fighting in the south and that you escaped the soldiers, so naturally I assumed you didn't want to be questioned by them."

"How do you know all that?" Marten was incredulous. Instinctively he glanced at the guides and then looked back to Marita.

"You told us. Myself and my colleagues; the guides, too. We saw you walking on the beach. You stumbled and fell and didn't get up. When we got to you, you were quite exhausted and exceedingly dehydrated. A little disoriented and frightened, too, when you saw the guides in their uniforms. Of course you had no way to know who we were."

Marten studied her carefully. "What, exactly, did I tell you?"

"That your name is Nicholas Marten and you are an English landscape architect in Bioko to study native plant life. You said you met a priest who took you up into the rain forest and showed you some of the flora you were looking for. You were returning to his village when fighting erupted there, the army trucks came, and the priest told you to run and you did."

Marten stared at her in disbelief.

"You have no memory of telling us, do you?" she said gently.

"No."

"Whether it's the truth is not my business." This time there was nothing gentle in her manner, nor any hint of impishness.

"It is the truth. Just the way I said it."

"Good, because you will want to repeat it when we get to Malabo."

"What do you mean, repeat it?"

"The army is going to question us when we arrive. They said so. It's why they ordered us to follow them."

"By us, you mean me, too?"

"Yes."

Questioning by army interrogators was the last thing Marten wanted. It was impossible to know how much they knew of his connection to Father Willy or if they had known about the photographs all along and had been trying to trap him and anyone he might have shown the photos to or told about them. Brutal or not, they were fighting a war and would do anything to get as much information as they could about what was going on and who was involved with arming the rebellion. Father Willy had been with the natives a long time and that made him a prime suspect in anything that might appear to be supporting the insurgency. The soldiers had seen Marten with him, and Marten had turned and run when they came after him. That in itself would make any question-and-answer session with them long and probably ugly, maybe even fatal.

He looked to Marita. "There's no need for me to make things difficult for you. Why don't you tell your driver to just pull over when we go around a bend in the road and let me off. They won't see it happen, and that way I'm out of your hair and you won't have to answer questions about me when they find out I wasn't part of your group to begin with."

"They know how many of us there are, Mr. Marten. If there were to be one less we would have to explain it and they would want to know why and then there would be more trouble all around. Even if we did stop and you got out, where would you go? Into the rain forest? How long would you be prepared to stay there? This is an island, Mr. Marten, and not terribly hospitable, as you already know. Whatever your private circumstances are, I would think it best that you come to terms with them sooner rather than later."

"You do," Marten said flatly.

"Yes, I do."

Marten looked off. He knew she was right and

that the best thing he could do would be to face whoever interrogated him and hope he could bluff it through. The idea of calling the president, using the direct-dial twenty-four-hour-a-day number Harris had given him, or calling anyone else for that matter, was not an option. This was not the United States, not Britain, not Europe. Demands to make a phone call would, he knew, be met with laughter and more likely with physical punishment. Maybe worse. He turned back to her. "I'll follow your suggestion."

"That being the case"—Marita grinned a little, and the impishness returned—"please tell me your story again precisely as you did before. That way we will all have everything comfortably in mind before you and we and the soldiers meet."

Marten smiled at her pluck. Here was a beautiful young doctor on some kind of mission of mercy or education or both in the middle of a poor-as-dirt country who understood something of the underbelly of the world around her and could smile about it even as she determined how to deal with it. People like that didn't come along very often.

12:42 P.M.

8

• Malabo, capital of Equatorial Guinea. 4:18 P.M.

Conor White stood alone under the arch of a public building, watching the street at the end of the block. Now and again people passed by. Mostly they were native women and children, their men seemingly elsewhere. The whites, Americans, Europeans, South Africans—mostly people in the oil business or in one way or another connected to it— were absent altogether, either still conducting the day's business or gathered in the bar of the Hotel Malabo, where most of them spent their free time. To them, neither Malabo nor the entire island of Bioko, the old Spanish Fernanado Pó, nor even Rio Muni, the Equatorial Guinea mainland across the Bight of Biafra from Bioko, was a place for civilized man. If you weren't in oil or somehow trying to profit from it, there was no reason in hell to be there at all.

• 4:22 P.M.

White pulled a handkerchief from his pocket, ran it over his neck, and then wiped his forehead. It was hot and humid as it always was, ninety-five degrees Fahrenheit when he'd left the air-conditioning of his motor home office/sleeping quarters ten minutes earlier.

The neighborhood here was a hodgepodge of old

colonial buildings in varying stages of disrepair. Most had crumbling archways and tattered or broken window shutters and front doors that looked as if they had been repaired by crate makers. All were topped by slanted, grooved metal roofs, the majority of which were in danger of rusting through. The buildings themselves, made of white concrete and two or three stories high, were, he imagined, probably built in the 1930s or '40s. No doubt once elegant and well kept, in all probability they'd remained that way until 1968, when Equatorial Guinea gained independence after one hundred and ninety years of Spanish rule and the series of brutal dictatorships began, slipping the country into a morass of untold riches for the few and deep poverty for the rest. The buildings now were inhabited by the latter and had not only fallen into sad disrepair but along the way had been painted a combination of colors that made no sense at all. One was faded yellow with an equally faded pink balcony, another a dreary white with one archway of light blue and another of muddy orange; still another was bright pink but had shutters that were salmon on one side and brilliant green on the other.

Conor White had been around the world more times than he could remember, and nothing he had seen quite matched the cheerless atmosphere of rust and decay and near all-invasive poverty that was Malabo, or at least the part of it where he stood now.

• 4:30 P.M.
Again his eyes went to the end of the block.

Still nothing.

They were to have arrived at four twenty-five. Where were they? What was the delay? He could radio, he knew, easily enough. Just reach into his jacket and click the piece on. Tell SimCo dispatch what he wanted, and in less than thirty seconds he would have location coordinates and a corrected, near exact time of arrival. But he didn't. There was no point in revealing his impatience, even to his dispatcher.

• 4:33 P.M.

Ten feet away a rooster wandered along the sidewalk, clucking around a dead palm tree and then strutting boldly across the cracked asphalt street under a collection of weathered low-hanging wires that dangled hazardously between metal telephone poles.

• 4:34 P.M.

Again White looked down the street. An old man turned the corner on a bicycle and came toward him. Behind him the street was empty. Patience be damned. He started to reach for his radio. Then—

There they were, rounding the corner and coming toward him: a muddied Army of Equatorial Guinea machine-gun-mounted Humvee followed in close order by two mud-crusted Toyota Land Cruisers and then a second army Humvee, the one that would have picked them up as a tail car when they entered the city.

White stepped back under the arch and out of sight as they passed. Seconds later the caravan pulled beneath the overhang of a crumbling two-story building across the street. Armed soldiers jumped from the army vehicles and pulled open the doors of the Land Cruisers. In a heartbeat the occupants of both cars were brought out and led into the building. They were eight in all. Four were young Spanish medical students he knew about. He had their names and passport numbers and home addresses in Madrid. Two others were uniformed native guides. The seventh was a young female doctor, from Madrid, whose personal information he had as well. The last was the individual he wanted most to see and was the reason he had come there and waited. At this point he had no information about him at all. What he knew was what he saw. A ruggedly handsome male Caucasian in his midthirties, about six feet tall, slim and dark-haired. He was the man the soldiers had seen with Father Willy Dorhn, the same man who had run from them in the rain forest. He was the real person of interest here. Someone who might well know about the photographs the priest had taken and the missing camera memory card that went with them.

White had wanted to see him in person, get a sense of him before the army interrogators took over. If the army didn't get the information he wanted, he would have to find a way to do it himself. Experience had taught him that if possible it was best to get a sense of your quarry before he had any idea that you even existed, especially when you had no information about him. It gave you a step up, a chance to see how he carried himself, what his attitude was, what he might be like physically and mentally if you had to go up against him. It wasn't much, but it was more than the other man had.

9

• 4:47 P.M.

The room was unbearably hot.

The soldier's uniform had no name tag, just gold oak leaf clusters on his epaulets. The best Marten could determine was that he was a major in the army of the Republic of Equatorial Guinea. He was big and powerfully built, well over six feet and easily two hundred and fifty pounds. A fearsome tribal scar covered most of the left half of his face, while a similar scar was on his right forearm. Taken together they gave him more the appearance of a bush warrior than a military officer. Yet none of it compared with his eyes. Dark brown and bloodshot, they were like those of the soldier who had come after him in the rain forest. Homicidal and wholly merciless, they were the gateway to the possessor's soul and something Marten would fear for the rest of his life.

"Speak into the microphone," the major commanded in a deep, heavily accented voice, sweat glistening on his forehead, the microphone of an old-style cassette tape recorder held inches from Marten's face. "State your name, profession, and place of residence. Then describe what took place yesterday when you were in Bioko South."

Marten was seated on a straight-backed chair in the center of a dimly lit room. Sweat soaked his hair, running down his neck and his face and into his shirt. To his left two solidly built uniformed officers stood erect and in silence. Beyond them, two more uniformed men guarded the door. The men at the door were clearly not officers but everyday soldiers, young and alert and eager. Their eyes locked on Marten, they seemed almost hungry, as if they were hoping he would do something so they could act on it.

All of them were dressed in the same sweat-stained jungle-green camouflage uniforms, their trouser legs bloused over heavy, laced-up combat boots. Each wore a dark red beret with some kind of bright yellow and black insignia stitched on the front. The major and the two officers carried sidearms, while the men at the door fingered light machine guns.

The room itself was large, its floor covered with cracked linoleum. An aging wooden table was just inside the door and had several old and rusted chrome kitchen stools standing alongside it. The walls were water-stained plaster, long ago painted a sickly green. What little illumination there was came from three bare lightbulbs that hung by frayed electric cords from the ceiling, and from the spill of afternoon daylight that crept in through broken shutters in the room's only window. A lone ceiling fan turned slowly above Marten's head, barely moving the stifling air.

Beyond all that, the thing that caught Marten's eye was a young male goat tied to a leg of the wooden table happily chewing on a stack of old newspapers. Whether it was a pet or regiment mascot or some kind of indigenous good-luck charm or was there for some other reason entirely, there was no way to know, but its presence seemed strange, even in a frightful place like this.

"Sir, speak into the microphone," the major commanded again. This time his voice resonated with impatience. "State your name, your profession, and place of residence. Then describe what took place yesterday when you were in Bioko South."

Marten hesitated, then began. The best thing, he knew, was to go along with them. Do just as they asked. "My name is Nicholas Marten," he said, patiently telling them what he had moments earlier when they'd first brought him into the room, taken his photograph and searched him, then took away his still-damp passport and wallet and the neck pouch in which he carried it. Immediately afterward the major demanded he tell them his name and what he did and where he was from. "I am a landscape architect. I live in Manchester, in the north of England."

Carefully, he went on with the rest, repeating the story he'd told Marita on the way there. It was a narrative, which, as he thought now, was something he must have quickly and subconsciously put together the day before when the soldiers were pursuing him through the rain forest and he had been certain he would be caught. A simple yet detailed explanation of who he was and why he was in Bioko.

"I came here on a five-day trip to study equatorial plants for possible inclusion in a tropical greenhouse a client would like to build on his estate. You can verify the date I arrived in Bioko by the stamp on my passport. I took a room at the Hotel Malabo for the duration of my stay. My things are still there."

Marten paused and casually looked around to see how the others were reacting. If they had relaxed. If they believed him. What might happen when he was finished. There was no response at all. The soldiers stared at him in silence, their focus and attitude unchanged.

Marten cleared his throat and went on. "While I was in the southern part of the island I met a priest who introduced himself as Father Willy Dorhn. He asked me about my travels, and when I explained my reason for being there he kindly offered to show me some rain forest vegetation I had not yet seen. Later, as we returned, we heard gunfire in his village. The father was very concerned about his people and left me to go to them. It was then the army trucks came. He looked back when he saw them, and I could tell he was frightened. He yelled at me to run for my life. Which I did. I had no idea what was going on, but the sound of his voice and the fear in his eyes was enough. I ran into the jungle with armed soldiers chasing me. Shortly afterward

I slipped from a cliff and fell into a river. The water carried me a long way. Then it became night, and in the morning I found I had reached the sea. I was lost and thirsty and hungry. I had no choice but to start walking, and I did. Sometime later the Spanish doctor and her medical students found me." Marten stopped and looked directly at the major. "You know the rest."

"Why would you be afraid of the army?" he asked flatly.

"When you are a stranger in the backcountry like we were and there is a lot of gunfire and the priest you are with, a man who very recently told you he had been serving the people here for half a century, tells you to run for your life, I would think it best to do so. I don't have to tell you that Africa is filled with bloody civil wars and untold massacres and incursions by armed men from neighboring countries. I had no idea who the uniformed men were. So I ran."

The major glared at him and seemed about to reply when the door suddenly opened and a hawk-faced, gray-haired soldier wearing the same kind of jungle fatigues as the others entered. Immediately the men in the room snapped to attention. At the same time, two other uniformed men came in. One carried a folding chair, which he opened and placed near Marten. The hawk-faced soldier looked at him, then sat down on it.

Immediately the major turned to Marten. "I would ask you to state your name, your profession, and place of residence and then to tell your story once again."

This time it wasn't a formal request as before, it was an order.

"Of course," Marten said politely and patiently, wholly aware of the hawk-faced soldier and how completely his presence affected the others. Whoever he was, he was dark-skinned but clearly not a black African like the rest. He looked more than anything like a sharp-featured Hispanic and was older than he first appeared. Fifty at least, maybe even sixty. Moreover, his uniform bore no insignia other than that of the Equatorial Guinea army. There were no service ribbons, no oak leaf clusters or stars or bars, no indication of rank at all. Yet clearly he was a superior officer, a colonel or even a general. Who he was or why he was here Marten had no way to know. But it didn't matter. He had been ordered to tell his story once more, and he did, being careful to leave out nothing.

"My name is Nicholas Marten. I'm a landscape architect. I live in Manchester, in the north of England. I came here on a five-day trip to . . ."

The whole time Marten talked, the hawk-faced soldier studied him. Watched his eyes, his hands, his body language, even the placement of his feet, as if something Marten might inadvertently do would reveal more about him than the tale he was telling.

And the whole time Marten ignored him, just looked at the major and repeated what, by now, he knew by heart. When he was done he sat back, his eyes still on the major, praying that was all, that he had passed the test and they would believe him and let him go.

"Thank you." The major smiled easily, and Marten relaxed. He had done everything they asked, genially and politely. Had cooperated at each step. Trouble was the microphone was still there, inches from his face. What else could they possibly want?

Suddenly the major's smile vanished and he leaned close. "Where are the photographs the priest gave you?"

"What?" Marten was caught completely off guard. How could they know about Father Willy's photos? It was impossible; there had been no one there but Father Willy and himself.

"The photographs Father Dorhn gave to you."

"I don't know what you're talking about."

"The photographs Father Dorhn gave to you," the major repeated.

"The father gave me no photographs."

The major stared at him for a long and very silent moment. Then, with a glance at the hawk-faced soldier, he looked back to Marten. "Stand up, please," he said.

Marten didn't move.

"Stand up. Remove your clothes."

"My clothes?"

"I am becoming impatient." The major's bloodshot eyes bore into Marten's. His face glistened with sweat. The tribal scar covering half of it looked more fearsome than ever.

Marten stood slowly. They'd searched him before and found nothing. What the hell were they going to do now?

He glanced around the room. Everyone in it, even

the goat, was staring at him. Suddenly the heat felt unbearable, and for a moment he thought he might faint. Then he recovered. If he was going to convince them he knew nothing of the photographs, he had to do exactly as the major had ordered and do it without fear or insolence. He had to prove he was a man of conviction no matter what they had in mind.

"Alright," he said finally. Immediately his hand went to his shirt. One by one he undid the buttons, then took off his shirt and dropped it by his side. Without hesitation he undid his belt, then opened his fly, unzipped his trousers, and dropped them.

The major stared at him impassively, then nodded at his undershorts.

You want those, too, Marten thought. Okay, you got them. Quickly he lowered his shorts and dropped them on the floor.

Now he stood naked, his clothing scattered at his feet. A white man alone in a sweltering, ramshackle room in the middle of a sweltering, ramshackle city, surrounded by seven armed black African jungle fighters, one hawk-faced ranking military officer of unknown nationality, and a goat.

10

"Where are the photographs the priest gave you?" the major said once again.

"I don't know what you are referring to," Marten said calmly. "The father gave me no photographs. And as you can see I am hiding nothing."

"You are hiding what is in here!" The major suddenly jabbed Marten's forehead with the tip of a massive finger. "What is in your mind, your head." Immediately he looked to one of the officers behind him.

In a blink the man stepped forward. Marten could see the swift grin, the glint in his eyes. He knew what was coming and that there was nothing he could do to stop it. Still he did his best to cover himself. It didn't work. The kick from the man's combat boot drove into his genitals like a piston. Marten cried out and dropped to one knee, gagging, coughing, retching. His head spun. The pain was excruciating, focused nowhere and everywhere at the same time. For a long while he stayed where he was, his eyes closed, gasping, praying for the agony to go away.

Finally he opened his eyes. When he did he found the major squatted in front of him, his sweating face inches away.

"I want the photographs," he hissed. "The photographs and the memory card from the camera that was used to take them. Where are they?"

What Marten saw in his eyes was pure hatred. Whether it was because Marten was white or because he was getting no information from him seemed not an issue. The major, like those here and the others from before—the soldiers who had slammed rifle butts into the heads of Father Willy and the two young boys and the ones who had chased him in the rain forest—were not so much soldiers as killers. Human life meant nothing. They wanted what they wanted, nothing less. Right now that was information regarding the whereabouts of Father Willy's photographs and the memory card from his camera, and those were things he couldn't give them. First, there was no way for him to know for certain whether copies of the photographs or the memory card itself still existed. Even if they did, he had no idea where they might be. Second, they had no evidence that he had seen the photos and were simply assuming it was true. That meant his continued denials of innocence were crucial because if they had any sense at all that he was lying they would torture him until he broke. Once he did, once he told them the truth of what had happened and what he had seen, they would kill him in an instant.

Marten brought his eyes up to the major's. "I don't know about any photographs or any camera or any memory card," he whispered. At the same time, he thanked God that Father Willy had had the intelligence to burn the photos on the trail instead of giving them to him.

"We shall see." The major grinned cruelly and stood up.

• 5:22 P.M.

The major went to the table, picked something off it, and came back. It was a tube, maybe two inches around and two feet long, and except for the twin metal electrodes protruding from one end, it looked like some kind of nightstick. It wasn't. It was an old-fashioned high-voltage cattle prod.

"Holy shit," Marten swore under his breath.

Suddenly hands grabbed him and he was flat on the floor on his back with the major standing over him. He brought the prod toward Marten's face, then pressed a button near the top of the handle. There was a stab of blue light and a loud crackling sound as electricity arced violently from one electrode to the other on the instrument's tip. The major grinned and slowly moved the prod down between Marten's legs to just brush his genitals.

"The photographs and the memory card and you go free."

Go free like hell, Marten thought. They'd find out soon enough that he couldn't give them what they wanted. Nor could they let him go afterward, no matter his condition, and have him start talking about what happened, so they'd have little choice but to get rid of him. All he could do was try to buy a little time and think of some other way to get out of the situation.

"I don't know anything about photographs or a memory card," he whispered. "Nothing."

"No?"

"No."

From the corner of his eye Marten saw movement. He turned his head. The goat was right beside
him. One soldier had it by the head. A second lifted
its tail. The major touched the prod to the animal's
genitals and pressed the button on the handle. The
loud snapping sound of high voltage was drowned
out by the goat's scream as its genitals and the mus-
cles around them contracted in wild spasm. The
goat shrieked and kicked wildly, trying to free itself
from the iron grip the soldier had on its head. It was
no good. The man was too strong. The major smiled
at Marten, then stuck the prod between the animal's
legs and touched the button again. And then again.
The terrified animal yelped and screamed in agony.
Then it kicked up violently, knocking the prod
from the major's hand, jerking away from the soldier holding its head. Then, bellowing and dragging
its hindquarters, to the laughter of the soldiers, it
circled the room desperately looking for an escape.
Finally it hid quivering under the relative safety of
the wooden table. Whereupon the soldier who had
been holding it walked over and knelt down as if to
comfort it. Instead he grinned, drew his pistol, and
shot it between the eyes.

"Cena," the major said in Spanish. Supper. He
retrieved the prod from where the goat had kicked it
and came back toward Marten.

Marten's eyes followed the prod, then shifted to
the major. "If I knew I would tell you," he said with
all the strength he could manage. "I don't."

"That is not a satisfactory answer, Mr. Marten.

Besides, it's early yet. Very early. I'm sure it won't be long before your memory returns." Slowly he ran the prod between Marten's legs, letting it come to come rest at the base of his testicles.

Just then the hawk-faced soldier raised his hand. Abruptly the major left Marten and went to him. A brief, muted conversation took place between them. When it was done, the major nodded and came back to Marten.

"Get dressed," he said.

Marten glanced at the other man, then looked back to the major.

"Get dressed," he said again.

A storm of relief rushed through Marten, but he dared not show it for fear this was part of the game. Make him think he'd been spared, then start the process all over again. Quietly he stood and then slowly dressed. Undershorts first, then trousers, then his shirt. The whole time he carefully watched the hawk-faced man, wondering what he'd said to the major and what was next.

In the next moment the major looked to one of the young soldiers guarding the front door. Immediately the man picked up Marten's passport case from the table and delivered it to him.

"There is a ten-o'clock flight to Paris this evening." The major put Marten's passport case in his hand. "You will be on it."

Marten stared at him, then looked around the room, wondering what they were doing, if this was some kind of trick. There was only silence.

"Thank you," he said finally and as politely as

possible, then started for the door. As he reached it the second young soldier flung it open.

Marten should have taken the gift he had been given and left as quickly as he could. Instead he stopped in the doorway and turned to look at the major.

"What happened to the priest?" he said quietly.

"Dead." The answer was sharp and stabbed across the room.

Marten had expected it to come from the major, but it had come from the hawk-faced soldier. It was the one and only time he had addressed him, and when he did he locked eyes with him.

"There were two boys—"

"Dead," the man repeated, his voice cold and flat. "Everyone in the priest's village is dead. It is a tragedy that no one seemed to know where the photographs were. Certainly one of them would have traded his life, or hers, or"—he purposely emphasized the next—"his mother's . . . or father's or . . . child's . . . for them if they had. It would have been a simple thing."

Marten said nothing. Then, with a glance at the major, he turned and walked out the door.

5:40 P.M.

11

Nicholas Marten stood in a tiny shower stall that was crammed, like the toilet, into a corner of his room. Head back, his eyes closed, he let the water run over him, relieved beyond imagination to be free of his army interrogators and on his way out of Bioko. At the same time, he thought of the cold bravado with which the hawk-faced soldier had told him of the village massacre.

How many had lived in that village? Sixty? Eighty? Maybe more. He wondered what was so extraordinarily valuable to the army about those photographs that they would expend so much effort and take that many lives trying to retrieve them.

The only answer that made sense was that they wanted them as proof to the world that an outside force was fueling the rebellion and that their deliberate actions in repressing it—highly criticized by human rights groups, the United Nations, and any number of countries—were justified. Still, if they were so eager to uncover the pictures and had not yet found them, why had they suddenly stopped their interrogation and let him go?

Part of the puzzle might have been the condition of his hotel room when he returned. The place had been thoroughly ransacked. Every piece of his personal belongings gone through, his bed stripped, the furniture turned over. They hadn't found the photos there, and they hadn't found them on his person, still that didn't answer the question of why they had let him go when they could have as easily killed him and buried his body somewhere in the rain forest where a missing man, no matter who he was, would never be found. A missed communication between them? Maybe. Goodwill? Not from men like that, particularly when they knew he'd seen firsthand what the army did to old priests and young boys and boasted about their slaughter of the villagers. So their freeing him had to have been for some other reason altogether. What that was he couldn't imagine.

• 7:10 P.M.

Freshly shaven and dressed in a clean shirt, jeans, and sport coat, Marten left his bags at the front desk and headed for the bar. He walked gingerly, his balls still swollen and achingly tender from the field-goal-like kick presented to him by the major's "specialist." What he wanted most was to have a gin and tonic, or two or three to kill the pain, and then get the hell out of there on the ten-o'clock flight to Paris. Yet suddenly there was doubt even about that. In the last half hour a tropical storm had whirled in from nowhere. Wind and rain pelted in never-ending sheets. The lights flickered and went off, then came back on. He'd been warned at the desk that the airport might close down.

"For how long?" he'd asked of the white, middle-aged desk clerk.

"For however long the storm lasts, señor. An hour. A day. A week."

"A week?"

"Sometimes, yes," the man grinned.

"The airport closes, you make sure I have a room. I don't want to sleep in the lobby for a night, much less a week."

"I don't know if that is possible, señor."

"You don't?"

"No, señor."

Marten reached into his jacket, took out a small roll of bills, and handed him a ten-thousand-CFA-franc note, the currency of Equatorial Guinea, which was somewhere in the neighborhood of twenty U.S. dollars. "Now you do."

"Of course, señor. If the airport closes you will have a room."

"Good."

Marten walked off and shuddered as he did. The last thing he wanted was to spend another hour, let alone a night or a week, here.

12

Noise and tobacco smoke hit Marten like a wall as he walked into the riot that was the Hotel Malabo's bar, a big, broad room furnished with rattan and packed to the walls with Westerners, most of them SimCo mercenaries and AG Striker employees. Both groups looked like they were straight out of central casting. The SimCo people were your classic badass tough guys, hard-drinking, cigar-smoking, black-T-shirt-and-camouflage-pants-wearing, shaved-headed combat veterans from probably a dozen different countries and as many wars. The Striker crew looked like field people—drillers, riggers, technicians, and the like. Most of them still wore their grease- and sweat-stained work clothes, lightweight jumpsuits with a big AG STRIKER company logo stenciled on the back, and unlike the SimCo people, not all were men.

Four women who looked like office staffers, folded umbrellas still wet from the rain hung over the backs of their chairs, sat at a nearby table drinking and talking among themselves, and once in a while looking off toward a hunky mercenary or oil driller. Here and there unkempt-looking women wearing low-cut, slit-to-the-thigh dresses like uniforms took up space at the long mahogany bar or sat at cheap rattan cocktail tables looking for any man who would pay for their attention.

Then there were the rest. Mostly they were men, ranging in age from middle twenties to late sixties. The majority of them wore tropical suits with dress shirts open at the neck. Some of the younger ones wore jeans or khakis with golf shirts under wrinkled, lightweight sport coats. Judging from their languages they seemed to be European or South African. Within a circle of twenty feet Marten heard smatterings of English, German, Afrikaans, Spanish, and Italian. His experience in his not-so-many-years-removed life as a homicide detective on the Los Angeles Police Department told him most were quick-buck artists—gamblers, manipulators, and hangers-on, whores of all trades—drawn to anywhere there was fast money to be made. And his sense of things during the few days he had been there told him there was plenty to be made in Equatorial Guinea. The dealings would be in drugs, guns, human beings, information—by the bundle or in snippets—anything at all they could sell for profit.

Marten pushed around a large man in a sweat-stained white suit and was trying to find the most direct way to the bar when he saw Marita and her medical students squeezed around a small corner table. She smiled and waved when she saw him. He grinned and nodded in return. He hadn't seen any of them since they had been separated and the soldiers had taken him off for interrogation, and he was happy to see they had been released and were safe. He stepped around two arguing AG Striker oil workers and went to their table.

"We were concerned about you, Mr. Marten,"

Marita said as he reached the table. "Please sit down."

"I'm alright, thanks." They made room, and he sat down gingerly. "What about you? Everybody okay?"

"We're fine," Marita said, then looked at her young companions. "¿Sí?"

"Sí," they nodded in agreement.

The four were people he knew only by their first names: the slim, ever-smiling Luis; baby-faced Rosa, a little overweight and looking like a wannabe executive secretary in oversized glasses and olive-colored sack dress; the quiet, chubby, seemingly overly serious Gilberto; and Ernesto, tall and gangly with an unruly mop of bright red hair and red Converse sneakers to match. Here, in this crowded, boisterous, smoke-filled room, surrounded by a crowd of hardscrabble players from a wholly different world, they looked a lot less like people who would soon be doctors than kids who should still be living at home and going to high school.

"They collected our things from the hostel where we were staying," Marita added, "and then brought us here, saying they would pick us up at nine and take us to the airport. We were told to leave the island tonight. From what they said we will be on the same flight you are taking."

"To Paris."

"Yes."

Marten smiled. "It's a pleasant coincidence." Some coincidence, he thought. From what he'd learned at the front desk, it was the only flight out for the next two days, and the army clearly wanted them all off the island as quickly as possible. He looked around the table. None of them seemed to have been ill treated. Still, they had been questioned, and he wanted to know what they had told whoever had done it. He wondered if the subject of the photographs had come up, or if they even knew about them. He turned to Marita. "What did they ask you?"

"They searched us and then wanted information. Mostly about you. How we came to be traveling together. What we knew about you. The things you said to us."

"What did you tell them?"

"The truth, of course. That we saw you walking on the beach and you collapsed and we went to help you. After that all the things you told us," Marita smiled conspiratorially, the impishness in her rising up, then she repeated almost verbatim what he had told them on the beach and what they had gone over in the Land Cruiser on the drive to Malabo. "Afterward they asked what we were doing in Bioko, but we had already documented our purpose with the proper authorities when we first arrived. So we were okay."

"That's all they wanted, nothing else?"

"No."

"Nothing about a priest?"

"No. Why?"

Marten shook his head. "Nothing." Apparently the matter of the photographs had not come up. Perhaps because they were satisfied with what he had told them and believed that the distance between Father Willy's village and the beach where he had been found was too great to have involved a conspiracy to smuggle the pictures out. If that were the case, then the pictures would not have been mentioned. No reason to alert others to their existence if there was no need; especially when that could only serve to complicate things later if some unforeseen problem arose, say, with the media and inquisitive reporters.

Suddenly Ernesto ran a hand through his pasture of red hair. "There was one other thing," he said in English. "When we collected our luggage we realized everything had been gone through, even our medical supplies. But nothing was missing. Why they did it none of us knows."

Marten half-smiled. "Don't feel bad, they went through mine, too. Looking for what, I don't know any more than you do." So they had been looking for the pictures. They weren't that incompetent. "I guess they have a revolution on their hands and aren't taking any chances."

At that moment a sudden gust of wind sent an avalanche of rain across a large window behind them. Seconds later a stronger gust rattled the entire building. Again the lights flickered, almost went out, then came back on.

"We'll be lucky if we get out tonight at all," Marita said with not well hidden apprehension. She didn't like being stuck here any more than Marten did. Too many things could still go wrong.

"That's what I was thinking," Marten said.

Immediately something off to one side caught Marita's eye, and she turned to look. Marten followed her gaze to see a tall, attractive woman coming toward them through the crowd. She was probably in her late thirties or early forties, had stylishly cut, shoulder-length dark hair, and wore expensive white linen slacks with a matching short-sleeve top. She also had the intense, almost severe air of someone used to being in charge and had something immediate and definitive on her mind.

With her was a handsome man in a tan suit with a light blue shirt open at the collar. He looked to be a little older than she, was well over six feet tall, had dark, close-cropped hair, and appeared to be more than physically fit. He, too, held the aura of authority. It was in the cut of his clothes and the way he carried himself: shoulders back, chest out; his movements smooth and fluid; his presence bordering on the aristocratic. It was a characteristic Marten had seen in some of his clients in Manchester, a studied military bearing born in the career officer ranks of the armed forces. There was something else, too, and it nearly took his breath away. He was one of the SimCo men he had seen in Father Willy's photographs transferring weapons to the insurgents in the jungle.

13

"I believe you are Mr. Marten," the woman said as she reached him.

Marten looked at them warily. "Yes, why?"

"My name is Anne Tidrow. This is Conor White."

"What can I do for you?"

"I'm a member of the board of directors of the AG Striker Oil and Energy Company," Anne Tidrow said. "Mr. White is head of the security firm we have retained to safeguard our workers in Equatorial Guinea. We understand that you were caught up in the rebellion in the south where a German priest was killed. Since Striker has many employees in various regions of Bioko, we are naturally concerned for their safety. Anything you could tell us about what you saw or experienced might help us be better prepared to protect our people."

"I went over the details at great length with army interrogators. Why don't you ask them?"

"Unfortunately the army does not share that kind of information with us, Mr. Marten," Conor White said, his accent noticeably British. "Might we have a few moments of your time? And in private, if you don't mind. This room is filled with large ears, and we wouldn't want to inadvertently create a climate of fear where there is none. Or at least where we hope there is none."

Marten hesitated. Here was a situation he could hardly have imagined. The oil company's chief security contractor, a man photographed supplying arms to the rebels, standing in front of him asking him to give him details of what he knew about the rebellion, and the woman with him, a member of Striker's board of directors, going so far as to mention Father Willy, though not by name. Maybe the army didn't share information with SimCo, but Conor White undoubtedly knew about the photographs and possibly that Marten had spent time alone with the man who took them. It meant that he, like the army, suspected Marten knew where the pictures were and wanted to retrieve them as quickly and quietly as possible. That explained Conor White and why he was here. What about Anne Tidrow?

It was interesting to wonder why she was even in Bioko, let alone here with White. There was little doubt she knew about the photos, too, or White wouldn't have dared expose his involvement with the rebels by bringing her along. So why would she be trying to protect SimCo when that was the firm her company had hired to safeguard its employees from the insurgency it was helping to fuel? It was the same question he had asked Father Willy.

"I came in here hoping to find a gin and tonic," Marten said finally. "Then I ran into my friends, and so far a waiter hasn't been by."

"Gin and tonic sounds good," White said. "Why don't we see about it at the bar?"

Marten nodded. "Why not?"

• 7:35 P.M.

Conor White led them to a corner of the bar that was away from the crowd and relatively quiet, seem-

ingly safely devoid of the "large ears" he had referred to. An aging Asian barman wearing a dark
toupee, who looked like he'd been there since the
building was erected, came over, and White ordered
drinks. As he did, Marten pulled back a worn rattan
barstool for Anne Tidrow.

"Thank you." she said, smiling.

"How did you know my name and that I was, as
you put it, caught up in the rebellion in the south?
Who told you?"

"My people," White answered for her. "We often
monitor army radio communications. It helps us
keep up on what's happening inside the country."

"It does until you get caught."

White grinned. "We are not in the business of get-
ing caught, Mr. Marten."

Just then the barman brought the drinks, and
White handed them around.

Anne Tidrow picked up her glass and looked at
Marten. "Perhaps you could tell us something of
your experiences during the fighting. What went on,
what you saw."

"I wasn't exactly in the middle of it." Marten
picked up his glass and took a solid pull at his
drink. "What I remember was seeing two little native boys come running along a very muddy road in
the pouring rain yelling for Father Willy Dorhn, the
priest you were referring to. A couple of minutes
later I heard gunfire from the village. The next thing,
a couple of army trucks full of soldiers showed up.
The first one stopped beside Father Dorhn and the
boys. Soldiers jumped out. One of them hit the
father with a rifle butt hard and knocked him down.

Maybe you don't know, but he was an old man. Another soldier did the same to the boys. One right after the other. I found out later all three of them died. The soldiers in the second truck came after me." Marten paused; then his eyes came up to hers and held there. "What else do you want to know?"

"Did you get to the village beforehand?" Now it was Conor White asking the questions. "By that I mean were you there earlier, before the rebels came?"

"I never said the rebels came. I'd met Father Willy several hours earlier, and he took me into the rain forest to show me some native plants. I'm a landscape architect. That's why I came to Bioko. To study the local flora for some clients back home. It was afterward, when we came down out of the jungle and were nearing the village, that all the trouble started. The father told me to run, and I did."

"Were you in his church? His living quarters?"

"Why?"

"Mr. White is just trying to get some sense of what was going on before the rebels attacked." Anne Tidrow took a sip of her drink and set the glass on the bar.

"You people keep telling me the rebels attacked. I never saw a rebel. Only soldiers."

"But you were in his church and his living quarters," Conor White pressed him.

"I met him in the village square, if that's what you want to call it." Marten deliberately locked eyes with White. "First it was the rebels. Now you've asked me twice if I was in the priest's church or his living quarters. Just what is it you're trying to find out?"

"If he was encouraging the rebellion. If you saw anything that might indicate that."

"No. I didn't."

"It might interest you to know the savagery has escalated greatly in the last weeks. The army is literally slaughtering suspected insurgents as well as their families, the elderly and women and children included, and afterward burning their villages to the ground. In response the people are butchering soldiers and bystanders alike. It is becoming very dangerous to have our people here, both mine and the employees of Striker Oil."

"Why don't you get them out?"

"Because if we did we might well not get back in again for a very long time. Striker has a major investment here. So, at the moment, that option is not realistic."

"Well, that's your business, not mine." Marten's eyes left White and went to Anne Tidrow. "If you don't mind, I've had a long couple of days. I want to join my friends at the table so that we're all together when the soldiers come to escort us to the airport. Maybe you haven't heard, but the army kicked us out of the country. We're leaving on the ten-o'clock flight to Paris, assuming it gets off. One way or another we've still got a lot of night ahead of us."

Suddenly the thunderous beat of a bass drum rocked the room. Instantly everything went silent. Even the storm seemed to quiet down. Anne looked to Conor White.

"Here we go again."

In the next second an honor guard made up of a dozen black African soldiers in gold-and-blue dress uniforms and wearing white gloves appeared in the main doorway. Each carried a gold-plated AK-47.

Again came the thundering boom of the drum. Immediately eight more soldiers in the same uniforms marched smartly into the room and stopped in unison. One had a large bass drum harnessed in front of him. The others carried gold-plated trumpets. In unison they raised them to their lips and blasted out what sounded like some kind of fanfare.

"President Tiombe is coming," Conor White said quietly. "He does this at whim, whenever it is his pleasure."

Marten looked toward the doorway as the drummer and trumpet soldiers stepped to the side and a lone black African in an elegantly tailored full-dress military uniform entered. He was tall and wide at the same time and visibly soft, giving more the appearance of a buffoon than the warrior-king of a merciless army. For an instant he surveyed the room, then without further hesitation started forward, accompanied left and right by the gold-plated-AK-47-carrying guards.

"What's going on?" Marten asked.

"He's making himself known to the foreign guests," White said. "He wants to be recognized as Equatorial Guinea's great host and benefactor."

Marten watched president/dictator Francisco Ngozi Tiombe work the room like a politician, choosing this person and that at random, shaking hands, chatting briefly, and sometimes touching them warmly on the shoulder as he moved on to the next. Thirty seconds and a dozen handshakes later he stopped in front of them.

"Good evening, Ms. Tidrow, Mr. White," he said in a low rumbling voice and in impeccable English. "I trust you are enjoying your stay."

"Yes, of course, Excellency, thank you," Conor White said, bowing slightly at the waist as he did. President Tiombe smiled, and then his eyes shifted to Marten.

"This is Mr. Marten, Excellency," White offered. "Unfortunately circumstances are such that he has to leave your most hospitable country this evening."

"I'm sorry to hear that, Mr. Marten." Tiombe smiled. "Please say good things about my nation and my people when you reach your home. I look forward to welcoming you personally the next time you visit Malabo."

"That is most generous, Mr. President." Marten nodded but did not bow. "Thank you."

Tiombe fixed Marten with a stare that could only be called chilling and then abruptly moved on.

"Now you can say you've met the president of Equatorial Guinea," Conor White said with a smile.

"All the more reason to be leaving." Marten finished his drink and set the glass on the bar. "I hope I've been some help to you."

"It was kind of you to take the time to talk with us," Anne Tidrow smiled.

"The pleasure was mine," Marten said and, with a nod to Conor White, walked off.

White waited until Marten was out of earshot, then turned to Anne. "What do you think?"

"He knows more than he's telling."

"I agree." White picked up his drink. "The question is what to do about it."

7:52 P.M.

14

• Headquarters, AG Striker Oil & Energy Company, Houston, Texas. Still Thursday, June 3. Noon.

A deeply troubled forty-seven-year-old Josiah "Sy" Wirth, chairman of AG Striker, stared out at the glare of the city from the window of his sixty-fourth-floor office. Tall and lanky, his face creased by time, the Texas sun, and the lifelong strain of intense ambition, he wore faded jeans, a weathered, pearl-studded western shirt, and ostrich-skin boots. He looked more like a cowboy just in from the range than like the top executive of a booming oil company.

"By all accounts, Mr. Loyal Truex landed his Gulfstream an hour ago," he said coldly. "Theoretically, he's on his way here now." Abruptly he turned from the window to look at Striker's general counsel, Arnold Moss, a sixty-two-year-old widower and long-ago-transplanted New Yorker, sitting in a chair across from him. "It doesn't take that long to get from Ellington Field to here. So where the hell is he? Lost? Or did he stop to get laid along the way?" Wirth sat down at his desk and picked up a large unlit cigar from a red, white, and blue ashtray shaped like the state of Texas.

Like his personality, like Texas itself, Wirth's office was huge, if coldly austere, all chrome and glass with pockets of overstuffed cowhide furniture arranged here and there in tidy groups for simultaneous separate conversations. A long side table held bottles of water, a stack of cheap Styrofoam cups, and a large thermos of coffee; a well-worn mesquite-topped bar stood in a far corner. In front of the window was the room's centerpiece, Wirth's enormous desk, ten feet long by four feet wide, its glass top an inch thick. On it were his essentials: an open laptop computer, a hand-tooled leather cigar box, a twelve-inch-high cigar lighter in the form of an oil derrick, the Texas-shaped ashtray, a slate gray telephone console, two lined yellow legal pads, an electric pencil sharpener, and four freshly sharpened number 2 Ticonderoga 1388 pencils lined up perpendicular to each other exactly two inches apart. Other than his executive desk chair and a mesquite credenza behind the desk itself, there was very little else. No photographs of wife and children. No bound volumes of corporate handbooks lining ornate bookshelves. No portraits of company founders on the walls, which, except for a large AG STRIKER company logo stenciled in raised gold leaf across from his polished-steel office door, were wholly bare.

A buzzer sounded on Wirth's console.

"Yes."

"Mr. Truex," a female voice responded.

"Send him in." Wirth said, then looked at Moss, "He's here."

"So I gather," Moss said as the door opened and Loyal Truex, founder and chief executive of the private security contractor Hadrian Protective Services, entered.

"Finally, the man himself," Wirth snapped. "Where the fuck have you been?"

"Traffic accident. Luckily not mine," Truex said in a quiet kind of southern drawl.

"Ever think to pick up the phone and call? Or don't you think this meeting's important enough?"

"You sound like my mother, Sy." Truex smiled easily, then plunked down on the arm of an overstuffed chair and made himself at home.

Loyal Truex was forty-three and just over six feet tall. With close-cropped black hair and the muscular build of the former U.S. Army Ranger he was, everything about him—calm, boyish humor, self-made wealth—reflected confidence. His clothes mirrored it: close-fitting, hand-tailored navy suit, open white shirt, plain-toed Italian dress shoes, diamond-studded gold bracelet on one wrist, Rolex watch on the other. That he had spent most of the morning circumventing bad weather while piloting his own Gulfstream jet from Virginia to Texas and after that inching through traffic for nearly an hour seemed to have had no more effect on him than Wirth's urgent summoning of him to Houston from his Manassas office at six that morning. Still, he was there as promised and ready to go to work.

Wirth got to it quickly. "The Bioko photographs."

"You want to know where we stand with them." Truex glanced at Arnold Moss, then looked back to Wirth. "It's the reason I'm here."

"I know where the fuck we stand with them. We don't have them! The reason you're here is because I want to know what Washington knows. How much you've told them or they've found out. How closely they've been monitoring this."

"As far as I know, Sy, it's still all in-house, yours and mine," Truex said quietly. "Communication with Bioko, with Conor White, is the same as it's been with you—all done over our own secure lines. The SimCo people in Malabo have been instructed to say nothing to anyone, and they won't. They're exceptionally loyal to White and closed-mouth anyway. On the other hand, if Washington has been monitoring the situation in a way we don't know— which I doubt, for the simple reason that this is a very recent, low-key development that would take time to filter down—I would have heard about it, slick, fast, and hard. As for the photographs themselves, White's best operators went after them and came up with nothing, so he brought in General Mariano's army unit."

"Mariano?" Wirth erupted. "Are you out of your fucking mind?"

"Easy, Sy." Truex put up a calming hand. "White's people were getting nowhere, so he asked Mariano for help. Only his sector knows about them, no one else. His men were told they were looking for unauthorized photographs taken by a village priest and anything found was to be brought directly to

Mariano himself. As far as I know, only White and a few villagers have actually seen them. Which is how White got them in the first place, through one of the villagers. The result of it all was that White's operators and Mariano's turned over every stone and tree root in the area looking for them, taking down a lot of people in the process. A hundred killed at least. So if the pictures were there they would have been found. But they weren't. What that means is there's a very good chance the priest destroyed them himself to avoid being killed." Truex smiled. "Which is probably why nobody's found them. Because they no longer exist."

"And maybe they do exist and are in some fucking place nobody knows about," Wirth spat, anger, impatience, and displeasure crawling all over him. The next came out of the blue. "Who the hell is this landscape guy, Nicholas Marten?"

"Apparently no more than he appears. An American expat visiting Bioko from England doing plant research for clients. He met the priest by happenstance. That's all we know."

"That's all you know?"

"Sy, we're working on it."

"I asked you to come here with hard information. You give me 'as far as I knows' and 'maybes.' And now you add the 'incidental information' that the army knows about them, too. Do I have to go over there and take care of this myself? What the fuck do I need you and White for? Shit!"

Abruptly Wirth pushed out of his chair and walked off, trying to digest the reality of what was going on. The information about the existence of the photos had come to them barely twelve hours earlier in Conor White's urgent e-mail to Truex. That White had known about them earlier and not reported it, and that he had enlisted a special section of the Equatorial Guinea army to help search for them, made things worse because now too many people knew about it. Worse yet, none of it had done any good. The photos were still missing.

Wirth reached the far side of his office, where the AG Striker logo was, then stopped and turned back. "If those photographs become public the whole Bioko field project is dead, and so is this company. If the media doesn't make certain of it, Washington will." He pointed his unlit cigar at Moss. "What the fuck do we do, Arnie?"

The New Yorker in him aside, Arnold Moss's thirty-odd years in the oil business had given him a shrewd appreciation for the complexities of life and a habit of taking the time to think things through. For a long moment he sat there in silence, doing just that.

"When this whole thing came together," he said finally, "in exchange for protecting our investment and interests in Equatorial Guinea, we agreed to give Mr. Truex and his Hadrian company seven percent of our gross profit from all crude oil pumped from the Bioko field until the year 2050. By our projections and his, that figure is staggering. That means Mr. Truex has considerable interest in making sure the photographs, if indeed they do exist, are not made public. Because if they are, as you correctly implied, Sy, Washington will simply void the contract, make certain our leases are terminated, and put together a new deal elsewhere. And we, along with Mr. Truex, will end up with nothing." Moss got up and went to the side table to pick up a Styrofoam cup and fill it from the thermos. Holding it, he looked back.

"That said, we have to assume the photographs do exist and will be publicly exposed. We have to act accordingly. Starting immediately the AG Striker and Hadrian companies have to distance themselves from SimCo and Conor White. Build a legal and public relations defense against them and be prepared to sever our relations with White and SimCo the instant the photos show up. How they're delivered, whether by this Nicholas Marten or by someone else or if they somehow just show up on the Internet, doesn't matter. Whatever is in them, whatever they reveal about White's people delivering arms to the rebels, it has to look as if it were SimCo's doing alone, that it was their agenda entirely and one we knew nothing about." Moss walked back to his chair and sat down.

"AG Striker is an oil field management and exploration company," he said, "nothing else. Hadrian is a contractor for us in Iraq only. Should it ever be proven that we and Hadrian were, in any way, involved with SimCo to exploit the revolution in Equatorial Guinea for our own gain, everything we've been blessed with and worked so long and hard to protect is over. Not only that, there is every chance the Department of Justice will look into it, with

Congressman Joe Ryder hanging over their shoulder. Which means not only very bad publicity and an enormous legal expense to defend us but the stark reality that some or all of us will go to prison. You, Sy, and Mr. Truex included. Should we look to Washington for help, they won't be anywhere in sight. To them, our agreement will have never existed. That's the way it is."

Josiah Wirth stared at his chief counsel in silence, then looked to Loyal Truex. "We send Conor White over, then what? Who protects us in E.G.?"

"We do."

"You?"

Truex nodded. "If it's done right, and Washington is convinced SimCo will take the fall cleanly, they'll approve it. They won't like it, but they'll approve it because of the sheer scope of the thing and because they won't dare risk losing what's there to the maneuverings of a foreign power. Once they do, we'll bring in a new contractor, one squeaky clean. Maybe Belgian or Dutch. I'll find out exactly who."

"That means telling them what's going on."

"Yes, it does."

Wirth stared at Truex, then again looked to Arnold Moss. "Tell him he's fucking crazy."

Moss shook his head. "He's not crazy, Sy, he's right. They should know what's happened and what we're doing to correct it. Despite what Mr. Truex has said, they may already know and wonder why we haven't told them. If they don't and find out later, they'll be understandably upset. Enough so that they might just cancel the contract anyway and make a deal with another oil company even if we're lucky enough to retrieve the photographs before something happens. Besides, if we include them now, they may be able to help."

"Arnie." Wirth's anger was building. "That's the same as telling them we can't control our own goddam business. Contractually we're in bed with them for years on down the road. We can't have them wondering what the fuck's next or they'll chop us off at the knees. Once that happens, forget ever having them go to bat for us again. And I mean ever! And it won't make a longhorn's-fucking-ass difference what party or administration's in power."

Moss smiled delicately. "Sy, you pay me for advice. This time I suggest you take it. Washington is not a group we can ignore and then apologize to later. We're not buying land or oil rigs here, we're helping facilitate a revolution. They need to know what's going on and understand that we would very much appreciate their help in resolving the situation. There are times in life when honesty really is the best policy. This is one of them."

Wirth stared at him. He hated all this. Hated that it had happened. Hated to have anything go this far out of his control. Especially when it revolved around something as simple and stupid as a few photographs snapped by a nosy priest. On the other hand, he knew he had to consider the counsel of Arnie Moss, a man he had known for years and to whom he had entrusted Striker's legal wrangling ever since he had become chairman of the company.

Finally he looked to Truex. "Get in your Gulfstream and go back to Washington. Call them from the plane, tell them you're coming and that it's important they wait for you. You should be in their offices by seven, maybe eight their time. When you get there, tell them what's happened and make me the bad guy, say that I wanted to go after the photographs on my own. That I hoped we'd retrieve them before anything came of it. But you disagreed and came here to talk me out of it because you felt it was important they know what has happened, not just because we're all partners in this but because you value who they are and what they believe in and want their muscle and help. You convinced me you were right and went back to meet with them. That will explain the time delay if they already know what's going on." Wirth turned to Arnold Moss. "You okay with that?"

"Yes." Moss nodded.

Wirth looked to Truex. "You?"

"Yes."

"Call me when it's done."

"You bet." Truex looked from one man to the other, then started for the door.

"Loyal," Wirth said, and Truex turned back. "Dracula Joe Ryder in is Iraq with a handful of other congressmen looking for any dirty crumb he can lay to us."

"I know."

"After you're through with Washington, go there. Find Ryder and hold his hand. Be as gracious as you can be. Kiss his ass without looking like it. Show him anything he wants. Make him feel we have absolutely nothing to hide."

Truex grinned. "There is no dirt, Sy. No cakes or crumbs, either. Never has been. We all know that, don't we?" With a glance and a nod at Arnold Moss, he pulled open the door and went out.

15

Sy Wirth and Arnold Moss waited for the door to close behind Truex. When it had, Wirth looked to his general counsel. "I agree with what you said about SimCo. We set up to distance ourselves from it and Conor White as quickly and quietly as possible. At the same time, we have to distance ourselves from Hadrian and Truex. Even if it means opening the door to Joe Ryder and his congressional commission and inviting them in. Even if it means giving back every penny of the nine-hundred-plus million we've made in Iraq. It's nothing compared to what we stand to make in the future."

Wirth crossed to the window and looked out at the garish midday brightness of the city. "We needed a private security contractor for our expanded operations in Equatorial Guinea," he mused out loud. "We felt Hadrian was already stretched too thin in Iraq. Also, there were some questions concerning our partnership there. Still, we trusted Hadrian and asked Loyal Truex to recommend a reliable contractor."

Wirth turned and looked at Moss directly. "SimCo was a small subcontractor to Hadrian in Iraq. Truex liked the company and its honcho, Conor White, who he'd worked with before and who had outstanding credentials. Because of that he introduced us. We liked what we saw in White and hired his company. How could we know SimCo was a front for Hadrian, which was trying to expand its operations into West Africa without the questionable stigma of Iraq? What Hadrian, through SimCo, was attempting to gain in firing up the insurgency in Equatorial Guinea we had no idea whatsoever. As you said, Arnie, AG Striker is an oil field management and exploration company, nothing else.

"Hadrian could try to deny it by saying we have a contract that says we helped create SimCo and why. But if they did, they would have to produce the contract itself, the hard copy of which, as we all know, is locked in a great big Mosler safe in one of the most secure buildings in the world. If they wanted to produce an electronic copy from Washington's database, they would have to have Washington's approval, and that is something that would never happen. If Truex were to complain to them privately later, his going there now, and then on to meet with Ryder in Iraq, would only make it look as if he knew there was trouble all along and was trying to get everyone on his side before it blew up.

"If somehow the photographs are made public before we get them, it won't be AG Striker that's under Joe Ryder and the Justice Department's laser beam, it will be Hadrian and SimCo."

Wirth went to the mesquite-topped bar in the corner, poured himself a shot of Johnnie Walker Blue, and drank it in one swallow. Then he locked eyes with Arnold Moss and swore an oath.

"I am not going to lose the Bioko field, Arnie. Not to Hadrian. Not to Conor White or Joe Ryder. Not to Washington. I'm not going to lose it to anyone."

16

• Air France Flight 959, Malabo Saint Isabel Airport
To Paris, Charles de Gaulle Airport.
Still Thursday, June 3. 10:30 P.M.

The seating in the economy cabin of the Airbus 319 was three and three divided by a center aisle, and the four-man army patrol that had escorted Marten and Marita and her people to the airport had commandeered one complete row for them. Window to aisle on the far side were Marita, Rosa, and Ernesto. Window to aisle on the other were Marten, Luis, and Gilberto. The flight had taken off during a lull in the storm, and the cabin lights had been lowered shortly after that. Save for the occasional passenger using an overhead light to read or work, most of the passengers slept, more out of relief to have escaped a long weather-related delay in Malabo than anything else.

Of them all, probably none was more thankful

than Marten. Emotionally drained and enormously relieved to be airborne out of the army's grasp, he only now realized the depth of his exhaustion. He'd been on Bioko for barely five days, but it seemed a lifetime. Still wired and restless, he tried to sleep, but it was impossible. Across the aisle, he could see the red-haired Ernesto awake, too, listening to something over a headset. A deep exhale and he turned to look out the window just as they broke through the lingering cloud deck into a clear, moon-lit night.

• 10:38 P.M.

He lay back and closed his eyes once more. They were still hours from Paris, and he wanted to sleep for as many of them as he could. To escape, for a time at least, everything that had happened in the last days.

Two minutes passed. And then four. And then eight. Marten sat up. Sleep wasn't going to come and he knew it. Again he looked out the window, watching as the plane banked, beginning its turn over the island. The darkness below played against the quiet whine of the engines, and for a moment he thought the combination might lull him to sleep. Then he caught sight of three reddish points of light on the ground. They were probably twenty or more miles apart in what should have been the deep black of heavily forested land. In his mind there was no question what they were. Burning vil-lages. If he was right, either the insurrection was escalating and moving quickly north, or President Tiombe's army was taking preventive action and destroying suspected rebel townships in a show of force. Maybe it was both. But whatever was happening, hundreds of people were being killed, and the rebellion—justified as it might be against Tiombe and his brutal, corrupt regime—was being made all the worse by Conor White's supplying of arms to the insurgents because the army's massive response to it was so barbaric. In Father Willy's words, "extreme, even savage cruelty." In Conor White's, "The army is literally slaughtering suspected insurgents along with their friends and families, the old and women and children included, and afterward burning their villages to the ground." To Marten it seemed as if the war were being purposely escalated on both sides. The question was, why and why now?

What had President Harris told him in England barely a week earlier? *"Father Dorhn has been in Equatorial Guinea for fifty years. If anyone knows what's going on there he does, and from his letter he seems to know quite a lot."*

Well, Father Willy did know a lot. And he was dead because of it. So were the two young boys with him. How many hundreds, maybe thousands of untold others had been annihilated in the course of things? How many were being killed right now, at this moment, twenty thousand feet beneath him?

Marten turned from the window, pulling down the shade as he did. As if somehow it would shield him from the horror below.

At almost the same moment a flight attendant entered from the first class cabin, abruptly pulling the separating curtain closed behind her as she did. For an instant Marten caught a glimpse of the handful of passengers seated there. To his surprise, Anne Tidrow was among them. She was dressed casually in dark slacks and tailored jacket and was in an aisle seat near the rear. Next to her was an older, gray-haired man in a business suit. Whether they were traveling together or were just seatmates there was no way to tell.

• 10:50 P.M.

Marten was angry and on edge and probably too tired to be trying to sort things out, but he kept at it anyway because he couldn't help it and because in this situation, his mind had no off switch.

"Tell them what you have seen!" Father Willy yelled just before he was killed.

By that he'd meant the photographs.

To President Harris and to Joe Ryder, especially, their significance would go far beyond showing SimCo mercenaries secretly arming the insurgents. The pictures would give immediate credibility to the theory Theo Haas had put forward to Joe Ryder about the Striker/Hadrian collusion in Iraq having been extended to Equatorial Guinea.

It was, he knew, pure speculation on his part. Still, he had seen what he had seen, and what Father Willy had so forcefully and tragically sent him to report. The trouble was that just telling them would

not be enough. He needed hard evidence—the photographs themselves and if possible the camera's
memory card. The same hard evidence the Equatorial Guinean government wanted as proof that an
outside force was fueling the rebellion. The same
hard evidence, he was certain, that Conor White and
Anne Tidrow had been after but for the opposite
reason: to keep their actions from being found out.

Clearly both sides believed the photos existed
and would do whatever was necessary to retrieve
them. But so far neither had apparently succeeded.
Even if Marten accepted their belief that the pictures did exist, he had no more way of knowing
where they were than the others. The whole thing
was, and remained, a mystery that only Father Willy
could resolve. And Father Willy was dead.

• 10:55 P.M.
For no particular reason Marten looked across the
center aisle to the passengers in the rows of darkened seats behind him. To his surprise he saw a
man in a striped shirt and white trousers sitting under a reading light watching him. At Marten's glance
he looked away, clumsily picking up a magazine he
had in his lap. He was heavyset and jowly, and Marten knew he had seen him somewhere before. Where,
he didn't know. A moment later his gaze shifted
across the center aisle. Two seats down another man
was awake and reading. He was dressed in tan khakis and a light blue golf shirt and was considerably
younger than the jowly man. Marten had seen him

before, too. In the airport maybe. Perhaps that was where he'd seen the other man as well.

No.

Suddenly he remembered where he'd seen them both. In the bar at the Hotel Malabo. The heavyset, jowly man in white he'd had to step around on his way in. The other had been sitting halfway down the bar when he'd been talking with Anne Tidrow and Conor White. If they were on the flight by chance, then why had the jowly man been watching him? Or had he been watching him?

• 10:57 P.M.

Marten turned out the light over his seat and again closed his eyes. He was starting to drift off when the thought he'd had earlier came roaring back. Why had the army interrogators suddenly put him on a plane and let him go when they could have as easily killed him and buried his body somewhere in the rain forest?

The reason had to be the photographs. They hadn't found them on Father Willy's person or in his church or residence or anywhere among the people in his village, or on Marten's person or in his belongings at the hotel, or in those of Marita and her students. As a result they might well have concluded he'd managed to send them to a safe haven off the island, maybe to someone on the mainland using something as simple as the regular mail. The last person they had seen him with had been the foreigner Marten. So why not assume the priest, instead of giving him the pictures to smuggle out, had told him where they were? If that were so they had simply used the police/military tactic some called "intelligence gain-loss"—why destroy a target when you can exploit it? Meaning it would have been foolish to kill him when it was so much better to let him go and follow him. And they had, putting him on the next plane out of the country and then planting someone on the same plane to tail him. Maybe the jowly man or the man in the golf shirt, or both, or maybe someone else entirely. The problem was—and even in his exhausted state Marten had to smile—they were grasping at straws, because Father Willy had told him nothing.

Once again he glanced over his shoulder. The light over the jowly man's seat was turned out. Not so for the man in the light blue golf shirt, who was still awake and reading. Forget it, Marten thought. Let them do what they want. You know nothing, so just forget it and go to sleep. He pulled the Air France courtesy blanket up around him and closed his eyes.

You know nothing, he repeated.

Nothing.

Nothing at all.

17

Marten waited at the luggage carousel with the other passengers from Air France Flight 959. Nearby, he saw Marita standing with her chattering medical students sorting through boarding passes and ticket wallets for luggage receipts. Directly across was the jowly man in the white suit and striped shirt, waiting, like everyone else, for the conveyor to begin. To his right, maybe a dozen passengers down, was the man in tan khakis and blue golf shirt. Both men seemed to be traveling alone. Now he saw Anne Tidrow move toward the carousel. The gray-haired man in the business suit who had been seated next to her in the first class section was with her. Suddenly he wondered if she had deduced the same thing as the army interrogators, that he knew where the photographs were, and was tagging along assuming he would lead her to them. If that were the case, he had not one group but two watching him. And both for no reason at all.

There was a whirring sound, and then the belt on the carousel started up. Seconds later luggage began appearing. Marten turned to look for his bag and found Marita and her students coming toward him. They had already collected theirs and were on the way out.

"Hi and bye." Marita grinned as she reached him. "We're on the next flight to Madrid. It leaves in thirty minutes. We barely have time to check our luggage."

"Then you'd better hurry," he said, then looked to all of them. "Thank you again for everything you did to help me. Maybe one day we can all—"

"Here," Marita pressed a page torn from a notebook into his hand. "My address and telephone number if you get to Spain. My e-mail if you don't." Her words tailed off shyly, but there was nothing shy about her impish smile. "Please call me if you have time. I want to know what happens to you."

"Nothing's going to happen to me. I'm going home and back to work and grow old, nothing else."

"You're not a 'nothing else' person, Mr. Marten." Their eyes met, and the impishness vanished. "I think you're one of those people trouble follows around." Once again she smiled. "We have to go. Please call me."

"I will," he said and nodded at the others.

Then they were gone, making their way through the rush of early-morning passengers and finally disappearing from sight.

Moments later Marten collected his bag and walked off, pulling the wheeled suitcase behind him. As he did he saw Anne Tidrow and her gray-haired, business-suited companion, their bags on a luggage trolley, moving toward the exit. Never once did she look his way. It made him think that he was wrong about her following him, that she had been on the same flight by coincidence and had no further interest in him whatsoever.

• 7:30 A.M.

Marten entered Musikfone, a small audio and electronics kiosk, that was up an escalator and down a window-paneled corridor from baggage claim. Outside, he had seen a bright morning sky filled with puffy clouds and the promise of a gathering weather front, but it was what was inside the store that was of far more interest—a display of iPods, Mp3 players, smart phones, and other electronic gadgets, plus what looked like a thousand headsets, battery chargers, connectors, and attachments. What he wanted was right in front of him—a shelf of inexpensive, throwaway cell phones and, next to them, prepaid phone cards.

His plan was simple: buy a throwaway cell phone, call President Harris on the private number he'd given him, and tell him about the photographs and what he'd witnessed in Bioko, then get rid of the phone, take the next plane to Manchester, and go back to work. If anyone was following him, good luck to them; their life would suddenly become very tedious and wholly uneventful. That is, unless they wanted to learn about flowers and shrubs.

Marten chose a dark blue cell phone and a prepaid phone card and headed toward the cashier. As he did, two things happened at once. Out of the corner of his eye he saw the jowly man in the white suit step into the store, glance around at the merchandise as if he were looking for something, and then leave. The second thing was infinitely more profound and hit like a lightning bolt.

"Fuck!" he spat out loud at the realization just as he reached the cashier, a pert young woman who looked no more than twenty.

"What did you say, sir?" she asked in accented English.

"Nothing. I'm sorry," he said and set the packaged cell phone on the counter. "Just the phone and the card, please."

• 7:38 A.M.

Marten walked down the corridor, throwaway phone and phone card in a plastic Musikfone bag tucked into his wheeled suitcase, barely aware of where he was or the people around him. How could he have been so blind, so naïve?

Father Willy had told him everything as they were descending from the rain forest in the seconds before they heard gunfire and the two boys came running and yelling.

"I trusted you, Mr. Marten, because I had to," he'd said. *"I could not give you the photographs because there is no way to know who you might run into when we part. Hopefully, you have clear memories of what you have seen and what I have told you. Take that information with you and leave Bioko as quickly as you can. My brother is in Berlin. He is a very capable man. I hope that by the time you reach him neither he nor your American politician friend will have need for you to tell them any of this. Tell them anyway."*

His brother have need for him to TELL THEM?

Of course not—when his brother would have the photographs *right in front of him!*

Somehow Father Willy had managed to get them to him, maybe via the regular mail as he'd thought earlier or maybe some other, even simpler, way. If he was right, and he was certain he was, that was where they would be—with Theo Haas in Berlin.

The trouble was, if he could figure it out, how long would it be before Conor White and/or the major and the hawk-faced soldier put things together? How long would it be before they looked into Father Willy's background and found that despite different last names and lives worlds apart, he and the famed novelist Theo Haas were brothers?

Once they did, the race would be on to get to Haas first. When that happened and the photos were retrieved, then everything Father Willy and his villagers had done and died for would either become a very public justification for the army to continue its barbarous rampage or vanish into thin air at Conor White's bidding.

To Marten, neither was acceptable. Theo Haas had to be reached and warned, told he was in grave danger and instructed to take the photographs to the police. On second thought, that could lead to unintended consequences if they fell into the hands of someone who recognized their importance and sold them to the tabloids or simply posted them on the Internet. If that occurred, the government of Equatorial Guinea would have achieved exactly what it wanted without having lifted a finger. No, he had to handle the whole thing delicately and with caution, while at the same time remembering that the life of Theo Haas might soon be in severe jeopardy. What Marten had, or hoped he had, was a small window of opportunity before the others realized who Haas was and what his brother, in all probability, had done.

He was in already in Paris. Berlin was a short plane ride away. He had to get there as quickly as he could and without attracting attention.

7:42 A.M.

18

• 7:45 A.M.

Marten walked hurriedly across the terminal looking for an electronic airline departure board and a listing of the next flight to Berlin. Suddenly the idea that someone might be following him, a thought he had dismissed as foolish only moments earlier, became a very real problem. The last thing he needed was for someone tailing him to see him board a plane to the German capital and report it.

He glanced over his shoulder.

No sign of the jowly man. No sign of the man in khakis and blue golf shirt. No sign of Anne Tidrow or her gray-haired friend. Maybe he was being overly cautious. If he was, so be it.

Thirty feet ahead was a departure board. Again he glanced over his shoulder. All he saw was strangers. Seconds later he was there and studying the departure list.

Twenty yards behind him a bearded young man in jeans and a *PARIS, FRANCE* sweatshirt with a backpack over one shoulder stopped and raised a hand casually to his mouth as if to stifle a cough.

"This is Two," he said quietly into a tiny microphone in his sleeve. "He's stopped at a departure board and is studying it."

"Thank you, we'll take it from here." A female voice came over a tiny headset in his ear.

• 7:59 A.M.

Marten entered a café area filled with travelers and went to the counter. He selected a croissant and a cup of coffee, paid the cashier, and went to a distant table near a large window overlooking the tarmac and sat down. He took a moment to collect himself, then casually looked around for someone he might recognize. He saw only faceless travelers and airport personnel. Finally he took a bite of croissant and a sip of coffee, then slid the Musikfone bag from his suitcase and took the packaged cell phone from it. Another sip of coffee and he tore open the packaging and brought out the phone. A moment more and he stood up, glanced indifferently around, then moved away from the table to stand near the window and flicked open the phone. He punched in an access number and the PIN code on his phone card. Quickly he entered a second access number.

"International directory, please, for Berlin." A moment later an operator came on. "Telephone number for Theo Haas, please," he said. "I don't have the address." He waited, then, "You're certain, no listing at all . . . I see. Yes, thank you."

He clicked off and looked around once more. Then, with a glance at his watch, he again dialed his access number and PIN code and punched in a second number. As he did, he turned his back to the room. An everyday traveler making a cell phone call.

• United States Embassy, Sussex Drive, Ottawa, Canada. 2:10 A.M.

A ringing telephone woke President John Henry Harris from an on-again, off-again sleep, his mind churning over the cumbersome details of a new trade agreement he'd come here to resolve with the prime minister of Canada and the president of Mexico. Through the fog of sleep he looked at the four telephones arranged on his nightstand. Two were hardwired. Two were cell, one red, the other slate gray. It was the gray phone that was ringing. He knew before he picked it up who was calling.

"Cousin," he said in the dark as he clicked on, tugging at a pajama top that had twisted awkwardly across his chest while he slept. "Where are you?"

"Paris."

"Are you alright?"

"*Yes.*"

"I was concerned. I've been briefed on the war in Bioko and the rest of the country. I'm glad you're safely out."

"*So am I.*" Harris could hear the emotion in Marten's voice. As quickly it was replaced by urgency. "*There are photographs of SimCo mercenaries, Striker's private security contractor in Equatorial Guinea, secretly supplying arms to the rebels. SimCo's headman, a Brit named Conor White, was one of them.*"

"What?"

"*Theo Haas's brother, Father Willy Dorhn, the priest you sent me to see, took them. He's dead. Murdered by the army. I don't know why White's people are involved with the insurrection, but they are, and I'm all but certain it's at Striker's directive.*"

"These photographs, they're clear-cut? There's no mistaking who the people in them are or what they're doing?"

"*No, none. I've seen them myself.*"

"Where are they? Who has them?" Harris flicked on a table lamp and swung his legs over the side of the bed.

"*That's what everybody wants to know. The E.G. army interrogators and Conor White himself. Nobody can find them, but I think I know where they are.*"

"Nicholas, cousin." The president got up and crossed the room barefoot. "I want, I *need*," he said emphatically, "to have those pictures in my

possession as quickly as possible and without anyone knowing. If the Striker people find out they'll
cover their asses in a hurry. Hadrian's, too. If they're
leaked to the media we'll have a major international
incident on our hands."

• Paris, Charles de Gaulle Airport.

"I'm aware of that." Marten turned from the window to look casually around as if he were in the
middle of a dull conversation. Satisfied no one was
within hearing distance, he turned back.

"It's just after eight in the morning, Paris time.
I'm going to try to make a nine-thirty flight to Berlin, where Theo Haas lives. His phone number is
unlisted. I need you to get it for me."

"I don't understand," the president said.

"I think his brother forwarded the photos to him.
He may have them in his possession and be planning to do something with them himself or he may
have them and not know it. If Father Willy sent them
by mail, maybe they haven't even arrived. I don't
think the others have considered Berlin yet because
he and Haas have different last names and there
would be no reason to make a connection. It means
I have a head start. At least by the few hours it takes
until they figure it out and get moving."

"Are you sure you want to do this?"

"Who else do you have?"

There was silence, and Marten knew the president was considering the ramifications of what
might happen if he asked for the help of the CIA or

other security agencies and because of it Hadrian or
Striker or both learned what was going on and where
and why.

"I will get you the Haas telephone number."

"Good. Now there's more," Marten pressed him.
"Haas may or may not have learned about his brother's death. Either way, he doesn't know me, so there's
no reason for him to trust me. But he does know
and trust Joe Ryder. Ryder needs to call Haas right
away and tell him to expect to hear from me. He
doesn't need to tell him what it's about, just say
I'm the person who met with his brother in Bioko
and that I want to meet with him as soon as I get to
Berlin."

*"Nicholas, Ryder is with a congressional group
in Iraq looking into the Striker/Hadrian situation.
I don't know how quickly I can reach him or how
soon he can get in touch with Haas."*

"I know you'll do the best you can. In the meantime I need Haas's phone number."

"Call me back in thirty minutes."

• 8:14 A.M.

Marten clicked off and turned from the window. As
he did he saw a familiar face watching him from a
balcony on the floor above.

Anne Tidrow.

Instead of feigning surprise, or turning away in
the hopes he wouldn't recognize her, she smiled and
waved easily, as if they were old friends. When he'd
last seen her she had been on her way out of the

airport with her gray-haired companion. Now she was back, apparently alone. If she was following him, this was the time to find out.

He smiled genially, then motioned for her to come down and join him.

19

• 8:17 A.M.

Marten watched her as she came down the escalator. Still in the dark slacks and tailored jacket she'd worn on the plane, she seemed slimmer, less severe, and more athletic than when they'd met at the Hotel Malabo. For the first time he noticed the long taper of her neck and the muscular strength of it. Clearly she kept in good physical condition and, from the way she held herself, was proud of it.

"I was on my way to the railway station for a train into the city when I saw you," she said as she reached him. "I wondered how you were after the long flight."

"Anxious to get home and back to work," he said lightly. "I have a flight that leaves in less than an hour."

"To England. Manchester, isn't it?"

"Yes. How do you know?"

"I also know where you work. The landscape design firm of Fitzsimmons and Justice." She smiled.

"Conor White told me. He has access to information most people don't."

"Why would either of you be interested in where I live or work?"

"Because, Mr. Marten, neither he nor I felt you were being completely honest with us when we talked in Malabo. We are concerned about our employees in Equatorial Guinea, and you seemed to have had some other reason for being there, aside from collecting information on plants, that is. So Mr. White did a background check on you and—"

"Found I was telling the truth," he said, finishing her sentence, "that I was in Bioko to look over native flora for clients at home." He paused, taking the slightest moment to study her. She was intelligent and equally bold and clearly used to getting whatever it was she was after. "I have to assume it's why you were on the plane, out of concern for your employees, following me to make sure Mr. White's background check was accurate. And why, instead of leaving the airport with your friend, you were watching me from up there." He gestured toward the balcony above.

She grinned. "I was leaving Bioko for Paris anyway. So I took the assignment."

"In that case, you should be happy to report that my flight to Manchester connects through London, so there's no need to chase me all the way there. That is, unless you're interested in property in the north of England. Have you been to Manchester before?"

"No."

"Well, if you should happen to come, I would be happy to show you around. Conversely, should you have need for landscape design for either your home or business in Texas, you know where to reach me. Fitzsimmons and Justice, Manchester, England. We're in the phone book and we're expensive, but we do excellent work. Now, if you don't mind, I don't want to miss my flight. Please give my regards to Mr. White." With that Marten nodded and started off.

"Which airline?" she called after him.

He looked back, "Why, you want to come with me?"

"No, but I might have you followed."

"Help yourself." He grinned. "British Airways." Then he turned and continued on.

• 8:22 A.M.

Marten's study of the departure console had been fortunate in more ways than one. In trying to find the next flight to Berlin, he'd also seen the next flight to Manchester via London, something he'd noted with envy because he would have much preferred going there. Nonetheless it had stuck in his mind and was a welcome immediate and reasonable destination to give to Anne Tidrow. He doubted she believed him, though. She'd been far too blasé in telling him that neither she nor White had fully believed him in Malabo. It had been the same when she'd asked what airline he was taking on his flight home. Maybe she'd been joking about having him followed, but most likely she wasn't. Clearly they believed he knew something about the photographs and weren't about to let go until they were certain, one way or the other.

The Air France flight from Malabo brought them to Terminal—or Hall, as it was called—2F. The British Airways flight to London left from Hall 2B at 9:10. That gave Marten precious few minutes to walk from one terminal to the other, buy a ticket to London, find a place where he could call the president back, make the call, and then get to the departure gate. Once there he would wait until passengers began to board, then suddenly duck into a nearby kiosk as if he needed something at the last minute, then go out the other side and make his way to Hall 2D and the 9:30 Air France flight to Berlin. It was a lot of maneuvering but hopefully enough to throw off Anne Tidrow or anyone else who might be following him and let him make the Berlin flight unnoticed.

The thing about Ms. Tidrow, when he'd caught her watching him, was that her reaction had been to simply smile and wave. Afterward, when he'd directly accused her of following him, she'd admitted it and said why. Or at least partially why. Honesty in situations like that was always best. Or at least partial honesty. The trouble was, most people didn't do it. They hesitated and made up a story and certainly didn't look you in the eye when they told you the way she had. Maybe that kind of confidence came from sitting on the board of directors of a large oil company or maybe it came from somewhere else. Just where, or what that was, he had no way of knowing.

• 8:44 A.M.

Marten stopped at the rear of the line entering the security checkpoint, then moved away and took the blue cell phone from his bag and a pen and small notebook from his jacket. He glanced around, then repeated the dialing procedures he had used earlier.

• United States Embassy, Ottawa, Canada. 2:44 A.M.

President Harris picked up at the first ring. "I just got off the phone with Joe Ryder. He'll be calling Theo Haas momentarily. Here's Haas's private number. You have something to write with?"

"Yes."

"030-555-5895."

"Thank you."

"After you've seen Haas, Ryder wants to speak with you. I do, too. Call me and I'll get us plugged in on some kind of secure conference call. Don't know just how it'll work yet because he's traveling, but I'll have it operating by the time you call." The president hesitated. "Nick, Nicholas, cousin. I did a quick run-through on your friend Conor White. He won his stripes as a top British commando. He's got the Victoria Cross and a chest full of other military honors to prove it. Be damned careful, huh? I wouldn't want to lose you."

"I wouldn't want to lose me, either. I'll call you when I have something to report." President Harris heard Marten click off. He looked at his watch. It was two forty-five in the morning. Eight forty-five in Paris.

20

• 8:48 A.M.

Marten showed his British Airways boarding pass at the security checkpoint, then set his suitcase on the luggage conveyor, took off his belt and put it in a plastic tray with a number of coins from his pocket, and stepped through the metal detector. A moment later he retrieved his belt and coins, collected his suitcase, and walked off toward his boarding gate, B34. Not once, from the time he'd stepped into line at the ticket counter until now, had he seen anyone in particular watching him. It didn't mean they weren't there. It simply meant he hadn't seen them.

• 8:50 A.M.

Ahead, to Marten's right, was Gate B34 where a long line of passengers was in the process of boarding the London flight. To his left were toilets, a combination bookstore/newsstand/convenience store, and next to it a sandwich shop. He continued purposefully on and joined the line at Gate B34.

Twenty feet in front of him a slim, athletically built middle-aged man in a sport coat and blue jeans stood in the crowd waiting to board and at the same time absently watched Marten come toward him. Now he raised his hand as if to stifle a cough or clear his throat.

"This is Three. He's just joined the passenger queue waiting to board," he said softly into a microphone in his sleeve.

A male voice floated through an earpiece barely visible in his left ear. *"This is One. Thank you."*

"What do you want me to do?"

"Stay with him and board behind him. Make sure he is on the aircraft when it pulls back from the ramp."

"Right."

Seconds earlier, by luck or by instinct, Marten had looked up and seen a middle-aged, athletic-looking man in sport coat and jeans, standing near the front of the line watching him and at the same time moving his lips as he held a hand to his mouth. Now Marten saw him drop his hand and casually move aside to speak with a uniformed British Airways agent near the boarding gate.

Right then he knew. Whatever he'd thought before, there was no question now, he was being watched. But by whom? Conor White and Anne Tidrow's people? Operatives under the direction of the Army of the Republic of Equatorial Guinea?

And there wasn't just one. The man had been communicating with someone, which meant there were two of them at least, maybe more.

• 8:52 A.M.

The ranks of boarding passengers were lessening rapidly as people entered the aircraft. The Athlete, as Marten had decided to call him, was still talking with the British Airways employee, gesturing as if he had some problem with his ticket or seating arrangement or something similar. Every so often he looked off, as if he were becoming frustrated with the direction of the conversation. That glance away and then back, Marten knew, was carefully calculated to keep an eye on him. See where he was in line. Make certain he was moving forward with the remaining passengers, whose number by now had dwindled to fewer than two dozen. Athlete or no Athlete, if Marten was going to get out of there, he had to do it soon.

"Excuse me." He turned to a young woman in line behind him. "I have a splitting headache and need to get something for it before I get on the plane. Would you mind holding my place in line? I'll be right back."

With that he was gone, leaving the boarding area and crossing to the bookstore/newsstand/convenience store on the other side of the corridor.

Immediately the Athlete turned from the airline

agent and raised his hand to his mouth. "He just left the boarding area and has gone into a newsstand across from it!" he blurted into his hidden microphone.

"Stay with him! Stay with him!"

• 8:55 A.M.

Marten entered the store in a rush looking for another exit. He pushed around a magazine stand and then past a rack filled with toiletries. No time to think about the Athlete—just find the exit and get out of there. But where? There was no other egress. In front of him was a wall of bestselling books. To his right, a large magazine rack. To his left, a floor-to-ceiling case of PARIS, FRANCE T-shirts and caps.

"Christ!" he said to himself and turned to look for another way out. As he did, the Athlete came into the store and stood in the entryway, his eyes scanning the room. Immediately Marten looked away. The only exit was the doorway where the man was. To use it he would have to walk right past him. The clock was fast ticking down. If he missed the Berlin flight, there was every chance people employed by Striker/SimCo or agents from the Equatorial Guinean army would be at Theo Haas's doorstep before he was. Athlete or not, he had no choice but to go out past him and go now.

He was turning, starting to move, when a nearby door suddenly opened and a female clerk came out of a back room pushing a service cart piled with magazines and boxes of candy. In an instant Marten was past her and into the room looking for a service exit. All he saw was shelves full of supplies.

Immediately the clerk came in behind him. "Sir," she said with a French accent, "you're not allowed in here!"

"Sorry," he said and turned back, disheartened. Then he saw an exit door to the side, a crash bar mounted across it just below a bright red warning sign.

EMERGENCY EXIT ONLY, it read, in French and English.

Marten studied it. Go through it and the alarm goes off. People come running from everywhere. Perfect.

8:59 A.M.

21

• 9:03 A.M.

Marten walked quickly, suitcase in tow, the blaring of the emergency exit alarm and the rush of security personnel toward the convenience store diminishing behind him as he left Hall 2B and moved through the throng of apprehensive travelers drawn by the sudden activity and toward Hall 2D and his destination, gate D55 and his 9:30 Air France flight to Berlin.

To his right, floor-to-ceiling windows looked out

on other terminals across the way. Through them he could see that the bright, cloud-pocked sky of earlier had become completely overcast and large droplets of rain were splattering on the glass. Suddenly, even as he rushed for the plane and at the same time tried to evade the Athlete and his unseen players, the idea of rain brought memories of the storm in Malabo that he had feared might keep him grounded there for days. It was a reflection that carried with it the haunting memories of Bioko itself: Father Willy and the young boys clubbed to death by army troops; the bodies of the woman and children caught in the branches of the floating tree; the venomous features of the soldiers murderously pursuing him through the rain forest; the deadly, piercing eyes and tribal-scarred face of the army major who had interrogated him; the preposterous entrance of President Tiombe into the bar at the Hotel Malabo and the awful, chilling stare with which he had fixed Marten as he moved on.

Only one word could express his feelings about all of it.

Anger.

The people of Equatorial Guinea were victims of machinery and measures and dynamics far beyond their control. More infuriating still was the numbing realization that there was so very little that could be done about it. Father Willy had tried, done the very best he could, and he was dead because of it. Yet the thing was, no matter the outcome, he had tried, which was what Marten, in his own way, was attempting here. If he could somehow retrieve the photographs and get them to President Harris and Joe Ryder, it might be ammunition enough to pressure Striker and Hadrian and SimCo to stop arming the rebels and at the same time force Tiombe to pull back his forces, a combination that could quickly lessen the barbaric scope of the fighting. It wasn't much, but if he could do it, it was something. And to Marten, as he hustled toward gate D55, that little bit of something meant everything.

• 9:07 A.M.

The Athlete was stopped midcorridor outside Hall 2B. Through the terminal's glass wall he could see the British Airways London-bound aircraft pull back from the gate. He lifted a hand to his mouth. "This is Three," he said quietly but with urgency. "Who's got him?"

"*This is Two. He came out of the gate area. Security swept in and we lost him. One?*"

"*I don't have him.*"

"There's three of you out there! Somebody had to pick him up! Four, where are you?"

Silence.

"Four, repeat, where are you?"

Silence.

"*This is One. Four isn't answering.*"

• 9:11 A.M.

Anne Tidrow watched Marten enter Hall 2D, then go into the boarding area, looking at the gate numbers

as he went. No one had had to tell her he'd been lying about his British Airways flight to London and
his connecting flight to Manchester. In the minutes
before he'd seen her watching him from the upper
balcony, she had seen him. He'd been about to enter a
café area in Hall 2B when he'd stopped a uniformed
Air France flight crew and asked directions. One of
them had pointed in the direction of Hall 2D. Marten
had nodded, then thanked them and gone into the
café, where he'd purchased coffee and a croissant
and soon afterward made a call on a cell phone.

• 9:15 A.M.
She saw him enter the section at Gate D55 and join
the line of passengers boarding flight 1734 for Berlin.
Ninety seconds later he handed an Air France gate
attendant his boarding pass, then entered the jetway
and disappeared from view.

A breath and she lifted her hand to her mouth as
if to stifle a cough.

"This is Four. I'm in Hall 2D. I thought I saw him
come this way, then he took the escalator down and
I lost him."

"*Roger, Four.*" The voice of One came back.

Anne Tidrow watched for a moment longer as the
last of the passengers slipped into the jetway and
the Air France people closed the door behind them.
She lingered a few seconds, then walked off. As she
did she took a cell phone from her purse, flicked it
open, then tapped in a number and waited for it to
ring through.

Past lives, fond memories, old friends.

By the time Marten reached Berlin and entered the city—by taxi, private car, public transportation, or even if he walked—she would know where he had gone and where to find him.

22

• Berlin Tegel Airport. Still Friday, June 4. 11:15 A.M.

Nicholas Marten exited Air France flight 1734 in a group of passengers. Suitcase in tow, he left the Gate A14 area and passed through the green NOTHING TO DECLARE customs archway into the crowded arrivals area, where people were gathered to meet travelers from incoming flights. Two minutes later he was outside in warm sunshine and walking toward the taxi area. A dozen paces more and he moved to the edge of the curb away from sidewalk traffic. He gave a quick glance around and unzipped the upper pocket on his suitcase and took out the dark blue throwaway cell phone. By now Theo Haas's private phone number was etched in his memory. He punched in the number and waited. The phone rang four times, and then a recording clicked on. A husky male voice that he took to be Haas's made a brief announcement in German. The recording ended and there was silence, followed by the usual beep signaling the caller to leave a message. For an instant he thought about identifying himself and mentioning Joe Ryder's name, then decided against it and clicked off. Who knew what other party might retrieve Haas's calls—wife, girlfriend, houseman, secretary? Maybe he talked about personal business with people he knew well, maybe he didn't. Besides, there was every chance Joe Ryder hadn't yet reached him. Or maybe he'd tried and like Marten got only a recording. No, Marten thought, better to wait, call him a little later in the day. Immediately he clicked off, slipped the phone into his coat pocket, then walked off toward the taxi queue.

A gray-haired, matronly woman wearing a light-weight summer coat watched him go. She had been in a group of others waiting at Gate A14 to meet arriving passengers and had followed him when he left. She'd seen him step to the curbside, take a cell phone from his suitcase, and make a call. Now she followed him again. Safely and at a distance. She stopped as he entered the taxi line, then watched as he got into a black Mercedes Metrocab. Number 77331.

11:35 A.M.

• Madrid, Barajas International Airport. Same time.
Tired, but happy to be finally home after a flight delay of nearly two hours in Paris because of mechanical problems, Marita Lozano and her medical-student charges—Rosa, Luis, Gilberto, and Ernesto—left Iberia baggage claim, passed through

the customs area, and went out into the arrivals hall on their way to the Metro that would take them into the heart of the city.

The area was crowded with friends, relatives, business associates, and others gathered to meet arriving passengers. Among them were perhaps a dozen limousine drivers, most of them in dark suits and white shirts, holding cardboard signs that were hand-lettered with the names of the clients they'd been hired to pick up.

"Marita!" Rosa was the first to notice. "A sign with your name."

Puzzled, Marita looked to the bank of limousine drivers. A handsome young man was holding a sign that read DR. LOZANO.

"Some other and richer Dr. Lozano." Marita said with a laugh and kept walking.

As they passed, the man suddenly approached. "Marita Lozano?"

"Yes."

"I have a limousine to take you into the city."

"Me?"

"Yes, and your friends."

"I don't understand."

He smiled. "It was paid for by the oil company in Bioko. To thank you for your work there and help compensate for your trouble with the army. I was instructed to take each of you to your homes."

Marita looked at him carefully. Something didn't feel right.

"That's very nice," she said politely. "But I think we'll just take the Metro."

"Please, doctor, the company insists. You have all had a very long trip."

"I don't know."

"Oh, come on, Marita." Rosa giggled. "We're all tired. It's very nice of them to do this."

Luis grinned. "Who wants to take the Metro when we have a limo?"

"Nobody," Ernesto added.

Marita hesitated a moment longer, still unsure. Rosa pressed her again. "Marita . . ."

Finally she gave in. "Alright, Rosa, we'll take the limo."

"Good." The driver smiled warmly, then took her bag and Rosa's and led them toward the exit.

23

• Berlin, Hotel Mozart Superior,
94 Friedrichstrasse, Room 413. 1:35 P.M.

Freshly showered and shaved, Nicholas Marten stood in the window looking down at the street below. He was barefoot and bare chested, wearing jeans and nothing else. The dark blue cell phone was in his hand. He hesitated for the briefest moment and then, for the third time since he'd checked into the hotel ninety minutes earlier, he called the number President Harris had given him for Theo Haas.

Again it rang through. After the fourth ring he again got the husky-male-voice recording. Again he clicked off.

"Damn it," he swore angrily. Where the hell was Haas? What was he doing? When would he be home?

Suddenly it occurred to him that the Nobel laureate might be traveling and not in the city at all. Then what? Try to have the president or Joe Ryder track him down? That could take days, even longer. In the meantime, where were the photographs, assuming Father Willy had indeed sent them to his brother? Where? Sitting in a branch of the Berlin post office? In Haas's home, just lying around, opened or unopened? Or did Haas have them with him? Was he at this moment preparing to reveal them as only an irascible world-famous writer could, and most likely would?

As quickly Marten thought of something else: that maybe Conor White's people or operatives from the Equatorial Guinea military hadn't been as slow to put Father Willy and Theo Haas together as brothers as he'd first thought. Maybe one group or the other had already reached him. If so he could be in grave danger or even dead. In what could only be described as an urgent, near-involuntary reaction, he lifted the phone and punched in Theo Haas's number again.

Once more the call rang through. Once more he listened as it rang four times. He was expecting the recording to click on once again when instead a male voice answered.

"Yes?" came a grumble in German.

"My name is Marten, Nicholas Marten. I'm trying to reach—"

"You've got him," Theo Haas said sharply in English.

"I would like to meet with you. Could I come to your apartment?"

"Across from the Tiergarten. Platz der Republik. The grassy park in front of the Reichstag. Five o'clock. I'm an old man in a green cap and carrying a walking stick. I'll be sitting on a park bench near Scheidemannstrasse. If you're not there by ten minutes past I will leave."

There was an abrupt click as he hung up and the phone went dead.

"Well," Marten said out loud and with relief. At least no one else had gotten to him. Not yet anyway.

• Platz der Republik. 4:45 P.M.

Marten came into the park early, determined not to miss Haas through some happenstance beyond his control. In front of him the Platz der Republik sprawled for nearly a quarter of a mile and was filled with seemingly hundreds of people taking advantage of a warm early-summer afternoon. To his right was the massive edifice that was the historic Reichstag, Germany's parliament building. He vaguely remembered that it had been burned down, purportedly by the Nazis in 1933, and was then rebuilt and reoccupied by the parliament in 1999 as a symbol of German unity following the Cold War. The words carved above its main facade in 1916 had been restored as well—DEM DEUTSCHEN VOLKE ("To the German people"). Maybe the historical significance of it was something Haas was trying to impress on Marten and the reason he chose to meet in its shadow. Or maybe it had no meaning at all. What was curious was why he had chosen to meet outdoors in public rather than in the privacy of his home, especially when he knew that what Marten had to tell him concerned his brother. He was known for being a "character," and so maybe it was a whim, or maybe he simply didn't want strangers in his home.

• 4:50 P.M.

Marten reached the far end of the park and turned back, staying close to the pathway that ran near Scheidemannstrasse. He looked carefully at every bench he passed, most of which were occupied, and then beyond them to the crowd in the park and what suddenly seemed like the impossible chore of sorting through them to find an old man in a green cap with a walking stick.

• 4:55 P.M.

He arrived at the Reichstag building and turned back, retracing his steps. Still no green cap, no old man with a walking stick.

• 4:57 P.M.

He stopped at the far end of the park and once again turned back. What if Haas didn't show up? All he could do was call him and hope to hell he answered and that someone else hadn't gotten to him in the meantime. It made him think of the ten-minute timetable Haas had given him. Why had he done that? Once again he wondered why the old man had insisted they meet in a place as public and crowded as this. Maybe it was simply that he felt safer meeting a stranger that way, especially in view of what had happened to his brother in Bioko. Still, a quiet restaurant or café would have accomplished the same thing.

Again Marten looked around. Still nothing. Then from the corner of his eye he saw a taxi suddenly turn out of traffic on Scheidemannstrasse and pull to the curb. A moment passed, and the rear passenger door opened and an old man in a green cap carrying a walking stick got out. He closed the door with a ferocious bang and started into the park and toward a nearby bench. It was exactly five o'clock. Theo Haas had arrived.

24

Anne Tidrow had been a good twenty yards behind Marten when he entered the park. She stayed with him until he reached the far end and turned back. At that point she stepped behind a group of chattering tourists and waited to see where he would go next.

She'd followed him to the Platz der Republik by
cab, watching him turn the corner from Friedrichstrasse onto the boulevard Unter den Linden and
walk several more city blocks until he reached the
historic Brandenburg Gate. There, he'd turned right
and then left before crossing into the park in front
of the Reichstag. It was then she'd left the cab and
pursued him on foot.

Her Lufthansa flight from Paris had touched down
in Berlin a little more than an hour after his. Immediately she'd called her "past lives, fond memories,
old friends" contact and learned that Marten had
taken a cab to the Hotel Mozart Superior and checked
in, and that very soon afterward a private investigator had taken up residence in the lobby, carefully
watching the comings and goings of people who
passed through it.

Twenty-five minutes later she'd checked into the
nearby Hotel Adlon Kempinski, keeping a taxi at
hire just outside. After a little more than three nail-
biting hours and numerous cell phone exchanges
with the private investigator in the Mozart Superi-
or's lobby, he called to tell her that Marten had just
left his key at the front desk and was on his way out.
Seconds later he reported that he was following him
up Friedrichstrasse toward Unter den Linden.

In less than three minutes—wearing dark glasses,
her hair pulled back, and dressed as a tourist in jeans,
athletic shoes, and a stylish denim jacket—she was
in the hired cab rushing in that direction, concerned
all the while that the investigator would lose him if
he suddenly hailed a passing taxi himself. And then

she'd seen him, just as he turned the corner and started down Unter den Linden.

She was now less than thirty yards away watching Marten approach an old man in a green cap with a walking stick who had just seated himself on a park bench. She saw Marten reach him and say something, then watch as the elderly gentleman studied him carefully before gesturing for Marten to sit down. She slowed, then stopped behind two boys kicking a soccer ball back and forth between them. She wanted to move closer in the hope of overhearing what was being said, but then determined it was too risky and stayed where she was. The last thing she needed was for Marten to look up and recognize her.

How long she stood there watching she didn't know. All around her was activity—the boys with the soccer ball, children at a birthday party chasing each other, people flying kites in the light wind, dogs scampering after tossed Frisbees, lovers walking hand in hand oblivious to the world around them. Others, many still in business clothes who looked as if they'd left work early for nothing more than to enjoy the late-afternoon sun, lounged on benches or lay sprawled in the grass.

Suddenly, not twenty feet from the bench where Marten and the old man sat talking, there was a loud explosion of firecrackers, thirty or forty or more going off at once. People cried out in surprise. Startled children shrieked. Dogs barked. Even Marten reacted, jumping from the bench and staring in the direction of the explosions. In the next instant horror struck. A young, curly-haired man in a black sweater appeared from nowhere and went to the old man on the bench. A knife flashed in his hand. A second later he dragged it across the old man's throat, stared at his work for a heartbeat, then ran off toward Scheidemannstrasse.

Marten saw the assailant just as a woman screamed. In an instant he was at the old man's side. He lifted his slumped head, held it gently, then slowly set it back down and raced off after the curly-haired attacker. In three steps he was at the curb. Then, dodging traffic, he darted hazardously across Scheidemannstrasse, and chased after him at a dead run heading toward the Brandenburg Gate.

5:16 P.M.

25

• 5:18 P.M.

Marten could see him forty yards ahead nearing the Brandenburg Gate. As he reached it he glanced back, and Marten saw his face clearly. It was young and thin, with wild narrow-set eyes under that great shock of black curly hair. Who was he? Why had he wanted to kill Theo Haas? And so viciously and in public? Had he been sent by Conor White? Or by the Equatorial Guinean army? Had he trailed him from his apartment? Did it mean someone already had the photographs and Haas knew it, and knew who they were, and they wanted him silenced quickly, before he told someone? If so, why hadn't he tried to kill Marten, too?

Marten ran harder, trying to stay with him. He saw the young man weave in and out through the cars, tour buses, taxicabs, and tourists congesting the area in front of the Brandenburg Gate. Again he glanced back. Again Marten saw his face. It was grim and wild and strangely triumphant. In that instant he had the gut feeling that he was chasing not a professional killer but a madman.

• 5:20 P.M.

Anne Tidrow was probably twenty seconds behind Marten and running nearly as hard. She saw him cut into a throng of tourists and then disappear within them. She kept going, pushing through the crowd, but not seeing him.

The sudden murder of the old man had thrown everything into turmoil. Who was he? Did he know about the photographs? If so, what had he told Marten before he was killed, and in what direction, if any, had he pointed him? If she lost Marten now and he went after the pictures instead of back to his hotel, she might never find out.

She kept on, taking the same route Marten had, moving into the thick of the crowd that was suddenly abuzz with tension in the wake of one man chasing another through them. She kept going, wishing now she had brought at least one of her contacts with her. For a moment she lost sight of him and almost panicked. Then there he was, less than a dozen feet in front of her, stopped in the congregation of tourists and beside a line of waiting taxis looking furiously around for the killer. Instinctively she started to look for him herself, thinking, like Marten, that he was hiding somewhere in the throng.

Suddenly came a violent rush of sirens. Green-and-white Berlin police vehicles screamed in from all directions. In seconds uniforms were everywhere, shoving through the crowd, looking for the murderer. For a moment she was uncertain what to do: confront Marten about the old man, in the event he darted off in the confusion and she lost him for good, or take a chance and stay back, see where he went next. Suddenly it made no difference. People were gesturing toward Marten.

The instant was horrific as both she and he realized what was happening. People had seen him tear through them in a wild rush. They thought he was the one the police were chasing and were pointing him out.

Anne moved, and fast. A half-second later she was at Marten's side, taking his arm. "Come on, darling," she said loud enough to be heard by people around her, "we're late." Abruptly she pulled open the door to a waiting taxi.

"Hotel Mozart Superior, right away, please," she said to the driver, then shoved Marten into the cab and got in beside him.

"Of course," the driver said in accented English,

then moved the taxi off quickly, closely following another cab through the melee. In seconds they were gone and traveling back down Unter den Linden in the direction of Marten's hotel.

• 5:24 P.M.

"Where the hell did you come from?" Marten stared at her, astounded by her presence, by everything that had just happened, and by what was happening now. "How did you know I was in Berlin, or where I was in the city, or where I'm staying?"

"I know everything, darling. You're keeping a lover. I want to meet her," Anne scolded Marten sharply and loudly enough to be heard by the driver. "In Paris you told me you were taking a British Airways flight to London. But that was after you'd already asked an Air France crew the directions to another gate. You do things like that, you'd better be careful no one sees you. Who, or what, should I expect to meet? Let me guess, a long-legged blonde, about twenty-four, with big tits."

Suddenly she looked up and saw the driver watching them in the mirror. "Would you please turn on the radio? We'd like to have some music."

"American?"

"Anything, thank you."

Immediately the driver turned on the vehicle's radio and tuned it to a satellite channel and U.S. country music boomed out.

Marten glared at her. "I asked you how you knew where I was and where I'm staying."

"You may remember that I sit on the board of directors of a rather large oil company. We have friends everywhere."

Marten glanced at the driver, then looked back to Anne and lowered his voice, uncertain the music would mask their conversation. "You followed me from Malabo to Paris to Berlin and now to here. Why?"

Anne looked to the driver and gave him a big smile. "I like it. Turn it up!"

He grinned back and did as she asked; the music blared.

Immediately Anne turned to Marten. "I want the photographs. And don't say 'what photographs?'"

"I don't know what you're talking about."

"Yes you do. And you know where they are. The old man told you."

Marten smiled evenly. "Too bad your hearing wasn't as good as your eyesight. The subject of photographs never came up."

Just then Garth Brooks's "Friends in Low Places" boomed from the taxi's radio, and Anne leaned in close. "I want the pictures, Mr. Marten. I'll pay you what you want for them."

"Whatever these pictures are, they obviously mean a lot to you. Why?"

"Don't play with me," she snapped. "You know what the pictures are of and who is in them. I want them back because the safety and well-being of our people in Equatorial Guinea depends on it."

"Which people are 'our people,' Ms. Tidrow? The fellow chasing me through Charles de Gaulle

Airport? The Striker Oil board of directors? SimCo mercenaries? Certainly not your friend President Tiombe or his army that is slaughtering people by the hundreds even as you and I cruise around Berlin."

"Striker Oil employees, Mr. Marten. People who work for us have always been treated as family. We guarantee their security anywhere they are working." She softened a little. "Please, Mr. Marten. The photographs are very important to me personally. I want them back."

"I still don't know what you're talking about."

"Then why did you tell me you were going to London and you came here instead? A few hours later you met with the old man in the park. That meeting was about the photographs. Who he is, or rather was, I don't know. Whoever he was, he told you where to find them. I don't know who you work for or why. But whatever they're paying you I'll pay you a lot more."

"Let me tell you something about the 'old man,' Ms. Tidrow," Marten said quietly. It was clear that neither she nor Conor White had yet made the connection between Father Willy and Theo Haas. It meant they were guessing that he knew about the photographs and where they were. "He was a rather famous German author who had written, among many things, several very good books on the design of city parks. You verified that I was a landscape architect, so it shouldn't surprise you that I changed my plans and came to Berlin when he agreed to see me at the last minute. I met him in the park so that he could discuss his work."

"I don't believe you, Mr. Marten." What little softness there'd been was suddenly gone.

"That's unfortunate, but you don't have much choice."

Just then the taxi pulled sharply to the curb and stopped. Immediately Anne turned to the driver. "What is it?"

The driver turned down the music, looked in the mirror, and smiled. "Where you asked to be taken, madame. The Hotel Mozart Superior."

In that next breath, Marten leaned forward and handed him a hundred-euro bill. "Please take the lady back to her hotel, or wherever she's staying."

Quickly he opened the door and looked to Anne. "Thanks for caring, darling. I'll get rid of her myself. Long legs, big tits, and all."

Then he was out of the cab and entering the Hotel Mozart Superior. A second later the taxi pulled away.

5:38 P.M.

26

It took Marten four minutes to get to his room and start putting his things together. Anne Tidrow's arrival had been a surprise, but nothing like the sudden murder of Theo Haas. Her personal motivations aside, her quick wit, spiriting him out of there when the crowd was pointing him out to the police thinking he was the man they were looking for, had been deeply appreciated. The trouble was, Haas had been a national icon and the hunt for his killer and anyone connected to him would be massive. He had to get out of Berlin and Germany as quickly as possible, before the police investigation began in earnest and witnesses in both the park and at the Brandenburg Gate began describing him in detail. There was something else, too. It wouldn't be long before the police would discover that Theo Haas and Father Willy were brothers and immediately wonder if the two murders were connected. If that were made public, Anne Tidrow, Conor White, and the E.G. army's hawk-faced officer would no longer be guessing why he had come to Berlin. They would know for certain.

What that meant, the police notwithstanding, was that very soon it would be exceedingly difficult, if not impossible, for him to leave Germany, let alone Berlin, without one of them close on his tail. And that he couldn't permit under any circumstance because now he did know, or at least thought he knew, where the pictures were.

Sitting on the park bench in the Platz der Republik, watching him the way Father Willy had in the rain forest, trying to judge whether or not to trust him, Theo Haas had, in a very roundabout way and in the manner of his brother, pointed him in the direction of the photographs: "Livros usados, Avenida Tomás Cabreira," he'd said with a smile. "The town of Praia da Rocha in the Algarve region of Portugal. A man named Jacob Cádiz. He collects things." Seconds later, before Marten had the chance to question him further, the firecrackers had gone off. A second after that the curly-haired man struck and Haas was dead.

• 5:47 P.M.

Marten finished packing his suitcase and zipped it closed. There would be no official checkout, no formal notice of leaving, nothing, just go and let the hotel track him down later. One final glance around to make sure he'd left nothing behind, then he went to the door, opened it, and froze.

"I believe this is yours, Mr. Marten." Anne Tidrow stood alone in the hallway. Immediately she pressed the hundred-euro bill he'd given to their taxi driver into his hand. "I can afford my own cab fare. May I come in?"

"I—" Marten hesitated.

"Thank you," she said and stepped into the room, closing the door behind them.

He stared at her. "Now what?"

"I have another taxi waiting. It's at the side door. I suggest we use it, and sooner rather than later."

"We?"

"After you left the cab, the driver turned his radio from country music to the news. It seems your murdered friend was not just an author but the famed Nobel laureate Theo Haas. A Nobel laureate who was last seen alive talking to someone in Platz der Republik who, according to witnesses, looked a lot like you. I'm sure that once our driver friend realizes it, he will be more than happy to describe that person to the police, then tell them who was with him and where he took them. Would you like me to explain it further?"

"No." Marten said. The police had moved more quickly and efficiently than he'd thought they would. It wouldn't be long before they'd know who he was and would be right here in this room collecting evidence. Like it or not, he and Anne Tidrow were suddenly joined at the hip. Worse, she had her teeth into him and wasn't about to let go, no matter the consequences. It gave him little choice but to go along with her.

"Just where is this other taxi taking us?" he said.

"My hotel."

"How do you know that afterward this driver won't inform the police?"

"Because I'm paying him five hundred euros not to."

5:50 P.M.

27

• Hotel Adlon Kempinski, Room 647. 6:15 P.M.

Marten stood near the window staring out. Not a hundred yards away, backlit by the late-afternoon sun, was the Brandenburg Gate with a number of police vehicles still clearly in sight. That they'd come back to the same area they had left barely an hour earlier was something he hadn't realized when they arrived because they'd come in through the luxury hotel's rear entrance on Behrenstrasse and then taken a back stairwell to avoid using the elevators.

He turned to look at Anne. She had her suitcase open on the bed and was hurriedly packing it. "Some choice of hotels. I count four police cars and three police motorcycles, and that's just those I can see."

She stopped and looked at him. "How did I know you were going to come this way? I just wanted a place reasonably close to yours."

"You should have stayed in Malabo. Better yet, Texas."

She smiled. "Look at it this way, darling. By now the authorities will have detained anyone they wanted to question, meaning that before long most of them will leave the area."

"Then what?"

"We go and get the photographs."

Marten suddenly flared. "You never let up, do you? Somehow you've convinced yourself that I know where they are and what's in them."

As quickly her eyes narrowed and she pushed back. "Stop playing games with me, Nicholas. You were going out the door with your suitcase when I showed up at your hotel. If the pictures were anywhere nearby you would have simply gone to get them and then come back to your room with nobody the wiser. That means they aren't in Berlin, maybe not even in Germany. But wherever they are, you were on your way to get them."

"I had my suitcase because I was going home," he said quietly.

"You were going home this morning, too, remember? You came to Berlin instead."

"I came to Berlin to see Theo Haas. He's dead. What else was I supposed to do? Believe it or not, I have a job waiting. My employers as well as my clients can be exceptionally demanding."

"Not as demanding as the police. They'll want to know why you met with Haas, and they won't buy your fairy tale about discussing park design. Once you tell them the real reason, and you will, they'll want to know what the photographs were of, and you'll have to tell them that too. Then we'll have the beginning of a major international incident and because of it the pictures, wherever they are, will be recovered. The police will see to it.

"You're not doing this on your own, darling. Not here, and you weren't in Bioko, either. If those photographs become public, whoever hired you won't like it, and neither will I. So cut the bullshit about not knowing. We don't have time for it. There may be a way out of this yet, but you can't do it without me, and you're not getting me without the pictures."

Marten had no idea what "a way out of this" meant. He knew that if he had to, he could get help by calling President Harris and telling him what was going on, but that was something he had to save as a last resort because if he did call him the president would do everything he could to get him out of there. That meant pulling strings, which was something that in itself could set off an international incident no matter how discreetly it was done, simply because of who Theo Haas was. Both the Berlin police and the German public would be outraged to learn that the chief suspect in his murder had been suddenly let go under pressure from the American government.

And one way or another they would learn, if by no other means than the long, invasive tail of the Internet. If that happened, pundits, bloggers, and almost anyone else would have a field day tracing the diplomatic maneuver to its "suspected" source. Even if it couldn't be proven the damage would have been done and what Anne Tidrow said about "whoever hired you won't like it" would be a helluva lot more than accurate because it would appear to the world that the president of the United States was trying to cover up a murder. Moreover, it could lead to the ultimate exposure of the photographs, which, when made public, would make it look as if the motive behind it had been to protect both Striker Oil and Hadrian. Clearly that was a scenario Marten couldn't let play out. So once again, and for now at least, he had little choice but to let Anne Tidrow run the show.

He plunked down on the edge of the bed. "What are we supposed to do while we wait for the police to go their merry way?"

"Turn on the television. Maybe you can learn what they're doing. If they're checking passengers leaving from airport, bus, and train terminals. If they're searching cars leaving the city."

"I don't speak German."

"You'll get the idea. It's television, it's not that hard."

"What are you going to do?"

"Take a shower."

"A shower?" Marten was incredulous.

"Most of last night was spent on an airplane. Today was spent chasing after you. I have the feeling tonight is going to be pretty damn long as well. So if you don't mind, I'd like to get cleaned up before it begins." Abruptly she went into the bathroom and closed the door.

"How do you know I won't just leave?" he called through it.

"Because I'd call the police if you did."

"They'd get you, too." There was no reply. He raised his voice. "I said they'd get you, too." Still no reply.

Then he heard the shower running.

6:25 P.M.

• 6:37 P.M.

Marten was sitting in a chair staring at the television when the bathroom door opened and Anne came back into the room, her dark hair twisted up in a towel, a thick white terrycloth robe pulled around her, her eyes on the TV screen.

"Did you learn anything?" she said.

Marten said nothing, just continued to watch the screen. She took a step closer. Whatever channel he was tuned to was broadcasting live remotes, cutting between stand-up reporters on the green of the Platz

der Republik, the Brandenburg Gate, and Polizeipräsidium Berlin, police headquarters, on Platz der
Luftbrücke. An on-camera correspondent outside
of the Polizeipräsidium suddenly put a hand to his
earphone, as if listening to a special instruction
from the studio, then quickly gave an introduction to
whatever was next. The video feed abruptly cut to a
media room somewhere inside the building where a
tall, steely, black-eyed man with a shaved head, wearing a black leather jacket, white shirt, and a tie, approached a bank of microphones.

"Ever hear of a Berlin detective called Hauptkommissar Emil Franck?" Marten asked without looking
at her.

"No."

"Well, that's him. A few minutes ago I saw him
on a video that was recorded at the Platz der Republik. He seems to be their top homicide cop and is
heading the investigation."

"What have they said so far?"

"That I'm the guy they're looking for."

"What?" Anne was flabbergasted.

"At least as far as I can tell."

"How can they know for sure? All they had was a
description."

"Somebody took my picture with a cell phone."

"Christ!"

"Amen."

"Do they have your name?"

"If they do, they haven't said."

Hauptkommissar Franck reached the microphones
and looked directly into the camera. He spoke first in

German and then in English and in a voice that was icy and without emotion.

"This is the man wanted for questioning in the tragic and shocking daylight murder of Theo Haas. We are asking the public's help in finding him."

A blurry image of Marten in the melee near the Brandenburg Gate popped on the screen. Franck's voice was heard giving a telephone number and e-mail address.

"Recognize me?" Marten's concentration was on the TV.

"Unfortunately, yes."

Immediately the same phone number and e-mail address appeared on the screen. After a long moment the picture faded to black. Several seconds later a photograph of Theo Haas appeared. Superimposed over it were the words VERBRECHEN DES JAHRHUN-DERTS.

"Crime of the century," she translated. "Crime of the fucking century."

Marten turned to look at her. "For some reason I don't think the rather generous bribe you gave the taxi driver who brought us here is going to be enough to keep him from suddenly going to the police."

"Neither do I."

28

Marten stood up quickly. "It's only a matter of time before they show up here. If I leave now, go out the back entrance the way we came in, you can deny it all. Tell them you met me on the plane from Bioko, we did a little flirting, and you followed me to Berlin for the fun of it. You had no idea I was going to meet with Theo Haas, let alone be around when he was killed. Moreover, you can describe the real killer to them. You know what he looked like as well as I do. Others had to have seen him, too, people the police may have already questioned and you can bring that up, it'll give you credibility. You're a wealthy American who sits on the board of a large Texas oil company. They're not going to do much of anything to you, especially once you convince them you just got caught up in an unfortunate coincidence and have no idea where I've gone. And it'll be the truth because you won't."

"It won't work." Anne was looking directly at him.

"Why? In ten seconds I'm out the door and vanished."

"Not without me."

Marten glared at her. "Don't start that again, not now. Not with this Hauptkommissar Franck on the trail. You get caught with me, you'll be locked up for as long as I am."

"I want the photographs, Mr. Marten. I'll take

my chances. Besides, as I said, there may be a way out of this yet, but you'll need me or it won't happen."

"How?"

"As my mother used to say, that's for me to know and you to find out."

Marten watched her carefully, then gave in. "Once again, I seem to be at your mercy."

"Then let's get to it." Immediately she dug in her suitcase, pulled something out, and tossed it to him. "It'll help cover you up. A little anyway."

Marten caught it and looked at it—a *Dallas Cowboys* baseball cap.

He looked at her as if she were crazy. "This isn't going to help."

"It's better than nothing, darling. Now collect your things, take a pee, and we'll get the hell out of here."

Abruptly Anne threw off her robe. Marten saw a flash of taut body, beautiful breasts, and pubic hair, and then she was pulling on underwear, jeans, sweater, and the jean jacket and running shoes she'd worn earlier.

Three minutes later they were walking out the Hotel Adlon's rear entrance, then turning onto Wilhelmstrasse in the direction of Unter den Linden and the Spree River. Marten wore the *Dallas Cowboys* cap and pulled his suitcase behind him like a tourist. Anne carried an over-the-shoulder bag taken from her luggage. In it were last-minute basics: clean underwear, toiletries, passport, credit cards, money, BlackBerry. Her suitcase had been intentionally left

in the room with the rest of her clothes, making it
look as if she fully expected to return.

7:07 P.M.

Hotel Adlon Kempinski, Office of the Concierge.
7:28 P.M.

"We have over three hundred rooms and seventy-
eight suites. It is not possible to know the physical
description of every guest." Paul Stonner, the Hotel
Adlon's proud, dark-suited, bifocal-wearing concierge, stood across from the shaved-headed, six-foot-
six Erster Kriminalhauptkommissar Emil Franck in
his private office. With Franck were his colleagues
Kommissars Gerhard Bohlen and Gertrude Prosser.
Bohlen was forty-one, skeleton thin, deadly serious,
and married. Prosser was thirty-eight, a sturdy, handsome blonde whose only marriage was, and always
had been, to the department. Gerhard and Gertrude.
Franck often referred to them as "the two Gs." Both
were top homicide investigators.

"Herr Stonner," Franck said coldly, his coal-
black eyes barely pinpoints in his head, "you are
going to bring your employees in here, and we
are going to do our best to find a match. Our man
here will describe them exactly as he has to you
and to us."

Franck looked to fifty-year-old Karl Zeller, the
white-haired taxi driver who had driven Marten and
Anne Tidrow from the Hotel Mozart Superior and
delivered them to the Adlon's rear entrance, by his
records, at precisely 6:02 P.M.

"We will be very happy to help as we can, Haupt-kommissar," Stonner said respectfully, "but how do you know these people were guests of the hotel?"

"We don't, Herr Stonner, but we are going to find out."

• 7:32 P.M.

The two walked quickly down Schiffbauerdamm, the roadway on the far side of the River Spree from Unter den Linden. Marten's suitcase was long gone, weighted down with chunks of concrete taken from a construction Dumpster near the Reichstag and tossed into the river. His own essentials—passport, driver's license, credit cards, cash, and the dark blue throw-away cell phone he'd used to call President Harris—he carried on his person.

• 7:34 P.M.

The river and city still glimmered in the warm glow of the long summer day. In a way the daylight helped because it enabled them to blend in with the tourists crowding the streets and cafés that sat on the quay above the Spree, where people could look out at the maze of tour boats plying the water. After sunset the crowds would lessen, making them more visible to the police who seemed to be everywhere—on street corners, on motorcycles, in patrol cars—in a massive search for the still-unnamed man whose blurred photograph Hauptkommissar Franck had shown on television.

In the half hour since they'd left the Adlon, Marten had said little, just turning this way and that at Anne's direction. Clearly she knew the city, at least this part of it, and was seemingly intent on taking them to some destination in particular. Just where that was and who would be waiting when they arrived were questions that made him as uneasy as the two that remained from earlier: how she had known where he was staying in Berlin and where he'd gone when he went to meet with Theo Haas. And then there was the business with the shower before they'd left the Adlon and the phone call she'd made from behind its closed door. At this point they all troubled him. As if he didn't have trouble enough.

"Where are we going?" he said abruptly.

"It's not far."

"Wherever it is, it's taking too long. We're giving the police too much time."

"I said, it's not far."

"What's not far? Bar, restaurant, another hotel, what?"

"A friend's apartment."

"What friend?"

"Just a friend."

"The one you called when you went in to take a shower?"

"What do you mean?"

"The shower was an excuse. The real reason you went in there was to make a call without me hearing."

"Darling," she smiled, "I wanted to get cleaned up, nothing more."

"Your BlackBerry was on the bed before you went in. It wasn't there afterward."

Anne's smile faded. "Alright, I did make a call. It was to my friend. To help us."

"Then why the secret?"

"It was personal. Do I have to explain everything?"

"Just get us there."

"We—" She hesitated.

"We—what?"

"Have to wait."

"For what?"

"She has to make arrangements."

"Arrangements?"

"Yes. She'll call me when it's ready."

"Who the hell is 'she'?"

Anne's eyes flashed with anger. "Understand something. The police are everywhere. There is no other place for us to go."

Marten didn't like it. Any of it. He pressed her hard. "Verbrechen des Jahrhunderts."

"What?"

"Verbrechen des Jahrhunderts. Crime of the century. That's what you translated from the television. You understand German. You know your way around the city. You had me followed from the airport. That's how you knew where I was staying. You had somebody watching the hotel, telling you the moment I left it and which way I had gone. It's how you found me in the park. Then with the police swarming all over you suddenly have to take a shower. And now we're going to a 'friend's'. A woman who has to make 'arrangements' first. What kind of friend is she, darling, when everyone in the city is looking for me, and probably by now for you as well? You told me to stop playing games; now it's your turn. You're not just Striker Oil. You're something else. Who? What?"

Ahead was Weidendamm Bridge where Friedrichstrasse crossed the river. Stairs led up to it.

"Take the stairs," she said quietly.

"I asked you a question."

Just then two Berlin policemen went by on motorcycles, slowing as they did. A half block later, they stopped and looked back, one of them speaking into a microphone mounted to his helmet. Abruptly Anne took Marten by the hand and pulled him around.

"Kiss me." She looked into his eyes. "And act like you mean it. Do it now."

Marten glanced at the police and then did. She kissed him back, long and hard.

The motorcycle cops watched, then rode off.

"The stairs," she said again and steered him toward them

7:40 P.M.

29

Two more motorcycle officers were waiting when they reached the top of the stairs at Weidendamm Bridge. Their machines were parked to one side, and they stood on the sidewalk chatting. Left was the way Anne wanted to go, but to do it they would either have to walk directly past the police or cross the street to the other side, which might well be interpreted as a deliberate move to avoid them. Instead Anne turned them right across the bridge.

As they went she leaned in and kissed Marten again, whispering as she did. "Ahead is the train station. As soon as we get there, go inside."

They didn't look back. If the police were following them, there was no way to know. Forty seconds later they were at the station and going inside.

"If they saw us go in and they're onto us," Marten said quickly, "they'll have cops watching every train. They probably do anyway. We have to get out, and now, but without getting on a train or going back out on the street."

"This way." Anne led them past the ticketing booths to a down escalator.

At the bottom she turned them left and then right and along a corridor that took them to an exit door at the far end. From there they crossed to the banks of the Spree as it wound through the city. Seconds after that they were at the top of a landing, then walking down a gangplank with a large group of tourists to board a double-decked tour boat named the *Monbijou*. The lower deck was a restaurant and already full, so the upper deck was where they were instructed to go. The upper deck, open to the view of anyone watching from another boat, a bridge, or from the banks of the waterway itself.

• Hotel Adlon, Room 647. 8:05 P.M.
"Get a technical unit up here right away," Hauptkommissar Emil Franck snapped at Detective Bohlen. Immediately the ghostly thin Bohlen clicked on a police radio and left.

It had taken Franck and his colleagues Bohlen and Prosser—with the help of the white-haired taxi driver, Karl Zeller, and concierge Stonner's excellent staff—little more than thirty minutes to determine the room number and identity of the woman Zeller had picked up from the Hotel Mozart Superior and dropped off at the Adlon's rear entrance at 6:02 P.M. With her had been a man who clearly resembled the person wanted by the police in the murder of Theo Haas.

"Her full name as registered is Hannah Anne Tidrow," Stonner read from a computer printout just handed to him by a young hotel employee in a navy business suit.

"Address: 2800 Post Oak Boulevard, Houston, Texas. She checked in at one ten this afternoon and requested an open departure date. She has stayed with us before. She used an American Express credit card in the name of the AG Striker Oil & Energy Company of Houston, Texas. The billing address and the address she gave are the same."

"When was the last time she was here?" Franck walked carefully around the room, looking at everything, touching nothing.

"Two years ago. March twelve through fifteen."

"Hauptkommissar." Detective Gertrude Prosser came in through the open door to the marble and polished-wood bathroom. "One or both of them took a shower. The hotel robe is still damp, as are three towels."

"Two pieces of luggage." Franck's eyes scanned the room. One of Anne's suitcases was on a luggage rack near the door; another was on the floor next to it. A pair of dark slacks, a designer blazer, two business suits, a pair of black dress slacks, an evening jacket, and a pair of expensive, somewhat wrinkled white linen slacks with a matching short-sleeve top hung in the open closet.

"Technical unit is on the way." Detective Bohlen came back in from the hallway.

Immediately Franck lifted a small police radio and spoke into it. "This is Franck. I want information on a Hannah Anne Tidrow of the AG Striker Oil and Energy Company of Houston, Texas. What she does there, her title, how she's involved with the company. If there is a recent photograph of her." He clicked off and looked to Bohlen. "Get a canine team up here as quickly as possible."

"Yes, sir."

"You and Prosser go to the Hotel Mozart Superior. Get the names and addresses of everyone who registered there in the last ten days. Then assemble the staff, give them a description of Hannah Anne Tidrow, and show them the suspect's photograph. Maybe they were only passing through or using the hotel as a way to throw us off, but if he was a guest there somebody will recognize him, and then we'll have a name, a room number, and an address."

"Yes, sir."

8:12 P.M.

30

• Monte De El Pardo, Spain. Same time.

The soil under the ancient olive trees was soft from a recent, unseasonable rain and made the grave easy to dig. A few minutes with a shovel and the job was done. Conor White lifted the corpse himself. It was small and delicate in his large hands. For a moment he studied it—the two tiny feet at the end of spindly legs, the unruly fluff of feathers at its neck, the proud twist of its beak, its gray wings, looking as if they could still take flight, neatly tucked back against its body. What kind of bird it was, or had been, he didn't know.

"I hope you had a good life, my little friend," he said reverently. Then, turning the creature over so that it would be on its side in the earth, he placed it gently in the grave and covered it over with soil. "Farewell and safe journey," he said with the same reverence. Then, shovel in hand, he walked off through the olive grove toward the farmhouse.

To his right he could see the A6, the main highway to Madrid, and the evening traffic on it leading to and from the city. A thick forest of conifers surrounded the house from behind and to the side, obscuring it from the roadway, while fallow, unplowed fields stretched out in front and to the right in an expansive fifty-acre semicircle. The farm was for sale and had been since its elderly owner had passed away more than two years earlier. So far there had been no offers to buy and no funds allotted for upkeep. As a result the olive trees had gone unattended. So had the mile-long dirt and gravel drive leading into the property, an ingress/egress that had been washed away in any number of places by winter rains and was mottled with rocks and overgrown with weeds. Yet, troublesome as it was, it had not deterred vandals from breaking into the house and taking anything and everything of value, leaving only the stove and toilets and a few pieces of unwanted furniture. The only other structure on the property was a dilapidated barn in a state of such disrepair that the only reasonable thing to do would be to knock it down and rebuild it from the ground up. Altogether, the location made an ideal setting for the interrogation that had been going on since he and his colleagues had arrived from Madrid via private jet from Malabo and then been driven here in a hired car some six hours earlier.

Six hours of questioning was a long time and had left the people being talked to both terrified and exhausted. Which was, perhaps, the reason he still had no answer to his queries, and why he'd walked out, to give them a rest and let them consider the gravity of their situation and to get some fresh air himself. It was then he'd found the dead bird in the shadows just outside the door.

• 8:18 P.M.

He was closer to the house now. Inside he could see the dull glow of a portable lantern one of his men had brought, correctly assuming the property no longer had working electricity. He looked up at a sky filled with red streaks and wisps of clouds as the sun set in the west. If he were the smoking man he once had been, this would have been the time he would have brought out a cigarette. But not now. Smoking was in his past, so he had nothing to use as a crutch except his own thoughts and emotions, which at the moment were deeply troubling.

This was hardly the situation he'd imagined when he took the job creating SimCo for Striker and Hadrian more than a year before, resigning from his own company to take a position that would be a major step forward in the highly lucrative world of private security companies. Not just a step but a leap, one that had begun with a ten-year contract with Striker Oil to protect their workers in Equatorial Guinea and that was renewable every five years afterward for the next fifty years. It was a situation that had instantly put him on a level with major private security firms worldwide, and that included Hadrian. But in that heady rush of expectation, neither he nor anyone else had foreseen the bizarre, even obscene, minefield that he and SimCo were in now. How graphically simple and stupid the whole thing with the photographs was. Almost as graphically simple and stupid as the Watergate break-in that brought down the Nixon administration almost a half century earlier. Yet it was as real for him as it must have been for Richard Nixon. But he wasn't a paranoid president locked up in the golden hell of the White House; he was a highly educated, seasoned warrior whose charge it was to bring the nightmare of the photographs to a fast and silent resolution before everything disintegrated because of it.

In the last hours he had heard from Loyal Truex—twice—and from Josiah Wirth, who, at this moment, was on his way to Europe from Texas on an AG Striker corporate jet. Coming, he was sure, for one reason alone, to look over White's shoulder and direct his every move. Both men had demanded to know where he was and how he was progressing and when, exactly, the problem would be resolved, as if he were a plumber called in to repair a broken toilet while a wedding party waited outside to use it. Both wanted it done yesterday, yet neither understood the complexity of finding the ghost he was chasing. Truex was trouble enough, but at least he and White spoke the same language. Wirth was entirely different, a man so driven, so egotistical, so rich, and so single-minded that it was impossible to view the world from any other perspective than his own. People like that easily became reckless, even foolhardy, especially when they began to lose confidence and feel things were slipping out of their control. As a result they left themselves wide open to their own brand of panic, one that easily led to judgments that could be hugely damaging and sometimes dangerous or even deadly, and not just to themselves but to people around them. And that was the last thing Conor White wanted.

Now or ever.

• 8:20 P.M.

In the growing twilight he could see the black Mercedes limousine that had brought the captives to the farmhouse parked under an overhang of trees. Its liveried driver and a similarly dressed local gunman, who had met White and the two SimCo mercenaries he'd brought with him from Bioko to Madrid and driven them there, were standing nearby smoking and chatting. Fourth and fifth hands if a problem arose inside the house. As if it would with the men stationed there: Irish Jack Hanahan, a former member of Sciathán Fianóglach an Airm, the Ranger Wing of the Irish army, with massive thirty-two-inch thighs, lightning reflexes, and fists like hams; and the wiry, almost too handsome French-Canadian with piercing green eyes, Patrice Sennac, at one time the CIA's top Central American counterinsurgent, a veteran jungle fighter, who had a long scar at the side of his mouth to prove it. Depending on the situation, either man could be absurdly polite or grimly lethal to anyone, friend, enemy, or whoever fell in between. Like those waiting for him to come back inside and begin the questioning once more—the young Spanish doctor and her four medical students. Five people who might very well know what the Equatorial Guinean army interrogators had failed to find out—the location of the photographs. Might very well know because Nicholas Marten would have had every opportunity to tell them: on the road to Malabo from where they had first met on the beach in Bioko South, or in Malabo itself at the hotel over drinks, or, last and most likely of all, on the long overnight plane ride to Paris.

White would have much preferred to have gone after Marten himself and left the doctor and her students to others, but that assignment had gone to Anne, who Truex, Sy Wirth, and Anne herself felt could get closer to Marten than he could. So instead he was given the secondary target, the five now inside the house.

The thing driving it all was urgency. Find the photographs and destroy them before they fell into what could only be referred to as "public hands." For White the pressure was all the greater because he was a prominent figure in any number of the pictures, and if they were made public everything he'd worked for all his life would be gone.

Everything.

Colin Conor White had been born in London, the only child of a young barmaid and George Winston White, a London railway worker who died of a heart attack several weeks after his son was born. Soon afterward Conor's mother, in grief and despair, left the city and went to live near her sister in a small two-room flat in Birmingham in west central England, where he grew up street-tough and all but impoverished. When he was eleven, and quite by accident, he discovered a farewell note tucked away in a cabinet above the kitchen sink in a long-forgotten box of memorabilia. In it, he learned that his father had not been a railway worker at all but instead a very married man. His name, what he did, and even the truth of the note were things his mother refused to discuss during an anger-filled confrontation, telling him in no uncertain terms that the idea was preposterous and that she had no idea who had written the note or where it had come from and warning him not to bring up the subject again.

Her heated denial only sent him digging for more. A careful examination of the London Transport Executive records, the railway authority at the time, determined that no worker named George Winston White had been employed there within two years of his birth. Eighteen months later and after considerable snooping, he discovered the man to be Sir Edward Raines, a handsome, silver-haired, longtime member of Parliament and former decorated officer in the British army who had lost an arm in the Battle of Crater during the Aden Emergency on the Arabian Peninsula in 1963. Raines, it seemed, was not only his father but was paying his mother a yearly stipend to keep silent about it.

Challenged again, his mother, quite irritably, kept to her original story, refusing to acknowledge any such person or arrangement. Moreover, the confrontation caused her to sink deeper into her own increasingly apparent mood of base self-pity. How dare he think a "somebody" such as Sir Edward Raines would even consider paying attention to a woman who barely had a grade school education and no breeding whatsoever? He could still hear the shrill, anger-filled ring of her voice:

"You should get it permanently through your head, Mr. Conor White, that neither me nor you will ever have that kind of social status and that you had best prepare yourself for a working man's life and not be making up silly fantasies about who you might prefer your father to have been. They will get you no further than the two-room flat we live in, if you're that lucky."

Maybe so. But fantasies or not, he had other ideas and had gone directly to Sir Edward himself demanding a confirmation of his paternity. Or rather he'd tried to. Each time he'd been rebuffed by an intermediary, Sir Edward refusing to even see him.

Powerfully built, sullen and angry, and little more than a street tough, Conor White's salvation had come through a determination to be as celebrated and socially acceptable as his father. Through a love of reading and the physical escape of rugby, which he'd played with a ferocity aimed directly at Sir Edward, he won a full scholarship to Eton College, where he excelled in English and was captain of the rugby team. Success there provided him entry and a scholarship to Oxford; upon graduation, he joined the Royal Military Academy Sandhurst determined to become an officer in the British Army. Not long afterward he managed an invitation to join the elite special forces unit known as the SAS. It was an invitation he jumped at because it promised the opportunity to become a frontline soldier in highly dangerous combat situations and, not so coincidentally, offered a playing field where, with luck and extreme courage he could become a military hero. The same as his father had been.

And for most of the last quarter century he had followed that path, building a stellar reputation as a top line operator in extremely high-risk situations across the globe. His SAS career alone, with an extraordinary run of decorations, was proof enough. Distinguished Service Order, or DSO, presented for meritorious service, valor in the face of the enemy, Iraq, 1991. DSO, Iraq, 1998. DSO, Bosnia, 2000. DSO, Sierra Leone, 2002. Victoria Cross, the United Kingdom's highest award for bravery, presented by the queen for duty in Afghanistan, 2003. DSO, Iraq, 2004. Then he'd moved into the private sector, where, even now, he remained a poster-boy hero with plans to one day run for parliamentary office. So to have it all come to a thundering end—his face smeared across the Internet and worldwide television, to be seen staring out from the covers of newspapers and tabloids everywhere as a lackey for an oil company intent on overthrowing the government of a third world country for its own gain, no matter how tyrannical the regime—was a humiliation he could and would not suffer.

• 8:22 P.M.

He reached the house and set the shovel alongside the front door, giving it a second glance as he did, wondering if more graves would have to be dug that night. A deep breath of resolve and he took a black balaclava from his jacket pocket, pulled it on, then opened the door and went inside.

The five "guests" were as he had left them, sitting in the glow of lantern light on a rustic wooden bench in the room that was once part kitchen, part dining area. By now he knew them by name—Marita, Gilberto, Rosa with the big glasses, Luis, the red-haired Ernesto. All were as pale, terrified, and silent as they'd been when he'd gone out. Except for Marita, they all stared at the floor. Her eyes had been on him the moment he stepped through the door. They were filled with defiance and hatred.

Irish Jack stood at the end of the bench, his arms crossed over his chest. Patrice was in front of them, feet apart, his arms behind him. Both wore the jeans and pullover sweaters he did. Both had automatic pistols in Kevlar holsters strapped to their thighs. Both wore the same kind of black balaclava he did.

"Who is ready to talk about the photographs?" White said in his crisp British accent.

"For the hundredth time, we cannot tell you what we don't know," Marita spat angrily.

Conor White looked at the frightened, sullen faces and scratched his head. "Maybe we're making this too hard," he said evenly and with that reached up and pulled off his balaclava. This was the first time he had been without it, and he could see their surprise as they recognized him from the bar in the Hotel Malabo. "Gentlemen"—he looked to Patrice and Irish Jack and nodded—"a little politeness, please. No reason to alarm these people any further."

Immediately both men removed their balaclavas and tucked them into their belts.

White moved a little closer. "You now see we are forthright and mean you no harm. All this has come about because of the civil war in Bioko. The photographs are very important to the oil company that employs us. Our job is to recover them, and right away. Once we do you will be free to go."

Suddenly Rosa looked up and boldly repeated Marita's words. "We cannot tell you what we don't know."

"No, I don't suppose you can." White hesitated for a moment, then looked to Patrice. "We need to speed this up."

"Yes, sir."

Patrice took a half step to stand right in front of them. He looked from one to the other to the other, turned toward Marita, then abruptly reversed his move and stepped in front of Rosa. A gasp went up from the others as a second later Irish Jack moved behind her to take hold of her shoulders in an iron grip White himself couldn't escape from.

"Marita!" Rosa cried out.

In the next instant Patrice slid the automatic from his holster and slid it up under her nose.

White looked to Marita. "Where are the photographs?"

Marita's eyes went to Rosa in horror, then came back to White. "For God's sake, we don't know! We've told you that over and over!"

"That's too bad."

Conor White nodded at Patrice. Irish Jack stepped to the side and Patrice pulled the trigger. There was an ear-shattering roar and Rosa's head exploded, her oversized glasses disappearing behind her, her body collapsing like a rag doll across the bench.

White gave them no chance to recover, just walked over to Marita. "The photographs. Where are they?"

Numbed, horrified, Marita simply shook her head.

"You're still telling me you don't know?"

"Yes. No. God! We don't know! Please! My God, please! Please!"

White looked at Gilberto and then Luis and then Ernesto. In the next instant he reached into a holster at the back of his belt and pulled a short-barrel SIG SAUER 9mm semiautomatic from it. In one fluid motion, he turned and shot Marita point-blank in the head.

8:27 P.M.

31

The tour boat *Monbijou* had left the landing at 8:02, motored up the Spree to a turning point, and was now headed back into a city beginning to come alive for the night. The initial fears Anne and Marten had had about being seated on the upper deck and therefore open to view from shore had been quieted by the sheer number of other passengers surrounding them, easily eighty in all plus two harried, white-jacketed waiters rushing back and forth to the lower deck to retrieve drinks and snacks in an attempt to keep the topsiders happy. If much of Berlin had been psychologically pained by the murder of Theo Haas, that mood wasn't evident here. In all probability that was because most of the passengers were English-speaking foreigners unaware of the emotional magnitude of the crime and its effect on the city.

Still, Marten was concerned, chiefly about the people seated nearby. He was afraid they might have seen his picture on television or be getting fresh information from the cell phones and other electronic gadgets seemingly everyone had despite the fact they had come on board to relax and enjoy the sights. Yet, so far at least, none had even looked his way, leading him to think that maybe Anne hadn't been as foolish as he thought when she'd tossed him the *Dallas Cowboys* baseball cap and told him to put it on.

The public aside, or even the police who might be watching through field glasses from the embankment as they passed, the thing that troubled him most was Anne herself. The questions he'd put to her earlier—who she really was and what her motivations were—remained unanswered, primarily because they were in public and trying to keep a low profile. So he'd let it go, at least for now.

For a time he'd simply watched the city as they passed by and thought about what he would do next, a sticky problem in itself because he both needed her and wanted to get rid of her at the same time. Then her BlackBerry had sounded. She'd answered and said quietly, "I am, yes. It's alright. No, not so far. Not certain just yet. Yes. Okay."

She'd clicked off immediately and was putting the device in her purse when it rang again. She clicked on, said a generic "Hi," gave the second caller very nearly the same information as the first, then clicked off and put the phone away. Afterward she'd smiled and kissed his cheek, taking his hand as if they were the lovebirds they'd portrayed to the police on the street. Not once had she mentioned either call.

If Marten had seen the text memo she'd sent earlier to Sy Wirth and copied to Loyal Truex and Conor White, he might have understood.

Meeting with our short-list candidate in Berlin. He is somewhat reluctant to join the firm so will need more time to help persuade him to change his mind. Home office execs joining us here to help in the process would only complicate things. More later.

What it had been was an affirmation that she'd trailed Marten to Berlin, had located him, and wanted no interference from any of them. That she had sent the text *before* the murder of Theo Haas only complicated things, because with Haas's death everything changed. Suddenly Marten had become a prime suspect in his murder, and very soon, if not already, the police would know she had been with him shortly afterward. Once they had traced them to the Adlon, they would know her identity as well. And what the hell would Messrs. Wirth, Truex, and White do about that once they learned of it?

But Marten had known nothing of that communication at all. What he would know was that in the last minutes she had received two brief calls that she had replied to ambiguously. Who they had been from or what they were about he could only guess, and she intended to leave it that way. Then, just seconds later, her BlackBerry had chimed a third time. She'd taken it from her purse, read a brief text message, then clicked off. What it had been about Marten wouldn't know, either, but from the way he looked at her, it was clear the run of recent communications was beginning to trouble him enough that she was afraid he might bolt from her the first chance he got. To ease his concern, and hers, she was about to tell him what had been in the text when the world around them suddenly got in the way.

"Would you mind, sir?" one of the white-jacketed waiters, a fiftyish man with curly eyebrows and a mustache, had stopped beside them. He carried a tray on which were balanced a half-dozen large glasses of beer and was looking directly at Marten, who, on the aisle seat, was closest to him.

"For the people next to your wife," he said with a smile.

"Sure," Marten said, taking one and then another of the glasses. One, two he handed them to Anne, who then passed them on to a middle-aged Australian couple seated next to them.

"Ten euros will make it," the waiter said.

The Australian woman dug in her purse and handed a twenty-euro bill to Anne, who handed it to Marten, who passed it to the waiter. Change came back the same way, and then a three-euro tip went back to the waiter, who said, "*Dankeschön*," and moved off to deliver the remaining beverages to a foursome two rows forward.

"Thank you." The Australian woman smiled at Anne.

"Our pleasure." Anne returned the smile, then gave it a minute and looked to Marten. Lowering her voice, she gave him the gist of the text message. "Our accommodations are ready, darling. Get off at the next landing."

8:38 P.M.

32

• Hotel Adlon, Room 647. 8:42 P.M.

Hauptkommissar Emil Franck watched veteran po- lice dog trainer Friedrich Handler lead two eager Belgian Malinois into the bathroom, remove their leashes, and show them the bathrobe and towels Anne Tidrow had used after her shower. Both animals nuzzled and sniffed and then for a moment stood motionless. Handler nodded, and as one they backed up, leaving the confines of the bathroom to explore the hotel room itself. In thirty seconds they had covered it, stopping first at the clothes closet, then moving to the chair near the television, then finally sniffing around the bed. An instant later they headed for the door. Handler leashed them again. Then, with a nod from Franck, he opened the door and they went out.

• 8:47 P.M.
The dogs led them down a set of rear stairs and to the Adlon's back entrance on Behrenstrasse. Outside, the Malinois turned left and then left again onto Wilhelmstrasse, tugging Handler and Hauptkommissar Franck in the direction of Unter den Linden. In less than a minute they had crossed the boulevard and were going in the direction of the Spree.

"*Hauptkommissar.*" A male voice came through a tiny receiver in Franck's right ear.

Franck lifted his police radio and slowed, letting Handler and the Malinois move ahead. "Yes."

"*Hannah Anne Tidrow is on the board of directors of the AG Striker Oil and Energy Company of Houston, Texas. The same AG Striker company that is under contract to the U.S. State Department in Iraq.*"

Franck looked puzzled. "She's currently on the board?"

"*Yes, sir.*"

"I want to know more about Striker. Where their operations are outside of Iraq. If they have offices in Germany or elsewhere in the EU. Next, do we have a make on her companion?"

"*Not yet, sir.*"

"*Yes, we do.*" Gertrude Prosser's voice suddenly crackled through his earpiece. "*His name is Nicholas Marten. He's a landscape architect from Manchester, England. Checked into the Mozart Superior just after one this afternoon.*"

"Landscape architect?"

"*Yes, sir.*"

"Find out where he was before he came to Berlin—if he came directly from Manchester or from somewhere else—and if he has a criminal record. I want to know about the firm he works for. How established they are, what kind of clients they have. All of this is to be kept confidential and within my department only. No information, I repeat, no information is to reach the media. Total blackout."

"Yes, sir."

"Hauptkommissar," Handler suddenly called to him.

"Yes." Franck clicked off and looked up.

Handler and the dogs were stopped at a construction Dumpster thirty feet ahead in a work area near the Reichstag. The Malinois were dancing in circles, confused.

"She stopped here," Handler said. "Spent a few minutes, then moved on. I don't know if the man was with her or not."

"Which way?"

"Toward the river, I think."

"You think?"

"There's too much construction debris and a great deal of plaster and cement dust. They've lost the scent."

Franck stared at him, clearly upset.

"I'm sorry, Hauptkommissar."

"It's alright, Handler. It's alright. We'll take it from here. Thank you."

9:12 P.M.

33

Anne Tidrow and Nicholas Marten walked quickly along Friedrichstrasse. Heads down, they dodged in and out of leisurely strolling pedestrian traffic as best they could without calling attention to themselves. Four minutes earlier they'd disembarked from the *Monbijou* at the Weidendamm Bridge dock on the city side of the Spree, then crossed back over it, going in the same direction they had earlier. The entire route, boat ride included, had consumed nearly two hours, while taking them in what was little more than a large circle that brought them right back into the city and the hornet's nest that was the police dragnet.

"This is crazy," Marten breathed as two motorcycle officers cruised slowly past surveying the pedestrians. "How much further?"

"We're almost—"

"You speak English?" A man with a closely trimmed beard suddenly locked step with them. He was maybe thirty and fashionably dressed in a beige suit and fitted black T-shirt.

They said nothing, just kept walking.

"English, yes? I'm trying to help you," he insisted.

Anne glanced at him. "What do you want?"

He smiled and lowered his voice. "I got some good stuff. Pure coke, none of this street shit."

"No, thank you."

"What about him?" he nodded at Marten. Marten kept his head down and said nothing. "She speak for you?" he pressed.

Still Marten said nothing, just kept walking.

"I'm talking to you, man. Come on, this is good stuff. Not easy to find."

"Please leave us alone." Marten glanced at him sharply, then looked away.

Suddenly the man narrowed his forehead. "I've seen you someplace before, and not long ago."

Abruptly Marten stopped, grabbed the man's collar, and pulled him close. "I'm a cop. A detective with the Los Angeles Police Department. Want me to pull one of the local gendarmes over, let him check you out?"

"Let go of me, man. Let me go!" The man squealed and tried to pull away.

Marten fixed him with a stare, then shoved him backward. "Get the hell out of here. Now!"

The man stared a half second, then turned and walked quickly away in the opposite direction, disappearing in the sidewalk crowd.

Anne looked at him and grinned. "A cop?"

Immediately Marten took her by the arm. "Wherever we're going, get us there as fast as you can."

• 10:10 P.M.

The apartment was utilitarian at best. The top floor of an old three-story brick building on an alley off Ziegelstrasse. There were two small, meagerly furnished rooms, plus a tiny kitchen and bath. The bedroom was in the back. It had a double bed, a worn overstuffed chair, and a chest of drawers. A small window opened onto an air shaft with an iron fire ladder that led to the roof. The other room, a kind of sitting room/dining room/library, was in the front, where two narrow floor-to-ceiling windows overlooked the alley with a glimpse of Ziegelstrasse at the end of it.

The chipped, red-painted cupboard in the kitchen had been recently stocked with a variety of canned soups and meats along with two boxes of dry cereal, a jar of mustard, and one of strawberry jam. The refrigerator held a pound of ground coffee, a small wheel of cheese, a liter of milk, some fresh-sliced ham, several apples, two loaves of dark bread, a half-dozen bottles of mineral water, and eight bottles of Radeberger Pilsner beer. In all, enough to keep them fed, as Anne said, "for several days or more."

"Several days?" Marten protested as they walked through the darkened front room to take refuge in the back bedroom.

"I'm doing my best to get us out of this mess. It's not easy. It may take a little time." Anne turned on a small bedside lamp. Its warm glow was welcome against the dark of the rest of the apartment, purposely kept that way to avoid drawing attention from the alley below. "You might even say thank you, for God's sake."

Marten's reply was slow. "Thank you," he said finally, then walked off down the hall to stand in the doorway to the front room and stare silently into it, alone with his thoughts.

"You're welcome," she said after him, then opened her purse and took out a designer T-shirt and started to undress. She took off her jacket and jeans, then her shirt and bra, folding them all neatly and setting them in a pile on top of the chest of drawers. She'd just pulled on the T-shirt when she felt a presence and turned to find him standing in the doorway looking at her.

"What the hell's going on?" he said quietly. "Whose place is this? Who are you?"

"I'm tired. I want to sleep," she said.

"Yeah, well I'm tired, too."

"Please, not now."

She was starting past him for the bathroom when he put an arm out and stopped her. "You've got ten seconds to answer my questions. You don't, I'm walking out. I'll take my chances with the police." His eyes were fierce and unrelenting, his mind clearly made up.

She stared back at him. "What do you want me to tell you?"

"About the company. About you. All of it."

"I wouldn't know where to start."

"Try the beginning."

She watched him a beat longer, then relented. "Alright." She went back to the bed and sat down cross-legged on it, still dressed only in the T-shirt and panties, the nipples of her breasts protruding smartly through the shirt's soft cotton. If it was provocative, she didn't seem to care.

"My father owned Striker Oil. He bought it when it was a small oil services company in West Texas in the 1970s. My mother died when I was thirteen. I was an only child. He raised me himself. Took me all over the world with him while he tried to build the business, which meant anywhere there was oil or oil companies who needed management or exploration services. We nearly went under more than once. Then it caught hold. He took Striker public and did very well. I went to college in Texas and then into business. I got married and divorced. Shortly afterward my father had a stroke and put me on Striker's board of directors because he knew I would protect the company and because I knew more about it than anybody but him. Then he had a second stroke, and I left my job to take care of him. I stayed with him for four years until he died." Suddenly she stopped. "Boring, isn't it? Why the hell don't we just leave it at that?"

Marten leaned back against the doorjamb. "What happened to the company then?"

She watched him for a long moment. He wanted to know everything and wasn't about to back down until he had it. If she was going to keep him with her, she had no choice but to continue.

"The people he brought in to run it, namely Sy Wirth and his hand-picked executives, got Wirth elected chairman and chief executive, bought back its shares, and took it private, getting rid of most of the board in the process. Afterward Wirth started developing friendships in Washington, which is how he hooked up with Hadrian to protect our oil field businesses around the world. Then Iraq happened, and he and Hadrian were right there. Almost from the start they were manipulating State Department contracts, hiring all kinds of subcontractors, double billing, using creative bookkeeping, all of it in a way that was almost impossible to track. I didn't like it and said so. The only reason they kept me on the board was because of my father's reputation with our employees and suppliers and other companies we did business with. I could yell to the horizon about what they were doing, but I knew it would do no good. They were arrogant and making hundreds of millions, so why should they change, even when they were under the spotlight of Joe Ryder's congressional committee. Conor White was—"

She stopped again, and he could see the anger rise in her, as if she suddenly realized she was telling too much. "I'm really tired. I want to go to sleep."

"Not yet."

She glared at him. "You're a fucking prick."

"Maybe. And maybe I just want to know what the hell I'm dealing with. Conor White what?"

"Conor White," she said deliberately, "was hired to create SimCo as a replacement for Hadrian in Equatorial Guinea so that whatever happened with Ryder's inquiry into what was going on in Iraq would in no way trigger an interest there."

"And you knew about it."

"I knew about it, but I had no idea he was involved

in arming the rebels. The man you saw me with on the plane was an independent auditor I hired to go over our books in Malabo to make certain there was absolutely no connection between the Striker/ Hadrian problem in Iraq and what we were doing in Equatorial Guinea. And as far as I know there wasn't, everything was legitimate. He finished his audit on the same day I learned about the photographs and the death of the priest who took them. I asked Conor about them, and he said they had to have been phonied up, Photoshopped or something, because whatever was supposed to be in them wasn't true. Still, phony or not, we had to get them back, quickly and quietly, before they became public.

"I didn't trust him then and I don't trust him now. I think the photos are real. Otherwise the priest wouldn't have been killed and the country so violently turned upside-down looking for them. What's more, I don't know that what White is doing isn't at the direct order of Sy Wirth and the people at Hadrian."

Marten watched her closely; her eyes, the movement of her body, anything that would tell him she was lying. He didn't find it. Still, she'd given him only part of it; he wanted the rest. "That takes care of the army, SimCo, and the top guns at Striker and Hadrian. Where do you fit in? We're not here now because you suddenly decided to take a vacation."

Anne took a deep breath. "I told you before, it was personal. I want the photographs to use against Wirth and Hadrian and Conor White. Threaten to turn them over to the Ryder Commission if they don't cease arming the insurgency and stop provoking an already terrible war. Maybe even more important to me personally"—her eyes filled with emotion—"I want to save what's left of the reputation of my father's company for him. For his memory.

"My mother got very sick when I was three. She was in the hospital for a month. She didn't recognize me or my father. Nobody knew what was wrong. Finally she came out of it. The experience scared the hell out of me. It did the same to him. I was very young, but I could see it. He was all but lost. I wanted so much to help him, but I couldn't.

"As I told you, my mother died when I was thirteen. It was brain cancer. She didn't live long, but it was awful for her and my dad. Like the first time, he tried to protect me from it while he was falling apart himself. How he kept everything together—me, himself, the company—I don't know. When she died, he and I went on together. It was his life and my life at the same time, and we went on like that until I went to college. But we never lost the closeness, not even later when I got married. I loved him very much. I respected him even more. I was holding his hand when he died." She paused, then let her eyes find his. "Is that enough explanation for you?"

"Almost."

Suddenly her anger roared back. "What the hell else do you want to know?"

"Whose place this is. Who you're relying on to get us out of Berlin. Who you had following me earlier so that you knew where I was and where I went when I left the hotel to meet Haas."

These were questions from before that so far she'd managed not to answer. But she knew he'd keep asking now until he had an answer, either that or he would simply walk out as he'd threatened.

"Things were arranged through old friends," she said quietly. "I lived in Berlin for eighteen months some years ago."

"Doing what?"

She didn't reply.

"Doing what?" he repeated.

"I was an employee of the U.S. government."

"As?"

"My job was classified."

"Classified?"

"Yes."

"Meaning you were an operative of some kind."

"I . . . worked for the CIA."

10:30 P.M.

34

• Harrington Lake, Canada, the official country retreat of the prime minister of Canada.
Still Friday, June 4. 4:35 P.M.

President Harris walked down a country path with Canadian prime minister Elliot Campbell, Campbell's wife, Lorraine, and Emiliano Mayora, the president of Mexico. The weather was warm with puffy clouds that occasionally darkened, suggesting rain later in the day. All were dressed casually for the walk that was purposefully about nothing, an opportunity for the leaders of the Americas north-ernmost countries to chitchat and spend a little unofficial time in one another's company before getting back to the formal discussions of trade and mutual security that brought them there.

A conversation about fly-fishing had seen Prime Minister Campbell and President Mayora move ahead of the others, leaving President Harris alone with Mrs. Campbell. Cute and perky, she took the opportunity to ask him how he was doing personally, gently reminding him that he was quite a handsome man who had not been seen publicly with a woman since the death of his wife during his presidential campaign some two years earlier.

"Frankly, I haven't had much time to think about it." President Harris smiled graciously. "This is a big job."

"That part I fully understand, Mr. President. Still, you do think about it. I saw the longing in your eyes as you spoke. For everything you do and have to do, you are lonely for companionship."

This time John Henry Harris's smile was more inward and delicate. "You're very perceptive, Mrs. Campbell, I am lonely. But my longing is still for my wife. I miss her a great deal. I do my best not to think about it."

"Mr. President," a voice suddenly called from behind them.

Harris and Mrs. Campbell turned to see Lincoln

Bright, the president's chief of staff, press through the gaggle of Secret Service agents following them and come quickly forward.

"Excuse me, Mr. President, Madame Campbell." Bright looked to the president. "Representative Ryder is calling from Qatar. It's important."

"I'll take the call," Harris turned to Lorraine Campbell. "Please excuse me for a few minutes. Tell the prime minister and President Mayora I'll catch up with you all shortly."

"Of course, Mr. President."

• 4:47 P.M.

President Harris took Joe Ryder's call over a secure phone in the comfortably rustic guest quarters of the Harrington Lake estate.

"You've heard what's happened in Berlin?" Ryder's voice was filled with concern.

"The Theo Haas murder."

"Yes."

"I know about it, that's all. Did Marten reach him before it happened?"

"Marten is wanted for his murder."

"What?" Harris was astounded.

"It's all over TV. In the Washington Post, New York Times, *and in about every other major paper as well as on the Internet. I realize you've been busy and probably not tuned in to this stuff, and certainly no one would advise you. There would be no reason to; they wouldn't know the connection."*

"My God, Joe, where the hell is he?"

"As far as I know, on the run in Berlin. There's a woman with him. So far they haven't released her name, or his, for that matter."

"Then how do you know it's Marten?"

"Someone took his picture with a cell phone. It's not a very good likeness. But it's him, or his double, without doubt. You showed me a photo of the two of you together when you suggested him for the job." Ryder hesitated. *"John, Mr. President. You can't get involved. You can't try to help him. Not even with your own people. You can't risk the connection."*

"I know, dammit. He knows it, too."

"What do we do?"

"Nothing. Just wait and hope to hell he finds a way to get in touch with me."

"Then what?"

"Something. I'm not sure. I'll work on it."

"What if he did kill Haas?"

"He didn't."

"You're certain?"

"Damned certain."

"I'm here for you, John. Whatever, whenever."

"I know, Joe, we'll work it out. And thanks. Thanks for being there in all this. I'll call you when I have news."

With that the president hung up and stared off, praying he was right, that Marten would find a way to get in touch with him. What he would do then, he truly didn't know. At the same time, he knew he'd better have something to tell him.

4:52 P.M.

35

Marten slumped in the worn overstuffed chair watching Anne sleep on the bed across from him. A bottle of the Radeberger Pilsner in his hand, he wore boxer shorts and the light blue sport shirt he had on when he'd gone to meet Theo Haas in the park.

He took a sip of the beer and looked restlessly up at the ceiling. The apartment was warm, and Anne slept with only a sheet pulled up around her. She'd invited him to sleep beside her for no other reason than that the bed was the only place to rest. Instead he'd chosen the chair, chiefly because it gave him a clear view of the apartment's front door. If anyone was coming through it, he wanted to see them before they saw him. Especially if they were police with orders to shoot.

• 1:32 A.M.

Marten took another drink of the Radeberger and looked at Anne across from him. He could just see her in the dark, sleeping on her side, her legs pulled up toward her chest in an almost fetal position. The CIA, he thought. Jesus, what department had she been in? Research, an operative, what? Whatever it was, it had certainly been important enough for her to still be connected to people who would shadow strangers for her, help her elude the police and provide a safe house and then somehow get them out, or at least try to get them out, of the city.

At forty-two, she was seven years older than he was, but looking at her now she might have been a child. She'd told him she'd been married, and he wondered if she had children herself. If so, how many? And how old? And where were they now? For all he knew they could be in high school or college or in their early twenties and out on their own.

• 1:40 A.M.

He finished the Radeberger and took the empty bottle into the kitchen. He was exhausted and wired tight at the same time. The idea of sleep seemed impossible. The murder of Theo Haas had been horror enough, but the combination of circumstances that made him a prime suspect was beyond imagination. That a top cop like Franck had been assigned to the case made it all the worse. His credentials aside, his physical bearing, his body language, and the intense look in his eyes as he'd addressed the television cameras had chillingly reminded Marten of his mentor on the Los Angeles Police Department, the late Commander Arnold McClatchy, who had been one of the most revered, relentless, and feared homicide detectives in California history. Like McClatchy, Franck had the entire department at his disposal, and like McClatchy, Marten was certain, once he'd taken on a case he wouldn't let go until, one way or another, his man was brought to the ground.

Then there was the other thought. Poor as his photograph was, it was everywhere. What if the guys on the LAPD still hunting him saw it and got in touch with Franck? Then what? A little cop-to-cop talk and suddenly a couple of detectives show up from L.A. waiting for Franck to get him. And when he does, he keeps it quiet and hands him over to them. The next day his body is found in a ditch somewhere. Nobody knows who did it. It would save the Berlin PD a big noisy trial and a lot of expense. It made him want to kick himself for blurting to the jerk-off dope dealer on the street that he was an L.A. cop. What if the police caught the guy and he brought it up?

It had been a stupid thing to do.

Just plain stupid.

• 1:42 A.M.

Marten set the bottle on the kitchen counter and was starting toward the bedroom when he heard sirens approaching. He stopped and listened. What were they? Fire? Ambulance? No, police, he was certain. They grew nearer. He went into the front room and stood beside one of the narrow windows to peer out at the dimly lit alley below. The sirens were closer still. He counted one, two, and then three, all traveling close together. Instinctively he listened for the sound of a circling helicopter. What would he do if they pulled up outside?

"What is it?" Anne called from the other room.

"Nothing. Go back to sleep."

Christ, maybe he should tell her to get up and get

dressed. But then what? Go out the tiny air-shaft window in the dark and up the fire ladder to the roof? Why? If the police knew where they were, they wouldn't have a chance to begin with.

He moved farther back from the window, giving him a view of the alley where it met Ziegelstrasse. The sounds grew louder, the shrillness bouncing off the old brick facades of the neighboring buildings. His heart was pounding. If they came, they came. Just give up. There was nothing else to do.

The sounds grew louder and louder. Then they were right there on top of him. He expected to hear the screech of brakes, the instant cutting of sirens, the slam of doors as armed police jumped from the cars. Instead he caught the briefest glimpse of flashing lights. And then, like that, they passed, taking their noise with them.

For a long moment he just stood there in the darkness listening to the pounding of his heart and the sound of his own breath. Suddenly he wondered about his emotional state, if things were beginning to get to him that shouldn't, or at least that he should have control over. Thinking, too, that this was no time or place for such fragility. It was far too dangerous.

"You need to sleep." Anne's voice floated out of the darkness nearby. He started and looked up.

He saw her in the light-spill from the streetlights, standing in the doorway watching him. Her dark hair tucked behind her ears, she was barefoot and still wearing nothing but the T-shirt and panties.

"You're overtired," she said quietly.

"I know." His voice was barely a murmur.

"Come to bed."

Marten stared at her.

"Please."

"Alright," he said finally, then left the window and followed her down the narrow hallway into the bedroom.

1:48 A.M.

36

• Berlin Police Headquarters,
Platz der Luftbrücke. 2:02 A.M.

"Why this took so long to reach me, I don't know. But I promise you I will find out." Hauptkommissar Emil Franck sat behind his serviceable steel desk in his very utilitarian office, his black eyes cold and unblinking.

Two uniformed motorcycle officers stood in front of him; Detectives Gerhard Bohlen and Gertrude Prosser were to his left. For a moment he stared at the motorcycle officers, then pressed the PLAY button on a digital recorder in front of him. A short silence was followed immediately by a recorded conversation between a motorcycle officer and a *Funk-betriebszentrale*, a central radio dispatcher at police headquarters.

MOTORCYCLE OFFICER: *West for West 717.*
DISPATCHER: *West 717, go ahead.*

MOTORCYCLE OFFICER: *Male and female pedes-*
trians with resemblance to fugitives on Schiff-
bauerdamm, approaching Weidendamm Bridge
at Friedrichstrasse. Copy.
DISPATCHER: *I have it, West 717.*

There was a several-second pause and then:

MOTORCYCLE OFFICER: *Ah, West for West 717,*
again, Dispatch. Cancel that. They're just two
lovebirds playing suck face.
DISPATCHER: *I have it, West 717.*

Immediately Franck's right index finger shot out
and punched the STOP button. The player went silent, and he looked up at the two motorcycle officers across from him.

"Your first call came at 19:38:44 hours," he
snapped at the officer designated West 717. "Why
did you cancel it?"

"It seemed like nothing. They saw us. They didn't
care. Hardly the style of fugitives, Hauptkommissar."

"How do you presume that? You said yourself
they resembled the suspects. How do you know what
they were doing or why? Schiffbauerdamm at the
Weidendamm Bridge is less than a twenty-minute
walk from the Hotel Adlon, and 19:38 was in the correct time frame." Immediately Franck's eyes shifted
from West 717 to the second officer.

"Did you agree with the evaluation?"

"Yes, Hauptkommissar."

"I want a report on my desk in five minutes. Exactly what those people looked like. What they were wearing. What they were carrying. And any other circumstance or particular either of you can remember. You may go!"

Both men drew up, saluted, then turned and left, their futures in the Berlin Police Department very much in doubt.

The door closed behind them, and Franck looked to Bohlen and Prosser. "Maybe they were our Mr. Marten and Ms. Tidrow, maybe they weren't. The time was right, the area was right. Handler's dogs lost them at the Reichstag construction site, a fistful of tossed rocks from the Spree. This 'suck face' couple was on Schiffbauerdamm at Weidendamm Bridge, also on the Spree and not far from the Reichstag."

Franck stood up from his desk and crossed to a huge sectioned map of Berlin mounted on a far wall. He stared at it for a moment as if to reassure himself of the Schiffbauerdamm/Weidendamm Bridge location, an intersection he could have pointed to in his sleep, the same as he could almost every other street and intersection in the city. But it was his nature to double-check, and he did. Then, assured, he turned back to his detectives.

"That intersection has two things in particular. Friedrichstrasse station and the river itself, which means tour boats. The moment I have the report from our very observant officers, I want investigators sent out to interview all station and train personnel and all tour boat crews on duty from 19:38 hours on.

They are to get people out of bed if necessary. If our 'lovebirds' were somewhere there, I want to know every detail of it. If they were in the station, which door they came in and went out. If they were on a train or boat, where they got on and where they got off."

• 2:25 A.M.

Franck stood alone looking at the map trying to assess where in the city Marten and Anne Tidrow might have gone and to put it together with the other information that had come in. Just after midnight he'd received an answer to his query about Marten's character and the architectural landscape firm where he was employed in Manchester, England. First, Marten was an American expatriate from Vermont who had no criminal record, rented a nice apartment, and paid his bills on time. Second, his firm, Fitzsimmons and Justice, was a long-established, highly respected business that catered almost entirely to municipal projects or private, mostly upscale clientele. Marten had worked there for more than two years following his graduation with an advanced degree from the University of Manchester. First-rate credentials all the way around. As for Hannah Anne Tidrow, she was not only a member of the board of directors of the AG Striker Oil and Energy Company of Houston, Texas, she was the daughter of the company's late chairman, Virgil Wyatt Tidrow. Moreover, Striker Oil, in partnership with the American private security contractor Hadrian LLC of Manassas, Virginia, had been working in Iraq under a U.S. State Department contract since shortly after the war began and was currently under the scrutiny of the United States Congress for alleged questionable business practices there. Further, Striker Oil did not have an office in Berlin or anywhere else in Europe. Lastly, Marten had arrived at Berlin Tegel Airport at eleven o'clock yesterday morning, coming in not from Manchester but from Paris. Barely two hours later, Anne Tidrow had arrived, also from Paris.

Franck stared at the map a moment longer, then went back to his desk and sat down. Why in hell, he thought, would two people like that come all the way to Berlin to murder Theo Haas and in a place as crowded and public as the Platz der Republik?

He turned to his computer and sent an URGENT e-mail to Detectives Bohlen and Prosser.

Please get more on Striker Oil activities outside the U.S. and Iraq. Also find out where Marten and Tidrow had been before Paris.

Done, he pulled a stack of reports toward him, the findings of more than two dozen investigators who had interviewed witnesses and bystanders at the Platz der Republik and the Brandenburg Gate shortly after Haas's murder. He opened the first and began to read. Maybe, hopefully, there was something somewhere in them that had been overlooked.

37

In two of the first four reports, three eyewitnesses—one at the Platz der Republik and two near the Brandenburg Gate—had made mention of a young, curly-haired man in a black sweater running through the crowd as if he were being chased. That was all, just that. Nothing about what he looked like, his size, or what he was wearing other than the sweater. It all three cases it was just a throwaway observation. Certainly nothing that would tie him in with Marten, Anne Tidrow, or the Haas murder. Nonetheless Franck made a note about it and reached for the fifth report. As he did his phone rang. He glanced at the clock on his desk and then picked up.

"Yes."

"Hauptkommissar." It was Gertrude Prosser.

"You should be home sleeping. A few hours at least."

"You are working."

"Yes, but I'm foolish. Go home, Gertrude. You can't work if you don't rest."

"Hauptkommissar." Her voice became urgent. *"I just received answers on two pieces of information you requested a short while ago. I think they should be regarded as confidential."*

"Go on."

"*You wanted to know where Nicholas Marten and Anne Tidrow had been before Paris. Answer, they had both come in on the same Air France flight from Malabo, on the island of Bioko, Equatorial Guinea.*"

"Equatorial Guinea?"

"*Yes, sir.*"

"The second piece?"

"*Striker Oil has oil field service and exploration contracts around the world. Lately they have expanded exploration activities on the island of Bioko and have hired a British private military contractor called SimCo to provide protective services there. And then I discovered something else.*" She paused, and he could feel the excitement in her.

"Go on."

"*A catholic priest, a Father Willy Dorhn, was killed in southern Bioko by members of the national army a day before Marten and Ms. Tidrow left there.*"

"So?"

"*Father Dorhn was the brother of Theo Haas.*"

"What?"

"*That's all I have so far. There is a major civil war building in Equatorial Guinea. Maybe they are all connected.*"

"Yes, maybe. Good work, and thank you, Kommissar Prosser. Go home and get some sleep."

Emil Franck hung up. This was a turn he would never have expected. Was it possible Marten and Anne Tidrow, and maybe her oil company, were somehow involved in the civil war in Equatorial Guinea? And had some part of it spilled over into Berlin via Theo Haas and his brother? If so, why? The questions puzzled and troubled him at the same time, and he suddenly wondered if this was something that should be handled by either the BND, the Federal Intelligence Service, or the BKA, the Federal Criminal Police, rather than his office.

But bringing in either agency would change everything. Their presence would be too unwieldy and have too much media coverage. As a result he might lose Marten and Anne Tidrow altogether. No, can't do it, he thought. For now, at least, he would do as Gertrude Prosser had advised and keep the information confidential.

Again he glanced at the clock on his desk.

3:09 A.M.

Time to lie down on the worn leather couch across from him and get some sleep himself. He closed the reports he'd been studying and was reaching to turn off his desk lamp when his personal cell phone sounded, announcing an incoming call with a musical ringtone a technical assistant had programmed, which he detested.

Who was it? His wife would have long been asleep. His children were out of the country, his twenty-year-old daughter spending a college year in China, his nineteen-year-old son backpacking in New Zealand. Very few others had the number.

The phone went silent, then rang again. He picked up and clicked on.

"Yes."

"I thought I'd find you working," a throaty female voice came back.

Franck paused, trying to place the voice. Then he did. "It's been a long time."

"We need to talk."

"When?"

"Twenty minutes."

"Same place?"

"Yes."

"Okay," Franck said, then slowly clicked off. He was right, it had been a long time. But putting things together, he knew he should have expected to hear from her.

3:12 A.M.

38

• 7:15 A.M.

Marten woke with a start. The bed beside him was empty. He looked around. The clothes Anne had taken off the night before to carefully fold and lay atop the chest of drawers were gone.

"Anne?"

There was no reply. He got up fast.

"Anne?"

He went down the hall, glanced at the open bathroom door, then went into the front room, then into the tiny kitchen. She wasn't there. It was then he smelled the coffee and saw the automatic coffee-maker on the counter near the sink. A freshly brewed pot was nestled inside it. A cup sat alongside. So did a note.

> *Back soon. Stay here.*
> *I have your passport.*

His passport? Maybe he had threatened to leave and take his chances with the police, but in truth, for the moment, at least, he was better off staying right where he was and letting her try to find a way to get them out of Berlin. Trouble was, by now she would be vulnerable to capture, too, and would know it, so where the hell did she go? Immediately came another thought. What if someone knocked on the door? Or had a key and just came in? Anne would have been able to handle things because she set it all up. He didn't even know whose apartment this was.

As if in answer to his concern, he suddenly heard voices in the alley outside. Immediately he went into the front room, stood by the window, and carefully looked out. A light rain was falling, and a number of people were entering the alley from the street under umbrellas. Most looked like they were college age or close to it. It made him think there might be some kind of school farther down the alley that had Saturday classes. If so, passport or not, it might be a place for him to hide, to blend in among the students, in the event the police began a house-to-house search.

• 7:19 A.M.

A small television sat on a bookshelf across the room. He went to it and turned it on, hoping for news of Hauptkommissar Franck's investigation. Quickly he ran through the channels. There was nothing but Saturday-morning television, cartoons and sports and travel shows. Finally he found an English-language news channel where someone was giving the weather forecast for Europe. He looked at his watch and then at the door, wondering what time Anne had gone out. The weathercast segued to an Audi commercial. He went back to the window and looked out. There were more young people hud-dling under umbrellas. By now a line had begun to form. What was going on, especially this early on a Saturday morning? Then commercials ended and the news resumed, and he went back to the TV to watch it.

The story being covered was about a car that had exploded on a country highway. All he saw was po-lice investigators and the burned-out wreckage of the car, and he assumed the location was somewhere in Germany. It wasn't. It was Spain. The car had been a limousine; its driver was among the dead. A bomb was suspected. The other victims were thought to be three of five people missing since they'd ar-rived in Madrid the morning before on a flight from Paris, Spanish medical personnel just returned to Europe from Equatorial Guinea. Their names were being withheld pending formal identification of the bodies.

"Please, God, no!" Marten froze in horror. In the

next instant he realized prayers and denial were use-
less. He knew exactly who the victims were—Marita
and her students. The coincidence was far too great
for it to have been anyone else. Shocked and sickened, he watched for a moment longer, then turned
off the sound and walked away. His senses numb, he
went into the kitchen and poured a cup of coffee,
then just stood there staring at nothing. Finally he
set the cup down and found his way into the bathroom.

He looked in the mirror. His complexion was
ghostly white. There were paper cups by the sink.
He filled one with tap water and drank it, then crum-
pled the cup and dropped it into the wastepaper basket. He went back into the front room to stare at the
TV still playing in silence. He saw one commercial
and then another. Next came a business news brief.
Then a replay of the story about the limousine explosion.

The initial account had reported the victims missing since they'd arrived in Madrid yesterday. Suddenly it occurred to him that if the police had the
bodies of the limo driver and three of the five missing people, where were the other two? And who
were they? Marita and one of the kids? Or two of the
kids, with Marita among the dead in the exploded
car?

Marten felt rage begin to heave through him. Unless there had been some terrible fluke of coincidence, whatever had happened had to have involved
the photographs. This was the doing of AG Striker
and SimCo. There was no point in even thinking it

might have been operatives from President Tiombe's cutthroat army. They might have had the will but not the kind of connections or swift response that a world-class mercenary like Conor White would have at his fingertips.

Meaning that what Anne had said about not trusting White and wanting to recover the photos herself in order to help slow the war and save the reputation of her father's company would have been nothing more than a excuse to get him to trust her. Meaning, too, that she most certainly would have known about White's activity in Spain. Maybe even helped orchestrate it. All of them making the assumption that, afraid something would happen to him, he had confided in Marita and the others and told them what the pictures were and where to find them. If that were so, it meant she didn't give a damn about anything but protecting the company.

Marten left the TV and stood near the window watching the line of people with umbrellas in the alley below. Immediately his gaze shifted to the end of it where it met Ziegelstrasse. It was the way Anne would come when she returned.

Where the hell was she?

7:33 A.M.

39

Sy Wirth's corporate Gulfstream G550 had had landed at Stansted Airport just after midnight. Immediately afterward a limousine had taken him into the city and to a private apartment in Mayfair. At 1:30 in the morning London time, he'd gone to bed. Four and a half hours later he was working out in the apartment's gym. At 7:07 he showered, then dressed in dark blue suit and tie, his accent and ostrich skin boots the only outward remnants of his Texas persona. At 7:30 he left the Mayfair apartment and was driven to the Dorchester Hotel on Park Lane. At 7:45 he was seated in a private dining room awaiting the arrival of his guest. Three minutes later that person arrived with fanfare—the brash, designer-dressed, forty-eight-year-old Russian oil oligarch Dimitri Korostin with a gaggle of bodyguards in tow. Within seconds the bodyguards were gone, and the two greeted each other as the old friends and business adversaries they were. They ordered breakfast and began to make the ritual small talk.

"How are your children, Dimitri?"

"They are well, already in college, if you can believe it. Oxford, Yale, and the Sorbonne." Korostin grinned, his Russian accent heavy. "Covering as many bases as possible given we only have the three. And how are you, Sy? Or are you again calling yourself Josiah, giving yourself some biblical dignity when you come to this side of the pond?"

"I'm in the oil business, Dimitri. I have no dignity, biblical or otherwise. Neither do you."

"So we stop talking about children and other bullshit and get to the reason you are here. What do you want to sell?"

"Trade."

"What for what?"

"I"—Wirth hesitated—"need your help."

"That can be expensive."

"Andean gas field lease, thirty-five years."

"Which one?"

"The Magellan, in Santa Cruz–Tarija."

"That is potentially a very big field." Korostin smiled. "Your trouble must be personal."

"Someone has a number of photographs and most probably the digital memory card from the camera used to take them. I want both recovered and returned to me with whatever package or packing they are in unopened."

"You're being blackmailed."

Wirth nodded.

"A woman. A man, perhaps."

Wirth nodded. Dimitri's inference was as good a cover as any. "Sex can be a nasty business."

"Surely you have your own people for these things."

"I'm not convinced my people are going to get it

done. For all its success the West is provincial. We have a tradition of trying to do things more or less the right way, even if it isn't always legal. It's a mind-set that doesn't necessarily work, especially if the situation is urgent. You, on the other hand, take the shortest route to the problem and more often than not have a satisfactory outcome. I need only mention the former KGB agent poisoned with polonium right here in London."

"The result is not always neat."

"But it works just the same." Wirth took a folded sheet of paper from his jacket and handed it to Korostin. "The Magellan/Santa Cruz–Tarija contract."

Korostin slipped on reading glasses and opened it.

The document was on simple everyday stationery. There was no letterhead, nothing to identify where it had come from. The words covered barely two-thirds of a page, the deal spelled out in the simplest terms, the particulars, everything. Josiah Wirth's signature was at the bottom of it.

"Everything's there," Wirth said. "The name of the principal person involved, Nicholas Marten. What I want done and how. When I have the items in my possession the Magellan/Santa Cruz–Tarija is yours."

Korostin read it. Then read it again and looked up. "You want to be kept informed of our movements."

"Each step of the way. I want to know where your people are and where Marten is. No action is to be taken on him until I am there, so that when the photographs and camera memory card are recovered they can be handed directly to me."

"That might be awkward."

"You are a gifted man, Dimitri, you'll find a way to make it work."

Korostin smiled. "If the items are as damning as your offer suggests, how do you know I will keep my part of the bargain and not turn them against you?"

"Small as we are compared to the giants, Striker Oil has any number of long-term oil and gas field leases around the world. Something you well know. You might want to do business with us again. As I said, you are a gifted man. You wouldn't jeopardize that opportunity."

Korostin folded the paper and slipped it into his jacket. "When do you want the work completed?"

"Yesterday."

40

• Berlin. 8:18 A.M.

Four people stood in the front room of a modest flat on Scharrenstrasse: Hauptkommissar Franck, Kommissar Gertrude Prosser, two uniformed policemen, and Karl Betz. A fifth person, Betz's wife, peeked anxiously through a door that led to the rest of the apartment. Betz was fifty-two, a little overweight, had a mustache and curly eyebrows, and was very nervous. He was also a waiter on the tour boat *Monbijou.*

Franck held up the official photograph of Nicholas Marten. "This is the man you served on the *Monbijou* last night."

"Not served, exactly, Hauptkommissar." Betz tried to smile through his uneasiness. "Actually he helped me serve. Along with his wife, that is. Or someone I took for his wife. They passed along a couple of glasses of beer to passengers seated next to them."

"But it was him, you're certain?" Franck pressed him impassively.

"He's the one you're looking for? The murderer of Theo Haas?"

"Is it the same man or is it not?"

"Yes, Hauptkommissar. It is the same man."

"And the woman with him was the one described to you by Kommissar Prosser?"

"Yes, Hauptkommissar."

"You said he was wearing something in particular."

"A Dallas Cowboys baseball cap." Betz smiled proudly. "I've been to Dallas. Dallas, Texas. I nearly bought a cap like that myself, but we were on a strict budget."

"Where did they board the *Monbijou*?"

"I'm not exactly sure. Lustgarten dock, I think."

"Where did they get off?"

"Weidendamm Bridge, the Friedrichstrasse crossing."

"At what time?"

Betz suddenly looked at the floor.

"At what time, Herr Betz?" Franck pressed him.

The waiter looked back, more nervous than before. "We did nothing illegal. It was a special tour for foreign travel agents. It ran later than usual. We had a special permit; you can look it up. The boat was crowded. I don't know how they got on, but they did."

"Herr Betz, I am not the waterway police." Franck was beginning to lose patience. "What time did they leave the boat?"

"Close to nine forty, Hauptkommissar. I looked at my watch as we docked."

"Nine forty."

"Yes, Hauptkommissar."

"Thank you."

8:24 A.M.

• 8:26 A.M.

Marten stood at the edge of the window looking down at the alley. Light rain still fell. The line of umbrella-huddling students inching forward seemed longer than ever.

Once, then twice he'd gone back to the television, turning the sound up, watching. Occasionally there had been repeats of the news story from Spain. If the Spanish police had more information on what had taken place there, they weren't making it public. The same was true of the news from Berlin. The investigation into the savage murder of Theo Haas

was ongoing. The police were asking the coopera-
tion of the public in locating the man "wanted for
questioning" in the killing. Again the fuzzy cell
phone photograph of Marten had been shown, and
with it a call in-number and e-mail address for con-
tacting the police if he were seen. After that came
the announcement that a media blackout had been
imposed. That part Marten found even more troubling than the continued exposure of his picture.
From his experience on the LAPD, a media blackout meant the police were on to a number of leads
that were potentially significant and that they
weren't about to disclose. Often that meant an arrest
was imminent.

He looked back to the front door.

Where was Anne? What was she doing that was
taking so long? What if—his heart caught in his
throat at the idea—something had happened and
the police had her? She had his passport with her.
How long would it be before they forced her to tell
them where he was? Maybe that was the reason for
the media blackout.

He felt sweat bead up on his forehead. Once
again he thought of Spain and the two people still
unaccounted for in the car bombing. He had to trust
that the Spanish police knew what they were doing
and that those missing would soon be found. Then
again, maybe not. Who knew how far the limousine
had traveled before it blew up? Maybe other police
agencies were involved and there was a jurisdiction
problem. Politics might figure in as well. Immediately the thought struck that the remaining two were

still alive somewhere else in the countryside and at that moment were being tortured in order to get information about the photographs. It was something the police would have no way of knowing. How could they? Christ, he had to alert someone. But how?

Just then the television crackled with more breaking news. He crossed the room quickly to watch it. The report was live from Madrid, where the police were about to make an announcement concerning their investigation of the limousine explosion.

An icy feeling of dread crept through him as he watched a police spokesman approach a bank of microphones, then address the waiting media in Spanish. A studio announcer provided a voice-over English translation. Two bodies, he said, had been found in a shallow grave at an abandoned farmhouse less than five miles from the car bombing. Another body had been found in a ramshackle barn nearby. All three had been shot in the head. The first two victims were women; the third was a man. Identification of the dead was pending.

Marten stared at the screen, numb and transfixed. Slowly he looked off to the window and the gray sky and drizzle and vague buildings beyond it. His memory was vivid. He saw the faces of Marita and Ernesto, Rosa, Luis, and Gilberto as they sat at the table with him at the Hotel Malabo during the howling storm; slept across from and beside him on the night plane from Malabo to Paris; remembered clearly his exchange with Marita when they all said farewell at the airport in Paris and she pressed a page torn from a notebook into his hand and smiled her impish smile.

"My address and telephone number if you get to Spain. My e-mail if you don't. Please call me if you have time. I want to know what happens to you."

"Nothing's going to happen to me. I'm going home and back to work and grow old, nothing else."

"You're not a 'nothing else' person, Mr. Marten. I think you're one of those people trouble follows around. We have to go. Please call me."

As if from far away he heard the sound of the television. A commercial for skin cream. Suddenly his head felt light. A wave of dizziness swept over him, and the room began to spin. In the next second he felt his heart start to race. Almost immediately he struggled to get his breath. Sweat seemed to engulf him. He felt hot and cold at the same time. He didn't know what was happening. He put a hand out against the wall to steady himself, gasping for air as he did. He felt trapped, as if the walls were closing in. He wanted to get out of there. Be outdoors in the open. Then the sound of his own voice rose above that of the television and the deep rasp of his labored breathing. It came from far inside and was powerful and intense and filled with rage and chanting a litany of names over and over like some demonic mantra.

Striker, Hadrian, Conor White, Anne Tidrow.
Striker, Hadrian, Conor White, Anne Tidrow.
Striker, Hadrian, Conor—

Suddenly there was another sound. That of a key being put into the front door. He pushed back against the wall and froze. A half second later the door opened.

"Nicholas?" a familiar voice called out. "Nicholas?"

Anne Tidrow.

41

He remembered seeing her close the door and lock it, then turn toward him. She had her purse and a garment bag over one arm and was pulling a cheap plastic rain cover from her hair. The rest he had little recollection of. All he knew now was that she was sitting in a chair by the television staring at him, her hair disheveled, the garment bag and her purse on the floor. And that he was leaning against the wall breathing deeply, his arms across his chest, trying not to look at her.

"Tell me what happened," she said quietly.

"I don't know."

"Tell me what happened."

"I—"

"Tell me."

Slowly his eyes went to hers. "I grabbed you by the throat and shoved you against the wall. Hard. And held you there."

"What did you say?"

"I didn't say. I asked."

"Asked what?"

"Why them?"

"And what did I say?"

"Who are you talking about?" Marten could feel his jaw tighten in anger. "You knew exactly who I was talking about."

"No. I didn't. I still don't."

"Fuck you."

"Tell me."

"You want me to spell it out?"

"Yes."

"The Spanish doctor and her medical students. I'll name them for you. Marita, Ernesto, Rosa, Luis, Gilberto. Marita wasn't even thirty. None of the students were more than twenty-three. They're all dead! Murdered! Somewhere outside Madrid. God only knows what happened before they were killed."

"Nicholas, I didn't know. Believe me. How could I?"

"I said—fuck you."

"It's the truth."

"Jesus God." Marten walked over to the window and stood beside it staring out. He felt like putting his foot through it and yelling at the people below that there was a real live murderer in here and they should call the police.

"You might have killed me," she said.

Marten's head came around like a bullet, his eyes filled with hatred. "I should have killed you."

"But you didn't."

"I should have."

"What did you do?"

"I took my hands away and let you go."

"What else?"

"I don't know."

"Yes, you do."

"No."

"You cried."

For a long moment Marten said nothing, just glared at her. "Yeah, well, fuck it," he said finally. "One way or another Conor White and your damned AG Striker Company killed them. Whether you helped him plan what to do and how to do it, I don't know. You do, but I don't."

"Nicholas," she said quietly, "I'm terribly sorry about your friends, I really am, but I don't know why you would think that I or Striker or Conor White had anything to do with it."

"Why? I'll tell you why. You thought I told them where the photographs were. You came after me, White went after them."

"That's not true."

"No?"

"No."

"Where is he now?"

"As far as I know, still in Malabo."

"You have his cell number?"

Anne nodded.

Deliberately Marten walked over and picked up her purse, then fished out her BlackBerry and dropped it in her lap. "Call him. Ask him where he is."

"Alright." Anne picked up the BlackBerry and punched in a number. She waited a few seconds; then they both heard a male voice on the other end. It was sharp and curt, the British accent unmistakable.

"Yes."

"It's Anne. Where are you?" She paused as he said something, then, "I just wanted to know where you were if I needed you." Another pause, then, "I'm still in Berlin. But don't come here. I'm alright. Never mind what you see in the media." There was a long pause as White said something more, then, "Yes, I think so. What?" Another pause, then, "No, I don't think, Conor, I know," she said testily, then finished. "I'll be in touch."

Marten watched her click off, then get up and put the BlackBerry away. "Where is he?" he said.

Anne hesitated.

"Where?"

"Madrid, Barajas Airport."

"Madrid?"

"Yes."

Marten leaned in so that his face was inches from hers. "The next time you talk to him, tell him from me that it was all for nothing. The people he killed didn't know a damn thing about the photographs. I never said a word."

Anne looked at him genuinely, even vulnerably. "Think whatever you want. But I didn't know. Whatever Conor White did, he did on his own, or maybe, as I said before, at the urging of Sy Wirth or the people at Hadrian."

Marten glared at her, then took a breath and crossed the room to again stare out the window. "When the hell are we getting out of here?"

"A van is picking us up"—she looked at her watch—"in five minutes."

"Where?"

"Outside, on Ziegelstrasse."

"A van is coming here?"

"Yes."

"To do what, run us right under the noses of the five thousand cops looking for us?"

"Hopefully."

"Hopefully?"

"The Hauptkommissar is getting closer. He must have interviewed people on the tour boat. Police are starting to put up roadblocks near the dock where we got off. If what I've put together doesn't work, we can both look forward to spending the next thirty years in a German prison."

Marten's eyes fixed on hers. "God damn you. Your company. Hadrian. Conor White. All of you."

"I'm sorry."

8:50 A.M.

42

The van had been there right on time, parked at the curb at the end of the alley where it met Ziegel-strasse. It was white and reasonably new. A man introduced by Anne as Hartmann Erlanger was at the wheel. He was probably in his late fifties and slim with thinning gray hair. He wore frameless glasses and a light brown cardigan over dark brown slacks, all of which gave him the appearance of a retired professor or antiques dealer, the role he seemed to be playing. Or at least that was what Marten remembered before he was ushered into the vehicle's rear compartment and past a collection of a dozen or so straight-backed antique chairs. Immediately Erlanger removed an interior panel to reveal a tiny, cramped space over the left rear wheel.

"Get in, please," he said in heavily accented English. "The police are stopping traffic at intersections, checking identification. I was lucky to get through. If we are stopped, please do not move, make no sound at all. Hold your breath if you can."

Marten climbed in and twisted around, trying to make his six-foot-tall body somehow conform to the microscopic area. Then Erlanger put the panel back in place. Marten heard him lock it, and like that he was alone in the pitch black.

He remembered hearing Erlanger speak to Anne

in English seconds later. "How is your German? There is every chance we will be stopped on the way out."

He heard Anne begin to say something in German, and then the driver's door slammed closed and Erlanger started the engine. Seconds later the van moved off.

Whatever else Anne had done, or hadn't, or was involved with, there was no question that she had balls. Apparently she was going to sit up front with Erlanger as they attempted to pass through Franck's roadblocks. Probably play Erlanger's wife or sister or niece. There was every chance she'd get away with it, too. Not just because of her attitude and determination and her ability to speak German but because of the way she looked—the reason she'd gone out early and the reason for the garment bag she carried when she came back. In the minutes before they went out to meet Erlanger she'd put her dark hair up under a blond shoulder-length wig and re-placed her jeans outfit and running shoes with a dowdy beige pantsuit and ugly orthopedic sandals. Her old clothes she stuffed back into the garment bag, then brought it with them.

Marten moved gingerly, trying to find some sort of comfort in his cramped, traveling prison. For a time he thought he had managed it and relaxed as best he could. Then the van hit a pothole in the road-way and he shot straight up, banging his head against the top of the enclosure. Seconds later they slowed and came to a stop. He heard a mix of voices and then that of a sharp-edged, authoritative male speaking

German. Erlanger's voice came next. They were at a police checkpoint.

Now what?

Suddenly he heard the van's rear doors open. Then someone climbed inside. He held his breath as Erlanger had asked. There was the scrape of the antique chairs as they were moved aside. Immediately there was a thump on the van's far wall, as if someone had hit it with a fist. Then came more. The vehicle's interior paneling was being checked. Seconds later there was a bang on the outside of the panel just above his head. In the next instant he heard Anne say something in German, her voice calm and accommodating. Several seconds passed, and then he heard footsteps retreating and the sound of the rear doors closing. There was another exchange between Erlanger and the authoritative male. A silence followed, and then the van moved off.

Marten exhaled.

One checkpoint down. How many more to go?

9:32 A.M.

• 9:40 A.M.

Hauptkommissar Franck sat alone in a dark gray Audi parked along Lichtensteinallee in the Tiergarten, Berlin's sprawling urban park. He stared blankly out at the drizzle and listened to the crackle of radio transmissions from his people in the field, most particularly the force he'd sent out in the last hour following his conversation with the *Monbijou*'s waiter. His description of the man and woman who had gotten off the tour boat at the Lustgarten dock, coupled with the reference he'd made to the Dallas Cowboys baseball cap the man had been wearing, all but matched the account the shamed motorcycle officers had given him in their report.

As a result he'd made a computerized grid of the surrounding area, then set up roadblocks at intersections and sent two hundred plainclothes and uniformed officers into it in a block-by-block search. Afterward he'd climbed into his car and driven here, then parked and waited.

Now he lifted a small container of orange juice, took a sip, and put it back in the car's cup holder. The gray sky, the drizzle. He should be home sleeping, especially after the long night. Under other circumstances the suspects would already be in custody. Meaning he could get up late, have a cup of coffee with his wife, then go to the gym before meeting with the media. But these weren't other circumstances.

"We need to talk." He still heard the throaty female voice he'd heard when he'd answered his cell phone in the early-morning hours.

"When?"

"Twenty minutes."

"Same place?"

"Yes."

The place had been a darkened café just off Taubenstrasse near Gendarmenmarkt Square. The time, 3:30 A.M. It had been just the two of them, half seen in a chiaroscuro of near black-and-white created by the spill from a streetlamp outside. Elsa was older, as he was, but still exhilaratingly handsome, intellectually and sexually. The sexual activity between them had stopped years before, and he knew better than to try to relight it. Especially now and under the circumstances.

"This Nicholas Marten," she'd said as she had walked behind the bar to pour them each a small cognac and then come around it to sit on a stool next to him.

"What about him?"

"Allegedly there are a number of photographs pertaining to the rebellion in Equatorial Guinea. They are why Marten came to Berlin, to collect them."

"What are they of?"

"All we've been told is that they are strategically important. Read into it what you will."

"By 'allegedly' you mean 'if they exist.'"

"We are assuming they do."

"What do you want from me?"

"Follow Marten. Find the pictures—the camera's digital memory card may be with them. If it is, retrieve both. Afterward eliminate Marten and anyone with him."

"To follow him, Elsa, I have to find him without his knowing. Something quite difficult in itself but complicated even more by the elevated profile of the case and the number of police personnel involved."

"It can be done, Emil. We succeeded before in the old days and under far more difficult circumstances."

"We didn't have the media curse we have now."

She hadn't replied, just stared at him in silence. He'd been given an order. Excuses didn't exist. Like the old days.

He remembered picking up his glass and taking a sip of the cognac, then looking at her directly. "Who is he?"

"Marten?"

"Yes."

"You mean other than a landscape architect?"

He'd nodded.

"As yet, we don't know."

"Before he came to Berlin"—there was no point in keeping it a secret from her; she might have known anyway—"he had been in Equatorial Guinea. So had Anne Tidrow, the woman we think is with him."

"Board member," she'd said. "Striker Oil Company. Houston, Texas. They have a large oil operation in Equatorial Guinea."

"So you do know."

"Tell me the rest, Emil."

"While they were there a priest was murdered. He was the brother of Theo Haas."

"Did either of them have contact with the priest?"

"I don't know. Any more than I know why Marten—"

"Murdered Theo Haas?"

"Yes."

"Did he murder him?"

"I'm not sure."

"Still, it is reason enough for you to kill him after you recover the photographs."

"Yes, if your information is correct and he knows where they are."

She'd looked at him with a steely silence, a gesture of condescension she'd employed for as long as he'd known her. Then she'd picked up her glass, drained it.

"I will give you further instructions as I have them," she'd said, then set the glass on the bar and looked at him once more—either remembering the old days or trying to judge whether or not she could still trust him, he didn't know which. "Please lock the door when you leave," she'd said finally, then stood up and walked out.

Her instructions had come two hours later, waking him shortly after he'd fallen asleep on his office couch. He was to meet a man in the Tiergarten on the southern edge of Neuer Lake at ten o'clock that same morning. He would be a Russian in his mid-forties, bearded and a little overweight. His name was Kovalenko.

43

• 9:48 A.M.

Marten felt the van lean to the right, then accelerate and even out. After that there was the quiet hum of the tires over the roadway and little else. If Anne and Erlanger were talking, he couldn't hear them.

Who Erlanger was or might be, Marten had no idea. His best guess was that he was one of Anne's German operatives from her CIA days in Berlin. It made him wonder when that had been. She was forty-two now. So how old would she have been when she left the agency to care for her father? Twenty-nine, thirty, maybe a little more. So for ten or more years at least she had stayed in contact with these people, not just Erlanger, but the woman whose apartment they had stayed in, and the person or persons who had tailed him from the airport and then told her where he was. Of them all it was the woman who'd provided the apartment and now Erlanger who were most on the spot. They were aiding fugitives and if caught risked serious prison time. On the other hand, if they had been operatives, or maybe still were, this was the kind of thing they did all the time, where connections were everything and loyalty and silence ran deep.

By Marten's estimate they had been traveling for nearly thirty minutes at good speed and without being stopped again, which meant they were probably on a major highway and headed for some town or city that lay outside of Berlin proper and its heavy blanket of police. Suddenly he began to wonder just where Erlanger was taking them and what would happen when they got there. Getting out of Berlin was one thing, getting out of Germany quite another, because there would be intense law enforcement presence at the airports, metro, train, and bus stations. Seemingly the only way out would be for Erlanger to drive them across the border himself.

Maybe that was his intention. Maybe Anne had worked that part out, too, but it was unlikely; since she still had no idea where the photographs were, it would be impossible for her to give Erlanger or anyone else a destination. Telling her where they were—"*if*" they were—was something he'd so far managed to avoid but was a subject he knew would come up as soon they reached their destination.

He'd known from the moment they'd left the Adlon that at some point he'd have to tell her something, especially when he realized that she might actually be able to get him out from under the grip of the police, but just how much to reveal was tricky. Tell her too much and she wouldn't need him, might even turn him over to Franck just to get him out of the way. Tell her nothing and he would get no farther than wherever Erlanger was taking them now.

The answer, he decided, was to wait and see where that was and what the circumstances were when they got there.

9:57 A.M.

44

They looked like Mutt and Jeff as they walked down a wooded path at the water's edge, their jacket collars turned up against the drizzle—the six-foot six-inch Emil Franck, alongside five-foot nine-inch Yuri Kovalenko. Kovalenko spoke a hesitating German. Franck's Russian was as passable. Consequently they held their conversation in English.

Their primary order of business: the photographs and, with luck, the memory card from the camera that recorded them. Neither man knew what the photos were of or if they even existed. What brought the two together was the promise of the objects' importance and the endeavor to retrieve them.

• 10:15 A.M.

The two turned a blind corner near an inlet, startling several ducks into flight. Franck stopped to watch them fly out over the lake, then land in the water a safe distance from shore. For a moment he stood there enjoying the simple pleasure of observing wildlife. Finally he reached into his jacket and took out photographs of Marten and Anne Tidrow. Marten's was made from a frame of the cell phone images circulated to the media; Tidrow's was from a Striker Oil web site.

Kovalenko glanced at them and put them in his pocket. "Thank you, Hauptkommissar. I have previously seen a photograph of Ms.Tidrow. Mr. Marten, I already know something of.".

"You are referring to his employment as a landscape architect in England and that he was in Equatorial Guinea when the brother of Theo Haas was murdered."

"Yes." Kovalenko nodded. "That and a little more."

"You have information we don't."

"At one time he was a homicide investigator in the Los Angeles Police Department."

"What?"

"Good one, too."

"How do you know this?"

Kovalenko smiled. "It's a long story, Hauptkommissar. Just appreciate that I do." His smile faded. "It is only a matter of time before your excellent police force apprehends both him and Ms. Tidrow. You realize we cannot have that happen."

"Perhaps he will get lucky and escape," Franck said flatly, and the two walked on. Tall German, short Russian. Gray sky. Incessant drizzle.

Kovalenko smiled thinly. It was safe to assume "perhaps" had little to do with it. By now Franck could have had a much clearer photograph of Marten to hand around. Say, one requested from British authorities, a copy retrieved from his passport or driver's license. But such a thing would only serve to make it easier for the public to spot him and alert the police. Alternatively, he might well have made arrangements that, in one way or another, would allow Marten and his companion to evade his own massive dragnet.

"Yes, perhaps he will get lucky, Hauptkommissar," Kovalenko said. "Perhaps indeed."

10:20 A.M.

• 10:28 A.M.

Conor White stared absently out the window of the tri-engine Falcon 50 as the chartered jet flew north toward Berlin. Thirty thousand feet below and through a broken cloud deck he could see Geneva and the Jet d'Eau, Lake Geneva's immense water fountain, spraying a cannon of water five hundred feet in the air. Yet neither the Swiss city nor the sight of the fountain registered. His thoughts were on Berlin and what would take place when he got there.

The whole thing in Spain had been an unfortunate, messy, and, as it turned out, wholly unnecessary exercise because, as he'd realized almost from the start, the Spaniards had no idea where the photographs were, or even what they were. Yet it was a situation he couldn't walk away from until he knew for certain. He'd pushed it as far as he could, and after that there was no turning back, so he'd finished it with the hope it was something that would not come back to haunt them. Had he had his way in the first place he would have gone after Nicholas Marten directly, but that had not been his assignment; it had been Anne's. And look what had happened.

As far as he could tell the only thing positive to come from her work was that she had proven that Marten did know where the photographs were. It had been confirmed when she'd called him at the airport in Madrid.

"Where are you?" she'd said. *"I just wanted to know where you were if I needed you."*

When he had told her, he'd asked where she was. She had replied that she was in Berlin and warned him not to come there and to disregard anything he saw in the media. It was then he pressed her about Marten, making sure he was with her and asking directly if the photographs existed and if he knew where they were.

"Yes, I think so," she'd said after an awkward hesitation. She'd affirmed it when he'd pushed her a second time, demanding to know if she was certain.

"Do you think or do you know?" he'd demanded.

"I don't think, Conor, I know," she'd snapped, then signed off.

White shook his head. If he had followed Marten, from the start, by now, police or not, he would have been close on his tail or maybe even had him alone, with Anne nowhere in sight. Either way the photographs would have soon been recovered and the whole nasty situation quickly resolved. But it hadn't happened. Instead he was on his way to Berlin not to confront Anne and Marten but to meet with Sy Wirth. For what reason he had no idea, except that Wirth was his employer and was about to act like it. Tell him what to do and how and when to do it.

It was Wirth, he knew, who had had the last word in allowing Anne to follow Marten and sending him to Spain. If he made the same kind of uninformed decisions again, it would be only a matter of time before the police had both Anne and Marten and the photographs. If that happened everything would come apart, and fast.

Abruptly he turned from the window to see Irish Jack and Patrice quietly playing cards across from him. Neatly dressed in jackets and ties as he was, they looked like professional athletes en route to their next game. Which in a way they all were; that is, if he could somehow find a way to keep Sy Wirth out of it. But for the moment, the Texas oilman was calling the shots and White would do his best to accommodate him, graciously and with his best Eton, Oxford, and Sandhurst manners, when they touched down in Berlin.

10:32 A.M.

45

• Potsdam, Germany. 10:40 A.M.

The van had been stopped for several minutes. From the dark of his hiding place in the compartment over the left rear wheel, Marten wondered what was going on. Erlanger had said something in German, and then the driver and passenger doors had opened and closed. After that there had been nothing. Had they reached their destination or had they been stopped by the police and silently ordered out of the vehicle at gunpoint?

Another minute passed, and then he heard the rear doors open and someone come inside. He held his breath. There was a noise outside the panel next to his head. Abruptly it was removed. He pulled back, expecting to see a man in uniform or even Hauptkommissar Franck with a dozen police crowded in the doorway behind him. Instead Erlanger's face came into view.

"Are you alright?" he said.

Marten heaved a sigh of relief. "Stiff and a little nervous but alright."

"I'm sorry. We had no choice. It was a means that worked quite effectively getting people out of the Eastern Sector during the Cold War."

"I could use a toilet, and in a hurry."

Anne, still in her blond wig and dowdy clothing, was waiting as he climbed from the van. For a fleeting moment she seemed as if she genuinely cared about his well-being and was grateful the trip was over and they had made it safely. As quickly, she was back to business.

"Come into the house," she said, then led him past some trees and up a gravel pathway to a two-story house that, from the surroundings, appeared to be in a quiet and leafy residential neighborhood.

Marten used the toilet and then opened the door and started down a hallway toward the front door, the way they'd come in.

"Here." He heard Erlanger's voice from a room behind him. He turned back and entered a small, wood-paneled office to see Erlanger alone and just getting up from a desk. Behind him was a window that looked out on a small garden.

"Where is Anne?" Marten asked.

"Upstairs. She'll be down in a moment. Would you like some coffee?"

"Yes, thank you," Marten said. Erlanger nodded and left.

Marten looked around. The room, like the little he'd seen of the rest of the house as he came in, was comfortable and worn, filled with a large collection of apparently well read books, knickknacks, and family pictures, as if whoever lived there had done so for years and had no intention of moving. Hardly the hideout of a man fearful of the police.

"Feeling better?" Anne suddenly walked into the room. Gone were the dowdy clothes and blond wig; back were her jeans, tailored jacket, and running shoes, her black hair twisted up in a bun at the back of her head. She looked sexy and impatient and dangerous at same time.

"Yes. You?"

"I'll be better when we're moving again. Where do we go from here?"

"Where is here, this house?"

"Potsdam. About a half hour outside of Berlin. It's Erlanger's home. He took a big chance bringing us to it. He'll still help, but we have to set things up as quickly as possible and get out. So, as I said, where do we go from here? Where are the photographs?

Neither I nor Erlanger can do anything more until you give me a destination."

"Does Erlanger know about the pictures?"

"No."

Marten closed the door. "The whole trip, while I was twisted up in the dark in that little compartment over the wheel well, I was thinking of the cost."

"Of what?"

"The photographs. How many people are dead because of them. Bioko, Spain, Berlin. Who knows who'll be next or where it will happen?" He crossed to the window and looked out.

"What are you getting at?"

"That the best thing would be to get in touch with Hauptkommissar Franck and tell him where they are." He turned to look at her. "Let the German government have them and do what they think is right."

"That's not a very good conclusion."

"Maybe not. But under the circumstances it will do."

Suddenly Anne flared. "Where are the pictures, Nicholas?"

"I want the war stopped, Anne," Marten snapped back, his eyes riveted on her. "At the very least slowed to a crawl. The photographs will do that. The world media will pounce. Reporters, camera crews, everything. And not just to Equatorial Guinea but to Houston, where they will be all over Striker management, and to SimCo headquarters in England. There'll be tough questions about what's going on. Blogs and talk shows will pick it up. Politicians will get involved because they'll have to. And the subject won't disappear the way it always seems to about the Congo or Darfur or other African theaters of horror because an American oil company and its private military contractor are at the center of it."

"I want the killing stopped as much as you do. I told you that before."

"You also said you wanted the photos so you could threaten to turn them over to the Ryder Commission if your friends at Striker and Hadrian and SimCo didn't stop arming the insurgency."

"Yes."

"How do I know your real goal isn't simply to protect Striker? Get the pictures and destroy them."

"It's not."

"How do I know?"

Anne glared at him. "I'll ask you what I did yesterday. How much do you want for the photos? Name your price, anything you want."

"Anything?"

"Yes."

"I want you."

"Me?"

"Yes," he said quietly.

Anne was astounded. "For Christ's sake, Nicholas, after everything this is about sex? You want to fuck me? Is that your price? Jesus God!"

"I don't want to fuck *you*," he said as quietly as before. "I want *you* to fuck your company."

"What the hell does that mean?"

"Conor White is prominent in a number of the photos."

"So. You've actually seen them." Anne smiled lightly as if she'd just achieved some sort of cruel victory.

"Some, not all." Marten stepped closer to her, as if to underscore the gravity of what he was telling her. "The point is Conor White is easily identifiable. Maybe you don't want to destroy the pictures, but he does because he's got a helluva lot to lose if they're made public. Who he kills or how he gets them doesn't seem to make much difference. One way or another he's already responsible for the deaths of Father Willy and his brother, to say nothing of my Spanish friends. If you have the photos, Striker board member or not, CIA or not, he'll kill you as quickly as he will me."

Anne's eyes darted over his face. "I still don't know what you want me to do."

"If I bring you with me and we get the pictures, we take them to Joe Ryder himself. You tell him who you are and who Conor White is and that you want to do anything you can to stop the flow of weapons to the rebels, hoping that the State Department can then pressure Tiombe into ordering his fighters to stand down.

"Of course, that will lead to his wanting to know more, and you'll tell him about SimCo as a front company for Hadrian, which in turn will make him go after the Striker/Hadrian enterprise even harder than he already is. If he can prove Hadrian and SimCo are providing arms to the rebels at Striker's behest, your Mr. Sy Wirth and the other decision makers at Striker, as well as Conor White and the people running Hadrian, will be in for a very ugly time. Prison wouldn't be out of the question for anyone, you included. You said 'anything,' Anne. That's the price, otherwise—"

Abruptly there was a knock at the door. Erlanger's voice came through it. "I have coffee. Should I leave it outside?"

"Give us a minute, Hartmann," Anne said and looked back to Marten. "Otherwise, what?"

"Otherwise I'll think you want the photos to protect your company and its investments in Equatorial Guinea. I'll assume they sent you because you're a very attractive woman and you might use that against me—the way you already have, taking off your robe in the hotel, kissing me in the middle of the street with the police watching, sitting in nothing more than panties and a T-shirt with your nipples showing through as you told me the story of your life. And because you were CIA you would know better than most what the hell you were doing and how to do it. You would have been trained for it."

For a moment Marten thought he was going to get slapped, but it didn't happen. Anne just stood there, breathing softly, staring at him in silence.

"That's the deal," he said finally. "Understand it?"

"Yes."

"Tell me you agree."

"How do you know you can trust me even if I do?"

"Because you just might be telling the truth about doing this for your father—for his memory, for the reputation of the company he built, and because you

loved him. And because there's always Hauptkommissar Franck if you're not."

He could feel her nails come up. Her stare cut him
in two, but she said nothing. Finally, she nodded almost imperceptibly.

"No, say it," he pressed her.

"I agree."

"To everything."

"To everything."

He looked at her for a long moment, judging her,
deciding the next step. "We'll need a plane," he said
finally. "Twin engine, civil aviation. Preferably a jet,
a turboprop will do. Fifteen-hundred-mile range."

"The pilot will have to file a flight plan. He'll need
to know where we're going."

"Tell him Málaga, on the south coast of Spain."

"Málaga?"

"Yes," he lied.

11:12 A.M.

46

• Berlin, 11 Giesebrechtstrasse. 12:55 P.M.

The meeting place was an expensive third-floor
apartment in a building in the western part of the
city near Kurfürstendamm. History books would
reveal that in the 1930s it had been a high-class
brothel called Salon Kitty. In the Second World War

it was still a brothel but used by the SD—the Sicherheitsdienst, the Nazi security service—for espionage, primarily the secret recording of private conversations between chic prostitutes, foreign diplomats, and German dignitaries who might become traitors. At the moment the space was being used for a conversation between two people unconcerned with that distant past—Sy Wirth and Conor White.

"How many men do you have with you?" Wirth sat back from a small table where coffee and an arrangement of fresh fruit had been laid out.

"Two," White said.

"Skilled?"

"The best."

"Are two enough?"

"For now."

"Where are they?"

"Outside, in the rental car."

Wirth reached over and lifted a silver coffee urn and poured himself a cup, gesturing to White to do the same.

"No thanks."

"Spain went poorly," Wirth said.

"You mean that we learned nothing about the photographs."

"Yes."

"We did as you asked. They had no idea what we were talking about. They and those we employed, a limousine driver and a local gunman, took the truth of what happened there into eternity." White looked to the Striker chairman for any sign of remorse, or sense that he'd made a mistake ordering the operation. As he expected he saw none.

"Then this Nicholas Marten is the only one who knows."

"Ask Anne."

Sy Wirth glared at him, clearly not happy being talked back to. "Anne's not here. I'm asking you."

"If the pictures exist, Marten knows where they are. That's what she said. Otherwise she wouldn't still be with him."

Suddenly Wirth shifted gears. "What went wrong at the airport in Paris when they arrived from Malabo? Anne had him in sight when the others lost him. Then she lost him, too. Except several hours later she found him here in Berlin."

"Apparently she lost him on purpose so she could go after him herself."

"Why would she do that?"

"Maybe she doesn't think the rest of us are capable. Maybe some other reason. I don't know."

Sy Wirth took a sip of coffee and held the liquid in his mouth, as if he were using the moment to think; then he set the cup down. "When was the last time you spoke with her?"

"This morning."

"What did she say?"

"Essentially what she sent in her text message yesterday—that she was in Berlin with Marten and not to come after her, and not to believe anything we saw in the media. As far as I know she's not been publicly identified. Or has she?"

"Not that I'm aware of. Not yet."

"Then the police must be on to both of them or they would have had her picture all across the German media, the way Marten's is." White kept his manner purposely calm. He was still upset with himself for telling Wirth to "ask Anne." His profound dislike of the Texan had ruled for the moment, and he didn't like it. He wouldn't make the same mistake again.

Wirth glanced at his watch and then stood. "I have to go. Bring your men here and wait for my call. Hopefully I'll have some idea where Anne is and if Marten is still with her."

"You will," White said flatly.

"Yes."

For the next few seconds White said nothing; finally he stood, all six feet four of him. "Where will this information come from?" he said respectfully.

"That's my business."

"You've hired a third party."

"No, Mr. White. I've simply made an arrangement."

"I see."

Now they were back to the beginning and White's deepest fear: that a man so rich, powerful, and single-minded, who was used to micromanaging everything, had suddenly distrusted everyone around him and turned elsewhere for solutions. That might be alright in a business deal; all you could lose was money. But in a situation like this he would be venturing into very cold and dangerous waters, and in doing so trusting people far more experienced, self-serving, and ruthless than he. It was a blueprint for disaster, and he was risking everything because of it.

You stupid bastard, White wanted to say. He didn't.

"I'll wait for your call, Mr. Wirth," he said politely.

Sy Wirth nodded curtly and, without a further word, left.

1:05 P.M.

47

• Potsdam, 1:10 P.M.

Hartmann Erlanger opened a cabinet near the window in his study, pulled a laptop from it, then set it down on his desk. He glanced at Anne and Marten sitting in chairs across from him, then opened it, touched the POWER button, and waited for the screen to come up. When it did he punched in several codes, then twisted it around so that it faced them and looked at Anne.

"This is what I downloaded yesterday after your call. It's two days old, so I don't know how much help it will be, but it's something. I'll leave it to you and Mr. Marten to decide the importance of it. I'm going out to try to resolve your situation. Arranging for a specific type of aircraft and someone to pilot it is difficult at best. More so under the circumstances and that the request was made at the last minute."

"Unfortunately, Hartmann, I didn't have the information until the last minute." Anne didn't need to glance at Marten; the barb was clear enough. "You know how appreciative I am for everything you've done and are doing. And the chances you've been taking all along."

Erlanger looked at her in a way that was very personal. "That's what friends and colleagues are for. I'll be back when I have more information. My wife is upstairs if you need anything." He held her eyes a moment longer and then left, closing the door behind him.

For a moment Anne sat there motionless, fully aware that Marten had seen the exchange between them. Then, without a word, she leaned forward and pressed a key on the laptop. In the next instant the screen came to life. They saw a graphic of the world globe, then a slow zoom in on West Africa.

"This is a classified CIA regional video briefing," she said. "Sometimes they come out daily. Other times less often, depending on urgency or need-to-know for handlers or assets in the field. Be warned, this stuff you won't see on television."

The video cut to a satellite view of Equatorial Guinea, taking in both the mainland and the island of Bioko. A narrator's voice was heard.

"The situation in Rio Muni, the nation's continental mainland, and on the island of Bioko, where the capital city of Malabo lies, is in increasing tur-

moil. Rebel forces are led by Alfonso Bitui Ada.
Popularly known as Abba, he is a schoolteacher and
member of the Liberal Party, the PL. Fifteen months
ago he was released after serving a ten-year prison
sentence for membership in the banned Popular
People's Party. Since then he has worked openly to
unite disparate tribes to protest against poverty, political corruption, and acts of physical violence by
the administration of President Tiombe."

Abruptly the video cut to greenish night-vision
footage of a poised, handsome, middle-aged man
with short graying hair, dressed in jungle fatigues
and addressing twenty or more rebel soldiers in a
jungle clearing.

"This is Abba, seen in clandestine footage taken
three days ago in Bioko as his forces moved north
toward the capital city of Malabo. What began little
more than ten weeks ago as organized protests
against the government in Rio Muni has become all-
out armed rebellion fueled primarily by the Equatorial Guinean army's savage acts of retaliation against
the demonstrators. The major tribes, including the
Fang, Bubi, and Fernandinos, have united behind
Abba. His strength is growing hourly. So, too, are
the causalities as Tiombe's military steps up its activity, engaging in increasingly brutal acts of reprisal against both rebels and civilians. To date estimates
of the dead range above four thousand."

Now the video cut to a gruesome daylight mon-
tage of burned-out villages and hundreds of dead
citizens. Many had been beheaded or horribly mutilated. Men, women, children, the elderly. Even

animals. Dogs, goats, cows; a horse, still saddled, slaughtered and left on the roadway.

"Jesus God," Marten murmured.

Immediately the images reverted to more clandestine night-vision footage, this time capturing army troops on a rampage through a village. Raw and terrible footage of soldiers executing civilians with machetes, pistols, rifles, and machine guns. There was a horrifying scene of a screaming woman being raped by five soldiers, one after another. A small boy ran in to try to pull the soldiers off. One of the soldiers grabbed him, turned him around, and made him watch. The boy's terrified struggle and reaction was tragic, especially when it was contrasted with the faces of rapist-soldiers who had finished with the woman and were standing back laughing. Then the night footage cut to a scene where army troops were using flamethrowers to set huts on fire. Suddenly a naked man ran from the darkness with his hands up, pleading for them to stop. The next instant a soldier turned the flamethrower on him, immolating him in a searing jet of burning gasoline.

"For God's sake, Anne, I can't watch any more! Turn it off!" Marten blurted and started to look away. Then— "Wait!" he all but shouted as the night-vision video cut to an older man in army fatigues standing imperially with a small group of heavily armed soldiers at the edge of the battleground watching the proceedings. He was hawk-faced and gray-haired and clearly not a black African like the rest.

"I know him!" Marten said. "He was there when they were interrogating me in Malabo. Who is—?"

In a near perfectly timed response the narrative answered Marten's query.

"This is Mariano Vargas Fuente, the former Chilean general known as Mariano, once a high-ranking officer in the notorious former Directorate of National Intelligence during the 1973 to 1990 dictatorship of the late General Augusto Pinochet. He is one of the world's best-known human rights abusers, convicted in absentia of torture and mass murder. Fled war-crimes prosecution and vanished into the jungles of Central America. Is thought to have been recruited by President Tiombe to personally supervise his counterinsurgency program in Rio Muni and Bioko. This is the first known confirmation that he is in Equatorial Guinea."

Immediately the video cut to a map of Bioko and showed the position of Abba's forces as they moved north, closing in on Malabo.

"Indicators suggest Tiombe is preparing to flee the country if Abba's forces continue to gain further ground. Analysts believe that Abba will take control of the government within ten to fourteen days. As of noon tomorrow local time the U.S. embassy will be closed until further notice. All nonessential personnel have been ordered to evacuate. The State Department has issued a warning to all U.S. citizens to leave Equatorial Guinea immediately."

With that the picture faded and the video ended.

Marten stared at Anne. "You wanted me to see that. Why?"

"I wanted us both to see it. So we can tell the same story to Congressman Ryder. And so that you will trust me the rest of the way. Trust that I want the killing stopped as much as you."

Marten was silent for a long moment; then he let his eyes find hers. "Does the term 'all U.S. citizens' include Striker personnel?"

"Abba's people are trying to get rid of Tiombe, not us. Our people have been confined to the company compound, which is heavily guarded by SimCo mercenaries. They're safe."

"Are they? Let me tell you something. General Mariano knows about the photographs. It's what they were trying to get from me during the interrogation. Or maybe you knew that."

Anne shook her head. "No."

"Just pray to God he doesn't order his butchers into your company compound looking for them. White's mercenaries wouldn't have a chance. And once they fall, God help the drillers, the tech people, the secretaries, the bookkeepers, and all the other Striker and SimCo 'little people' I saw in the bar at the Hotel Malabo. Especially if Tiombe's killers come in with flamethrowers." Marten paused, anger and outrage eating away at him. "What the hell have you people done in the name of profit?"

Anne said nothing.

"It's alright, darling," he said. "Don't look for an answer. Don't even try to make one up. Because there is none."

1:37 P.M.

48

President John Henry Harris sat in shirtsleeves listening to Lincoln Bright, his chief of staff, run through the day's abbreviated appointment schedule: three White House meetings, one of them with the secretary of state just back from meetings in India and China, then helicopter to Camp David and talks with his chief financial advisers about the ongoing crises in the economy.

The briefing over, Bright left, and the president leaned back to stare out the window, watching as they passed over Lake Ontario and entered American airspace. He'd had an early breakfast with Canadian prime minister Campbell and Mexican president Mayora at the Harrington Lake compound, then immediately departed. In four hours he would be at Camp David to spend the rest of the weekend enmeshed in critical budget details and preparing for a Monday morning meeting with the governors of a dozen states who would each come looking— begging was a better word—for additional funding beyond what they already had been given.

Still, and for all the importance of the secretary of state's report and the crises with the economy, other things weighed heavily. A phone call from Joe Ryder in Iraq had come before breakfast with Ryder telling him his fact-finding team had met with an unexpected twist when Hadrian's Loyal Truex had arrived unannounced, boldly and generously offering to throw the Striker/Hadrian doors and books wide open and inviting Ryder and his colleagues to look over anything they liked. Acting as if, in Ryder's words, "he had come at the last minute to hide everything in plain sight." Which apparently he had, because so far they'd found nothing more than they already knew.

Then there had been his morning security briefing, where he'd asked about the situation in Equatorial Guinea and was told that President Tiombe's army was heavily engaged with the insurgent forces while at the same time committing terrible atrocities against the civilian population under the guise of hunting down rebel leaders. The army's brutal tactics aside, analysts expected Tiombe's government to fall within days, and by then Tiombe and his family and staff would have fled the country.

"To go where?" he'd asked.

Reports had been inconclusive, but Tiombe was known to have residences in several parts of the world, Beverly Hills among them. The president's reaction to that had been simple and drawn a laugh. "I hope to hell he doesn't do that." But there was nothing funny about any of it. Immediately he called in Lincoln Bright and instructed his chief of staff to get in touch with Kim Ho, secretary-general of the United Nations, and ask what he could do to press the UN to intervene in the situation in Equatorial Guinea, and then to call Pierre Kellen, president of the International Red Cross, and ask what

the United States could do to help on a humanitarian level.

The thing was, no matter how concerned he was
about the plight of the Equatorial Guinean people, he
knew he dared not show too much personal interest
in the war itself because to do so would risk pricking
up ears in the national and international intelligence
and diplomatic communities. They would be more
than curious to know why he had singled out that one
area when so many other parts of the African conti-
nent were suffering under similar circumstances,
and they might well send people to look into it. That
was something he couldn't afford. The last thing he
needed was to have covert interests poking deeper
into what was going on and risk having one of them
come up with the photographs before they were
safely in his or Joe Ryder's hands.

Having such far-reaching power and for so many
reasons not being able to draw on it was one of the
hells of his office and made the trouble with Marten
all the worse. Six weeks earlier he would have sent
Hap Daniels, his Secret Service special agent in
charge, a man he trusted completely and who knew
Marten well, to Berlin to sift through the goings-on.
Daniels was canny enough and experienced enough
to find a way to let Marten know he was there and
where to find him without the police or anyone else
learning about it, no matter how deeply Marten was
hidden. Once contact was made, Daniels could get
him the hell out of there, and then both could go
after the photos. But in the those six weeks Daniels
had undergone heart bypass surgery, and he was at

home on medical leave and in no shape to be working that kind of assignment. David Watson, his replacement, was a likable, able man but one Harris didn't know well enough to send on a mission that would be delicate at best. Moreover, Marten didn't know him at all and so would have no reason to come out of hiding even if Watson made himself known. That left no one at all the president could turn to for help.

"Dammit," Harris swore out loud then glanced at his suit coat thrown over the seat across from him. He'd put it there himself, making sure it was in reach. Tucked into an inside pocket was the thing he'd carried everywhere since he'd left Washington: the cheap slate gray cell phone that was his direct and only connection to Nicholas Marten. That was, if Marten called, because he had no way to contact the throwaway cell phone or phones Marten would be using.

He'd hoped all the while Marten would get in touch with him, but he hadn't. Probably because of the police, or because he was hurt, or even—he hated to think—dead. Or maybe he was just in a situation where phoning anyone was not possible. Or maybe because he had nothing to tell him. What was the thing he'd said when they'd last spoken? *I'll call you when I have something to report.*

Whatever the reason, the gray phone remained silent, and the stillness was gut-wrenching. It was more than the urgency to find the photographs, or the gnawing reminder that it was he who had sent Marten to Equatorial Guinea in the first place. The thing was he cared about Nicholas Marten enormously. What they had been through together, barely a year earlier in Spain and the close friendship that had come out of it, made them almost like brothers. More than anything he wanted him out of harm's way. It made him think what it must be like for a parent of a missing child, imagining the worst and waiting and hoping and praying that the phone at your elbow would suddenly come to life and that your daughter or son would be on the other end with a "Hi, Mom" or "Hi, Dad," all perky and safe and sounding as if nothing at all had happened.

"Damn it to hell," John Henry Harris spat out loud to the smooth, indifferent walls of Air Force One's presidential cabin. Then he stoically reached for a breakdown of the federal budget and went to work.

49

• Potsdam, 6:20 P.M.

Marten, Anne, and Hartmann Erlanger stood in an open field near Erlanger's van shading their eyes from a late-afternoon sun that at long last had poked through the drizzle and overcast. Their attention was on a twin-engine Cessna 340 as it dropped down through broken clouds, then flew at treetop level until it neared the far end of a private airstrip. Seconds

later its landing gear touched the tarmac and it
roared past them, giving them a glimpse of its fuselage registration, D-VKRD. The aircraft slowed as
it reached the end of the runway, then turned and
came back toward them.

"Piston engine. It's the best I could do, all things
considered." Erlanger crushed a cigarette butt under
his heel, then picked it up and put in his pocket. "It
will get you wherever you're going within the pa-
rameters you gave me. Maybe not as fast as you
would like, but you'll get there just the same."

"It's fine, Hartmann, thank you," Anne said.

He looked at her the way he had in his study earlier, and she smiled and put a hand to his cheek.
Plainly there was a history between them, one they
didn't seem to mind sharing, to a degree at least, with
Marten. How profound it was, or if Erlanger's wife
was aware of it, there was no way to know.

The roar of the Cessna's engines deafened as it
neared and came to a stop. Then the pilot shut them
down, and for a moment the silence was almost as
profound. Almost immediately the chirp of birds and
the buzz of insects filtered back. All around was
deep forest. The only cuts through it were the airstrip
itself and the gravel road they had come in on. Not
once had Erlanger brought up the subject of whose
property it was, but clearly he had access to it.

The pilot's door opened, and a woman in a flight
suit climbed down. She was blond, maybe thirty-
five, and attractive in a matronly sort of way.

"Her name is Brigitte," Erlanger said. "Tell her
where you want to go and she'll get you there. Don't

tell me, I don't want to know. Neither of you saw me. None of this took place." Abruptly he turned to Anne, the warmth and tenderness of moments before suddenly gone, replaced instead by a cold professionalism. "Stay away from the old contacts," he warned. "You got away with it once. For your sake, don't try it again." He stared at her for a moment longer, then glanced at Marten and turned and walked to the van. Seconds later he got in and closed the door, then started the engine and drove off.

Never once did he look back.

6:50 P.M.

• Berlin Police Headquarters. 7:05 P.M.

Hauptkommissar Franck took the call on his private cell phone and immediately left the room. Detectives Bohlen and Prosser and the dozen other top investigators with them stopped what they were doing as he went out, watching in silence as the door closed behind him. They'd spent the last eight hours shoulder to shoulder with the Hauptkommissar in the dark of this high-tech situation room deep inside the building surrounded by rows of computers with floor-to-ceiling monitors sorting through mountains of information provided by officers tracking reports coming in from the field.

Franck had called them there just after ten thirty in the morning when the all but certain capture of Nicholas Marten and Anne Tidrow in the neighborhood near the Friedrichstrasse/Weidendamm Bridge had failed. The Hauptkommissar had faced them angrily and forcefully, dressing them down and citing their failure and his own, clearly and harshly.

"I was put in charge of this operation," he'd said. "I am responsible for the decisions that failed. The suspects are still at large. Failure a second time is not acceptable. To me, to you, or the people of Berlin and Germany. I hope that is quite clear."

The effect had been powerful and shaming and embarrassing, putting everyone on edge and spreading through the entire department within minutes. It was why, when he answered his personal cell phone and so abruptly left the room, the people there held their collective breath. Perhaps it was a major breakthrough, a tip from one of the untold number of informants only the Hauptkommissar knew. Perhaps in short order he, and then they, would learn where the suspects were and as quickly mobilize and within the hour bring the entire ordeal to a close.

• 7:12 P.M.

"I don't like so many people involved," Franck stood on the sidewalk outside the building on Platz der Luftbrücke talking on his cell phone, his back to passersby. "It will be a billiard game, you know that, one playing off two, two playing off three, who knows where it stops. Unpredictable, volatile at best, dangerous all around."

"*You are at the top of your game when it's like that.*" Elsa's throaty voice came back to him. "*You should enjoy it, you always have. Besides, they expect it. It's why you were called and not someone else.*"

"Yes. Alright. I understand," he said finally. "Yes. Yes. Of course." With that he clicked off.

Hauptkommissar Emil Franck's persona had been established early in his career as that of a man who was most successful when he worked alone. Between the ages of twenty-four and twenty-seven he had single-handedly ended the vocations of nineteen public enemies. Ten were in prison, the rest dead. The media, even his colleagues, both then and now referred to him as Berlin's "Cowboy," its "Dirty Harry," and it was that role he would play to Detectives Bohlen and Prosser and the others in the situation room when he returned. Something had come up, he would tell them. Something he would take care of himself. Their instructions would be to continue on the course he had laid out for them that morning, an intense continuation of the massive and very public manhunt for the killer of Theo Haas. There would be no announcement that he had left. The media would be told only that he was coordinating the effort from his headquarters office and was unavailable for comment. No other details would be given. It was that simple.

50

Sy Wirth clicked off one of the two BlackBerrys
he'd carried with him since he left Houston and
picked up a freshly sharpened number 2 Ticonderoga 1388 pencil. He made a brief note on the last
of the half-dozen yellow legal pads on the writing
table in front of him, on which he had scribbled
twenty-odd memos, the result of several hours' worth
of business calls. Done, he looked at his watch, then
picked up the BlackBerry he'd just used, the one he
called his everyday phone and utilized for business
and personal calls. He was about to punch in a number when there was a knock at the door.

"Yes," he said impatiently.

"Room service, Mr. Wirth."

Wirth got up and opened the door. A uniformed
waiter pushed a rolling table with a covered platter,
a carafe of coffee, and a bottle of mineral water into
the room. He was starting to set it up when Wirth
intervened.

"I'll take care of it," he said brusquely and gave
him a twenty-euro bill.

"Thank you, Mr. Wirth. Guten abend." The man
nodded and left, closing the door behind him.

Wirth lifted the silver cover from the platter,
glanced at the club sandwich beneath it. Ignoring it,
he went back to the desk, picked up the everyday

BlackBerry, punched in a number, and waited for it to ring through.

"*Yes.*" Dimitri Korostin's voice filtered through his earpiece.

"Well?"

"*You sound nervous, Sy.*"

"How long are you going to keep me waiting around? What's the status of our project?"

Korostin laughed. "*Your status is that you're anxious and on edge. My status is that I'm getting a blow job. Afterward I'm going to dinner with friends. I think my lifestyle is better than yours, Sy. Excuse me a minute.*" Suddenly there was dead air, as if he'd clicked off. A full two minutes later he came back on. "*Sy, you there?*"

"Fuck you and your blow job."

"*Relax, Sy. Like they say, your order has been processed. I will have information for you before midnight. Fair enough? I wouldn't want to disappoint you and risk losing the Magellan/Santa Cruz– Tarija gas field. Would I?*"

With that Korostin clicked off, leaving Sy Wirth alone with his two BlackBerrys, half-dozen legal pads, coffee, mineral water, club sandwich, and unease.

• 8:20 P.M

Hauptkommissar Emil Franck turned his Audi down a service road near Tegel Airport in the last rays of warm summer-evening sunshine. Sunshine that, after the gray skies and drizzle of the morning should have cheered him a little at least. But he was in no mood for cheer. Apprehending Marten for the killing of Theo Haas had been one thing, but since the photographs and the rebellion in Equatorial Guinea had come into play it was clear that something far more complex than the murder of a Nobel laureate was taking place. As he had said on the phone, it would be a billiard game. Kovalenko was already in it. Moscow was watching. God only knew where it would go from there.

Ahead he could see a maroon Opel parked at the side of the road next to a security fence. All around was the thunder and whine of jet aircraft approaching or taking off from the airfield. He slowed, then pulled up behind the Opel and stopped. Two men were in it. Kovalenko and a driver. The Russian said something to the other man, then opened the door and got out and walked back to the Audi.

"So, our friend is now airborne and in a piston-engine Cessna," Kovalenko said as he slid in next to Franck.

"Fuselage registration D-VKRD," Franck said. "Flight plan filed to Málaga. They will have to stop for fuel at least once."

"You've done well, Hauptkommissar. I know how valuable informants can be. I trust you will see that he or she is well rewarded."

"Things have a way of taking care of themselves."

Kovalenko smiled. "True, Hauptkommissar. It is—" Kovalenko's voice was drowned out by the roar of a Lufthansa Airbus taking off. He waited until the sound died away and then continued. "It is safe to leave your car here?"

"Why?"

Kovalenko smiled again. "Nothing against Berlin law enforcement. It's just that I have a driver. We'll take mine."

"To where? We're leaving from here. From Tegel, yes?"

"No, Schönefeld."

"I don't understand."

"I cannot think as Moscow does." Kovalenko shrugged. "What can I tell you? You should see the hotels they put me up in."

Franck studied him for the briefest moment. He didn't like the sudden change of arrangements. Kovalenko was supposed to have arranged for a private jet that would leave from here, from Tegel. Now the plan had shifted to Schönefeld Airport in Brandenburg, south of the city. It would be a waste of time to ask why. He'd been through this kind of thing often enough in the past, in "the old days," before the wall was torn down. One didn't ask why, just did what Moscow ordered.

"Alright," he said finally. They got out of the Audi, Franck pulled a small overnight bag from the rear seat, then closed the door and locked it. Thirty seconds later they were in the Opel and heading south toward Schönefeld Airport.

8:32 P.M.

51

• Cessna 340, D-VKRD, somewhere over
Southern Germany. Cruising speed 190 mph.
Altitude 26,170 feet. 9:35 P.M.

They had been flying for nearly two and a half hours,
with Anne and Marten sitting impassively in plush
leather seats behind the pilot, the blond, handsome
Brigitte. Before they took off she had courteously
filled them in with her full name—Brigitte Marie
Reier—and a little of her history. She was thirty-
seven and had flown in the German air force. She
was a single mother of twelve-year-old twins. The
three lived "temporarily" with her brother, his wife,
and their two children, and everyone got along, more
or less. And that had been that. Afterward she was
back to the business at hand, telling them there was
bottled water and sandwiches and a thermos of coffee in the pullout tray beyond the seats. There was a
tiny toilet facility between the pilot and passenger
compartments, she said, but if they could, they might
be better off waiting until they made a fuel stop—
or stops, depending on head- or crosswinds—and
they could pee or whatever at that time. That had
ended it. Immediately she'd helped them on board,
climbed into the cockpit, then started the engines
and taken off. Little or nothing had been said since.

Brigitte aside, it was Anne who had kept the silence, sitting back, hands in her lap, staring blankly

out the window. When Marten had asked her if she wanted something to eat or drink she'd not even looked at him, simply shook her head in reply. His first thought was that now they were finally up and away and out of the immediate grasp of the police she was troubled by her promise to meet with Joe Ryder, show him the photographs—presuming they found them—and reveal the clandestine business workings of Striker Oil, Hadrian, and SimCo. To promise it was one thing because it was nothing more than a pledge written in air. To actually carry through and do it was something else because she not only risked publicly damning her father's reputation but might well face a federal indictment herself. Both were cause enough for her to withdraw while she tried to find a way out of her commitment, yet for some reason he didn't believe that was what was troubling her. It was something else entirely.

Then he realized what it was—Erlanger's cold warning before they got on the plane and the silent, stony way he'd walked away afterward and driven off.

"Stay away from the old contacts, he'd said. *You got away with it this once. For your sake, don't try it again."*

From Marten's view it was hard to tell what it had meant to her. Maybe she'd been in love with him once, or still was, and had expected some kind of romantic good-bye. A kiss or an affectionate hug, or something in between, a physical gesture that would confirm that he still had feelings for her. On the other hand, there could have been more to it, something left unsaid that Marten didn't understand, something that frightened her more than it upset her. Which, as he thought about it now, was more likely because the look in her eyes had been more fear than hurt.

"Mind if I ask you something personal?" he smiled gently.

For the first time she looked at him. "It depends what it is."

"What Erlanger said at the airstrip just before he left. It affected you a great deal."

"The Erlanger thing is past," she said coldly. "Let's drop it."

Marten watched her. The Erlanger thing wasn't past at all. Moreover, the abrupt way she'd answered and the look in her eyes when she'd done it told him he'd touched a nerve she didn't want touched. And he'd been right—whatever it was, the heart of it had been fear. Of what, he didn't know, but clearly it was important. It didn't surprise him that she didn't want to discuss it, but maybe there was another way to come at it, especially if he could learn a little more about her.

"What if we just talk about something else?"

"Why?"

Marten grinned. "Well, it's going to be a long night, and I don't think Brigitte brought along a stack of magazines."

Anne leaned back in her seat and studied him. "What would you like to talk about?"

"Don't know." He said with a shrug. "You said you'd been married. How's that for starters?"

"Twice."

"Twice?"

"Don't look so shocked. I've got friends who would think that's nothing more than spring training."

"I'm not shocked, just surprised."

"At what?"

"Your lifestyle doesn't seem to reflect home, hearth, and motherhood once, let alone twice."

"If you're asking if I have a home, yes, I do. As for children, no, I don't. Neither husband was suited to be a father, and I don't think I'd have made much of a mother, either. Besides, I couldn't have them."

"That's more than I needed to know."

"So now you do. And now it's your turn. How many times have you been married?"

"Never."

"Why is that? You're not a bad-looking guy."

"Thanks."

"It wasn't a compliment, it was a question."

"The only two women I ever really cared enough about to go down that road with did other things."

"Like what?"

"One I met in England. She suddenly ran off and married the British ambassador to Japan."

"The other?"

Marten hesitated, then stared into some private distance that was his own.

"Well?" Anne pushed him a little, hoping to hear some kind of colorful, lurid gossip. She got something else entirely.

"She died a little more than a year ago. She was young and married. Her husband and son had been killed in a plane crash a few weeks earlier. We grew up together. We were childhood sweethearts. I loved her very much."

"I'm sorry." Anne was taken aback, embarrassed by what she had done. "I didn't mean to intrude like that." Suddenly she became gentle and very human. It was a side of her he hadn't seen before.

"You couldn't have known."

"May I ask what happened?"

"She was . . ." Marten looked off again, the pain and loss and anger still there. "Murdered."

"Murdered?"

"She was purposely given an incurable staph infection. It's a long, complicated story. Thankfully for her it's over."

"But it's not for you."

"No."

For a long moment Anne said nothing, just let him sit there in the privacy of his thoughts that she knew were millennia away. The only sound was the hum of the Cessna's engines.

"What was her name?" she said finally.

"Caroline."

"She must have been beautiful."

"She was."

10:02 P.M.

52

• Berlin. The apartment at 11 Giesebrechtstrasse.
10:47 P.M.

"We're leaving now, Mr. Wirth. I'll confirm when we're airborne." Conor White clicked off his Black-Berry, then clicked back on and punched in a number.

Across from him, Patrice and Irish Jack were already on their feet, putting away the cards they'd been playing, packing up, getting ready to leave.

"This is White." He spoke into his BlackBerry. "File a flight plan for Málaga, Spain, and get clearance for takeoff. Wheels up in forty minutes."

"Málaga?" Sennac said, his eyebrows raised, his Quebecois accent pronounced as always.

"*Oui,*" Conor White nodded as he clicked off.

Irish Jack grinned. "Good pubs, good babes, good beaches. Merrily we roll along."

"Jack," White cautioned, "we're not on holiday."

"Aw, don't spoil the fucker for us, Colonel." He winked at Patrice. "What we got to do won't take but a short few minutes. Will it now?"

"It shouldn't," White said deliberately and with none of the Irishman's humor. "And won't."

"You're right, Colonel, it won't." Patrice glanced at Irish Jack, a warning to back off the levity. They'd known White's obsession with recovering the photographs from the beginning. If they needed a reminder they needed only to remember what happened in the farmhouse outside Madrid. The grilling of the young Spanish doctor and her medical students had gone on to the point where White had had enough. Removing his balaclava and telling them to remove theirs had been a signal that they would give them one last chance to cooperate and that would be it. Killing one captive in front of others was an age-old means of attempting to terrify those left into divulging information when they had so far refused to provide. It hadn't worked, and White ended it on the spot. Afterward he'd sincerely apologized to the three horrified students who remained, saying he had taken up too much of their time, and told the limo driver to take them back to their homes and parents in Madrid, knowing full well Patrice had rigged the limousine to explode twelve minutes after the engine was started. Seconds after they'd gone, White went into the barn where the Spanish gunman who'd brought him there waited with the car, and shot him where he stood.

For a professional soldier like Conor White to be fixated on accomplishing a mission was one thing. The depth of his passion was something else entirely. He'd told them soon after the interrogation of the Spanish doctor and her students had begun that they had no idea where the pictures were and or even what their captors were talking about. But he'd gone on with the questioning anyway. Then personally managed their deaths.

Over the years both he and Irish Jack had lived and fought alongside extremely cruel and often fanatical men, but nothing matched what Conor White had done in Spain. He was clearly mad, and in a way neither of them had ever seen before, not even on the battlefield. Still, they would follow him into hell simply because they knew something larger was going on, the substance of which they, as foot soldiers, wouldn't know about or be told. Whatever it was, it was clearly important enough for White to be giving everything within him to successfully execute. You took orders from men like that, fought alongside them and didn't ask questions. It was what he and Irish Jack had signed on for and the kind of professionals they were.

• Ritz-Carlton Berlin, Suite 1422. 10:55 P.M.

"*Málaga.*" Dimitri Korostin's call had come ten minutes earlier. His message had been to the point and exceedingly brief. "*They will probably arrive sometime after four in the morning, maybe later. The plane is a piston-engine Cessna 340. Its fuselage registration is D-VKRD. If there's a change I will inform you. Sweet dreams. Get your own blow job and don't worry so much.*" With that he'd hung up.

Sy Wirth was still at the writing table, his chin resting in his hands, his yellow legal pads piled up beside him, the remains of his club sandwich on a side table.

"*Cessna 340. Fuselage registration D-VKRD. Flight plan filed Berlin to Málaga, Spain. ETA sometime after four in the morning.*"

It was the information he'd passed on to Conor White, secure in the fact that if the Cessna changed course Dimitri would report to him within minutes, and in turn he would alert White. But until then White was to keep a safe distance behind and follow Marten's Cessna directly to Málaga. Something he would do without question because that was the directive Wirth had purposely given him.

Let him go first. Give him time to get there, Wirth thought. It has to look as if he's doing this on his own, that he's out to protect himself, SimCo, and Hadrian at all costs and that Striker has no knowledge of it whatsoever.

Wirth glanced at the two BlackBerrys on the table beside him. The first was his everyday phone. The other had a little piece of blue tape on the bottom to distinguish it. Calls made from it were rerouted through the Hadrian Worldwide Protective Services Company's headquarters in Manassas, Virginia, making it appear as if they had originated from there.

It was the device he'd been using to contact Conor White since the meeting with Hadrian's Loyal Truex and Striker's chief counsel, Arnold Moss, in Houston when both companies had agreed to distance themselves from SimCo. The same meeting where, after Truex left, he'd told Moss it was time to distance themselves from Hadrian as well. Hence any calls he made to Conor White would be on telephone company records as having come directly from Hadrian. It was a concept he had devised himself, the system and means of execution very quietly put into play by a friend in the Houston office of the FBI.

• 11:07 P.M.

Wirth looked at his watch, then picked up his main BlackBerry and alerted the pilots of his Striker-owned Gulfstream on standby at Tegel Airport to be ready for takeoff in two hours. Done, he set the alarm on his watch for midnight, then got up, crossed to the bed, lay back, and closed his eyes, determined to get even a few minutes of sleep. It didn't come easily. His mind and senses overrode it.

In addition to normal air traffic, by one thirty there would be four more planes in the air, all headed for Málaga: Marten's piston-engine Cessna and three chartered jets—Conor White's Falcon 50, another with Dimitri's people on board, and his own Striker Gulfstream. A lot of money, a lot of men, a lot of aircraft to recover a single batch of photographs.

53

• A LEARJET 55, somewhere over Southern France. Fuselage registration LX-C88T7. Airspeed 270 mph. Altitude 39,000 feet. Pilots, 2. Maximum passengers, 7. Actual passengers, 2. Sunday, June 6. 1:25 A.M.

Emil Franck could see Kovalenko hunched over a cell phone in the darkened forward cabin, every once in a while nodding and gesturing with his free hand. His first thought had been that he was in conversation with someone in Moscow—his wife or his children, or perhaps a mistress. Yet the idea that it was a domestic call was doubtful because it was almost three thirty in the morning Moscow time. A more credible scenario was that he was engaged with a superior, discussing the mission at hand and the details of what would happen if and when they recovered the materials they were after.

They'd lifted off from Berlin/Schönefeld just after nine thirty and two hours later gone into a holding pattern, a wide circle over the southern city of Toulouse that swung as far out as the Pyrenees on the French/Spanish border, waiting for the slower Cessna carrying Nicholas Marten and Anne Tidrow to catch up so they could follow it into Málaga or wherever else it might touch down. Wherever else because they knew Marten was not foolish enough to file a flight plan that would tell anyone exactly where he was going.

Franck looked to the laptop he'd been monitoring off and on since they'd left Berlin. On it, superimposed over a map of Western Europe, was a tiny green dot that represented the location of Marten's Cessna, the information relayed by a powerful thumb-sized transmitter hidden inside the aircraft.

The setup was part of a complex operation carried out quickly and efficiently after his meeting with Kovalenko that morning at Neuer Lake when he'd tapped into his vast underground network of informers and several hours later learned of an urgent request to charter a fast plane—a jet or turbo-prop—to fly two passengers from a private airstrip near Potsdam to Málaga, Spain, early that evening. Quickly, he'd turned the fast-plane request into one for a slower aircraft, the piston-driven Cessna 340, then had the transmitter installed after the plane had been secured and was being serviced.

His current calculation put the Cessna some two hundred and fifty miles behind them, flying south-west at approximately 190 mph, the speed it had been averaging since he first turned the laptop on and picked up the plane's location. It meant they were still on course for Málaga. Nothing had changed.

• 1:30 A.M.

Franck put the laptop aside and leaned back, hoping to get an hour or so of sleep, a prospect he knew was unlikely. Sleep in situations like these was not part of the drill. He glanced at the overnight bag on the seat across from him. In it was a fresh shirt, socks, underwear, a toothbrush, and a razor all tucked neatly alongside a Heckler & Koch MP5K compact submachine gun, which, along with the Glock 9 mm automatic Kovalenko carried in a holster clipped to his waistband, had been locked inside a storage compartment on the aircraft when they boarded.

Who the hell was Kovalenko anyway? A man with FSB credentials—the Federal Security Service Ministry of Internal Affairs—who had arrived on-scene in Berlin quicker than magic, literally within hours of his early-morning meeting with Elsa in the darkened café near Gendarmenmarkt Square, as if he'd already been in the city looking for Marten. And maybe he had. Franck might be a top cop in Berlin, a Hauptkommissar of Hauptkommissars, but he certainly didn't know everyone or everything, and besides, he hadn't heard from Elsa in ages. So there was no telling who or what she had been involved with since. She might well have been working with Kovalenko for years. That the Russian had known Marten from before, when he'd been a homicide investigator in Los Angeles, was a curiosity in itself. Stranger still was how they should both end up here circling over France at the orders of Moscow waiting for him to retrieve what were thought to be extremely important pictures. How had Elsa put it when reminding him Marten was wanted for the murder of Theo Haas?

"... it is reason enough for you to kill him after you recover the photographs."

Which, other than his official role as the primary German investigator charged with apprehending Marten for Haas's murder and his connections to the international law enforcement community that might be of help in the event Marten eluded them on the ground, was the reason he was there. Retrieving the photos for Moscow was only part of it. Once done—*if* done—Kovalenko and the pictures would disappear, and he would be left to clean up. Eliminate Marten and whoever was with him—in particular the Texas oil woman, Anne Tidrow, and/or anyone else who got in the way. That way there could be no trace back to Moscow, no hint that Russia was in any way involved.

• 1:37 A.M.

Franck glanced at the laptop's screen. The Cessna was no longer moving. Instead its dot was frozen on the screen inland from the sea near the French city of Bordeaux. He sat up fast. As he did, he saw Kovalenko coming toward him.

"The Cessna has stopped," he said quickly. "Did the transmitter crash? Did the plane?"

Kovalenko grinned. "Neither, Hauptkommissar. They've put down at Bordeaux-Mérignac Airport, most likely for fuel. An understandable delay. Nothing has changed."

"What is our own fuel situation?" Franck said calmly, unhappy with his show of alarm and Kovalenko's patronizing response.

"For now, more than adequate, Hauptkommissar."

Franck squinted in the dim cabin light trying to see the Russian more clearly. Deliberately he changed the subject. "You told me you knew Nicholas Marten from before, that he had been a homicide investigator in Los Angeles."

"I was there investigating a case involving the murder of Russian nationals. We had some dealings together. He had a different name then."

"Why did he change it and move to another country and take up another profession? Corruption?"

"He's not a policeman at heart, Hauptkommissar. I think he wanted to wholly extricate himself from that world. He preferred to see the beauty in life instead of bearing such close witness to the horror of what the human race does to itself every day."

"Yet now he's going to become part of that same horror."

"It is his fate, Hauptkommissar." Kovalanko pointed a finger skyward. "Written long ago in the stars. At least he will have had a few years of peace and, hopefully, joy."

"You believe in fate, Kovalenko?"

Kovalenko smiled. "If I didn't, I, too, would be out planting flowers. Who the hell wouldn't? If it weren't for fate, everyone in the world would be out planting flowers. It would seem a very reasonable thing to do. Few, like Marten, recognize what's happening and do something about it. The rest of us merely accept it and simply go about the business at hand." The humor left Kovalenko's eyes. "Until, as Marten is about to discover, our true fate catches up."

"And then?"

"And then—that's that."

1:45 A.M.

54

• France, Bordeaux-Mérignac Airport. 1:50 A.M.

Marten crossed the lighted tarmac in the area dedicated to civil aviation. A dozen planes were parked equidistant from each other. All dark. Locked for the night. The thirteenth, the Cessna D-VKRD, was farthest out, its interior lights on. By now it would have been fueled and ready for takeoff. Anne and their pilot, Brigitte Marie Reier, having used the terminal's toilet facilities and had something to eat, would be in the plane waiting for him.

Before, he'd purposely stayed back, remaining with the aircraft, letting the women go inside first. There'd been no real reason, other than to be polite and wanting to stretch his legs, and to be alone and think. And for a brief time he had, reflecting back on his conversation with Anne.

Memories of his late, beloved Caroline had moved him deeply, as had the horrors of Equatorial Guinea. The deaths that occurred there screamed out, leaving nothing but unfathomable anger and damning hatred for the carnival of perpetrators. All of it complicated by his own mental and physical exhaustion.

The truth was he was coming apart. He'd thought he'd left the savagery of violent death behind when he'd begun his new life in England. Then, from nowhere, he'd been thrust headlong into a world far darker and more monstrous than anything he'd seen on the streets of L.A. Suddenly he was afraid he was no longer capable of operating in it, that the self-protective, steel-edged coping mechanism every homicide cop develops to deal with murder on a daily basis had left him. If he was to continue, he would need that attitude and those skills. Without them, he might very well be killed himself and take Anne along with him. Especially if he had to go up against Conor White and whatever mercenaries he was sure to have accompanying him.

Instinct told him to walk away now. Say to hell

with Anne, the photographs, Joe Ryder, even the president. Leave the Cessna where it was without a word or a note or anything. Just find his way back to Manchester and the quiet beauty and emotional safety of his life there. Make believe none of this had ever happened.

He might have done it, too, or at least tried, if he hadn't suddenly been jolted by the thundering roar of a corporate jet taking off less than two hundred yards from where he stood. He'd watched it disappear into the night sky, its exterior navigational lights quickly fading to nothing. In that moment he heard Erlanger's words again.

"Stay away from the old contacts. You got away with it this once. For your sake, don't try it again."

Maybe they'd gotten away with it and maybe they hadn't.

Immediately he thought of the jet aircraft he'd requested and then of the slow '54 Chevy of a Cessna they'd been given. Had it been all that was available or was there some other reason?

In the next second he'd gone to the plane and walked around it, looking at the engines and under the wings, then examined the fuselage and tail assembly as best he could in the faint light. Afterward he climbed inside and poked around in the same way, looking under the instrument panel, the seats, the small luggage area, anywhere some kind of electronic transmitting device might have been planted. Then he'd heard the women coming back and quickly finished, stepping out just as they arrived.

A few insignificant words passed between them,

and then it was his turn to go into the terminal. He'd used the restroom, then found a cafeteria area with Wi-Fi hookups and given the lone young man he found working at a laptop twenty euros to borrow it for a few moments—"to check my e-mail and stuff." In those minutes he'd done what he'd not had the chance to do since Theo Haas had been murdered, clicked on Google Maps and pinpointed the location of the town Haas had pointed him toward, Praia da Rocha, in the Algarve region of Portugal's south coast. He'd found it nestled among the myriad of small beach communities near the city of Portimão. The nearest major airport was in Faro, which was close to the Spanish border and probably not two hundred miles from Málaga. Importantly, there were rental car facilities at the airport, most of which opened at six in the morning.

Faro was close enough to Málaga for Brigitte to radio a last-minute amended flight plan to Málaga air traffic control saying her passengers had requested she give them a tour of the coastline and would return to her original flight plan when they had finished. Not an unusual request for civil aviation traffic. So, if he chose to bypass Málaga, Faro would be the clear option. Anne could rent a car, and they could take what on the Google map appeared to be no more than a thirty-minute drive to Praia da Rocha. So he had a workable alternative, but he would wait until they were approaching Málaga before he made a final decision.

55

"We have clearance for takeoff?" Marten was looking at Brigitte as he climbed into the Cessna. She was sitting at the controls studying navigational charts under a high-intensity cockpit light. Behind her, he could see Anne watching from the darkened cabin.

"Yes, sir," Brigitte said.

"Then let's go."

"Yes, sir," she said again.

Marten slid past her on his way to his seat. As he did he saw the two women exchange glances.

"What was that for?" he said as he buckled in.

Anne raised an eyebrow. "How long does it take to pee?"

Marten grinned. "Sometimes it works right away and sometimes it takes a little coaxing."

Brigitte turned out the cockpit light and the lights of the instrument panel in front of her came to life. There was a sharp whine as she touched the ignition. A second later the port engine caught, then the starboard, and with a roar of propellers the Cessna moved off.

Marten waited a moment, then looked to Anne and lowered his voice, the lightheartedness of seconds earlier gone. "I specifically requested a faster plane. We didn't get it. Whose idea was that, yours or Erlanger's? Or was it someone else?"

"What are you talking about?"

"I asked you before about what Erlanger said in Potsdam before we took off. You didn't want to discuss it. With all your connections in Berlin, he, or whoever arranged for the plane, could have found the kind of aircraft I wanted. It didn't happen. And for one reason. They gave us a two-hundred-mile-an-hour Cessna so they could use a five-hundred-mile-an-hour jet to track us. That way we couldn't outfly them in the event we changed course. They know the kind of aircraft we're in, its registration number, who our pilot is, our flight plan, everything. Not to mention this."

Marten took a small black box from his jacket and held it out to her. "Looks like a Hide-A-Key, doesn't it?" He slid it open and took out a thin, flat object about four inches long and an inch wide. A tiny red light blinked off and on in the center of it. "I found it under the copilot's seat. Just clipped in like whoever did it didn't have much time."

She looked at it and then at Marten. "It's a bug, a transmitter."

"I don't suppose you knew about it."

"No."

"I didn't think you would," he smiled cynically. "I'm sure whoever put it there did it just to make sure we didn't get lost." Abruptly his demeanor hardened. "What does the CIA have to do with this? And don't say you don't know. I could see it in the way you looked at Erlanger when he spoke to you. He was warning you about something, and it upset you a great deal. What was it?"

Brigitte swung the Cessna sharply right and onto the runway, then accelerated for takeoff, the roar of its twin engines earsplitting as the plane gained speed. Ten seconds, then twenty and thirty, then they were up, the lights of Bordeaux-Mérignac Airport disappearing beneath them.

Anne glanced at Brigitte, then looked to Marten and lowered her voice. "I'm not sure how much Erlanger already knew or what he had just learned. But I put it together with something that happened that last night at the hotel in Malabo. As I was leaving for the airport I saw Conor White meet with a man in combat fatigues. He was armed and unshaven and looked as if he'd been in the rain forest for several days if not more. They talked briefly and then left together. I assumed he was working for SimCo, but I'd never seen him there before."

"What do you mean 'there'? Malabo?"

"No. Not anywhere SimCo people were. Malabo or anywhere else on Bioko. Not on the mainland, Rio Muni, either."

"But you had seen him somewhere before."

"Not just seen him, I knew him, when I was active CIA in El Salvador. His name is Patrice Sennac. He's French-Canadian and was then a top contract agent. He's a first-rate jungle fighter whose specialty is insurgency and counterinsurgency. He'd fight for one side in the morning and the other in the afternoon, working one against the other. Neither side knew."

"Jungle fighter?"

"Yes, why?"

"He's tall and very thin. Wiry."

"How did you know?"

"He was in several of the photographs."

Anne said nothing, just looked at him in that fearful way she had when Erlanger spoke to her at the airstrip.

"You think White brought him in specifically to help arm Abba's rebels but kept him out of sight until you left because he knew you would recognize him and ask what he was doing there?"

Still she said nothing.

"Is that what you think happened?"

"Yes," she said finally.

"Meaning you're not sure if he's a SimCo employee or if he still works for the CIA. And if he does, then Conor White might work for them, too, another contract agent with a top security clearance, comfortably inside in the Striker/Hadrian household with neither of them knowing, like the two sides in El Salvador."

Anne nodded.

"I don't understand. Striker/Hadrian is a State Department issue, not national security or intelligence. If it was, the CIA or FBI would be doing the investigating, not the Ryder Commission. You were in the Agency. Why would it be involved at all, let alone to that degree?"

She shook her head. "I don't know. But if it's true and somehow Erlanger found out, maybe through his own poking around, which is his nature . . . You understand? He did what he was told and brought in the Cessna instead of a jet—then tried to warn me away. I doubt if he knew about the bug."

Marten stared at her. "I think you do know."

There was the briefest moment when Anne did nothing at all. Finally she glanced at Brigitte, then looked back to Marten, her eyes cutting into him, her voice low and fiery. "I said I don't know and I meant it. I've told you everything. There is nothing else. Understand?"

Marten didn't react. She could get as mad as she wanted, he wasn't about to let go. "Let's assume that what you've said is true and get back to the photographs. You and your friends at Striker want them. Maybe for different reasons, but you both still want them. No doubt the Hadrian people do, too. So do the Equatorial Guinean army, Conor White and his pals at SimCo, and now the CIA. It's starting to play like some kind of comedy where all kinds of crazy people are chasing after the same thing. Or a darker, more murderous one, if they're just as insane but don't laugh much. It should be entertaining, but it's not. A civil war is going on. People are being butchered by the hour. What I saw myself was bad enough. The CIA video pushed it over the top."

Again Anne glanced toward the cockpit—if Brigitte had heard over the engine noise, she didn't acknowledge it. Anne looked back to Marten and softened. "Those things we saw on the video are as raw in my mind as they are in yours and won't go away. Your ragging on me as if I'm hiding something does nothing but get me mad and doesn't help anybody. I've told you the truth all along, and if you don't believe it we can stop right here. When we land I get out and walk away. Then the whole thing is in your lap. You deal with it."

Marten said nothing, just searched her eyes. He didn't know what to believe except that as much as he might have delighted in the idea of her walking away before, he didn't now. Whatever the Erlanger thing was, it was too important to abandon.

"What if I told you I did believe you. And probably have all along."

"Then I'd say I'm not so sure I believe you."

"Then that puts us in the same fix. Neither of us knows what to believe." Marten looked at her a second longer, then at the bug in his hand and the blinking red light in the center of it. "You know how to disable this thing?"

"Yes."

"Good." He said with a smile. "I'll tell you when."

2:37 A.M.

56

• Learjet 55, in a holding pattern over the Bay of Biscay just off Bilbao, Spain. Airspeed 310 mph. Altitude 27,200 feet. 2:52 A.M.

Emil Franck was slouched in his seat, half dozing, thinking of his children on their own, continents away, and at the same time watching the green dot showing the Cessna's progress on the laptop in front of him. From somewhere in the dimness of the cabin behind him he heard Kovalenko talking in Russian, presumably on his cell phone. The conversation was brief. He heard him sign off and in a moment came forward and sat down across from him.

"Moscow has just informed me that two other jet aircraft are tailing the Cessna," he said.

"What?" Franck sat up quickly. "What aircraft? Who are the people involved?"

"One is the chairman of the Striker Oil and Energy Company. The other plane has been chartered by the head of the private security firm hired to protect Striker's interests in Equatorial Guinea. His name is Conor White. He's a Brit, a former colonel in the SAS."

"Striker is after the photographs, too."

"So it seems."

"If mercenaries are involved it means weapons."

"Probably."

"Why two planes? Why aren't they traveling together?"

"I don't know."

"What is the origin of the information? How did Moscow get it?"

"I wasn't told."

Franck stared at him. It had been a long time since he'd had Moscow thrust into his life. He didn't like it.

"What *were* you told?"

"To keep them informed of Marten's position."

"Which they, in turn, will pass on to some nameless entity who then forwards it to Striker and White."

Kovalenko nodded.

Franck glanced at the slowly moving green dot

that was the Cessna on his laptop, then stood and walked partway down the aisle between the seats. He stopped and turned back. "Moscow is trying to serve its own interests without ruffling someone's feathers. So they give you this information as a way of telling us to make sure these dual problematicals don't get the pictures before we do."

"Yes."

"Just how are we to accomplish that?"

"Moscow has left it to us. And I leave it to you. You are famous for your 'creative thinking,' Hauptkommissar. Besides, we are in Europe, not Russia. Things are different here."

Franck stared at him. He hated these Moscow people.

"Well?" Kovalenko pushed him.

"We let them follow the Cessna to Málaga and see what Marten does. I guarantee you it's not his final stop. But then you know him better than I do. What is he thinking?"

"By now it's reasonable to assume he knows, or at least thinks, he's being followed. That means he will find some way to get where he's going despite that handicap. He has a rather determined personality and is quite clever at using it."

"So?"

"I seriously doubt he would set down in Málaga. He doesn't file a flight plan for all to see and then follow it to the letter. Unless he's going to some place around the corner, which I also doubt, it would be too obvious. On the other hand, if he did land and was still some distance from his target—even if he had arranged for a car—ground travel would be undependable and he would be easy to follow."

"You think he'll stay in the air until he's close enough to where he's going to make ground travel expedient. A reasonably short distance. An hour's drive or less, either as you say, in an arranged car, or in a rental."

"Yes," Kovalenko nodded.

"Then we assume he will divert somewhere along the way. Since these other two aircraft are relying on us for his position, it's very unlikely they will have him in line of sight. When he changes course we only need provide them with what information we think appropriate."

Kovalenko smiled thinly. "Give them a little but not too much. A balancing act, Hauptkommissar. For Moscow's sake."

"And ours."

3:07 A.M.

57

• Cessna 340, just north of Madrid. Airspeed 190. Altitude, 25,600 feet. 3:30 A.M.

Anne was asleep or at least pretending to be, curled up in her seat and breathing easily, her seat belt loose over her waist. Marten sat next to her, pretending nothing. He was wide-awake and wired, every bit of him considering what to do about whoever might be following them, and then about Anne herself. No matter what she'd so vociferously said about telling him the truth—about wanting to stop the war, the importance of her father's memory, even her promise to meet with Joe Ryder once they had the photos—the rest of it was just too iffy: the CIA connections; Erlanger and whoever else had helped them in Berlin; the sudden appearance of the former CIA jungle fighter, Patrice; the hidden transmitter on the plane; her own past as an Agency operative. Who knew what she really believed or where her true loyalties were? Too much was at stake to keep trusting her.

Meaning that it was best to do what he'd threatened before, get rid of her and go off on his own. Have Brigitte land in Málaga as planned. Go into the terminal with Anne, tell her he needed to use the men's toilet facilities, and then simply disappear, find a way to get the two-hundred-odd miles to Praia da Rocha any way he could. Bus, train, even hitchhike. The 1985 Schengen Agreement had ended border checkpoints in most of continental Europe. The official Berlin police photograph of him had been fuzzy at best, and by now he had a day and a half's growth of beard. All of which would help in the event his picture was still in the media, or if the Spanish and Portuguese police were on alert. All in all, it might work very well.

And he would have done it. Except for one thing; the Erlanger question.

The thing Anne had refused to reveal about his

warning that had made her more intense, troubled, and determined than he'd seen her since they'd met. Whatever it was was a powerful intangible, one he was certain involved some larger truth about Striker and Hadrian and their operation in Equatorial Guinea. Because of it he was extremely hesitant to abandon her; if he did, something of great consequence might slip through his fingers. At least that was what he thought now and chose to believe. What he would do was revert to his original plan, land at Faro and have Anne rent a car, then together make the short drive to Praia da Rocha. Of course, that strategy raised other potential problems, especially if the airports were, as he'd considered, on alert and the authorities were looking not only for him but for her as well. It also made the question of what to do about whoever was tailing them critical.

He thought a moment longer, then unbuckled his seat belt and slid into the empty copilot's seat next to Brigitte.

"Are we on time and on course?"

"Yes, sir. I estimate we'll have wheels down in Málaga at a few minutes past five."

"What's the weather?"

"Overcast with a low cloud deck."

"How thick is it?"

"Nine hundred feet, sir."

"Will it affect our landing?"

"The deck is solid, but no, sir, no problem with the landing."

He smiled. "Thank you."

3:57 A.M.

58

Conor White hunched forward in his seat. Headset
on, his laptop open with a street map of Málaga on
the screen, he was listening to Málaga air traffic
control. Behind him, Patrice and Irish Jack had laid
out their choice of weapons: two nine-and-a-half-
inch fixed-blade, partially serrated jungle knives and
accompanying nylon sheaths; two compact, lightweight, highly modified M-4 Colt Commando submachine guns with sound and flame suppressors
and six 45 mm thirty-round magazines for each—
firepower 750 rounds per minute; two Beretta 93R
burst-firing 9 mm automatic pistols, with six twenty-
round magazines for each. And then there were
Conor White's armaments: a similar nine-and-
a-half-inch fixed-blade jungle knife; two modified
Heckler & Koch 9 mm MP5 submachine guns with
sound and flame suppressors and eight thirty-round
magazines, firepower 800 rounds per minute; and
one short-barrel SIG SAUER 9 mm semiautomatic
handgun with four ten-round magazines that he
used as a backup "hide gun," kept under his jacket in
a slim polymer holster at the back of his belt. This
was the gun he had used to kill the young Spanish
doctor in the farmhouse outside Madrid and, soon

afterward, the driver of the hired car, whom he'd shot at point-blank range in the dilapidated barn.

• 4:52 A.M.

They were ninety miles out. Marten's Cessna, D-VKRD, had already been cleared to enter the Málaga landing pattern. By White's calculation, that should put the Cessna on the ground in about fifteen minutes, or approximately 5:07 A.M.

He had one man in the control tower and two in the terminal, one at the entrance from the tarmac, the other at the exit onto the street. A fourth and fifth waited in cars just outside, one near the taxi line, the other near the car rental agencies.

Once Marten landed, the plane would taxi to the terminal area, where he and Anne would disembark. Assuming the Berlin police hadn't put out a Europe-wide APB for Marten, which would have the Spanish police closely watching arrivals at every airport, the two would simply enter the terminal, walk through the green NOTHING TO DECLARE customs door, and go into the terminal proper. There they would either take a taxi, rent a car from an airport agency, or use some other form of transportation yet to be determined. Anne might even have a car waiting. Whatever the case, once they left the terminal they would be followed by one or both of the men outside—and soon thereafter by himself, Patrice, and Irish Jack traveling in a dark green SUV that would be waiting for them at the edge of the tarmac, an SUV courtesy of Spitfire Ltd., a Madrid-based private security contractor that served most of the Iberian Peninsula—Spain, Portugal, Andorra, Gibraltar, and a tiny French territory in the Pyrenees—and was owned by a former SAS major, one of his closest friends.

For no particular reason, White thought of his father, Sir Edward Raines. For everything he had—money, political and military esteem, legitimate family of wife, daughter, two other sons, three grandchildren—the one thing he did not have was the Victoria Cross, which was the honor White treasured most. It was not only hugely prestigious, it put his name ahead of his father's in British military history. But while queen and country had proudly and publicly saluted him for it, his father had not. He had been invited to the ceremony but had not come. Nor had he phoned, faxed, e-mailed, or written. It had been a golden opportunity for him to recognize his bastard son without ever saying it. The simplest of gestures. A handshake, a look in the eye, a word of congratulations would have been enough. It was the prize he coveted most of all, but it had not happened.

And now, at this moment, and for a reason he was unable to understand, the lack of recognition pained him more than it ever had in his life. It was a hurt that had been assuaged a hundred times over in combat when the face of the enemy had suddenly become that of his father and he'd struck at it with every ounce of fury he had. It was why he had been so successful in battle. Why he had received the Victoria Cross and the sea of Distinguished

Service Order medals. It was why he would succeed again in the hours and minutes immediately
ahead, because this time the enemy who would
wear the face of Sir Edward Raines would be the
person who stood between himself and ruin. Nicholas Marten.

*"Cessna D-VKRD, you are in the landing pat-
tern. Please change radio frequency to 267.5."* The
voice of an air controller suddenly crackled over his
headset.

"D-VKRD. Going to new frequency, 267.5," he
heard the Cessna's female pilot reply.

"Copy to 267.5, D-VKRD."

Abruptly White's radio went to static as the Cessna
pilot changed radio frequency. He took off the
headphones and looked over his shoulder to Patrice
and Irish Jack in the seats behind him.

"They're on approach, gentlemen. Workday's
about to begin," he said sharply. "Saddle up."

4:55 A.M.

59

• Cessna, D-VKRD, on approach to Málaga International Airport. 5:02 A.M.

Marten looked at his watch, counting down the time. Anne was awake now, watching him in the dimly lit cabin.

"Where do we go from here?" she asked quietly.

"That will depend on Brigitte." Abruptly he undid his seat belt and climbed into the copilot's seat next to her, just as he had an hour before. Below he could just make out the cloud deck in the beam of the plane's landing lights. It was steel gray and forbidding, stretching out like some enormous glacier.

"How long before we're in it?"

"About eight seconds."

Marten glanced over his shoulder at Anne, then back out the windshield. He held his breath and counted down. Five, four, three, two— Then they were in it. The clouds swirled around them. He turned to Brigitte.

"This is what I want you to do."

                                                      5:05 A.M.

• SimCo Falcon, 3C-B797K, 5:12 A.M.
Conor White felt the main landing gear hit; then the plane's nose angled over, and the front gear touched the runway. He saw the lighted terminal flash past,

then heard the scream of the three Garrett turbofan engines as the pilot put them into reverse thrust. The plane slowed quickly. Another few seconds and they were at the end of the runway and coming back around. Instantly he was out of his seat and at the window looking for the Cessna as they taxied for the terminal. Patrice and Irish Jack were up, too, their weapons packed away in a pair of dark green and yellow sports-equipment bags, peering out, ready to go. All they saw was darkness and parked aircraft.

"Where the fuck is he?" Irish Jack was on edge. "Where the hell did he go?"

White was already on his cell phone talking to his man in the tower. "Where's the Cessna that just landed?"

"The landing was aborted at the last second."

"What?"

"The pilot reported radio trouble. Said she would refile a landing request."

"Where did she go?"

"Don't know. Her radio is still out."

White glanced at Patrice and Irish Jack. "Son of a bitch used the cloud deck to dance out of here. He knows he's being followed." He turned back to the phone. "Refile us for immediate takeoff, then get me a reading of the Cessna's transponder code. I want a location of that aircraft."

"It may take a little time to find, sir. There is a lot of traffic in the area. Cessna's not the only airplane up there."

"My friend." Conor White's voice was filled with

rage, "I can't follow a plane when I don't know where the hell it went! Find it. Find it fast! Find it now!" Conor White clicked off and looked to Patrice and Irish Jack. "Shit!" he said.

5:24 A.M.

• Learjet 55, forty miles out from Málaga.
Airspeed 310 mph. Altitude 14,200 feet. Same time.

Emil Franck turned his laptop off and then back on and waited for it to reboot, just as he had done moments earlier. The green dot giving the Cessna's position had suddenly disappeared from the screen, and he held his breath, hoping the problem was with the laptop's software. Up front, he could see Kovalenko talking excitedly to the pilots and knew the software had nothing to do with it. They'd had the Cessna on their screen, too, and called for Kovalenko seconds after it had vanished from Franck's. Clearly something major had occurred. Abruptly Kovalenko left the pilots and came toward.

"Marten's aware that he's being tracked," he said. "The Cessna was on approach, then suddenly veered off in a cloud deck and reported radio trouble. There is something of a disorder in the Málaga tower as a result."

"The transmitter was new. It was functioning perfectly."

"And then it went dead. Almost at the exact same moment the pilot aborted her landing. Either it was found and disabled or simply stopped working at a convenient moment. But whatever happened makes no difference. The Cessna is gone. Málaga tower is attempting to locate it by its transponder reading, but it will take time. Maybe a few minutes, maybe a few hours. Who knows?"

Kovalenko suddenly leaned in close, his face inches from the German detective's, his eyes seeming to pull back into his skull in a way that was wholly unnerving. "Hauptkommissar, that little tracking device, no bigger than your pinky finger—its condition and where it was placed on the aircraft were your responsibility."

"I neither selected it nor placed it. I simply ordered it done and it was."

"It was your responsibility, Hauptkommissar. The Cessna is gone. So is Marten."

"Then I will find him."

"If he's not already on the ground somewhere and vanished. Then where will we be, Hauptkommissar, you and I? Most particularly to Moscow."

Franck's black eyes flashed angrily at Kovalenko's attempt to shift the blame to him, but he said nothing. Instead he stood up and slid a cell phone from his jacket, then punched in a number.

"At this point they won't have much fuel remaining," he said quietly, then turned to the phone as a male voice answered. "This is Franck. I want an immediate Europe-wide aeronautical APB on a Cessna 340, fuselage registration D-VKRD, last seen approaching AGP, Málaga Airport, Spain. Contact me with the coordinates the moment the aircraft's transponder signal is located or when the pilot requests permission to land, whichever is first. I want infor-

mation only. No contact is to be made with the aircraft itself. All agencies are requested to stand by for
further instructions. No action is to be taken without
my permission. Confirm."

"Roger, copy. Confirmed, sir."

Franck clicked off without another word, then
looked to the Russian. "If, as you suggest, Nicholas
Marten manages to land somewhere without our
knowledge, then recovers the photographs and dis-
appears into the mist, we would be dealing with the
concept of fate we discussed earlier. Yours and mine
especially, as far as Moscow is concerned. To para-
phrase you, Kovalenko—we go about the business
at hand until our true fate catches up and then—
that's that. Put more directly, unless something happens within a very short time, we will both soon be
dead."

5:31 A.M.

60

• Cessna, D-VKRD. Airspeed 190 miles per hour.
Altitude just over 11,200 feet. 5:57 A.M.

"Where are we?" Marten was talking to Brigitte
without looking at her, his eyes on the sparkling
lights of a city below.

"Passing over Gibraltar. Following the coastline
west, as you asked."

"Good."

"It would be helpful if you told me where you want to land."

"I'll tell you when we get there. The same as I've I said all along."

"Yes, sir."

It was still nearly an hour to sunrise. Faro, Marten had to remember, was in Portugal, not Spain, and the time zone there was an hour earlier, meaning it was now approaching five in the morning Portuguese time. From what he remembered of the Google map he'd studied earlier, Gibraltar was probably a hundred and fifty miles from Faro in a direct line. By following the coast they could easily add another forty or fifty miles to the trip. Meaning it would be sometime after six when they reached Faro, and that was important. If they arrived too early, the airport terminal would be relatively quiet, making it difficult for two people arriving by private plane to walk in off the tarmac unnoticed. Faro was the hub airport for the popular Algarve region of southern Portugal, and the later they got there, the better the opportunity they would have to mix in with the tourists and business people arriving or departing on early-morning flights. The trouble was, by taking a longer route, fuel became a problem, and they were low on it as it was.

Marten glanced at the gauge on the instrument panel. It read close to empty.

The last thing he wanted was to put down somewhere between where they were and Faro, because the minute he gave the order to land, Brigitte would have to contact the tower, and once they were down they would be vulnerable. Never mind that the people in two planes he suspected had followed them to Málaga might still be on their tail; if Brigitte was a CIA plant arranged through Erlanger in Berlin, she might well silently alert someone on the ground and an operation to tail them would be in force when they arrived. That kind of chance he was prepared to take in Faro because he knew exactly where they were going afterward; he'd just have to hope they could find a way to leave the airport quickly and unnoticed. But landing at an unknown airport along the way was no good. He looked to Brigitte.

"How soon before we need fuel?"

"An hour. A little more if we throttle back and slow down."

"Then slow us down," he said without hesitation. If they made it to Faro they would be landing on fumes, but it was a chance he was willing to take.

"I hope you know what you're doing." Anne's voice rang out from behind him.

He turned to look at her. She was sitting back, her arms folded over her chest. "I'm not exactly in the mood to end up in the Atlantic." She smiled demurely.

"If it makes you feel any better, neither am I."

"How comforting." She smiled again.

"Isn't it?"

6:00 A.M.

61

"I understand, Conor, there was nothing you could do," Sy Wirth said with uncharacteristic calm, his ear to his Conor White–only, blue-tape BlackBerry. "I assume you're still on the ground at Málaga?"

"Yes, sir," White's voice came back. *"There's a lot of traffic. The tower is having difficulty picking up the transponder signal from the Cessna. It's a complicated procedure that's out of my hands. Even my man in air traffic can't force it. I've pushed him as hard as I can. We're cleared for takeoff the moment we isolate the signal."*

"I'll call you back." Abruptly Wirth clicked off, set the blue-tape BlackBerry on the worktable in front of him, and picked up his other BlackBerry. Immediately he punched in a number and waited for it to connect through.

"I know, Josiah, they've lost the signal. My people are on it." Despite the hour Dimitri Korostin was right there, clearly expecting his call. *"It's much too early to have to deal with your problems. You're making me begin to think an Andean gas field is hardly worth it."*

"A field the size of the Santa Cruz–Tarija is worth as many problems as you have to solve. That is, if you still intend to deliver as promised. So fuck you, and find out where the hell Marten's plane is."

"Fuck you, too. I'll let you know when I have something." With that the Russian clicked off.

Sy Wirth set the BlackBerry down and poured himself a cup of coffee from the thermos the flight attendant had provided. When he had it, he sat back and tried to relax. He could worry, but it wouldn't help. Dimitri's people were in the air and on Marten's tail. So far, and despite Marten's clever maneuverings, they'd tracked him every step of the way, so there was no reason to believe they wouldn't pick him up again soon. There was little doubt Conor White and his team would find him in due course, too, but Dimitri's people would find him faster and with a lot less noise.

Unfortunate as losing the Cessna's signal was, it was strangely working in his favor and was why he hadn't raised his voice to White. Why upset someone who's helping you without knowing it? By pressing his man in Málaga air traffic control, he was unconsciously leaving a big fat footprint for the authorities to follow once the business with Marten was done. The same hefty footprint he'd left in Madrid when he hired the limousine and driver to pick up the Spanish doctor and her medical students at the airport and take them to the isolated farmhouse, and then later when he used the Falcon charter to take him from Madrid to Berlin and now back to Spain.

When all was said and done—when Dimitri's people had delivered the photographs and gone, and from Dimitri's reputation and actions so far there was little reason to think they wouldn't succeed, with Marten and Anne dead in the process—the person left twisting in the air would be Conor White. And there would be nothing he could say without incriminating himself further. Even if he pointed the finger at Wirth, claiming he was the mastermind of all this—of arming the rebels and then of directing the search for the damning photographs, which included the interrogations in the farmhouse outside Madrid—his case would fall apart because there would be no photographs and any claim of direct communication between the two of them would end only in a trace back to the general number at Hadrian headquarters in Virginia. An allegation of a clandestine meeting between the two of them at the former bordello in Berlin would be indefensible as well. The apartment had been rented by phone and charged to a SimCo account in England under the name Conor White. On the morning of the day in question Josiah Wirth had been in a meeting with the Russian oil oligarch Dimitri Korostin at the Dorchester Hotel in London. It was true he had gone to Berlin later and taken a suite at the Ritz-Carlton Hotel, but that had been to meet with an associate of Korostin's who had had to cancel at the last minute. He hadn't even been aware that White was in the city. Sometime after one the next morning he'd left the German capital in the company Gulfstream for a series of business meetings in Barcelona.

It was on the way there that he would hear about the tragedy in whatever town or city where Dimitri's people caught up with Anne and Marten, and where White and his gunmen would be found by the local authorities and accused of their murders. Authorities who would have gone there on a tip from the Spanish police, who would have been anonymously alerted to White's probable complicity in the Madrid farmhouse murders and have been warned that he was on his way to wherever this place was to settle some grievous personal account with Striker board member Anne Tidrow.

Depending on the timing, Wirth would either go to the location directly from Barcelona or divert his flight en route, shocked and outraged at White's involvement with what had happened there and at the Madrid farmhouse and mourning the death of a dear colleague who was the daughter of Striker's late and much loved founder.

Wirth took another sip of coffee and looked out the window to see the first streaks of day beginning to brighten the eastern sky. Suddenly he felt exhausted, as if all of the anxiety, intensity, and travel of the past days had caught up with him. He'd slept little and knew he would need all the clearheaded energy he could muster when things began to happen. If he could sleep now, even for twenty minutes, it would be a godsend. He put the cup down and lay back, closing his eyes. Just relax, he told himself. Don't think about anything. Don't think about anything at all.

6:28 A.M. Spanish time

62

- Cessna, D-VKRD. Airspeed 130 miles per hour. Altitude 4,500 feet. 6:15 A.M. Portuguese time.

Marten glanced at Brigitte and then looked back at Anne. She was watching him without expression, as if she were fed up with his maneuverings and seriously wondering if he really did know what the hell he was doing. He turned back, saying nothing. This was no time to get into it again. Not when they had come this far and were so close to their objective. Or at least what he hoped what their objective would be.

A short while earlier they had passed into Portuguese airspace and were hugging the coastline, where the sunrise was providing a stunning view of the numerous beach communities dotting the Algarve region. Faro would be one of them. By his calculation, ten to fifteen minutes ahead at most.

"Mr. Marten—" Brigitte said over the drone of the engines.

"Fuel, I know."

"We have to put down, and soon."

"I understand," he said, knowing they were lucky to have come as far as they had. He was still concerned about giving Brigitte their destination too soon for fear she would somehow signal ahead and operatives would be waiting for them when they arrived, but unless he wanted to land on one of the beaches along the way, he had no choice but to tell her now. "Can we make it to Faro?"

"Yes, sir. I think so."

"Then do it."

"Faro?" Anne said behind him.

He turned to look at her. "Yes, darling, Faro," he said, smiling warmly. "Anything else?"

"Not at the moment."

"Good."

There was a roar of engines as Brigitte swung the Cessna out over the sea, radioing the Faro tower with a request to land. Seconds later she looked to Marten. "Portugal has no passport control for flights originating inside Europe."

"Yes, I know."

"Once we reach the terminal you'll go directly inside, pass through the NOTHING TO DECLARE door, and walk into the arrivals hall. Then you're out and gone, and I refuel and fly back to Germany. It's as simple as that."

So Brigitte did know something of their situation. At least enough to know Marten might be concerned about having to show identification when they landed and be thinking what to do about it when they did. The question was, was she being helpful? Or purposely trying to lull him into a sense that he had nothing to worry about after they'd landed, and in doing so throw him off guard for whoever might be waiting to follow them?

"I hope it's as simple as that," Anne said.

Marten looked over his shoulder. "So do I."

6:22 A.M. Portuguese time

63

- Striker Oil Gulfstream G550. Nearing Málaga.
Airspeed 470 mph. Altitude 28,300 feet.
7:35 A.M. Spanish time.

Sy Wirth had slept soundly for an hour, then suddenly woke with a start and immediately picked up his BlackBerry, trying to reach Korostin. He got only the Russian's voice mail. Angry, he started to call Conor White, then decided against it. There was no reason. If Korostin knew where the Cessna was, he would have alerted him. If he didn't know, there was little chance White would either. If he did, he would have already been in touch. So there was nothing to do but wait; one of the things he hated most.

Finally he got up and went to the lavatory. Afterward, he came back and sat down, then abruptly took a yellow legal pad from his briefcase, picked up a freshly sharpened number 2 Ticonderoga 1388 pencil, and scrawled a brief memo to himself for a dialogue later in the day with his chief counsel, Arnold Moss.

1: Prepare to quickly and publicly disavow any connection to Conor White, Marten, and Anne once the photos are recovered. Whatever happens, White acted wholly on his own, or— (check with Arnie) as previously discussed re:

*separate clandestine Hadrian/SimCo
relationship—with no involvement by Striker
whatsoever. White should immediately and
very publicly be terminated (he will go to
jail anyway) and SimCo reorganized for
continued operation in E.G. (Side note:
SimCo's a good operation with personnel
already in place in E.G. No need to completely
dismantle it.)
2: As above, prepare quick, smart, well-placed
public relations spin, esp. in D.C., to make
Striker look like the victim in the White/Hadrian
debacle.
3: Prepare to dissolve all business in Iraq.
Organize legal defense team against any and all
ensuing actions by White, Loyal Truex/Hadrian,
and the Ryder Commission.
4: Analyze Striker's worldwide operations,
prepare to reconfigure to make E.G. and the
Bioko field the centerpiece within 6–12
months.
5: Prepare—*

Suddenly his everyday BlackBerry chimed. Immediately he picked up.

"Faro, Portugal," Dimitri Korostin's voice spat
at him. *"They landed about five minutes ago."*

"Your people are there?"

*"We have an agreement, Josiah. I deliver as
promised, no matter what you may think."*

"Thank you, my friend."

"Fuck you, too!"

Dimitri clicked off; so did Wirth. A moment later he picked up the blue-tape BlackBerry and speed-dialed Conor White.

"Yes, sir." White's voice came back. *"I'm still on the ground in Málaga. No update on Marten as yet."*

"Call me back. The connection's breaking up."

"Yes, sir."

Eight seconds later Sy Wirth's other BlackBerry chimed and he picked up, the one with blue tape silent at his elbow.

"Conor, they've landed in Faro, Portugal," he snapped quickly and with urgency. "You get off the ground now, you can be there in less than an hour. Call me when you touch down. I should have more for you by then."

"Faro. Yes, sir."

Wirth clicked off, and a smile crept over his face. At long last the game was coming to an end.

7:47 A.M.

• SimCo Falcon, Málaga International Airport. Same time.

"Faro." White stood in the cockpit doorway, the BlackBerry still in his hand. "Fast as this thing will go. Give me a wheels-down ETA as soon as you have it."

Abruptly he turned and went back into the cabin. Patrice and Irish Jack were waiting for him.

"Faro," he said again, then slid past them and into his seat and buckled in. Seconds later the first, then the second and then the third of the Falcon's turbo-fan jet engines came to life. Almost immediately the plane started to move.

White clipped on his headset, listening to the conversation between his pilot and the tower; then he looked to Patrice. "Get in touch with Spitfire/Madrid. Tell them we want an SUV waiting on the Faro tarmac when we get there."

"Yes, sir." Patrice nodded and slid a cell phone from his pocket.

"Where'd you get the info, Colonel?" Irish Jack grinned with the kind of enthusiasm he always had when he knew action was near. "Same little bird that's been feeding us all along?"

"Same little bird, Jack. Same little bird." White sat back as the Falcon banged over the tarmac toward the runway. Irish Jack liked to use playful, almost childlike descriptions of people or things. Where that came from he didn't know, probably his youth. That aside, White was well aware that both Irish Jack and Patrice knew it was Sy Wirth who had been communicating with him all along.

That was alright for them, but for White the bigger question was, where was Wirth getting his information? Just who was this third party he'd brought into the picture, and how was he keeping tabs on Marten and Anne with such speed and accuracy? Whoever it was was either extremely sophisticated or highly connected, or both. He didn't like it, and it made him think once again that Wirth, with his blind, self-confident arrogance, had blundered into something far over his head. If so, he was being dragged face-first into it as well. But at this point there was nothing he could do about it because whoever it was held all the cards. Right now he was the tail on the dog.

7:53 A.M. Spanish time

64

• Portugal, Faro International Airport. 6:55 A.M.

Marten and Anne entered the terminal separately, mingling with the passengers from arriving commercial flights he'd hoped would be there. He looked behind him. Through the glass doors he could see Brigitte move the Cessna off to refuel for her return flight to Germany. Whether she had alerted anyone on the ground was impossible to know.

• 6:57 A.M.

Marten was a dozen paces behind Anne with travelers in between as they approached the green NOTHING TO DECLARE archway and the exit door beyond it leading to the arrivals hall. Here and there armed Portuguese Airport Authority police stood in pairs watching the flow of travelers. Marten kept moving, paying them no attention. Ahead, he could see Anne doing the same. Then she was there, passing under the archway and walking into the arrivals

hall. Seconds later he passed through it himself un-
challenged. Simple as that, just as Brigitte had said.

• 7:00 A.M.

Marten caught up to Anne near the main entrance,
blending in with the controlled chaos of morning
travelers coming and going and keeping a watchful
eye on another pair of airport police standing just
inside the doors, one of them with his hand on the
leash of a large black Labrador. Sniffer dog, Marten
thought, looking for travelers carrying drugs or ex-
plosives.

They had no luggage at all; everything was carried
on their person, the same as it had been after they'd
left the Hotel Adlon in Berlin. Anne had her basics—
toiletries, change of underwear and sleeping T-shirt,
passport, credit cards, money, BlackBerry and phone
charger—in her shoulder bag. Marten's passport, his
toothbrush, the dark blue throwaway cell phone,
and his wallet with his British driver's license, credit
cards, and cash were neatly distributed between his
jeans and his summer-weight sport coat.

"Where do we go from here?" Anne said quietly
and with a furtive glance toward the police and their
dog.

Marten steered her toward the main entrance.
"Out the front door, then look for a bus into the city."

"Bus?"

He looked at her sardonically. "Don't tell me
you're above using public transportation."

She shot him an indignant glance. "My father and

I rode buses for years when we were traveling and trying to build the business. There was no money for anything else. But in case you've forgotten, buses are narrow enclosed places filled with people who just might watch TV or surf the Net or read newspapers. I have to think that by now your friend the Hauptkommissar will have spread your name and picture all over the EU. Maybe mine, too."

Marten ignored her protest. "After the bus we're going to need a car."

"Are you going to rent it or steal it?"

"*You* are going to rent it."

"Me?"

Marten glanced at her. "I can't risk using a credit card and having my name show up in some kind of commercial data bank," he said quietly. "Anyone looking for me would know exactly where I am."

"What about anyone looking for me?"

"We'll have to take that chance."

Again came the indignant look. "We will?"

"Unless you want to walk. Where we're going isn't exactly around the corner."

They were still in the crowd when they moved past the police and the sniffer dog and out into bright sunshine. Two police cars were parked on the far side of a center island directly across from them, with three uniformed officers standing nearby chatting and keeping their eyes on the terminal entrance.

"There are car rental agencies here at the airport." Anne moved a step ahead of Marten. "It's crazy to risk being seen on a bus."

"True. But not so crazy when one considers that airport rental agencies and taxicabs are the first place anyone following us will look." Marten nodded toward a city bus as it pulled to the curb not twenty yards in front of them. "They'll look but they won't find. By the time they think to check the agencies in the city we'll be long gone." He glanced back at the police. "I hope."

"To where?"

Marten shook his head. "Not yet, darling."

"Still don't trust me, do you?"

"No."

7:10 A.M.

65

• Faro, Montenegro district. Still Sunday, June 6. 8:12 A.M.

Nicholas Marten stuffed his hands in his pockets and walked across the street to a small tree-lined park and sat down on a bench. In the distance church bells tolled for Sunday Mass. Somewhere nearby was the faint odor of cultivated garlic. Marten looked around for the decorative plant, curious as to what variety it was and where it was. Farther down two elderly men played chess under a large almond tree that he estimated was at least forty years old.

For a moment he did nothing but sit there. Finally

he turned and looked across the narrow street behind him to the Auto Europe rental car office where
Anne was, and had been for more than ten minutes,
hopefully just because that was how long it took to
rent a car, not because the use of her credit card had
attracted the police as she had feared. He turned
back, then stood and strolled deeper into the park.
He'd been casual enough for long enough. He
glanced at his watch.

8:18 A.M. in Faro.

3:18 A.M. in Washington, D.C.

• Camp David, Maryland. Aspen Lodge,
the presidential cabin. 3:20 A.M.

A musical ringtone jolted President John Henry
Harris from a deep sleep. It took a moment before he
realized the sound was coming from the slate gray
cell phone on the table at his elbow. The phone he had
long prayed would ring. He stared at it almost in
disbelief, then snatched it up and clicked on.

"Nicholas!" he blurted. "Are you alright? Where
are you?"

"Faro, Portugal."

"Portugal?"

"Is it safe to talk? Are you alone?"

"Yes." The president sat up quickly.

"I don't have much time."

"Go ahead."

*"You know about Theo Haas, about the Berlin
police?"*

"Of course."

*"I didn't kill him. A young man did. I chased af-
ter him. He got away in a crowd. People thought
I was running from the murder scene."*

"I believe you. It's alright."

*"Just before Haas was murdered he gave me a
clue as to where the photographs were or might
be. A man named Jacob Cádiz, in the Portuguese
beach town of Praia da Rocha. There's a woman
involved."*

"I know. Anne Tidrow. Striker Oil. Her father
founded the company. For a time she was in the CIA."

"You do your homework."

"I try."

• Faro.

Marten turned his back as two cyclists in bright
jerseys moved past him to join a group of six other
riders waiting at the far end of the park.

"She's with me now, across the street, with luck
renting us a car. Next comes the crazy part. I'm
not so sure she isn't still with the Agency. Her old
connections got us out of Berlin and then Germany
courtesy of a former operative who arranged for a
private plane. We were being tracked, and our pilot
may well have tipped off whoever's on our tail to
where we landed. Meaning that at this point, I don't
know who's who or what's what with anyone."

*"Does Ms. Tidrow know about this Jacob Cádiz
or Praia da Rocha?"*

"Not yet."

"Can you get rid of her? Go there on your own?"

"That's part of the problem. She says she's concerned with her father's reputation and the reputation of the company. That she doesn't like where its directors have taken it, especially in Iraq and with the Hadrian company. The photographs and the company's culpability in the civil war in Equatorial Guinea pushed her over. While we were in Berlin she agreed to meet with Joe Ryder after we recover the photos and tell him what she knows about the Striker/Hadrian situation in Iraq and Equatorial Guinea. That is, if we get them, if they're there at all. There's another thing, too. She learned something from a former CIA operative in Germany that shook her up and that she won't talk about. Whatever it is it may be even more valuable than the photographs. I'd like to think the Agency is very quietly trying to protect its friends at Striker and Hadrian and at the same time trying to prevent what could turn into a major international incident. But somehow I think it's more than that, and she knows what it is. All of them are reasons why I can't just walk away from her.

"Then there's the flip side. It could all be a game just so I'd keep her with me. If so, and she set me up? You understand? We get the pictures, then the CIA swoops in, and she and they and the photos are gone and I'm hung out to dry for the murder of Theo Haas."

"Nicholas, you don't have to put yourself at risk any more than you already have. Leave her and get the pictures and get out of there."

"I can't."

"Why?"

"I just can't," Marten said definitively, then glanced at the old men playing chess and then at the Auto Europe car rental agency across the street where Anne was.

"Does she know of my involvement in this?"

"No."

Suddenly the door to the Auto Europe agency opened and Anne came out. She shaded her eyes from the sun and looked around, clearly wondering where he was. Marten stepped back into the shadow of a large stand of tall conifers that seemed the centerpiece of the park.

"What is it?" Harris said at his silence.

"Nothing." Marten watched her for the briefest moment, then turned back to the phone. "Call Joe Ryder and tell him what's going on. When I have the pictures, or don't, I'll let you know. In the meantime find some place where Anne and I can meet with Ryder that won't draw attention. A good-sized city somewhere near here would be best. A place we can get lost in if someone's following us. I know it means pulling Ryder out of Iraq, but he can travel a lot easier than we can."

"It's going to take a little while to put all this together. Let me call you this time. I don't like not being able to reach you anyway. Give me your cell number."

Anne crossed the street and was coming into the park. Marten moved farther back into the conifer grove. The last thing he needed was for her to see him on the phone and then to question him about it, wanting to know who he'd been talking to and why. Immediately he turned his attention back to the president.

"Better let me do the calling. I run into trouble, someone else gets the phone, and you call? If it's the Agency there's every chance they'll trace it straight to you even if you hang up right away."

"Give me an hour."

Anne passed the old men playing chess and was approaching the trees where he was. She was noticeably concerned and looking around, as if she were afraid that he'd run out on her.

"One last thing." A jagged intensity came into Marten's voice. "Have you seen the latest regional CIA briefing video on Equatorial Guinea?"

"No."

"Find a way to get it without the request seeming to come from you. Then watch it alone. That'll answer why I'm doing what I am. You won't need more."

Anne was almost there, thirty feet away at most.

"I have to go, my friend. I'll let you know what happens." With that Marten clicked off and slid the phone into his jacket, then walked out from the behind the trees to meet her.

8:53 A.M

66

"I trust you got a car." Marten took the initiative the moment he reached her. If she'd seen him talking on the phone or even sliding it into his jacket he didn't want her asking who he was talking to and why. Better to keep the conversation on her and what was going on and hope she wouldn't bring it up.

She nodded toward the rental agency. "It's parked in front."

"No questions about you? Who you were? How long you wanted the car? Where you planned to go?" He started them down the path and toward the street where the rental was.

"I said I was a tourist. I wanted it for a day or two, maybe more. That was it." Suddenly her eyes flashed and she pressed him. Hotly. "Where the hell were you? I was looking all over. You were in this rush to get out of Faro, then you disappear into the woods. What were you doing, climbing trees?"

"I was looking for something." Marten glanced around. The old men were still playing chess. Farther down a pair of young lovers lay in the grass, seemingly with no care in the world but themselves. A man of forty or so in jeans and a light sweater played with a small leashed monkey near the park's entrance. For now, that was all.

"Looking for what?"

"Huh?" he brought his attention back to her.

"You said you were looking for something. What was it?"

"Garlic."

"Garlic?"

"Ornamental garlic plants, *Tulbaghia violacea*. They're growing here somewhere. I smelled them, I just couldn't find them."

Anne was incredulous. "We're trying to get out of here and you're looking for plants?"

"You may remember that flora interests me a great deal. It's my profession. The reason I was in Bioko. It's also a world I'd be very happy to get back to, and the sooner the better. So yes, garlic. You don't believe me, take a deep breath, tell me what you smell."

"You're serious."

"You act as if I'm making it up. Go ahead, sniff."

"Oh, for Christ's sake."

"Sniff."

"Fuck," she said and then inhaled.

"What do you smell?"

"Garlic."

Marten grinned. "Thank you."

• 9:30 A.M.

The car was a silver Opel Astra with an automatic transmission. Marten took the N125 highway toward Portimão, some forty miles west. If Hauptkommissar Franck had put out an EU all points bulletin to apprehend Anne, or if her bank accounts were being electronically monitored, so far nothing had happened in the short time since she'd used a credit card at the car rental agency. And if whoever was following—CIA operatives or Conor White and maybe this Patrice—they hadn't made themselves known either, at least that he was aware of. Still, he kept close watch on the rearview mirror.

"Okay. There's just the two of us, we have a car, and we're on our way," Anne said abruptly, the light banter of before gone. "Where the hell are we going?"

Marten knew he had stalled as long as he could. "Rental agent give you a map?"

"Yes."

"Open it and look for Praia da Rocha. It's a beach town near Portimão."

"Praia da Rocha."

"You know it?"

"No."

"Neither do I."

9:35 A.M.

67

• Learjet 55, on approach to Faro International Airport. Airspeed 190 mph. Altitude 2,420 feet. Same time.

After thirty years of police work Hauptkommissar Emil Franck's connections across Europe ran deep. Some were legitimate, some criminal, others somewhere in between. Marten's Cessna had barely touched down at Faro when Franck learned about it from the Policia Judiciária at the airport, who quickly made several calls spreading the information. It worked like a charm.

A cousin of Judiciária police inspector Catarina Melo Tavares Santos was a desk employee of the Auto Europe branch in Faro's Montenegro district. Santos's physical description of Anne Tidrow fit perfectly with the woman who had rented a silver Opel Astra barely half an hour before. She'd had to wait fifteen minutes until her supervisor went on break before she could access the rental records and confirm the identity of the Opel's renter. At the same time, she noted the car's license number, then went outside, clicked on her cell phone, and spoke directly with her cousin. It was Inspector Santos who was on the phone with Hauptkommissar Franck now.

"New silver Opel Astra, four door, license number 93-AA-71," Santos said, *"rented in Montenegro at 8:57 A.M. by one Anne Tidrow of Houston, Texas. Marked down for an open-ended rental. Suggested time frame, twenty-four to forty-eight hours."*

"Destination?"

"None was given, sir."

"Obrigado, Inspector," he said. *"Obrigado."* Thank you.

Franck clicked off and looked at Kovalenko. "They are thirty minutes to an hour ahead of us," he said with a quiet confidence that bordered on condescension. "A car will be waiting when we touch down. I suggest whatever call you need to make, you do it now. Moscow must be waiting to hear from you."

"Yes, Hauptkommissar, they must be." Kovalenko's eyes zeroed in on Franck's. "Breathlessly."

9:43 A.M.

• **Portimão. 10:18 A.M.**
Marten turned the Opel south, circumventing the city. He'd judiciously watched the rearview mirror for most of the trip. If they were being followed there was still no sign of it. Nor had there been any close-in air traffic, helicopters or civilian aircraft, to suggest they were being watched from above. Satellite tracking was always a possibility via the car's GPS system, but satellite operators would have had to have been alerted, and that was something that took time and required several layers of authorization before it would be put into effect. The thing was, at this point, they seemed to be ahead of their pursuers, and so the complications almost didn't matter. He was too close to the end to do anything but go for it and hope everything worked out. Still, he knew he had to be ever cautious of Anne and remember how much was at stake all the way around. If he could wish for anything now it would be a gun, the more powerful the better.

• **10:20 A.M.**
The distance from Portimão to Praia da Rocha was short, two miles at best. They were traveling south under a high sun. Mist rolling in from the sea intensified the brightness and gave everything a dangerous

glare, making it hard to see without squinting. To their left was the wide estuary of the Rio Arade that flowed from the inland mountains to Portimão and from there into the Atlantic between Praia da Rocha on the western shore and Ferragudo on the eastern. They were almost there, and Marten felt his pulse rise in anticipation. All they had to do now was drive into the city and, with luck, locate Avenida Tomás Cabreira and then this Jacob Cádiz at a *livros usados*, which Marten had roughly translated as a used-book store.

• 10:32 A.M.

Avenida Tomás Cabreira turned out to be Praia da Rocha's main drag. It was jammed with hotels and shops and restaurants and overlooked jagged sea cliffs and a beach far below that was dotted with rows of bright umbrellas and an uncountable number of semidressed beachgoers.

• 10:50 A.M.

They had driven the avenue itself twice and now were doing it again. What they saw this time was what they had seen before. Traffic, tourists, the *Hotel da Rocha*, the *Hotel Jupiter*, restaurant *La Dolce Vita*, restaurant *A Portuguesa*, restaurant *Esplanada Oriental*, bars, outdoor cafés, curio shops, a bank, a pharmacy, and several bakeries. But no bookstores, new or used.

"Used books. You're sure?" Anne asked.

"That's what Theo Haas told me."

"No name for it."

"All he said was livros usados, Avenida Tomás Cabreira, and a man called Jacob Cadiz." Marten knew he couldn't expect to just show up and go right to the store. Still, it should have been easy enough to find on a main street like Tomás Cabreira. But clearly it wasn't here. So where was it? Closed? Moved to another location? Or had it never been here? Had Haas wholly distrusted him and sent him on a road to nowhere? If so, had he come all this way for nothing? Were the photographs still somewhere in Berlin?

"Christ," Marten swore under his breath. He glanced around. A group of teenagers waved cheerfully, no doubt tickled by what seemed to be lost tourists who were chugging down the street for the third time in less than ten minutes. The driver of a car behind them honked impatiently, then suddenly sped up, passed in traffic, and cut sharply in front of them. Still no used-book store. Marten looked at his watch: 10:55 A.M.

The longer it took to unravel the puzzle, the more important time itself became. Slowed as they were and with no goal in sight, they were giving whoever was following them every opportunity to find out where they had landed and then pick up their trail. If they were CIA they would have had assets on the ground to begin with. Assets who could easily tap into car rental agency records, find Anne's name and what make of car she had rented and its license number. Once they had that, finding them would relatively easy; then all they had to do was lie back and watch until they recovered the photos. Then what? If one of them happened to be Conór White, they could look to the same fate that had befallen Marita and her medical students in Spain. More than ever he wished he had a gun.

"Pull over," Anne said suddenly.

"Why?"

"Just pull over."

Marten did, sliding to a stop in a bus zone. Without a word she got out and approached two elderly men chatting outside a bar. They looked at her and then at each other, then back to her. The first man, plump, with a wrinkled hat and a dark suit with even more wrinkles, smiled. Then a finger came up and he pointed behind them and up a narrow alley. Anne grinned and nodded, then patted him gently on the cheek and came back to the car.

"The store is called 'Granada.' Up the alley in the back."

"How the hell did you do that?"

"You may remember I was in El Salvador, darling." She slid in next to him. "A little Spanish goes a long way in this world, even in Portugal. Besides, a good CIA op, retired or not, can sell almost anything to anyone. It's in their blood."

"What did you sell?"

"A smile . . . from a not so unattractive forty-two-year-old woman."

10:59 A.M.

68

Ten minutes earlier Sy Wirth had checked in, gone to his room, and immediately put in a call to Dimitri Korostin only to get the Russian's voice mail. It was the fourth call and voice mail response in the thirty-odd minutes since his Gulfstream had touched down at Faro International Airport. Each time he'd left word for Korostin to call him back immediately. So far he'd had no reply.

He called again. Once more he got the voice mail. This time he left no word, just clicked off. This was crazy. They'd been in contact ever since he'd left Berlin. Now, at the most crucial moment of all, there was nothing but silence.

Conor White's Falcon had landed, and he and the others were at the airport waiting for word and ready to go. But to where? Korostin's men should have long ago been on the ground. By now, theoretically at least, they would know where Marten was. But theoretically was just that, nothing. He couldn't send White after Marten if he didn't know where he had gone. And he couldn't know that without Korostin telling him. The whole thing was very nearly a replay of what had happened when Marten dodged them all at the airport in Málaga, disabling the hidden transmitter and flying off for parts unknown. Now he was on the ground somewhere here with all kinds of land routes open to him. If they'd lost him this time there was every chance he would recover the photographs and disappear into the countryside. Then what? Sit back and wait for the pictures to be made public?

Then, and maybe darker still, there was Korostin himself. He knew how important the pictures were. What if his people already had Marten? If they retrieved the photographs and looked at them out of sheer prurient interest expecting to see illicit sex, it wouldn't take long for them to realize what they really had, and Wirth would never know until it was too late. By then Korostin would have not only the pictures but also the Santa Cruz–Tarija gas field. Depending on what he did with the photos—turning them over to the Russian government would be the worst—he might very well lose the Bioko field as well.

He went into the bathroom and washed his hands and face, then stared at himself in the mirror. What had he done? The idea that Korostin might somehow double-cross him had never entered his mind. This was his own doing. His alone. Even his chief counsel, Arnold Moss, had no idea he'd made a deal with Korostin. Only Conor White knew someone else was involved, but he had no idea who it was.

Wirth cursed himself with every word he knew. Why he had so blindly trusted the Russian? Inviting him to secretly partake in the greatest triumph of his life had been insane. It was like taking a lover and trusting her with all kinds of intimate secrets only to have her destroy your marriage and family and afterward run off with the company.

Half panicked and full of rage, he went back into the other room and picked up the BlackBerry, determined to try Korostin again. No sooner was it in his hand than it rang.

"Yes," he snapped.

"Josiah, you call me every five minutes. You're giving me a headache. Where the hell are you?" Dimitri Korostin's voice rumbled through the receiver.

"Faro. Where the hell are your people?"

"There and gone."

"To where? Do they know where Marten is?"

"They have rented a car and left the city. That's all I know. When I have more I will tell you."

"That's not good enough."

"Josiah, it's all I have. Trust me."

"Trust you?"

"Yes, trust me." Korostin paused. *"I think maybe you are getting nervous again. Don't, there is no need."*

"The terms of our contract, Dimitri. I am to be there when the pictures are recovered. They are to be brought directly to me unopened."

"I think I was right about the pictures compromising you. Very personal, yes? You and a woman. Or several women. Or men? Doing what, Josiah? We're all human. We do things. We aren't perfect. What makes these photographs so special you can't live another hour without them?"

"That's my business."

"Josiah, you will be there when the pictures are recovered. They will be delivered to you right away. The terms of the contract. You have my word."

There was a click and Wirth's BlackBerry went dead.

• 11:15 A.M.

Sy Wirth sat at a corner table in the hotel's Santo Antonio restaurant staring blankly out over the harbor. The two BlackBerrys were on the table in front of him, the one with the blue tape closest. A waiter came and took his order—coffee and fresh fruit. Maybe he was being crazy. Maybe Dimitri had been right when he told him to calm down. There was a big payoff for him, so why would he double-cross Wirth, especially as he had promised during their meeting in London that the Santa Cruz–Tarija gas field could be the first of many deals they might work on together. Why would he do something stupid and jeopardize the future? Moreover, the photographs would have to be in some kind of package, meaning that he and his men might not even look at them. Just deliver them as promised. They would know what they were because Marten would have them in his possession.

So take it easy, he told himself. Calm down. So far everything they had plotted from Berlin to here, even with the delays, had worked. Now came the waiting game; it happened in almost every business transaction, and as anxiety-provoking as it was, it wasn't unreasonable.

He glanced at the blue-tape BlackBerry. Conor White was nearby and waiting. He could wait a few minutes longer.

Wirth picked up the other BlackBerry, hit the speed dial, and called Arnold Moss's personal cell phone. It was almost five twenty in the morning in Houston. Whether Moss was up or not made little difference. If things were going to come off as planned, at some point soon White would go into action, and Wirth needed to officially cover the state of affairs. It was something his general counsel would understand immediately and afterward dictate for transcription to be included in the Striker corporate record under MINUTES OF THE DAY.

"Good morning, Sy." Moss picked up at once. If he'd woken from sleep it wasn't evident. *"Where are you?"*

"Faro, Portugal."

"I thought you were headed to Barcelona."

"I was. Conor White called several hours ago telling me he was on his way here and asked me to meet him. I've only just arrived. He said it was urgent but didn't say why or what it was. From the sound of his voice I'd say it was more than urgent, it was critical. Frankly I'm hesitant to call him because I don't know what's going on. I'd rather have him come to me and explain it."

"You think Hadrian should be advised?"

"Probably. But again I don't know. Hadrian and SimCo have their own arrangements. If what's going on here has to do with Striker, I'm completely in the dark about it."

"Have you heard from him since you arrived?"

"No. Not yet."

"If he asked you to meet him the way he did, I'd say Hadrian should be advised right away. Let them get in the middle of it, or at the least advise us as to what's going on. Want me to call Loyal Truex?"

"No, I'll do it. He still with Joe Ryder in Iraq?"

"Yes."

"Go back to whatever you were doing, Arnie. I'll be in touch later."

"Good luck."

"Indeed."

Wirth clicked off just as his breakfast came.

"Will there be anything else, sir?" his waiter asked.

Wirth looked up. "Not just now, thank you."

"Yes, sir."

Wirth watched him go, then picked up the Black-Berry, looked at it, and set it back down. Loyal Truex was in Iraq. Wirth's story would be that he had tried to get through to him but couldn't get a connection and so would try again later. Meaning no call would be made to Truex until the photographs had been recovered and Nicholas Marten and Anne Tidrow were dead, with Conor White and his men in the custody of Portuguese authorities charged with their killing and the suspicion of their involvement in the Madrid farmhouse murders. All of it topped, as Wirth would put it to Truex, by the chilling sense that because White had asked him to meet him there and because of what had happened to Anne, he'd meant to kill him, too. That way, and quite clearly, Truex would have been informed of the extent of Conor White's derangement.

11:09 A.M.

69

• Praia Da Rocha, Livros Usados Granada. 11:12 A.M.

Bright and steamy hot outside, inside the Granada used-book store was dark and cool with classical music playing softly in the background. There were five small, interconnecting rooms, each with floor-to-ceiling shelves and large floor bins, all of them crammed to overflowing with thousands of used books in a dozen or more languages.

A thirty-something woman with short dark hair and wearing a light summer dress was behind the checkout counter as Anne and Marten came in. Beyond her Marten could count eight people scattered throughout the rooms, browsing, reading. If there were more he couldn't see them.

He casually slipped a *Livros Usados Granada* business card from a wooden holder near the door and was about to approach the woman at the checkout counter when a roly-poly man in thick glasses with a great mane of gray hair appeared from a back room. He was probably in his late fifties and wore a black short-sleeved polo shirt with LIVROS USADOS GRANADA stenciled in white over the left-hand breast pocket. Marten could see two worn volumes tucked under his arm as he passed from one room to the next coming toward them. When he reached the adjoining room, he stopped to converse with a slim blond woman in white jeans.

Anne nodded toward him. "Cádiz?" she mouthed.

"Maybe," Marten said quietly. "Watch the door," he warned, then went into the other room.

Entering, he looked around absently, then poked through some books in a center-of-the-room bin while the man and the blond woman carried on a conversation in Portuguese. Finally the woman decided she wanted neither book, thanked the man, who by now clearly appeared to be the proprietor, and promptly left. He watched her go, then turned to take the volumes back to wherever he had gotten them. As he did, Marten approached him. "Excuse me, do you speak English?"

The man turned back. "What is it you want to know?" he said quietly in what sounded like everyday American English.

"Are you Jacob Cádiz?"

"Why?" He looked at Marten carefully.

"A friend sent me to find him."

"Man or woman?"

"A man."

"My name is Stump Logan. Originally from Chicago. What do you want with Jacob Cádiz?"

"As I said, a friend—"

"Who?" Logan cut him off. "What's his name?"

"Does Cádiz work here?"

"What is your friend's name? Why did you come to my shop looking for Cádiz?"

Marten glanced at Anne, standing near the cashier in the outer room. Roly-poly and bespectacled or not, Stump Logan was no pushover. And he wasn't just a guy transplanted from the Windy City. His edge, the way he looked at you, gave him the feel of a rough-hewn social worker or maybe an old Chicago cop, or something in between. Whatever it was, Marten felt he had to take the chance and tell him the truth. He looked around and then back to Logan.

"My name is Nicholas Marten. Theo Haas gave me Cádiz's name and pointed me here to your store. I was with him in Berlin just before he was killed. The police think I did it, but I didn't. I knew his brother, too, Father Willy Dorhn. I met with him just a few days ago in Bioko. I was there when an army patrol killed him. Theo sent me here to find Jacob Cádiz. He said he would have something I might find useful. It has to do with the civil war in Equatorial Guinea."

Stump Logan stared at Marten for a long moment, reading him. Suddenly he nodded toward Anne. "She with you?"

"Yes."

"Get her and come with me."

Stump Logan's backroom office was as full of books as the rest of his shop—piled on shelves, on the floor, everywhere and anywhere there was room. Still he had managed to squeeze in an old steel desk and chair and two folding chairs in front of it. He ushered Marten and Anne toward them, studying one and then the other as they sat down.

"I knew Theo for thirty years," he said finally. "He wouldn't have told you to look up Cádiz on a lark. What he sent you to find I don't know." Logan reached for a notepad, scrawled an address on it, and gave it to Marten. "Number 517 Avenida João Paulo II. Follow it to the end, then look for an old wooden gate and a gravel drive down to the beach. That's Cádiz's house. He won't be there. How you get in is your business."

"Thank you, Mr. Logan. I mean it sincerely." Marten stood, and Anne got up with him. "If anybody comes, we were never here."

"Mr. Marten." Stump Logan peered through his thick glasses. "I knew Father Willy very well. I visited him in Bioko more than once. The two treasures of his life were his brother and the people he served in Equatorial Guinea."

"I saw that for myself. I understand," Marten said.

"So do I. Theo Haas did not send you here without reason."

11:25 A.M.

70

Wirth was back in his room and had just finished brushing his teeth when his BlackBerry sounded. Immediately he answered.

"Yes."

"*Praia da Rocha. Four-door silver Opel Astra, license number 93-AA-71,*" Korostin said tersely. "*By the time you reach it my people will have found Marten. By the terms of our agreement, Josiah, I will tell you where.*"

"Thank you." Wirth clicked off.

It was time to move.

He went into the bedroom and picked up the blue-tape Blackberry. Two calls would be made from it. The first would be to Conor White, letting him know where Marten had gone, giving him a description of the car, and telling him he would give him an exact location in Praia da Rocha when he had it. The second would be made once he knew White had reached Praia da Rocha. It would be a text message to an FBI informant in Spain arranged by his friend in the FBI's Houston bureau who had originated the transmission system for the blue-tape BlackBerry. The text would be a simple "OK." At that point the informant would call Spanish authorities, implicating

Conor White in the Madrid farmhouse murders and telling them he was armed and dangerous and thought to be in Praia da Rocha, Portugal.

Wirth glanced out the window at the swarm of pleasure boats plying the Sunday waters of Faro harbor, then lifted the blue-tape BlackBerry and punched in Conor White's number.

"Yes, Mr. Wirth," White's voice came back sharply.

"The city of Praia da Rocha. On the sea near Portimão. I'm on my way now."

"I need a location."

"I will have it by the time you get there."

"Yes, sir."

11:45 A.M.

• The House at 517 Avenida João Paulo II. 11:50 A.M.
They found it, as Stump Logan said, through an old wooden gate and down a gravel drive. Marten opened the gate by hand, drove the Opel through, then closed it behind them and started down the driveway.

They could see the house at the bottom. It was single story, made of stone and white stucco with a red tile roof, and was very nearly on the beach itself, no more than a hundred feet up from the high-water mark. Jagged sea cliffs that rose straight up from the sand surrounded most of it, giving a feel of isolation and extreme privacy. For all the bustle of the town's nearby beaches, there was nothing here but sea birds and slowly lapping waves.

Marten rolled the Opel to a stop at the end of the

driveway, and he and Anne got out. They studied the house for a moment, then looked around. There was no one in sight, either on the beach or up the driveway behind them.

"Let's do this fast," Marten said, and they moved toward the house. Sand had blown up in shallow drifts over the front walk, and a loose awning swung from its anchorage over a front window, seemingly torn free by the wind. Stump Logan had been right—whoever Jacob Cádiz was, he wasn't there and hadn't been for some time. Nor apparently had anyone else, at least since the wind had started moving the sand and awnings around.

Marten started toward the front door, then decided against it and led Anne around to the side of the house. Most of the windows had blinds that had been drawn against the sun, suggesting this was a vacation retreat of some kind and Cádiz had closed them when he left.

They were turning back for the front door when Marten noticed a small window that did not have a shade. Peering in, they saw a narrow hallway that looked as if it were an extension of the front entry-way. Partway down it was a small wooden drop-leaf table stacked high with mail, as if someone had deposited it there for Cádiz upon his return. A neighbor or caretaker perhaps.

Mail.

Suddenly Marten remembered what he'd thought during the flight out of Malabo—that the reason the army hadn't found the photos on Bioko was that Father Willy might have sent them to a safe haven somewhere off the island, perhaps in something a simple as the everyday mail.

"Front door," Marten said quickly. They went to it, and he rang the doorbell. No answer. He tried it again. Still nothing. Once more. Same result. He looked to Anne. "CIA give you training in breaking and entering?"

"Yes, but most of it I learned it on my own." Anne bent down and picked up a fist-sized rock. Quickly they went back to the window.

She looked at him. "Just hope to hell there's no alarm system."

"Darling, break the damn window."

Three sharp hits with the rock and the glass cracked. They stopped and listened. No alarm. Marten nodded at Anne, and she hit the glass again. Once more and there was a hole big enough for Marten to reach through and take out the remaining shards. Seconds later they climbed inside.

"Anyone here?" Marten's voice echoed through the room. There was no reply, and they moved toward the front hallway. To the left was a small study lined with bookshelves. It had a round desk with an ergonomic chair in the center. A desktop computer and printer sat to one side. Beyond that was a kitchen and eating room that faced the sea.

"Anyone here?" Marten called out again, and they went into the front hallway, stopping at the wooden table and the stack of mail overflowing it they'd seen from outside.

Most of it was bills, newspapers, magazines, and advertising circulars. By the postmarks the pieces seemed to have been deposited there off and on over the last four to five weeks.

Marten swore under his breath as he went through it quickly. "Nothing. Nothing at all."

He sifted through the rest, increasingly concerned that no matter what Stump Logan had said about Theo Haas having sent him to Cádiz for a reason, Haas had been playing him for a fool and their trip had been for nothing.

"Wait," Anne said abruptly. Several more pieces were on the floor, hidden by a leaf of the table. They were bigger, three boxes and four large envelopes. She sorted through them quickly. The bottom-most piece was a thick padded envelope addressed to Jacob Cádiz and postmarked from Riaba, Equatorial Guinea, sometime in late May. The exact date was hard to read.

"This, maybe!" she said with a rush and handed it to him.

Marten looked at the postmark. "Christ," he breathed and anxiously tore it open.

"Yes. Yes!" he all but shouted as he slid out a plastic-wrapped bundle of Father Willy's photographic prints, color computer copies like those the priest had shown him in the rain forest. There were twenty-six in all, and all of them the damning Bioko/SimCo stuff.

The first few were duplicates of pictures he had seen before: the helicopter set down in the jungle clearing with men in the doorway unloading crates of weapons to natives who in turn were loading them on an open-bed truck. Among the faces was a very familiar Caucasian in tight black T-shirt and camouflage fatigues.

"Recognize your friend Conor White?" Marten asked, then went to the next photo that showed two more Caucasians. They had buzz-cut hair, were wearing the same black T-shirts and camouflage gear, and were standing in the helicopter doorway.

"Patrice," Anne said, pointing to the man on the left. "The other's Jack Hanahan, a onetime Ranger in the Irish Army. Conor keeps him with him almost all the time. Calls him Irish Jack."

Marten stared at the picture, fixing the men's faces in his mind. "You knew who these people were, but you had no idea any of this was going on," he said quietly but with an edge that was clearly accusatory.

Anne reacted. Fiercely. "Of course I knew what was going on. The whole thing was my idea. I love to watch thousands of people kill each other. It beats the hell out of Texas football. You want to get more into it? Fine. We can fight about it later. Right now let's take this stuff and get the hell out of here."

Marten stared at her, waiting for her to give him some small clue that she *had* known what was going on, or at least to soften. She did neither.

"Alright," he said finally, "sorry."

"You better be."

"I am." Immediately he picked up the photographs and started to slide them back into the plastic wrapping. As he did, a white letter-sized envelope slid out. It had been folded over several times and sealed tight with an elastic band. He slipped off the band and unfolded it, then turned it upside-down. A small, thin rectangle dropped into his hand.

Anne and Marten looked at each other.

The camera's memory card.

"As I said, let's take this stuff and get the hell out of here." Anne started for the door.

"No," Marten said abruptly. "Father Willy didn't print every picture. I want to see what else there is."

"Now?"

"Yes, now."

"Why?"

"Because there's a computer in the other room and because there may not be a chance later. And because when we call Joe Ryder, I want one of us to be able to tell him what's on it."

"What do you mean—one of us?"

"In the event your Mr. White and his friends show up and one of us gets killed."

12:16 P.M.

* * *

71

• 12:17 P.M.

Marten sat down at the round desk in Cádiz's study and booted up the computer, then looked for a port to slip the card into.

"It's here," Anne said and slid an external card

port from behind several books near the CPU and set it on top of the tower.

Marten was about to load the memory card into it but found one already there. He started to slide it out. Anne stopped him.

"Let's see what's on it. There may be more. Something Father Willy sent earlier."

She moved in behind him. Marten clicked the photo icon, and images on the card came to life. On it was a series of everyday snapshots. The beach in front of the house, sea birds, the house itself, inside and out, and, as they moved on, a heady number of nude or nearly nude twenty-something women sunbathing on a beach, seemingly taken with a hidden camera.

"Jacob Cádiz has quite an eye." Marten grinned.

"Stop drooling, darling. There's a little bit of urgency here. Take that card out. Put the other one in."

Marten popped out the card, slid the other out of the white envelope, and loaded it into the port. In seconds they knew it was the card Father Willy's photos had been printed from. They hunched closer to the screen as Marten started to click through them. It was then they heard a car pull up on the gravel outside.

"Cádiz," Anne said.

"Or maybe a friend or housekeeper. Or—"

"Conor White wouldn't come up that way. Neither would the others."

Abruptly Marten shut down the computer, then put the memory card back in the envelope with the photographs. "Use the front door. Say we were looking for Cádiz and found it open and the window broken."

• 12:23 P.M.

The glare from the midday sun was blinding as they came out, and both squinted against it. The vehicle that had driven in was stopped behind theirs, a dark gray Peugeot sedan. Two people were visible in the front seat. Then the driver's door opened and a tall man stepped out, a Heckler & Koch compact submachine gun in his hand.

Hauptkommissar Emil Franck.

"Jesus God," Marten said and looked around expecting to see more police. He saw none. Then the passenger door opened and Marten let out a sharp breath as a slightly overweight, bearded, and very familiar figure stepped into the Portuguese sunshine.

"Good afternoon, tovarich. It's been a long time."

"Yes, it has," Marten said in astonishment.

"Who is he?" Anne asked quickly.

Marten kept his eyes on both men. "Yuri Kovalenko. An old friend from Moscow." What the hell was going on? What did Kovalenko have to do with this? "Why are you here?" he said. "What do you want?"

"I think you should ask the Hauptkommissar."

Emil Franck answered before Marten had the chance. "The photographs."

"What photographs?"

"Those, in the package under your arm. The postmaster confirmed that he personally delivered mail to the house on a regular basis. Among the pieces was a large envelope sent from Equatorial Guinea, which he remembered because of the stamps." Franck smiled forcefully. "He often did personal favors for Jacob Cádiz. He liked him."

If Marten was wary before, he was more so now. "Why are there no other police?"

"They know I prefer to work alone. It makes less noise."

"Then why him?" Marten indicated Kovalenko, then looked back to Franck. "Who else does the Hauptkommissar work for? Mother Russia? Hadrian? SimCo? Or is it Striker Oil?"

"The photographs, please." Franck lifted the Heckler & Koch and started toward them.

"The Hauptkommissar and I met in Berlin." Kovalenko started forward as well. "Later we had a dialogue with an old friend of Ms. Tidrow. You seem to have found our transmitter. By shutting it down you succeeded in helping to throw off the others following you. There are others, you know. They may well be on their way here now." Kovalenko's eyes went to Franck and then back to Marten. He kept moving, slowly, carefully, keeping pace with the German.

"Your photographs seem to be quite a popular attraction. The reason why we are here so soon and the others are not is that the Hauptkommissar is highly respected inside the European Union, especially where the police are concerned. We knew you were on approach to Faro quite some time before you landed. We knew you had rented a car in the city. What make, what color, its registration number." Again Kovalenko looked to Franck, then back to Marten. "You shouldn't have driven so many times along Avenida Tomás Cabreira or parked your car where you did. The local police are very good at following up on things. They told us where you went. The postmaster helped with the rest."

Suddenly Anne understood why there were no police. "Nicholas," she said, "the Hauptkommissar is CIA."

Kovalenko half-smiled. "Is that true, Emil? You have another employer?"

"Only those you know." Abruptly Franck twisted the submachine gun toward Anne. "Please step away from Mr. Marten."

Marten started to move between Anne and the German.

"Don't, tovarich," Kovalenko warned. Suddenly he was sliding a Glock automatic from his waistband.

Marten froze where he was.

"The photographs, please." Franck was right in front of him, the machine gun leveled at his chest. "You are wanted for the murder of Theo Haas. You were found here and refused to surrender. No one will be surprised that you were shot because of it."

"Give him the pictures, tovarich," Kovalenko said quietly. "Do it."

Franck saw the Russian suddenly step behind him. In a millisecond everything that had happened since they'd met in Berlin flashed across his mind in a hellish collage. Kovalenko's every move, every gesture, even his attitude had been choreographed to perfection: the arrogance, the measured antagonism, the egotism and competitiveness that seemingly came with the job; the constant references to, and deferral to, Moscow; the fear of reprisal, his personal conceit. All were in character and were expected and put him off guard. They knew he was a double agent and probably had for decades, even before the Berlin Wall came down.

A split second later the Glock in Kovalenko's hand came to a rest behind his ear. The steel felt cold. He wanted to do something, but it was too late. *Until our true fate catches up and then—that's that.* He thought of his wife and children. Prayed they would be alright without him. Then he heard a *pop* and there was a flash of searing white light.

The body of Hauptkommissar Franck dropped to the ground as if some terrible force of gravity had overwhelmed it. Marten and Anne jumped at the suddenness of it.

"Ms. Tidrow was quite correct, tovarich, the Hauptkommissar was CIA." Kovalenko kept the Glock in his hand. He was calm, wholly matter-of-fact, as if nothing out of the ordinary had happened. His tone and his manner were the same as they had been years before when he'd done very nearly the same thing from point-blank range and in front of Marten in St. Petersburg, Russia.

Immediately he retrieved Franck's machine gun, loosened its strap, and threw it over his shoulder. Done, he looked to Marten.

"If you would help me please, tovarich." He

twisted the Glock toward Franck's body. "I'm afraid you will have to carry him yourself."

Marten stared at him, then handed Anne the photographs, picked up Franck's body, and carried it toward the Peugeot.

Kovalenko opened the trunk, and Marten laid Franck inside. He looked at him just as Kovalenko closed the lid. The once fearsome über-cop with the shaved head, leather jacket, and immense reputation was now stone dead with half of his skull blown away. A mutilated corpse, nothing else. Murdered where he had stood. How many times had he seen that as a homicide investigator in L.A.? Someone who had been alive one minute was lifeless the next. Yet this was different. Franck had not been killed at random, or because he was a gang member, or for money or drugs or over a woman, but for something much larger. The same something Father Willy and Marita and her students and God only knew how many hundreds or thousands of Equatorial Guineans had been killed for. Maybe Theo Haas, too, but he still wasn't sure about that. The trouble was, he had no idea what that something was.

Oil?

Maybe.

At the moment it was the god of everyone on the planet. But something didn't fit. SimCo was arming the rebels, not trying to protect Striker's workers from them.

"The photographs, tovarich." Kovalenko turned the Glock automatic toward Anne and the envelope in her hands. "Any number of interested parties thought he might have mailed them. They were right. Let's get out of this sun and see what they are."

Marten looked at him and then at the Glock. "After all this time you need that with me?"

Kovalenko smiled. "For now, tovarich, I think it is best."

12:35 P.M.

72

Ninety seconds later they were inside the house, the front door closed, standing in the hallway. Franck's submachine gun was slung over Kovalenko's shoulder, the Glock still in his hand. Anne and Marten stood in front of him, the envelope open, the photos spread out on the wooden table. Marten turned them over one by one.

"Him," Kovalenko said suddenly and pointed a finger at a photo of Conor White. "This man is Conor White."

"I know," Marten said.

"He's one of those following you."

"As I suspected."

"You know him, then?"

"I met him in passing." Marten glanced at Anne.

"Be very careful, tovarich. He is a highly decorated former British combat officer with a great deal to lose personally if these"—he touched the stack of photos—"are made public."

"I know that, too."

Anne was staring at Kovalenko. "Who else is following us?"

"Two of his fighters." Kovalenko reached out a finger and pushed aside the photos until he found the one he wanted, the one showing Patrice and Irish Jack in a helicopter doorway. "These."

Anne exchanged glances with Marten, then looked back to Kovalenko. He wasn't telling her everything. "You said 'others.' Who are they? Your people? Who and how many?"

"As far as I know, only one, Ms. Tidrow. The head of your own company."

"Sy Wirth?"

Kovalenko nodded. "He is, or at least was, traveling separately and feeding information about your position to White and his men. Where any of them are now I don't know."

"Where did Wirth get this timely information he was passing on?" Marten said, then deliberately looked at Anne.

"Don't even think it," she snapped. "I haven't talked to him since we were in Malabo." She nodded at Kovalenko. "Why don't you ask him how he knows all this."

Kovalenko smiled easily. "Moscow."

There was no smile from Marten. "I should be surprised, but I'm not. I suppose Moscow knew about Jacob Cádiz, too."

"It took a little time, but yes."

"Why would Father Willy send the photographs to him and not his brother? Was he that close a friend?"

Kovalenko cocked his head and grinned. "You honestly don't know."

"Know what?"

Kovalenko's free hand swept around, indicating the house. "This is the place Theo Haas came to work and get out of the Berlin cold and the public spotlight of a Nobel laureate. He didn't want people coming around bothering him, so he used the name Jacob Cádiz. He spoke Portuguese well; few people knew." Abruptly his expression changed. He put the photos aside and picked up the folded white envelope with the camera's digital memory card inside. "What is this?"

Marten didn't answer.

Kovalenko unfolded it and slid out the card. "Ah," he said, smiling, "the cake's frosting." Suddenly his eyes found Marten's. "You've looked at its contents."

"Some, not all."

"Where is the computer you were using to view it?"

"In the other room," Marten said quietly, still trying to understand what Kovalenko was doing here and why Moscow was involved.

"I was assigned before I knew you were in the middle of it," Kovalenko said as if he had read Marten's thoughts. "Moscow has been watching the developments in Equatorial Guinea closely. She is always intrigued when a Western oil company shows undue interest in an area and begins building up its operation there, especially in West Africa, where there are potentially large untapped reserves. If something should prove of value it would be strategically unfortunate if other countries, especially the Chinese, got to bid on it first. I'm sure you can appreciate that kind of thinking. It's merely good business."

"So one would think."

73

• 12:54 P.M.

Marten glanced at Kovalenko, then powered up Jacob Cádiz's computer and slid the memory card into its port. Anne was in a chair to his right. Kovalenko sat on a stool to one side and behind them, the Glock in his hand, Franck's Heckler & Koch machine gun still dangling from his shoulder.

"Let's see what we have, tovarich," he said as the screen came to life. Marten touched the mouse, and a photograph popped up on the monitor. It had been taken with a long lens and apparently from a hidden vantage point in the brush. It was a portrait of a bizarre picnic in the jungle. Six white wicker chairs were pulled up to a long table covered with a white linen cloth, two on either side, one at either end. Fine china, silverware, and expensive wineglasses sat atop the table. White-gloved soldiers in the dress uniform of the Army of Equatorial Guinea stood by as waiters. Another of them carved a huge roast on a serving table nearby. Two more, in full dress and seemingly of high rank, were seated along one side of the linen-covered table. Opposite them were Conor White's lieutenants, Patrice and Irish Jack, dressed in their trademark tight black T-shirts and camouflage pants. Several more SimCo mercenaries stood in the background, their muscular arms crossed over their chests. All had buzz cuts and wore wraparound sunglasses and had automatic pistols strapped to their thighs.

Conor White himself wore a tailored white suit with an open-collared starched white shirt and sat at one end of the table. Another man sat at the far end, his back to the camera.

"Go to the next," Kovalenko said.

Marten touched the mouse, and the next photo came up. In it the other man was revealed. He was older, had jet black eyes, and wore the dress uniform of an Equatorial Guinean army general.

"Mariano," Marten said, surprised.

"Generalissimo Mariano Vargas Fuente. You know him?" Kovalenko marveled.

"I had the pleasure of being interrogated by a unit of the Equatorial Guinean army. He sat in on the party."

"You were lucky not to be butchered on the spot. He's Chilean. Was once an officer in the Directorate of National Intelligence under Augusto Pinochet. He was personally responsible for the death squads and the unspeakable horrors they committed. Thousands of people vanished under his watch, and then he suddenly—"

"Disappeared into the jungles of Central America," Marten finished for him. "Or so I was told. How did he get to Equatorial Guinea and when?"

"He was living under an assumed name in southern Spain. That was until your friend Conor White recruited him for the Equatorial Guinean army."

"White?"

"Yes, but secretly. President Tiombe thinks he did it alone. Sought out Mariano and paid him a fortune to run the E.G. counterinsurgency."

"Why?" Marten was mystified.

"For Mr. Tiombe to demonstrate to the people that this is how he handles troublemakers."

"He doesn't know White set it up?"

"Probably not."

Marten looked sharply to Anne. "Did Striker Oil order White to arrange the Mariano contract?"

"I don't know. Maybe it was Sy Wirth's doing with Loyal Truex pulling strings. Maybe White did it for his own reasons. However it happened, I had no knowledge of it."

"There seems to be a lot you don't know about your own company."

"That's why I'm here with you, darling, to find out." Anne's stare could have split Marten down the middle.

"Tovarich," Kovalenko said, mildly amused at their spat. "It makes no difference who ordered it. The thinking behind it was tactical. Fire up the insurgency through the army's brutal repression of it. Slaughter or terrify anything that moves, and do it theatrically. Men, women, children, the elderly, even animals. Burn them alive if you can. It brings the rebels together with astonishing fervor. Word of it would give the insurgents sympathy from the outside. If the world were to—"

"Burn them alive?" Marten cut him off sharply. "You've seen the CIA briefing video."

"True." Kovalenko nodded. "Hauptkommissar Franck worked both sides of the fence at the same time, for us and for the CIA. We knew, of course. So while he watched us, we watched him. The minute he learned that the priest killed in Equatorial Guinea was Theo Haas's brother, he requested the video briefings and began viewing them. The transmissions were simple enough for us to intercept and copy. I must tell you in all candor that we, too, were appalled by what we saw and what General Mariano was able to carry out so efficiently. Yes, we could leak the video, but who knows if blogs or other Internet aficionados don't already have it in hand? So why not let one of them take credit and keep us out of it. Besides, even if the video is never released, Tiombe's reign is nearly ended. Abba's rebel forces are too strong and impassioned for him to survive."

Marten stared at Kovalenko. What the hell was so important in Equatorial Guinea that it would make White recruit someone like General Mariano and at the same time draw the attention of both the CIA and Russian intelligence, or whoever Kovalenko was working for—which was something he had never been able to find out, not even years before when their lives had been so profoundly intertwined.

Oil, as he had thought earlier?

Maybe. But oil was being found almost every-where in West Africa, so that in itself it didn't seem enough to warrant attention like this. There had to be something more. Something else.

"You are puzzled, tovarich," Kovalenko said. "You would like some explanation as to what all this is centered on."

"Yes."

Kovalenko gestured with the Glock. "I think Ms. Tidrow might enlighten you. In this case I would believe what she tells you." He looked at Anne and smiled gently. "It's alright, you can tell him. We know."

Anne's eyes locked on Kovalenko's. There was no doubt at all that he did know and that Moscow knew, so there was no point in keeping it from Marten, not now.

"In that case, I will," she said and turned to him. "A little more than a year ago Striker engineers dis-covered a massive oil reserve beneath the one we were already drilling. It's huge, probably fifty times bigger than the entire Saudi field, comparable in size to the North American Great Lakes, with a re-fining capacity of more than six million barrels a day, or roughly four times that of the Saudis. It's large enough to supply oil to three-quarters of the world for the next century.

"As soon as the find was confirmed, Sy Wirth called a meeting at Striker's Houston headquar-ters. Loyal Truex was there representing Hadrian as Striker's top security contractor. So was I and a handful of others, including Arnold Moss, our chief counsel. The general consensus was that the find was worth billions, if not trillions. But there was something else—it could be an enormously strategic energy supply for the United States, freeing us from any reliance at all on OPEC. Truex warned that it wouldn't be long before the CIA learned about it and did something to bring their protective influence to bear." Anne glanced at Kovalenko as if to say, *I'm sure you know what I'm talking about.* Immediately she looked back to Marten.

"He meant it was important for us to take the first step and get them on board right away. Sy didn't like it at all. He wanted no part of government interference on any level and said it was Truex's job, not the CIA's, to guard the find. The meeting ended on that note. As chairman and CEO of a closely held company like Striker he all but controls the board of directors and whatever else happens in the company. So if he wanted the find kept inside the company, it would have been. But now it seems clear the CIA was made aware of it anyway, maybe by Sy himself at some point, or Truex, I don't know. Who did it and when doesn't make any difference. The fact is the Agency is apparently doing everything it can to take command of the situation, including the retrieval of the photographs." Again Anne looked at Kovalenko. "How Moscow found out, I don't know either."

Marten was dumbstruck. So it *was* oil, an ocean of it.

"That's why no operatives from the Equatorial Guinean army followed me from Malabo," he mused out loud. "They were under Mariano's control and on the same side as SimCo, so they let Conor White do it instead." Suddenly he pushed back from the computer console and stood up.

His eyes went from Anne to Kovalenko, and then he looked away, trying to put it all together, to shape it into some coherent whole. Finally he stood and crossed the room to stand with his back to them.

"Tiombe controlled everything for years. Took the profits from the pumped crude and built riches for himself and his family while letting the people wallow in poverty. Finally they got angry and started to make demands on the government with Abba as their leader. Tiombe didn't like it and sent his troops in and the war began. Then Striker, already with leases in the area, had this massive find." Abruptly he turned to face them.

"Why risk losing it to Tiombe, who might cancel the leases and throw them out of the country while he worked on a better deal with some bigger player?" Deliberately he looked to Kovalenko. "Maybe a country like China instead of a midlevel American oil company. Better to have the CIA in your pocket and help Abba. Send in Conor White and his mercenaries with armaments; become his friend and ally while at the same time secretly setting up Mariano on the other side to brutalize the army's response, thereby firing up the rebels even more and bringing in hundreds more fighters."

Marten came back across the room. His voice and manner, cold and cynical. "In two months or three or four, Tiombe is gone and Abba is in place, highly beholden to both SimCo and AG Striker. At White's suggestion, and Abba's agreement, the army will be dissolved, replaced by SimCo mercenaries, who will begin to mold Abba's ragged fighters into a national police force. Another couple of months and the people start to share in the oil wealth so long denied them. A little of it, anyway, but much more than they ever would have had under Tiombe. Clean water starts to flow. New roads, hospitals, decent housing, and schools are announced. A few months later construction begins. Then the big find is revealed, with the geologic details provided for authentication. Once that happens the shock wave will be enormous, politically, economically, and emotionally, as the West, especially, breathes a collective sigh of relief. Right?"

Kovalenko nodded. "And no outsider can touch it—not BP, not Shell, not Exxon/Mobil, not Russia, not China, not anyone—because Equatorial Guinea is a sovereign nation and because no one can compete with the power that much oil will bring. Overnight, tiny, poverty-stricken Equatorial Guinea will become the paradigm for a modern, peaceful, very successful third world country.

"The catch is that no matter what the public perceives, in essence, the country, its leaders, its army, its grateful population, and its biblical sea of petroleum will be owned not by its inhabitants but by Striker Oil, and will continue to be owned by it for the next hundred or more years."

Marten looked to Anne. "Is that what your father had in mind for the company's future? Fiscal growth through slaughter. Expansion by flamethrower."

Anne's eyes, her entire being, suddenly turned to fire. "You son-of-a-bitch bastard," she hissed.

"I simply asked you a question."

"No," she snapped. "It's not what my father had in mind!"

"The world changes, tovarich," Kovalenko interrupted, "and not always for the better." Immediately he stood up. "Time is short and I must leave. You have come a long and perilous way for the photographs, and so you may have them. I will take the memory card." Again he gestured with the Glock. "Would you please remove it from the computer and hand it to me?"

Marten looked at the gun. "If that's what you want, that's what you get," he said flatly, then went to Jacob Cádiz's desk, leaned in, and popped the memory card from the external port that rested on top of the CPU unit. He glanced at Anne, then looked at Kovalenko.

"Maybe you'd like it better if I put it in the envelope it came in." Marten's tone was acidic, even sardonic. "Make it neat and tidy and easy to carry so you won't lose it."

"Thank you, tovarich. You are most considerate."

Marten shuffled through the pile of photographs, found the letter-sized envelope the memory card had been in, and dropped the card into it. Folding it, he snapped an elastic band around it and handed it to the Russian. "Sealed with a kiss," he said.

Kovalenko smiled broadly and stuffed it into his pocket. "As always, it was good to see you, tovarich. Though too many years have passed. Your dear sister, Rebecca, is well and still in Switzerland?"

"Yes."

"Give her my regards. Perhaps one day we will all holiday together."

With a nod at Anne, Kovalenko started for the door.

"One more thing, tovarich," Marten called after him. "Why did you kill the Hauptkommissar when you could have strung him along for years longer?" Kovalenko turned back, the Glock still in his hand. "You had an unknowing mole in both the CIA and the Berlin police," Marten said. "He would have continued to be of immense value."

"Once we had the photographs he was to kill you and Ms. Tidrow," Kovalenko said quietly. "It was his assignment. It would have been bad manners for me to let that happen. Don't you agree?"

Abruptly he slid the Glock into his belt, then took Franck's Heckler & Koch machine gun from his shoulder and leveled it at them. Marten's eyes went to it; so did Anne's.

"So you do it, instead of him," Marten said coldly. "Then everyone's out of the picture."

"After all we have been through together, tovarich? You embarrass me with your distrust." The roundish, bearded Russian gave a great teddy bear grin. "What I think is that you will have trouble still. Especially from this Conor White. More so now that the photographs are in your possession." Immediately his free hand went to his belt. He lifted the Glock from it and tossed it to Marten, then slid an ammunition clip from his jacket pocket and flipped it to him as well. "Fifteen-round magazine. A simi-

lar magazine is in the pistol, except that one round
has been used. It means you have twenty-nine shots
left." He paused and let his eyes go to Anne; then
they came back to Marten. "Your rental car—four-
door silver Opel Astra, license plate number 93-AA-
71. The Portuguese police have that information."

"As the late Hauptkommissar said."

"They will not be watching now because he had
called them off. But be very careful where you go
next, tovarich." Kovalenko let the slightest grin escape. "I trust we remain the best of friends and that
you will not use my own weapon against me. If you
did you would then have two bodies to explain." He
nodded at Anne, then, just like that, turned for the
door and was gone.

They watched through the window as he walked
up the gravel driveway to the Peugeot with Franck's
body in the trunk. A moment later he got in, started
the engine, and drove off.

Marten waited until he disappeared from view at
the top of the driveway, half expecting a phalanx of
police to suddenly materialize and start down toward them. It didn't happen. Most likely because
Franck, as Kovalenko had said, had called them off.
He gave it another thirty seconds, then went down
the hallway and began gathering the photographs.

Anne was watching the driveway. "Conor and his
men won't be far behind."

"White's not our only concern." Marten slipped
the pictures into the plastic wrapping and then into

the envelope. "Kovalenko's got to leave the car some-where. Once Franck's body is found, every cop in Europe will be looking for us thinking we killed him. And there won't be a lot of confusion about where to start. Right here."

1:21 P.M.

74

• Still Praia Da Rocha, the Santa Catarina Fortress. Same time.

The old fort was at the eastern end of Avenida Tomás Cabreira and on the banks of the Rio Arade near its mouth, where it emptied into the sea. It had been constructed in 1621 to defend the cities of Silves and Portimão from Moors and Spanish pirates. Now it was little more than a tourist attraction, a series of ancient stone buildings and a small chapel devoted to St. Catherine of Alexandria, its terrace giving sweeping views of the Atlantic, the river, and Praia da Rocha's beaches and sandstone cliffs. It also was a place for Josiah Wirth and Conor White to meet while they tried to put together what went wrong and if there was yet a way to do something about it.

Some fifty yards distant, Patrice and Irish Jack sat in a black Toyota Land Cruiser in the fortress's parking lot watching them. They could see Wirth pacing back and forth on the terrace talking vigorously into his BlackBerry while White stood patiently nearby, the bright sunshine reflecting like a shimmering wall off the sea behind them.

Irish Jack lifted a pair of binoculars and pointed them in their direction. Immediately both men came into close focus. A second later, Wirth clicked off the BlackBerry and stared off in disgust.

"Maybe your friend has nothing to report, Mr. Wirth, and that is the reason he hasn't been in contact." Conor White was deliberately composed and accommodating, desperately trying to remain civil to a man he wholly detested. "Maybe his people were on top of Marten and he sidestepped them, like he did all of us in Málaga. Maybe he's still somewhere here in Praia da Rocha. Try your friend again. He might be in a dead zone, or something's wrong with his cell. Maybe by now he has it working and knows something."

"He isn't in a dead zone for more than an hour. There's nothing wrong with his cell, either. He's not taking my calls because he doesn't want to."

"Then something went wrong with Anne and Marten."

"Nothing went wrong," Wirth spat angrily, then lifted the BlackBerry again and walked off to stare out at the Atlantic where a dozen or more sailboats were passing by in some sort of regatta.

White could see him punch in a number, then wait

while it rang through. Seconds later he clicked off, then clicked on again and apparently tried another number.

What happened between the time Wirth had given them Praia da Rocha as Marten's destination and the time they arrived to take care of him, there was no way to know. But at this stage Wirth was clearly in a state of what White called controlled emotional upheaval. Not much different from the behavior he'd observed over the few months he'd known him. Yet his emotional state now was the worst he'd seen and the cracks were beginning to show. Clearly he felt he'd been double-crossed, cut out of the picture at the last moment. Not only was he outraged that it had happened, he didn't know what the hell to do about it.

Before, when they'd been close on Marten's tail, when they'd finally learned where he'd landed and then gone, there had been every expectation that they would soon recover the photographs and their fears would come to an end. Seemingly that was no longer the case. If whoever this third party was that Wirth had engaged to track Marten down had intercepted him along the way and retrieved the photos, he/she/they would have known something of what was in them from the beginning. Meaning they had planned all along to recover them for their own purposes. Meaning, too, that White's long-held fear that the Striker chairman had gotten in far over his head had suddenly become a horrendous reality. If he'd hated Josiah Wirth before, he hated him more now than anyone he'd ever met. And that included his father.

"Conor," Wirth called sharply, then turned and came excitedly toward him. "An envelope has been sent to my hotel in Faro."

"The photographs?" White felt a jolt of impossible hope, as if some wild ray of good fortune had suddenly and unbelievably shined down from above. Maybe there was a chance yet. Maybe he had been wrong. Maybe Wirth wasn't the fool he thought.

"All I was told was that an envelope was being messengered to the hotel." Wirth started for the parking lot and the black Land Cruiser. "We won't know what's in it until we get there."

• 1:42 P.M.

75

• Livros Usados Granada. 1:47 P.M.

Stump Logan was behind the checkout counter as they came in. They were hot and sweaty and looking as if they had just walked a considerable distance in the midday heat and done so quickly.

"I wonder if we might use your office for a few minutes," Marten said intensely, squinting a little as his eyes adjusted from the bright sun outside to the relative darkness of the store. Anne was just behind him.

"My office," Logan said flatly, peering through his thick glasses, first at Marten, then at Anne, and then back to Marten. Marten had a large padded envelope tucked under his arm. Something he hadn't seen on the couple's first visit.

"Actually I think Anne would like to use the rest-room first," Marten said. "That is, if you have one."

Logan studied him a moment longer, then looked at Anne. "All the way to the back and down a flight of stairs into the basement. It's not much, but it works."

"Thank you." Anne glanced at Marten and went off in the direction the book dealer had sent her.

Logan lifted the glasses and looked at Marten intently. "You're in trouble."

"More than a little. I'm afraid we need your help, and badly."

Just then a middle-aged couple came in and began to look over the books in the front of the store. "Why don't you see to them," Marten said quickly. "If it's alright, I'll wait in your office."

Logan nodded toward the back. "You know where it is."

"Thank you."

Marten walked off. Other than the couple who had just entered there were no other customers. The only employee he saw was the thirty-something woman with short dark hair and a light summer dress who'd been at the checkout counter when they'd come in the first time. She was on the far side of the room with her back to him, intent on rearranging a display of books.

It had all been planned. They'd left the rented Opel in a parking area near the beach, then walked

to the only refuge they knew, Logan's bookstore.
The whole way they'd looked for both the police
and Conor White, who they knew had to be closing
in on them in one way or another. The idea had
been to get to Logan's store as quickly as possible,
then get him alone, tell him as much of the story as
was necessary, and ask for his help. They were taking a chance, but there was nowhere else to go, and
he'd helped before. Now they were praying he'd do
it again, if for no other reason than his past relationship with Theo Haas and Father Willy. The idea of
sending Anne to the restroom had come to Marten
as they entered—give him a chance to work Logan
singly, man on man, before she came fully into the
picture. At least that was what he'd told her. What
he really wanted was to find a way to be alone for a
few minutes so that he could call President Harris
and tell him where he was and what had happened.
He hadn't been sure how he would do it, but then
the middle-aged couple had come in and the problem had been solved, at least for the moment.

Just ahead was the door to Logan's office. Marten
opened it and went in.

1:59 P.M.

• 8:59 A.M. in Camp David, Maryland.

President Harris had been sequestered in a small
study off his bedroom for the last two hours. Note
pad and pencil at his sleeve, he was taking yet another maddening pass, trying to cut fat from the pro-
posed new federal budget when the slate gray cell

phone on the table next to him rang. It startled him, and for a moment he did nothing; then it rang again. Immediately he realized what it was, and picked up.

"Where are you? What happened? Are you alright?" he spat emotionally, the words run together like a jet stream of consciousness.

"Praia da Rocha. The back office of a used-book store."

In ninety seconds Marten told him everything. Recovering the photographs. Striker's massive oil find in Bioko and Moscow's knowledge of it. That Anne was still with him. Kovalenko's arrival with Franck and subsequent killing of him. That Franck had been working for the CIA. His own fear that a huge police dragnet would be put out for him once Franck's body was found. Everything, that was, but the business about Kovalenko and the camera's memory card. That was something that could wait for later.

"What about Joe Ryder?" Marten asked at the end.

"He's left Iraq and is on his way to Rome and then Lisbon, where he'll meet you," the president said. "He'll be at the Four Seasons Ritz, but not until tomorrow morning at the earliest. He has a dinner tomorrow night with Lisbon's mayor. The whole thing has been played as a courtesy call on his way back to Washington. The mayor's wife and Ryder's support the same international charity, so it's a logical cover. It's a long way from Iraq to Portugal, so you should have more than enough time to get to Lisbon even if you have to slow it down. The question is, police or not, can you do it? Can you get there?"

"What about a safe house?"

"One has been set up for you in Lisbon, a small apartment in the old part of the city, the Bairro Alto"—Harris picked up a notebook from the table and opened it—"number seventeen Rua do Almada. Ask for a woman named Raisa Amaro. She lives in a flat on the first floor. She knows you're coming. It's not fancy, but it'll do until Ryder arrives. Go there and stay there. He'll know where you are and how to get in touch. So again, can you get there? If you don't think so, I'll try to arrange something else."

"We'll get there."

"Good. Call me the minute you're safe. I'll take the information you gave me and work on it. If the oil field is what you say it is, the find is hugely strategic. No matter what you think of them, Striker's done a great job of keeping it quiet. Still, the handling of the rest from here on in, your end to mine, has to be done with extreme caution. None of this can get out."

"Cousin," Marten warned, *"don't go near the CIA. Something is still very wrong."*

"The Lisbon station chief already knows Ryder's coming. But that's all he knows. Ryder will be under the protection of the State Department's Regional Security Office. The RSO will coordinate his movements, but they won't know about you or Ms. Tidrow. Joe Ryder's pretty resourceful. He'll find a way for you to meet him alone."

  "Thank you, my friend," Marten said quietly, gratefully.

  "You're the one to thank, cousin. Take damn good care of yourself. Good luck and Godspeed."

• 2:06 P.M.

Marten clicked off just as Logan's door opened. Anne came in, followed by Stump Logan.

  Anne looked at the cell phone in Marten's hand, then at Marten. "Are we disturbing something?"

  "An old girlfriend."

  "An old girlfriend? Right now, in the middle of all this?"

  "Well, yes . . ."

  "How old?"

  "Let's just say—from a long time ago."

  "And she still has your number?"

  "And how." Marten grinned a little, then slid the cell into his jacket. Abruptly the grin faded, and he looked to Logan. "Please close the door."

  He waited until Logan did, then looked at him directly. "A Berlin policeman followed me here investigating the murder of Theo Haas. He was killed at Cádiz's home by a man who was with him and who later drove off with the body in the trunk of his car. Once it's found the police will blanket this whole area, thinking I killed him. As I said earlier, all of this has to do with the civil war in Equatorial Guinea. Ms. Tidrow and I have a meeting tomorrow in Lisbon that hopefully will—"

  "We do?" Anne interrupted him in surprise. Her

look told him everything. She knew what the phone call had been about, that he had somehow arranged for them to meet with Joe Ryder in Lisbon. It was clear, too, that she realized she had little choice but to go through with her promise to meet him. At least for now.

"Yes, we do," he said emphatically. Immediately he turned back to Logan. "That meeting may well change the course of the war. But none of it will happen if the police have us in custody."

"You want me to help you get to Lisbon."

"Yes."

Logan glanced at Anne, then looked back to Marten. "Suppose you did kill the policeman. Theo Haas, too. Maybe even Father Willy. What if everything you've told me is a lie? I help you and the police find out, then what?"

"That's something you have to decide for yourself. Theo Haas put this whole thing in motion to begin with because he was concerned for his brother's safety and because of what he had uncovered in Bioko. He's the reason I went there to meet with Father Willy and why I came here looking for Jacob Cádiz. It's also the reason I was followed to his house by both the German policeman and the man who ended up killing him, a high-level Russian security operative. They were supposed to be on the same page but weren't." Marten pushed harder. "What I'm telling you is the truth. If it wasn't, Ms. Tidrow and I could just as easily have tried to get to Lisbon on our own. We came to you because you knew Theo Haas and Father Willy and what kind of men they were. You've lived here a long time, you know how things operate. We've got to get out before the police close in or we won't get out at all, and everything we've worked for, what Father Willy died for, will have been for nothing. Please, I'm begging you. Can you help us? Will you help us?"

Stump Logan took off his thick glasses and wiped his eyes, then put them back on. "It might be a grave error on my part, Mr. Marten," he said finally. "But yes, I will try to help you."

2:13 P.M.

76

• Faro, Hotel Largo. 2:30 P.M.

Sy Wirth and Conor White came in the front entrance and went straight to the front desk, leaving Patrice and Irish Jack to wait outside in the black Toyota SUV. At this point Wirth had wholly abandoned the idea of keeping his distance from White. Too much was at stake, emotionally and physically, if the package Korostin had promised contained the photos and the camera's memory card as he hoped—as the Russian had indicated when he'd so surprisingly and belatedly reached him as he stood with White at the Santa Catarina fortress in Praia da Rocha.

"You will find the terms of the contract have

THE HADRIAN MEMORANDUM [373]

been fulfilled, Josiah," he'd said with quiet assurance. "Everything is in a large envelope that is on its way by messenger to your hotel in Faro now. Things didn't quite work out as planned. I apologize. We'll do better the next time." That he'd clicked off with no mention of either Marten or Anne didn't matter. If the contract had been fully executed, the whole thing would be over anyway. What had happened to the others would be irrelevant. He would immediately destroy the photographs and the memory card, and they could all breathe a monstrous sigh of relief. Afterward White and his men would simply fly back to Malabo, and he would return to Houston.

"I'm Mr. Wirth, room 403. You have a package for me," he said to a tallish red-haired woman behind the front desk.

"Yes, sir." She turned and disappeared into a back room.

Wirth glanced at Conor White. Then the woman came back carrying a large padded envelope and handed it to him.

"How was it delivered?" he asked.

"I believe a taxi driver brought it, sir. I was at lunch at the time. I can check on it for you."

"No matter," he said and with a nod at White walked off toward the elevators.

Wirth pushed the button, the elevator door slid open, and he and White entered. Immediately he pushed the fourth-floor button and the door started to close. Suddenly it pulled back and a young couple entered. The man held the hand of a little boy. His wife, or at least the woman with him, was noticeably pregnant. Both smiled and nodded politely as they entered. Neither man responded.

They rode up in silence. Second floor. Third. The car stopped at the fourth, and they all got off. Wirth let them walk off down the corridor in front of them; then he and White followed. At room 403, Wirth stopped and slid his keycard through the slot in the door. A green light flashed, and the two men entered.

"Lock it," Wirth said and went anxiously to a writing desk near the window. The moment he reached it, he tore the envelope open and dumped its contents on the desk. "What the fuck?"

There were a dozen eight-by-ten photographs. Eleven were cheesecake photos of naked women in various pornographic poses. The twelfth was of Sy Wirth himself, the official corporate photograph of Striker's chairman standing alongside the company logo in the lobby of its Houston headquarters.

Apart from the photographs were two letter-sized envelopes. Enraged, Wirth ripped open the first and took out a small, thin rectangle, the size of a digital camera memory card. The trouble was, it was no memory card but a tourist trinket, a refrigerator magnet. Printed on the front in bright, happy red letters was the phrase FOND MEMORIES OF FARO, PORTUGAL.

"Fucking Russian cocksucker," Wirth breathed, his face as crimson as the letters on the magnet. Immediately he picked up the second envelope. Angrily he ripped it opened and looked inside. White could see the color drain from his face.

Slowly Wirth turned the envelope upside down

and a half-dozen or more torn pieces of paper fell onto the tabletop, landing among the cheesecake photographs, his official Striker portrait, and the Faro refrigerator magnet. White had no idea what it was. Sy Wirth had known instantly. It was what was left of the agreement for the massive Andean gas field, the Magellan/Santa Cruz–Tarija, he had given to Dimitri Korostin at the Dorchester Hotel in London in exchange for finding and returning the photographs and the memory card.

"What is it?" Conor White was staring at him.

Wirth's eyes came up to meet his. "I thought I was dealing with a friend. I wasn't."

"You said something about a Russian. What did you mean?"

Wirth glared at him. "I said nothing about a Russian. Nothing at all."

"Are the Russians involved?" This time White didn't hold back anything. "Is that what happened?"

Wirth didn't reply.

"Do they have the photographs?"

"I don't know."

Suddenly Conor White's vast experience and education—at Eton, Oxford, the Royal Military Academy Sandhurst, his long career as a frontline British combat officer and then a top-level professional mercenary soldier—came fully into play. Wirth's blundering had struck an immediate and terrifying chord, the stakes of which, even moments earlier, he could never have imagined.

"Mr. Wirth," he said emphatically, "I suggest you try to reach Anne and find out where she is. If she's with Marten, if she's not. Maybe she'll answer, maybe she won't. But if we can find out what happened, we may well learn something about the rest of it. In the meantime one of us needs to call Loyal Truex and tell him what the hell's going on. God help us if the Russians have the photographs, because if they do they will have all the evidence they need to prove what they may have already guessed about what Striker is doing in Bioko.

"We're talking about a massive amount of oil, Mr. Wirth. Massive. They will want it, all of it, if for no other reason than to keep it out the hands of the West. Once they start formulating a plan and communicating between themselves, the Chinese will find out. And they will want it, too. Either or both will create some kind of excuse for an armed intervention into the insurrection, basically to get hold of the country for themselves. They do that and it will be seen as a bona fide threat to U.S. national security, and Washington will have no choice but to try and stop them." White paused as a chilling apocalyptic anger raged through him. "You might have damn well planted the seeds for a major war, Mr. Wirth. Major."

3:08 P.M.

77

• 3:34 P.M.

Stump Logan turned the battered green-and-white
1978 Volkswagen bus onto the A2, the Auto-estrada
do Sul, and headed toward Lisbon, by now less than
a hundred miles to the north. Logan had reasoned
that it was best they get out of not only Praia da
Rocha but the whole Algarve region before Hauptkommissar Franck's body was found. Fortunately
it was Sunday afternoon, and hundreds of people
would be leaving the beach communities for the trip
back to the cities, Lisbon especially. So he left his
employees to watch the store, packed up everyone
pretty much on the spot, and joined the traffic exo-
dus heading north out of the Algarve.

"Packed up everyone" was an all-inclusive term.
By that Logan meant himself, Anne and Marten, and
his five dogs, which for all intents were his family.
Two sat in the shotgun seat next to him; a white Wes-
tie and a golden retriever/poodle mix. Behind him,
on the floor between Anne and Marten and the large
envelope Marten so carefully guarded, was Bruno,
a coal black 130-pound two-year-old Newfoundland
who affectionately rested his not so inconsiderable
head in Marten's lap. The last of the five were an aging Old English sheepdog called Bowler, who kept to
open space behind the seats where Anne and Marten
sat, and Leo, a young, frisky eighty-pound Bouvier
des Flandres, whose self-appointed duty seemed to be

a constant patrol between Anne and Marten and Bruno, and Bowler behind them.

• 3:40 P.M.

Anne heard her BlackBerry ring for the fourth time in the last half hour. The previous three had been from the same number—Sy Wirth's BlackBerry— and she simply hadn't answered. Each time she'd drawn a look from Marten, but he'd made no comment. The latest call was again from Wirth; this time it was a text message.

Anne. Sy. Very concerned about your safety. I've tried calling with no luck. Where are you? Are you alright? Extremely important I speak with you. Please get in touch immediately.

She looked at Marten and showed him the screen. "He's the one who called before. I didn't answer because I knew who it was. He's the last person I want a conversation with."

"But this time you clicked on."

"I knew it was text. I wanted to see what he said."

"Can he find you because of it?" Marten said.

"No. I switched off the GPS feature from the application settings before I left Paris. If I wanted them to know where I was, I wanted to be the one who told them."

"Do you know where Wirth is now?"

She shook her head. "I tried earlier, but it didn't work. So I imagine he did the same thing."

Just then Leo, the Bouvier, poked his head over Bruno's head, which was still parked in Marten's lap, and looked up at him, seemingly intent on knowing what was going on.

"Fellas, it's getting crowded. Go play somewhere else, huh?" Marten said and pushed both dogs away. As he did, he felt the press of the Glock automatic Kovalenko had given him, which he'd tucked into his waistband under his jacket before they left Cádiz's house. He glanced at Stump Logan at the wheel, then looked to Anne and lowered his voice. "Wirth will know we landed at Faro. By now he's getting desperate, wondering what happened after that. It's why he's trying to reach you, hoping you'll tip your hand. I think we have to assume White and this Patrice and probably the other fellow, Irish Jack, are with him."

"Police!" Stump Logan warned suddenly. Marten looked up to see the bookseller's eyes glued to the rearview mirror. Both he and Anne turned to look behind them and saw two helmeted, uniformed police on the motorcycles coming up fast.

"Relax and watch your speed," Marten said evenly, then turned to innocently ruffle Bruno's head, an everyday dog lover stroking man's best friend. Anne eased around, then looked over at Marten and smiled as if she were enjoying his interplay with the dog.

Seconds later the police were abreast of them, one on either side. The rider on the left glanced in as he rode. The rider on the right did the same. It went on that way for what seemed an eternity. Finally Marten looked over and nodded politely at the rider on the right. In the next instant and almost as one, they accelerated off to disappear in the flow of traffic ahead.

Logan looked in the mirror. "Lucky," he said, "very lucky." Then he clipped on the headset to an iPod he had next to him, tuned in to something, and drove on.

Anne and Marten exchanged glances but said nothing. The police might have sped off, but their sudden arrival and close scrutiny were deeply troubling. There was no way to know if Franck's body had been found and if the authorities were already looking for them, the motorcycle officers part of a much larger dragnet. Even if they weren't, it was only a matter of time before it happened. What made it worse, and Marten hadn't even thought about it until now, was that the Glock Kovalenko had given him was the weapon used to kill the Hauptkommissar. Not only did he have it on his person, with the lone fatal shot fired from the otherwise full magazine, his fingerprints were all over it.

And then there was Sy Wirth. Wherever he was when he had tried to reach Anne—surely Faro, maybe even Praia da Rocha—he was too close. That Conor White and his mercenaries would be with him exacerbated an already highly dangerous situation because of their reach and connections and deadly expertise. He had only to remember what had happened to Marita and her medical students outside of Madrid to remind him what kind of people they were.

What had President Harris said about the CIA

station chief in Lisbon? That he would know Joe Ryder was coming—

"But that's all he knows. Ryder will be under the protection of the State Department's regional security office, the RSO. They'll coordinate his movements, but they won't know about you or Ms. Tidrow."

Maybe not, unless White was CIA. If he was, it wouldn't take much for him to learn that Ryder had abruptly left Iraq and was on his way to Lisbon and to find out where he would be staying when he arrived and then realize why he was going there. If that happened, things would get a lot darker. And quickly.

Suddenly something large and black appeared in front of Marten and he was shoved back hard against his seat. The next instant brought a nauseating wave of hot doggie breath. Bruno had suddenly leapt up, throwing both forepaws against Marten's chest, knocking him backward and holding him there. Now his large, drooly face was inches from Marten's and he was staring at him with a look of deep sympathy, as if somehow he had sensed the fear and turmoil going on inside him and had determined to share his concern.

"Thanks, buddy, you're a real pal," Marten said gratefully, then lifted the Newfoundland's big paws and eased him back to the floor. Afterward, he patted him gently on the head. "If I was going home I'd ask Stump if I could take you with me. Unfortunately, I've got other things to do first."

3:48 P.M.

78

They came in on the A2 *Auto-estrada*, passing the towns of Palmela, Fernão Ferro, and then Almada on the southern bank of the Tagus River. Then, still in a crush of heavy traffic, they were across the towering 25th of April Bridge—an edifice that was a near replica of San Francisco's Golden Gate Bridge—and into the city, staying on the main highway, Avenida da Ponte.

Marten leaned forward to talk to Stump Logan. "We're looking for the Bairro Alto section. Rua do—"

Instantly Logan put up a hand for silence, then yanked off his iPod headset. "Don't," he said sharply, looking at Marten in the mirror. "I don't want to know, period. Area, street address, who you're meeting. Nothing at all." With that he slipped the headset back on and drove on in silence.

Four or five miles later he took an exit near the Zoological Gardens, then turned left and then right onto Rua Professor Lima Basto. Another twenty yards and he pulled to the curb and stopped.

"Down there and around the corner"—he pointed a finger at the windshield—"is Terminal Rodoviário de Lisboa, a central bus terminal where the motor coaches from the Algarve come in. Get out and walk to it; go in from the coach entrance and then out the front door. Nobody will stop you, unless by now the police have the German policeman's body and your faces are plastered all over. If they do, you're as good as dead anyway. But if they don't and somebody sees you and remembers you later, they'll think you came into the city by bus. The police come to me afterward and ask if I was in Lisbon, I'll tell them yes, I was, I had to pick up some books from a fellow used-book storekeeper—which I will do before I leave. Unless we had plain bad luck with those motorcycle cops, there'll be no way they can prove I drove you here. All I can tell them is that you were in my store looking for a Jacob Cádiz and that you came back later looking for my help in getting out of the city. To where, you didn't say. I told you there was nothing I could do. You left, and that was the last I saw of you."

"Sounds reasonable," Marten said.

"Good. Now, if you don't mind, I have some books to pick up before I head home."

They left it that way, with Anne and Marten on the street and Stump Logan and his dogs driving off in his thirty-odd-year-old VW bus, having wished them good luck and saying he was glad to have been of service.

Marten glanced around, then started them quickly down the sidewalk toward the bus terminal.

"This Bairro Alto section that you asked Logan about," Anne said. "You know where it is?"

"No, we're going to have to find it. Get a street map or something."

"What's there?"

"A safe house."

"Safe house?"

"Yes."

"And then tomorrow a meeting with Joe Ryder."

"Yes."

"The 'old girlfriend' you were on the phone with in Logan's office. She set it up."

Marten nodded.

"Who the hell is she that she can orchestrate all this?"

"Just a friend."

"No, not just a friend. Someone who can pull top-level strings, and quickly. Things like this don't just happen."

Marten glanced around again, watching the traffic, looking for police.

"Who are you really, Mr. Nicholas Marten? Who do you work for?"

"Fitzsimmons and Justice. Landscape architects. Manchester, England."

"That's not a good enough answer."

"For now it will have to do."

5:20 P.M.

79

• Four Seasons Hotel Ritz Lisbon,
Rua Rodrigo da Fonseca. Same time.

CIA Chief of Station (COS)/Lisbon Jeremy Moyer
worked Sundays when he had to, and this Sunday
was one of them. Four and a half hours earlier he'd
taken a call at home from Newhan Black, deputy
director of the CIA, asking him to go into the embassy and pull up a file on a case officer named
Fernando Coelho and when he had it to call him
back right away.

What it meant was "Go to the office immediately
and call me back over a secure line." Clearly whatever Black wanted to discuss on this summer Sunday afternoon—one o'clock in Lisbon, eight in the
morning at CIA headquarters in Langley, Virginia—
was urgent.

Twenty minutes later Moyer was in his private
office, door locked, secure phone in hand. When
they established contact Newhan Black's first words
were: "I'm not going to tell you everything that's going on, and it's probably better that you don't know.
But this is what I want done."

Now, at nearly five thirty in the afternoon, Moyer
sat at a small cocktail table in the Ritz Bar sipping a
Dubonnet on ice and chatting with forty-year-old
Debra Wynn. Wynn was chief of the U.S. State Department's Regional Security Office and, like Moyer,

based in the U.S. Embassy/Lisbon. She was responsible for coordinating all security for the embassy, visiting guests, and dignitaries. In this case they had a CODEL, a congressional delegation, in the person of Congressman Joe Ryder of New York, chairman of the House Oversight and Government Reform Committee, coming into the country.

"What I would like, Debra, is to go over the Ryder situation." Fifty-one-year-old Moyer fit well into the hotel's posh surroundings—neatly trimmed graying hair, navy blazer, pin-striped shirt open at the neck, khaki trousers, oxblood loafers—one embassy official having drinks with another at the hotel where an important U.S. politician was due to arrive the next day. "The congressman, coming here as he is, makes him a very high-profile target. That he's passing through on his way back from Iraq doesn't help. As you know, I would have preferred to have him stay at the embassy."

Wynn looked at Moyer directly. She was handsome and athletic, a twenty-year State Department veteran who'd come up through the ranks, as Moyer had. The difference was, her personality was far more guarded. While he drank Dubonnet, she chose iced tea. "The choice of where to stay was his," she said.

"I know. And it's why I came here, to look around for myself and to offer you some assistance."

"You think he needs it?"

Moyer took a sip of the Dubonnet and used the government-employee-speak of someone more senior in rank than the person being addressed. "I hate to think what the result would be if something happened."

In other words—what her career and life would look like if she had been offered CIA help in protecting Ryder and turned it down, and then, as Moyer said, something happened.

Wynn looked to the glass of iced tea on the cocktail table next to her, then picked it up and held it without drinking. "How many of your people should I expect?"

"One."

"One?"

"Sometimes in one man you get ten." Moyer smiled. "When are your people scheduled to secure the congressman's room?"

"Tomorrow morning at seven."

"My man will be there at six thirty. He is to be afforded freedom of movement. Your people will understand."

"You mean he won't be taking orders from us."

Moyer nodded.

Debra Wynn smiled courteously. "Does he have a name?"

"Carlos Branco. But he will use another name then."

"He's a local. Portuguese."

"Yes. You know him?"

"Just the name."

"He's been in the business for a long time. He knows the city and his way around it better than any of us, and the congressman will be visiting a number of venues before he has dinner with the mayor." Moyer took another sip of the Dubonnet, then set the glass down and stood to leave. "One last thing. Ryder is used to RSO security, so let him think my man is one of yours. There's no need to alarm him."

"Is there a need for alarm?"

"It's a precaution, nothing more."

Debra Wynn nodded; again came the courteous smile. "Then, thank you."

"We do what we can." Moyer nodded and walked off.

She watched him leave the bar area and go out into the lobby. His driver met him, and they left.

Moyer had said he'd come there to look around and to offer some assistance. Look around? He'd been stationed in Lisbon for more than three years. The Ritz was an international gathering spot, a place he'd been in and out of countless times. The assistance he was offering could as easily have been offered over the phone. The real truth was he'd come there to meet her in the venue where Joe Ryder would be staying for the purpose of gaining information. The "looking around" had been primarily into her eyes when he told her he wanted to place one of his operatives among hers. There had been no question that she would accept his offer, but he'd wanted to see if she knew more about Ryder's visit than she was telling. Clearly something was going on and the CIA was involved. Whatever it was, it would require a security clearance and pay scale far higher than hers. So what he'd seen in her eyes would have been what he expected. Nothing. Whatever Congressman Ryder's visit was really about, she didn't know. And didn't want to.

5:52 P.M.

80

• SimCo Falcon 50. 5:57 P.M.

Conor White looked at Patrice and Irish Jack in the seats across from him. They were calm and relaxed, patiently waiting for the plane to touch down and the next act to begin. White wasn't quite as comfortable or composed.

Abruptly he shifted his weight and looked out the window as the chartered jet began its descent into Lisbon, a city he'd been to a dozen times or more—but never in a situation like this, where his entire future rode on luck. He had no doubt whatsoever that soon, maybe within hours, the pictures would be made public and, in the hands of the Russians, in a most demonic way. Meaning that aside from the terrifying specter of a superpower showdown in Equatorial Guinea, what he had feared from the beginning would finally come to pass—that his career, and therefore his life, were essentially over. The blame he put fully on Sy Wirth and his stupid, colossal meddling. If it would have accomplished anything at all, he would have killed him right there in the Faro hotel room. But there had been no point because things were beyond the control of either of them. Instead he'd simply watched as Wirth, in what could best be described as a violent stupor, picked up one of two BlackBerrys on the room's writing desk and started to call Loyal Truex in Iraq to tell him what had happened. At the same time, the other BlackBerry sounded. Wirth looked at the one in his hand—one with a small piece of blue tape on the bottom—and, seeming to realize it was not the device he had intended to use, quickly put it in his pocket and answered the other. Truex had been on the line, excited and at the same time agitated. At that moment things began to happen, fast.

The first part was information, most of it coming from Truex.

Joe Ryder had suddenly been called away from a close inspection of the records division of Hadrian's central facility in Baghdad. Less than thirty minutes later his plane had taken off for Rome, the first leg of a hurried return trip to Washington. But Rome, Truex had learned, was not his final destination in Europe. Lisbon was. The purpose of his Lisbon visit? A courtesy call on Lisbon's mayor. It was bullshit. A man like Ryder, who'd gone all the way to Iraq for a hands-on inspection of the Striker and Hadrian operations there, accompanied by several members of his commission, an audit team, and their support staff, and who then suddenly abandoned everyone and everything to hurry back to Washington alone and for reasons unknown, does not stop to make a courtesy call on the mayor of

Lisbon. Clearly he was going to the Portuguese capital for some other and very specific reason. And since Marten and Anne had been in Portugal that day, it was more than reasonable to presume that the three were planning to meet somewhere there. That same logic taken a step further, especially in light of the haste of Ryder's departure from Baghdad, suggested that it was possible, even probable, that they had somehow snatched the photographs from under the Russian noses and were readying to turn them over to Ryder. It was equally probable that Anne— almost certainly to avoid prosecution—had agreed to brief Ryder on the Striker/Hadrian/SimCo arrangement in Equatorial Guinea and the Striker/Hadrian dealings in Iraq. Either or both reasons made it a meeting neither Striker nor Hadrian could afford to have take place.

For Conor White it was a defining moment. For the second time in hours he'd been given a massive injection of hope that the photographs might still be retrievable. With it came the feeling that maybe his torment would, at long last, be over and that finally everything would be alright. It was the kind of sentiment he'd so often longed for as a boy. That no matter what he had done or what had happened, his father would somehow manage to be there, to put his arms around him and hold him and tell him everything would be alright. That he was there for him, and always would be. Even if it was a lie. Just to see him and hear it and feel it even once would have brought untold joy.

Less than an hour after Truex's call, they'd lifted

off from Faro for Lisbon. Once again, Wirth had taken the Striker corporate Gulfstream, leaving the tri-engine Falcon 50 to White and the others, with Wirth promising to update them with more information the moment he received it. Ten minutes after takeoff White's BlackBerry had sounded. Wirth had the data.

"Ryder is staying at the Four Seasons Ritz," he'd said. *"He'll arrive sometime tomorrow morning. His dinner with the Lisbon mayor is at eight in the evening. I don't have a location yet. A man named Carlos Branco will meet you on the tarmac in Lisbon at Air Terminal Two in the civil aviation area and take you to an apartment on Rua do São Filipe Néri, which is close to the Four Seasons. Go there and wait until you hear from me. Branco is a freelancer, a total professional. He'll be working with you. It was set up by Truex, not me, so trust him. We'll get out of this yet, Conor. We'll look back and laugh."*

"Yes, sir, Mr. Wirth," he'd replied flatly. "We'll look back and laugh."

• 6:05 P.M.

White heard a thump as the Falcon's landing gear came down. Then it banked and came around on final approach. As it did he could see the tarmac and terminals at Portela Airport and then Lisbon itself. Down there somewhere, among the tree-lined avenues and city squares, beneath the acres of red-tile rooftops—either now or sometime later tonight, certainly by tomorrow when Ryder arrived—would be Nicholas Marten and Anne and, he prayed, the photographs. All he had to do was find them.

• Portela International Airport, Terminal 2. 6:19 P.M.
"Conor White?" a slim, fortyish, dark-haired man wearing a Hawaiian shirt and blue jeans met them on the tarmac as they came down the Falcon's stairway.

"Yes," White said cautiously.

"My name is Carlos Branco. I have a car waiting."

• 6:30 P.M.
A metallic gray BMW 520 touring car left the terminal and passed through the civil aviation security gate. Moments later it turned onto Avenida Cidade do Porto and headed into the city.

White sat in the right rear seat, with Patrice between him and Irish Jack. Branco rode up front next to the driver. He'd taken them directly to the car and waited as they put their luggage and two dark green and yellow sports equipment bags into the trunk. As they drove off, he mentioned something about the weather and rain showers that were due over the next few days. After that, they rode in silence.

• 6:38 P.M.
As Branco's driver brought them into the city in a swirl of traffic, White began to feel a surge of energy.

With it came a churning of thought, and he began to wonder where in the city a meeting between Anne and Marten and Joe Ryder might take place, and how, and at what point, they might best deal with it.

• 6:52 P.M.

The BMW entered the Marquês de Pombal round-about at the top of the lush, tree-lined Avenida da Liberdade. Immediately the driver swung up the hill past the green of the city's sprawling Eduardo VII Park.

"There," Branco said, a long, narrow finger pointing out the window to the right.

Directly above them and looking out over the city like some modern, box-shaped sentinel was the place where Ryder would be staying. The Four Seasons Hotel Ritz.

6:54 P.M.

81

• Bairro Alto, the upper town. 7:12 P.M.

It was still nearly three full hours until sunset. Nicholas Marten stood in a shaft of sunlight at the far end of a small, leafy park, one foot on a stone bench, the envelope with Father Willy's photographs tucked under his left arm, Kovalenko's Glock 9 mm automatic in his waistband under his jacket. Anne sat on another bench some thirty feet away casually feeding a congregation of pigeons from a box of crackers she'd bought at a variety store in the tourist-jammed lower old-town Baixa district fifteen minutes earlier. Around them were a dozen or so others—chatting, reading, playing cards, people just enjoying the long summer evening. Whether they were visitors or locals it was hard to tell, but whoever they were, none seemed to be paying either Anne or Marten any attention.

Directly across from the park was Rua do Almada, a narrow cobblestoned street fronting a block of four- and five-story apartment buildings. Number 17 was the third building down. Its second- through fourth-floor apartments had floor-to-ceiling windows that opened onto narrow balconies decorated with ornamental iron railings. The fifth, or top, floor had no balconies or railings at all, only large windows that, like those on the other floors, looked out onto the street below and the park across from it where they were.

• 7:16 P.M.
Marten glanced at Anne and nodded toward number 17. She responded with a slight shake of the head, then went back to feeding the pigeons. They were hot and tired from the nearly ninety-minute trek they had made across the city from where Stump Logan had dropped them. Their destination, hopefully with a message from Joe Ryder waiting for them, was

only feet away across the cobblestones. But for all the good it did, they might as well have still been in Praia da Rocha. Dangerous as it was for them to stay out in the open, Anne's sense was that it was even more foolhardy to simply walk up to the front door and knock on it without first surveying the building and its surroundings.

"See what vehicles come and go," she'd said as they neared. "If they pass by more than once. Who goes in and out. If someone is watching from the windows or from the windows next door or from farther up or down the street. If a pedestrian or some- one on a bicycle goes past, taking special interest in the building as they do. Look carefully at the people in the park. See if any of them are watching from there."

"Anne." Marten's reply had been impatient and emphatic. "Only one person knows we're coming, Raisa Amaro, and she's inside. We have to get off the street."

"Not yet, darling," she'd said with finality and crossed into the park to feed the pigeons and watch the building. For how long, she hadn't said.

Frustrated, indignant, yet knowing he couldn't very well grab her by the hair and drag her into the building, Marten had reluctantly followed, taking up the position on the bench where he was now.

Their journey to Rua do Almada had begun the moment Stump Logan drove off. Following his di- rective, they'd gone to the nearby main bus depot,

Terminal Rodoviário de Lisboa, crossed into the bus arrival/departure area, and entered through the ARRIVING PASSENGER doors. Taxis and public transportation were immediately available outside the main entrance on the far side, but Marten had been hesitant to use either for fear of leaving a trail that could be followed. Instead he'd bought a street map from a terminal vendor and they'd left on foot.

Ever wary of police patrols and deliberately trying to avoid appearing as a couple someone might remember later, they'd kept to opposite sides of the streets and avenues as they moved deeper into the city. With little sleep and even less to eat since they'd left Berlin, the walk had seemed interminable. The last twenty minutes especially had been a slow, lingering ramble through the crowded Baixa quarter, with Anne, on the far sidewalk, acting more like a tourist—poking her head into this store and that—than someone trying to get to the safe house on Rua do Almada.

Finally Marten had abandoned caution, crossed over, and taken her by the arm. Then, map in hand like a vacationer, he led her up a steep cobblestone street into the fashionable Chiado district and its rich blend of outdoor cafés, antique stores, and stylish shops. If Anne had had any intention of lingering there, Marten hadn't let her—with the single exception of a small, elegant, five-star hotel on Rua Garrett that she'd gone into, to, as she'd said, "use the loo."

Ten minutes more and up another sharply inclined street and they entered the Bairro Alto, the upper town, where Rua do Almada was. Another five and they entered the park across from number 17 where they were now, and where they had been for almost fifteen minutes of waiting and watching.

Marten looked at Anne again. She ignored him. This time it was enough. He walked over and leaned in close. "Nobody's gone in, nobody's come out. Not a single person has walked by. No vehicle has passed more than once. No bicycles, either. It's time we go in. Now."

Immediately she got up and walked a little way off. The pigeons followed; so did Marten. He started to say something, but she stopped him.

"Congressman Ryder's coming to Lisbon," she said quietly without looking at him. "That means the U.S. Embassy will have been informed. Which means the CIA/Lisbon chief of station will know."

"He might know he's coming, but he won't know why."

Abruptly she turned to look at him. "Don't you suppose that by now he knows we were in Praia da Rocha and just might suspect that since Mr. Ryder is all of a sudden coming to Lisbon we just might be too, and for some reason other than seeing the sights?" She stared at him a half beat, then went back to feeding the pigeons.

"Erlanger, in Berlin," she said, still without looking at him, "was CIA. You wanted to know about his manner at the airstrip in Potsdam. He was trying to warn me that the Agency was actively involved and whatever I was doing I'd better stop. And then we found out that Hauptkommissar Franck was an operative. Conor White's friend Patrice was CIA and maybe still is."

"Yes, and maybe White is, too. We've been through that."

"Nicholas—" Something caught her eye and she looked off. A well-dressed elderly couple sitting nearby was watching them intently. She smiled politely, then gently turned her back to them and looked to Marten.

"It all has to do with the photographs," she said quietly and almost offhandedly, as if she were simply discussing the weather or where they might go for dinner. "If Erlanger knew about them, I don't know. But clearly Franck did. He brought Kovalenko along because he had to, but he would have killed him afterward, the same as he planned to do with us."

"You're saying the Agency wants to make sure Ryder doesn't get them."

"Yes."

"Why?"

"I don't think they would particularly delight in the idea of someone—one of their own former operatives, or an expat American landscape architect, or even an esteemed U.S. congressman—having graphic proof that a private security contractor conspired to provoke a revolution in a third world country, especially one that resulted in the deaths of thousands of its citizens, to benefit an American oil company. Franck's job was to kill us after he got the photographs. What makes you think that order isn't still in place?

"The Agency has long arms, Nicholas, and very good hearing." She nodded across the street toward number 17. "What if they're already in there waiting? Or will be told where we are once we go inside? Who knows who this Raisa Amaro is, anyway?"

Just then the elderly couple walked slowly past, the gentleman walking with a cane and tipping his hat as he passed, his wife holding his arm.

Marten waited for them to move out of hearing, then abruptly turned to Anne. "Joe Ryder's expecting to contact us through whatever means Ms. Amaro has set up for us. We try to reach him now—if we can reach him—and tell him our fears, he'll want to change his plans. If he does, the people with him will want to know why, and he'll have to tell them something, which can only make things worse when he tries to find a way to connect with us. We have to take the chance that your Lisbon chief of station, Sy Wirth, and White and his friends don't yet know we're here or, if they do, where we are."

Anne looked off. She didn't like it at all.

In the next instant a distinctive white-and-blue car with a thin red stripe running the length of it drove slowly past. A single word was painted on it—POLICIA. Seconds later two motorcycle units followed, their helmeted, uniformed riders carefully surveying the park as they went by. A moment of stillness followed, and then two more motorcycle units came by, this time on the far side of the park.

"May I suggest another storm front?" Marten

asked quietly. "The very real possibility that Franck's body has been found and that the authorities are keeping it quiet until the Portuguese police and maybe their counterparts in Spain, France, and Italy have been alerted and given the order to locate and take into custody the two persons the Hauptkommissar was investigating for the murder of Theo Haas. The same two persons the police know he followed to a beach house in Praia da Rocha that was owned by a certain Jacob Cádiz."

Anne smiled thinly. "You're saying we should take a great leap of faith and introduce ourselves to this Raisa Amaro as quickly as possible."

"Sooner, darling. Sooner."

7:34 P.M.

82

• 7:45 P.M.

"There are just you three, no more?"

"Yes."

"A car and driver will be outside whenever you have need. Supplementary transportation is available with a ten-minute-or-less response time."

"Good."

"I know you are armed. Will you need additional armaments?"

"Unlikely, but it would depend on the situation."

Conor White and Carlos Branco stood on the balcony of a modest fourth-floor apartment on Rua do São Filipe Néri. In the distance, long shadows cast by the setting sun accentuated the wide Tagus River and the boat traffic on it. Illuminated, too, in bright yellow light, was the towering Golden Gate–like 25th of April Bridge carrying vehicles to and from areas to the south, the Algarve among them.

Inside, through the sliding glass door, they could see Patrice and Irish Jack in the living room. They were already comfortable in jeans and tight black T-shirts, drinking coffee and playing cards. Over the rooftops on the building's far side rose the Four Seasons Ritz, where Congressman Ryder would make his base sometime the next morning. It was a four-minute walk at most, thirty seconds by car.

White studied Branco carefully, as if trying to take his full measure. How much experience he had, his thought process, the way he moved. If he could fully trust him. Clearly what Sy Wirth had told him—that Loyal Truex, not himself, had set this up—seemed to be true. From all appearances he was a skilled professional. It was one of the very few things Wirth hadn't screwed up. The speed of it meant that Truex had been in direct contact with Washington and that Branco's hire would have been done by Lisbon's CIA station chief. It was a roundabout, but in intelligence terms, correct way of keeping White out of any direct contact with Washington. That way they all were protected, which had been the idea from the beginning.

"What do you see?" Branco asked calmly.

"An accomplished resource whose name is not on the Agency payroll or listed anywhere on its books or records. A freelancer for hire who is paid out of the chief of station's private account and is used to working that way."

"Good." Branco smiled.

"How much do you know about what's going on?"

"Little to nothing. I'm a simple painter who has been assigned to Congressman Ryder's RSO security detail. My job is to help set up his quarters at the hotel before he arrives and then be with him for the rest of his stay."

"Painter? As in paint him as a target."

Branco smiled. "Make sure all of his communication lines are bugged and that he is under real-time surveillance wherever he goes."

"You are aware there are two others involved."

"A Nicholas Marten and a Ms. Anne Tidrow. At some point they will attempt to meet with the congressman. When that happens, I am to pull back and take the RSO detail with me. Then you and your cardplaying friends will move in and do whatever needs to be done."

Again Conor White studied him. "You know Lisbon well."

"You are asking if I know how and where to work our threesome into an isolated situation but so they won't realize it. And in a way where there can be no interference from the police or problems with accidental witnesses."

White nodded.

"In a city like this there are all kinds of unexpected

trapdoors. One only needs to know when they will be needed, and after that how to put them in play."

"You can do that."

"I am, as you said, an accomplished resource. Preparation is everything. It's a discipline in which I am quite skilled."

White crossed the balcony to look out at the river. For a long moment he stared at it, his mind elsewhere. Finally he turned back to Branco. "Do you know what Marten and Anne Tidrow look like?"

"I was provided with Marten's British passport photo and the Tidrow woman's corporate photograph. By now, either through the passage of time or on purpose or both, they will have changed their appearance. We will have to take that into consideration."

"They will be coming over that"—he nodded toward the 25th of April Bridge—"from the Algarve. Maybe they're already here, maybe not. When they are here, now or later, can you find them?"

"Undoubtedly the congressman will know how to reach them and will do so at some point after he arrives. His room will be bugged, his cell phones monitored the minute he lands. When he makes contact, we can move."

"Carlos." White took him by the arm. "I don't want to wait that long. Marten and Anne are the principal targets. If we can locate them before the congressman gets here, we won't need to involve him at all. It would be much cleaner that way." He paused and then smiled deliberately. "It's something you might find quite lucrative."

"You mean a bonus."

"Yes."

"Paid by who?"

"Me to you, personally. Fifty thousand euros in cash within thirty-six hours of the job's completion. No one else will know. Not your chief of station, not even my own people."

"How can I be sure you will keep your word?"

"You know who I am. You would have checked on me before you took the assignment. A man in our line of business who doesn't honor his promises doesn't last very long, and I've been around for quite some time."

"I can't guarantee success."

"Then we will return to the original plan. You understand, of course, that if that were to happen you would be out a lot of money."

"I will do what I can."

Again Conor White smiled. "I know you will."

8:02 P.M.

83

• 17 Rua Do Almada. Same time.

Who Raisa Amaro really was or worked for was impossible to know, at least in the first few minutes—and, Marten guessed, probably not even in a lifetime. What she did do was play the part of the discreet hostess exceedingly well. Which was how she had met them at the door. Elegantly dressed in a tailored navy suit under a shock of coiffed red hair, she'd introduced herself, inquired about their trip, then immediately taken them up in a small elevator to the sensual luxury of a top-floor apartment, acting all the while as if the sole purpose of their visit were an illicit affair.

French born and sixty-something, she was barely five feet tall; her livelihood seemed to revolve around the careful managing of this single piece of real estate that was little more than a very private stage designed for sexual intimacy. She expounded on the richness of her service by explaining that should a third-party plaything be required—male or female—she would be happy to provide one at short notice. In essence, Raisa Amaro was a handsomely paid madam of the first order who guarded the apartment as well as the front door to the building herself. A building, she explained, that she owned outright. If the edifice's other tenants knew about her top-floor arrangement, they said nothing, knowing full well that as the proprietor Raisa—as she asked to be called—could and would evict them at any moment and for any reason at all, no matter what local ordinances there were against such things.

"Everything you will need for your stay is here. A day, a week, or longer, whatever is your pleasure," she'd explained in French-accented English as she'd gracefully shown them around the expansive one-bedroom facility. "Marble bathroom with Jacuzzi tub, bidet, dual-head shower, imported soaps, perfumes, extra-thick towels with more in the linen closet, terry robes more luxurious than in any hotel in Europe. The bed is king-sized, the sheets silk, the pillows and comforter goose down. A wide selection of condoms is in the cabinet next to it."

At that Marten and Anne had exchanged glances as the term "safe house" suddenly took on an entirely new meaning.

"There is a small hotel-type safe in the clothes closet; instructions on the door will tell you how to use it. The television in the front room receives one hundred and twenty channels in any number of languages. Breakfast is when you ask for it. If you want something you don't see, pick up the phone and dial one-one. It is a direct line to my apartment on the ground floor." At that point she'd led them into the kitchen.

"In the refrigerator you will find paté, cold cuts, a selection of cheeses, milk, champagne, and mineral water. Fresh fruit and desserts are on the side table. The coffee is automatic, ready to brew at the touch of a button. The telephone is there next to the refrigerator. There is another in the bedroom. The number is unlisted and is changed regularly. Use it to make and receive private calls. The line is patched through a commercial laundry that I own and where I do the books, so there is no record of any calls coming or leaving here."

"I'm expecting a friend to be in touch. I wonder if he might have called before we arrived?" Marten asked carefully and with a glance at Anne, hoping her fears about Raisa had been calmed. From her return look it seemed that for now, at least, they had been. Still, he wasn't quite sure about the situation. Neither Raisa nor the apartment was anything like he had expected, especially after the president had told him—*"It's not fancy, but it'll do until Ryder arrives."*

"There." Raisa pointed toward a small boxlike piece of equipment next to the kitchen phone. "An old-style answering machine. It lights up with a number when a call has come in." She walked over and looked at it. "Right now it reads zero. So, no, there have been no messages."

"What about a door key?" Marten asked.

"On the table in the entryway. It opens both the door to the apartment and the front door downstairs. Make sure both are locked behind you when you come or go. There are two"—she smiled—"in the event one of you needs some air. Quarrels and misunderstandings do come up, even at the most unlikely time."

"Thank you," Marten said, and they walked out of the kitchen and toward the front door.

"One other thing," Anne said, as if it were an afterthought. "A computer or laptop with an Internet connection. At some point I will need to do a little work."

"This is an old building, and the Internet we do not yet have. Soon, we hope." She glanced at Marten, sizing him up, then looked back to Anne. "If I were you I would have left my work at home."

With that she'd bid them good night and left, closing the door behind her.

Anne looked around at the sensual opulence. "I'd like to meet this old girlfriend. The string-puller who set all this up. She must be something."

Marten grinned. "She is."

"I bet." She crossed to look into the bedroom, then turned back to Marten. "I'm tired and hungry. I could use some champagne and something to eat and a shower. In what order I don't know. And then, if you don't mind, I want to get some sleep. Alone."

"You don't think I planned this?" Marten raised an eyebrow. "There are far less dangerous ways to get a woman into bed."

"Let me tell you something, darling. If a woman wants to have sex with you, she'll let you know." She fixed him with a deliberate stare. "Now be a good boy and turn on the television like you did in Berlin. Out of a hundred and twenty channels you ought to be able to find one that will give us some clue as to what's going on in the world. Say, with Equatorial Guinea, or Joe Ryder's trip to Lisbon, or maybe even what happened to Hauptkommissar Franck."

With that she walked off and into the kitchen. A moment later Marten heard the refrigerator door open. Seconds after that there was the distinct pop of a champagne cork. Then there was silence. Two full minutes anyway.

"What are you doing?" he called finally.

"Drinking," her voice came back.

"You do that alone, too?"

"Right now, yes."

"I'd be careful if I were you. It could lead to a whole series of bad habits."

Anne didn't reply, and Marten didn't carry it

further. Finally he picked up the TV's remote control and sat down on an overstuffed chair.

Click. He turned on the television.

Forty-seven channels later he found a Portuguese news station. A man and woman shared an anchor desk. Almost immediately the station went to a commercial. A half-dozen commercials later the picture came back to the male anchor and then quickly morphed into a photograph of Hauptkommissar Emil Franck. Next were live photos of a burned-out car near an apparently desolate beach with police and emergency vehicles everywhere. A female correspondent in a Windbreaker was doing a stand-up. The whole thing was chillingly reminiscent of the television news coverage and video of the burned-out limousine in Spain that had led to the discovery of the bodies of Marita and her students.

"Anne," he said quickly over his shoulder.

"I know. The Hauptkommissar." Her reply was sharp and close by.

Marten turned to see her standing near the door, her purse over one shoulder, one of the room keys in her hand. He stood up in surprise and alarm. "Where are you going?"

"I took down the phone number here. I'll call you later." Immediately she twisted the lock, pulled open the door, and was gone.

"Jesus Christ!" Marten blurted and went after her.

84

He came out into the hallway on the run expecting to hear the whir of the elevator. He didn't. It was silent. Then he heard sounds in the stairwell beside it. Abruptly he looked over the side. She was already two flights down and moving fast.

He took the stairs two at a time. Down three flights, then four. He caught up to her on the ground floor in the entryway near Raisa's apartment just as she reached the front door. He grabbed her and pulled her back.

"What the hell are you doing?"

"Going out." She wrenched free of his grip.

"To where?"

"To think. To be alone."

"You can do that in the apartment. Go in the bedroom. Shut the door. I won't bother you."

She said nothing, just stood there staring at him, breathing heavily. He saw fire and fear and uncertainty in her eyes. At the same time, there was a deep, almost animal-like resolve. She was going to do whatever it was she had set out for, and he knew keeping her from it would be next to impossible. Still, he had to try. He couldn't have her going out in the streets, not now. Not after Franck's body had been found.

"Want to talk about it?" he said quietly.

"You wouldn't understand."

"Give me a chance."

Her eyes fixed on his. All the emotions were still there. "I have something to do. Please don't interfere."

"You get caught by the police, we're both done. Joe Ryder won't try to help. He wouldn't dare even acknowledge us. If Conor White and his friends get you, you won't live an hour."

"Then I better not get caught," she said coldly. In an instant she was past him and out the door and into what was now twilight. Marten watched her cross quickly into the park and then she was gone, swallowed up in the shadows.

"Quarrels and misunderstandings." A familiar voice rang out from behind him. Startled, he whirled around.

Raisa stood in the doorway of her apartment, her arms folded over her chest. The navy suit was gone. In its place she wore a rose-colored silk robe and red slippers that nearly matched her hair. "The thing I warned you about a short while ago. At some point she'll come back. And when she does, she'll want to fuck you. You can be sure of it."

Marten cocked his head. "What did you say?"

"You heard me, my love."

Of course he had, but it surprised him nonetheless. What she had said and the way she'd said it—easily and without embarrassment—as if she were one of those people who just knew things. Suddenly he saw her not so much as the provider of a safe house, or the professional madam she'd turned out to be, but rather some kind of diminutive French-born earth mother. One who might or might not be more than a little crazy but who understood life and human behavior in ways others might not and wasn't above verbalizing it.

"I saw her face," Raisa continued, "her eyes, her demeanor. Something troubles her a great deal. It's why she left, to try and resolve it. When she does, or even if she fails, she will come back completely drained by whatever has happened and be looking for a release of the most profound kind. In my experience nothing does that better than a good fuck, especially when it's done with someone you like and trust." Raisa Amaro smiled tenderly. "Be gentle with her. But not too gentle. For a little while at least she will want to forget everything. Good night, Mr. Marten."

With that she gathered her robe, went back into her apartment, and closed the door.

Marten stood frozen. Whatever Raisa said about Anne coming back and what would happen when she did hadn't fully registered. Nor had whatever reason had caused her to leave. What overrode everything was the danger out there on the street. He damned himself for having let her go. Instinct told him to go after her right then. Find her quickly. Fight with her if he had to but bring her back before the police or Conor White and his people found her. The trouble was, if he rushed out after her he would have to guess where she'd gone and in doing so would have no choice but to ask strangers if they'd seen her. Something that multiplied the risk to himself a hundredfold. It was a gamble he didn't dare take. Joe Ryder was counting on him to deliver the photographs; so was the president.

He went to the door and looked out toward the park. The evening lights had come on, and he could see a few people still mingling there. Anne was not among them. He watched for a moment longer, then finally turned and went back up the stairs to the apartment.

9:18 P.M.

85

• Four Seasons Hotel Ritz, the Ritz Bar. 9:20 P.M.

Sy Wirth sat alone finishing his second Johnnie Walker Blue over ice. An attractive woman in a green dress walked up to the bar, ordered a Black Russian, and smiled seductively at him. He didn't respond. Instead he signed his tab, then got up and made his way through the bustling lounge area toward the elevators in the lobby. It was nearly nine thirty at night local time, almost three thirty in the afternoon in Houston.

• 9:24 P.M.

The elevator door opened; Wirth stepped out and walked down the hallway toward his tenth-floor room. His electronic key unlocked the door, and he went in. A hallway light was on. So was one on the nightstand beside the bed. The maid had turned down the sheets. A writing desk was in front of a large sliding glass door that opened onto an outdoor terrace overlooking the dark expanse of Eduardo VII Park.

He sat down at the desk and turned on the lamp, then slid the two BlackBerrys from his jacket pocket, put the one with the blue tape aside, and picked up the other. A deep breath and he punched in a number in England that automatically forwarded the call to Striker general counsel Arnold Moss's personal BlackBerry in Houston. It rang three times before Moss picked up.

"*I thought I'd be hearing from you,*" Moss said immediately.

"Where are you?"

"*In the office, where else?*"

"You alone?"

"*Yes.*"

Wirth ran a hand through his hair. "Truex has gotten Washington involved. I'm in Lisbon. So is Conor White. Anne and this Nicholas Marten are either on their way or have already arrived. They're going to meet with Joe Ryder somewhere here tomorrow. Most probably to give him the photographs and have Anne tell him what she knows about our operations. White's already got an Agency freelancer on board to help stop them."

"*Carlos Branco.*"

"How the hell do you know that?" Wirth was startled. "Truex tell you?"

"Newhan Black."

"Black called you?"

*"He wants us out, Sy. He didn't want to talk to
you. Thought I should deliver the news. It only
happened a little while ago. It's why I didn't call. I
wanted to think."*

"Stop thinking." Wirth shoved back from the
desk and stood up. "This is what we're going to do."

"You didn't tell me the Russians were in this."

"They aren't anymore."

"How the hell did they get involved in the—"

"I tried an end run. It didn't work." Wirth crossed
the room, reached the far side, then turned back. He
was angry. At the world. "Not everything pans out,
Arnie. In the end you hope you come out a step
ahead of even."

*"Sy, leave it alone. We've got to cut our losses
while we can. Close the whole operation down. Get
out of Equatorial Guinea."*

"What's the matter?" Wirth's anger flared. "The
game gets a little rough and you suddenly start
whimpering? Whose side are you on, theirs or ours?
I told you a long time ago I wasn't going to lose the
Bioko field. I haven't changed my mind."

*"Jesus, Sy. The whole thing's crumbling. The
walls are coming down. Black's given us the opportunity to walk away. He'll protect us. We have to do
just that."*

"Arnie, listen to me." Wirth was emphatic. "We're
going to execute what you and I discussed in Houston. Joe Ryder's due here in the morning. I'm staying at the same hotel he is and am going to request

a meeting with him. Just the two of us. He'll see me if for no other reason than the Iraq situation. I plan to tell him exactly what he's going to find when he gets the photos, then turn it right back on Truex. Tell Ryder it was all his game, his and Conor White's, one we knew nothing about. We had no idea that they were helping to arm the revolution until we heard about the photographs.

"Their plan all along seems to have been to covertly expand their influence in West Africa by using us as cover while they backed Abba and his people, giving them whatever they needed to overthrow Tiombe. Something they were certain Abba could do if he had the weapons. Then suddenly the photos came into play and a whole new enterprise presented itself, one worth hundreds of millions if not billions."

Again Wirth crossed the room. "All they had to do was get hold of the pictures and exploit them. Play Striker as the bad guy who ordered it done. Make it look as if we had backed the overthrow of the country for our own benefit. If they did it right, the exposure would kill Striker publicly and politically, and we'd have to pull out, forfeiting our leases." He walked across the room once more and then again.

"In the chaos afterward, Truex would convince Abba that he had no experience finding and extracting oil. With Abba's blessing, he would resurrect the leases in Hadrian's name with the promise that he'd find someone who did have that experience, first and foremost the Russians, who'd been hovering there the whole time. Then he'd sell the leases to them for an enormous fee and leave, staying lily-white in the process.

"The trouble was, they didn't have the photos but they knew who did, and they came to Lisbon to get them at any cost whatsoever. They hired a freelancer named Carlos Branco to take care of Anne and Marten and recover them when they went to meet with Ryder, kill Ryder, too, if necessary. I found out what was going on and confronted White and tried to stop him. He refused and threatened to kill me if I said anything or got in the way. That was when I knew I had to go to Ryder myself. He doesn't have to know anything about Black or the Agency. They'd deny it anyway if it came up."

"*Sy, you're out of your mind. Don't touch it! Stay the hell away from Joe Ryder!*" Moss warned in alarm and anger. "*Black's given us the green light to leave cleanly and quietly. He'll let SimCo, even Hadrian, take the fall, and then plug in another U.S. oil company to pick up the pieces. He's not stupid, he won't lose the Bioko field, it's too damn important. So forget Joe Ryder and get the hell out of there. Now. Tonight. Walk away from it. Just walk away.*"

"Arnie." Wirth kept pacing, not even aware of it. In his mind he was in Houston and face-to-face with his general counsel, a man he saw now as little more than an employee. "I run Striker Oil, not you. I'm the one who brought the company to where it is. I'm the one who decided to take the chance and explore Equatorial Guinea and then negotiated the long-term leases with Tiombe's people. I'm also the same fucking guy who told you from the start he was not going to lose the Bioko field. Not to the Agency, the Russians, or anybody else. Newhan Black doesn't want to talk to me, then fuck him. You call him and tell him just what I've told you and what I'm going to tell Joe Ryder.

"You're right when you say Black's not stupid and the find is far too strategic for him to risk. Still, he can't chance having the photos get out, so he'll let Branco, White, and his men get rid of Anne and Marten, then take the pictures and fade into the woodwork. Not long afterward, somebody they all know and trust will show up and they'll disappear. Just like that. White, his gunmen, Branco, and the photos. That same day or maybe the next, Truex will go down, an accident of some kind, and the Bioko field will remain the legal property of the AG Striker Company. Much easier for the Agency that way. After all, we're the oil company with the long-term leases. The others were just hired gunmen. Hired gunmen are dispensable. Long-term leases for an ocean of oil are not."

"Sy, you're crazy to think you can pull this off! You're playing with fire."

"I am the fire, Arnie. I'll call you after I meet with Joe Ryder."

9:46 P.M.

86

- 9:52 P.M.

The rain was everything. Off-and-on showers had been forecast for the next few days and were expected to begin after midnight. But just after dark a storm front moved in and a steady rain began to fall. To Marten it was serendipitous, and he used it as an excuse to go out after Anne.

He'd found an umbrella stand in a cubbyhole near the apartment's front door with three large umbrellas tucked into it. Several hats and caps had been in a nearby closet. As with almost everything else, and in a most thorough way, Raisa Amaro had provided her guests with solid protection against nature. Now, with the Glock automatic in his waistband and using the night and weather to help veil his movements, he ventured out.

Umbrella held overhead, jacket collar turned up, a bucket hat borrowed from the closet pulled over his ears and several-day growth of beard adding to his prayer that neither a passing police patrol nor White's people, however many of them there might be, would recognize him, at least initially, he let Raisa's front door close behind him, then crossed Rua do Almada and went into the now deserted park.

Six minutes later he crossed Rua da Flores, leaving the Bairro Alto district and entering the Chiado section, backtracking the way he and Anne had come. It was the only thing he could do considering that neither of them had been in Lisbon before today. His guess was that she had to have seen something in passing that caught her eye, a place she felt she could retreat to later. For what purpose he had no idea whatsoever.

Her fear of the CIA seemed to be at the core of everything. But what she thought she could do about it somewhere out here on a rainy Sunday night in a city she barely knew mystified him. Yet whatever she was so intent on doing was, as he'd told her, beside the point if she ended up in the custody of the police or dead at the hands of Conor White. Still, concerned about her as he was and as angry with her as he'd been, at another time and place he might have let it ride, have let her take her chances and get whatever it was out of her system while he stayed in the apartment riding herd on the photographs and keeping out of sight himself. But he no longer had that luxury. Not now, not after President Harris had so compellingly stirred the pot.

Twenty minutes earlier, and still in the apartment, he'd used his dark blue throwaway cell phone to call Harris—at Camp David or the White House or wherever he was—on his own throwaway cell. There had been no answer. He'd tried again to no avail. Then, seconds later, the apartment's phone had rung. It startled him and he hesitated. Finally he picked up, sure it was either Anne or Joe Ryder.

"*It's me,*" an unfamiliar voice said.

"Who is me?" he said warily.

"*Cousin Jack. I was in a meeting when you called. I'm in another room using a laptop with a special voice-filtering IP service that's very difficult to intercept.*"

Marten relaxed. "You wanted me to let you know when we got here. I was waiting for Ryder's call. I thought maybe this was it." He made no mention of Anne, just let the president assume she was there with him.

"*He's still in Rome. You may not hear from him until tomorrow morning.*" Immediately the president's demeanor became more serious. "*The Portuguese police have found the body of the German policeman, Emil Franck.*"

"I know."

"*I asked for a detailed report on it. He was shot once in the back of the head. Then his body was put into a car and driven to a beach somewhere near Portimão where the car was set on fire. No mention was made of this Russian, Kovalenko, you talked about.*"

"I wouldn't think so. He's very good at what he does."

"*When you called from the bookshop you told me Moscow knew about the Bioko field. If they already knew, why was he with the German?*"

"The photographs. Franck was coming after them for the CIA. The Russians knew about them, but they didn't know where they were. They hoped he would lead them to the prize. Franck was a double agent. He had no choice but to let Kovalenko come along."

Marten heard the president hesitate, as if he'd suddenly had an even more troubling thought. *"The photographs. You do have them."*

"Yes. He let me keep them, probably hoping the police would find me and think they were the reason I murdered Theo Haas."

"He came all that way for the pictures, killed the policeman, and then let you keep them?" The president was incredulous.

"Not exactly."

"What the devil does that mean?"

"Kovalenko took the memory card from the camera that was used to photograph them. There's far more damning stuff on it than just the pictures that were printed. A lot more."

"So, in essence, he does have them."

"He thinks he does. But when he gets to where he's going, plugs in the card, and brings the pictures up on a screen, he's going to find he's got a whole lot of pictures of half-naked young women Theo Haas secretly photographed while they were sunbathing on the beach near his house. I switched cards on him. I have the original. No one knows but you, not even Anne. Both are locked away in the room safe here."

Marten could almost see the president grin. Then abruptly he spoke, his voice even more somber than before.

"What the police haven't made public is that you and Ms. Tidrow are the prime suspects in Franck's murder."

"That doesn't surprise me. They know we were in Praia da Rocha this morning. They don't want to make it public and drive us underground, then have us get away, like in Berlin."

"This is different than Berlin, Nick. You're now not just a murderer but a cop killer. So is she. Raisa Amaro is a very smart, very gifted and trusted woman. She'll keep anyone away from where you are. So both of you, stay right there. Don't do anything until you hear from Joe Ryder."

"Right." Marten still said nothing about Anne leaving.

"Not just right, crucial. I finally saw the CIA briefing video from Equatorial Guinea. I was sickened as you were. I'm meeting with the secretary-general of the UN tomorrow to see what we can do to intervene or at least bring in humanitarian aid. But there's something else, and why we have to get you both out of there as quickly as possible and before the police or anyone else finds you.

"We need the photographs and whatever else is on the camera's memory card as hard evidence. But we also need the sworn testimony of Anne Tidrow to establish beyond question that Striker Oil, the Hadrian Company, and SimCo conspired to arm the revolutionaries for their own gain."

"I'm not sure she knew what was going on at the time."

"Maybe not, but she certainly knows enough about the inner workings of Striker and its relationship with Hadrian to give the attorney general's office a solid base to work from. Whatever she can give us is more than we have.

"One more thing. You said Franck was a double agent and the Russians knew it."

"Yes."

"Do you know if they have seen the CIA video?"

"They have. Kovalenko told me they intercepted it and copied it."

Marten heard the president sigh in despair. *"That seriously exacerbates what we've worried about from the start. If the pictures are made public and at the same time the Russians leak the video, I can guarantee you very few in this world, our own citizens included, will see the U.S. as anything but a murderous exploiter who has used the mercenary forces of an American oil company to further its own political ends. We will then be in the extremely delicate position of having to prove our innocence beyond any doubt whatsoever to an outraged global public. A feat that will be all but impossible without Ms. Tidrow's presence and testimony.*

"There's something else, too. The very real possibility that Kovalenko or agents working with him will come after you again once they discover you've switched memory cards. They will want the real one. So I repeat. Stay where you are and wait for Ryder's call. He'll be protected by his own RSO security detail, and the CIA will leave it at that. They'll get you out and onto Ryder's plane. We'll take it from there." The president hesitated, then finished. *"I got you into this pickle, Nick, and I'm doing everything I can to get you out. But unfortunately I can't guarantee success. Most of it's going to be up to you, and Joe Ryder and his people."*

"I realize that."

"Then, as I said before, good luck and God-speed. And keep Ms. Tidrow close."

"Yes, sir, I will," Marten said. The president clicked off.

Marten let out a breath.

And stared.

At the empty room.

• 10:10 P.M.

Lost in thought, still rattled by the president's directive and his own guilt at letting Harris believe Anne was safely with him, Marten stepped blindly from a curb. Immediately there was a flash of headlights and a loud blare of horn, and he jumped back as a city bus passed inches from his nose. He swore out loud, then ducked low under his umbrella and crossed the street, moving deeper into the Chiado district looking for any sign of Anne.

For all the rain and dark and the fact that it was Sunday night, it was still summer, and even though most shops were closed, here and there he found an open café, a bar, a restaurant, a specialty shop selling souvenir T-shirts, coffee mugs, key chains, cheap cameras, and the like. She had to be in one of them because there was nothing else. But which one? And how far had she gone before she found what she wanted? Whatever that was.

10:13 P.M.

87

• 10:18 P.M.

The text message was sent from CIA Chief of Station/Lisbon Jeremy Moyer to Carlos Branco's Black-Berry in an electronic heartbeat.

Striker Oil American Express credit card used at Hotel Lisboa Chiado, Rua Garrett, 9:57 P.M.

• 10:19 P.M.
The same message was forwarded by Branco to Conor White. And, after a moment's hesitation, from White to Sy Wirth.

• 10:20 P.M.
Wirth had a one-word reply.
Respond!

• 10:24 P.M.
Nicholas Marten walked out of Casanova, a small blue-and-white-tiled restaurant permeated with the distinctive odor of delicately seasoned roast pork. Raising his umbrella against the rain, he walked on, his eyes scanning either side of the street for pedestrians. He'd counted twenty tables inside Casanova; six had still been occupied. None by Anne.

Describing her to the English-speaking head waiter proved fruitless. No one resembling her had been in the restaurant all evening, let alone within the last hour. A quick use of the toilet facilities toward the kitchen area in the rear—a covering act to see if the restaurant had a second or private dining room—had been unproductive as well. The place was small. What you saw when you entered was what there was.

• 10:35 P.M.

A visit to a café further down the street and then a bar and shortly afterward a souvenir shop had had the same result. No Anne, nor anyone looking like her, had either come or gone within the past hour.

He moved on, the wet streets reflecting the vivid colors of lighted store signs and the headlights of passing traffic. By now he was walking along Rua Garrett and nearly out of the Chiado district. Ahead, and down a steep cobblestoned street—he recalled from earlier—and he would be in the even more densely populated Baixa quarter. He was about to turn the corner and start down when two things came to mind at almost the same moment.

The first was something Anne had asked Raisa as she had shown them around the apartment.

"One other thing. A computer or laptop with an Internet connection. At some point I will need to do a little work."

Raisa's reply had been that as yet the building had no Internet connection. It was a reality Anne had accepted with little more than a nod.

The second was something that had happened earlier as they'd climbed from the Baixa quarter and turned onto Rua Garrett, where he was now—when Anne had suddenly ducked into a small, elegant five-star hotel to use the loo. At the time it had seemed completely reasonable, but putting the two pieces together now he wondered if she hadn't been doing something more than just taking a pee. Maybe she'd been deliberately checking out the hotel to see if it had Internet service, a service a five-star hotel might very well provide even if some of the surrounding neighborhoods did not. But why? She had an Internet connection on her BlackBerry.

Still . . .

Abruptly Marten turned back, retracing his steps on Rua Garrett. The hotel had been small, stylish, and on the left. Where was it? What had it been called? He walked on. Suddenly the rain came down in earnest. He huddled close under the umbrella and moved on. Seconds later he stopped. Not fifty paces ahead he saw it.

HOTEL LISBOA CHIADO

His blood came up in a rush, and he started toward it.

10:46 P.M.

88

The sound of a piano greeted Marten as he entered the small foyer. It seemed to be coming from a bar partway down an elegant wood-paneled hallway that led to the main desk area in the rear. On the left and in between was an elevator. A stairwell was just past it. Not the best architectural layout for a hotel, but probably done to work within the structural confines of a building that looked to be eighty years old at least and might once have been a private residence.

Marten closed the umbrella and walked down the hallway to glance into the bar. A young black man in a white suit sat at a piano effortlessly playing a medley of show tunes for the dozen or so patrons congregated there. As in the other places he'd visited, Anne was not among them.

He turned back, looked in the direction of the main desk, and headed for it. As he did, the elevator in front of him opened and three people stepped out. Their backs to him, they walked in the same direction he was going, toward the main desk. Two were clearly hotel employees, both in dark suits, one older than the other, the concierge, maybe. The third was a slim, fortyish, dark-haired man dressed in jeans and a Hawaiian shirt.

"I understand she checked in, but where is she now?" the Hawaiian shirt asked emphatically.

"I don't know, sir. I'm sorry." The older man was genuinely apologetic. "Maybe she went out for something she needed. She had no luggage. She said it had been lost at the airport and was to be delivered here. So far it hasn't been."

"But she did go to the room."

"Yes, sir. The night clerk showed her to it. You saw that for yourself."

"All I saw was that someone had used a hand towel in the bathroom. It could have been anyone."

"I'm sorry, Mr. Tidrow. It's all I can tell you."

"She's my sister, you know. She's not well. She was supposed to call the moment she checked in."

"I appreciate the situation, sir. We will alert you the moment she returns."

At the word "Tidrow" Marten stopped where he was. They were already here, looking for her. How could they have known? Unless she'd been foolish enough to use a credit card and her accounts were being electronically monitored. But then credit cards, plus a little cash—certainly not enough for a room in a hotel like this, four hundred euros a night at least, probably more—would have been all she had. Moreover, she would have known that there was every chance her accounts were being watched and that if she used any of her cards they would know where they had been used and when, almost instantly. It meant she'd come there, done whatever she'd had to do, and then left before they could get there. But why? What was it that was worth the risk of exposing herself like this?

Use of the Internet?

Maybe he was wrong. Maybe she'd come there for some other reason entirely. He looked around. On a side table near the bar entrance was an arrangement of hotel brochures. Quickly he crossed to it, picked one up, and opened it. In the list of hotel amenities were the words *High Speed Internet Access in All Rooms.*

Again he saw the fire and fear and uncertainty in her eyes just before she'd left Raisa's apartment building and disappeared into the night. Alright, maybe the Internet was what she'd been after. But what information had she hoped to get that wasn't already available to her via her own BlackBerry?

He slipped the brochure back in its cradle and looked down the hallway. The man in the Hawaiian shirt had stepped away from the others and was on a cell phone.

Get out of here, now! Marten thought.

Head down, he started for the front door. As he did, it opened and two men in suit coats came in. One was strongly built and well over six feet; the other, tall and very slim. Marten barely glanced at them as he passed, but in that instant the breath went out of him. The big man was Conor White. The other was the French-Canadian jungle fighter, Patrice Sennac.

Breathless, umbrella in hand, Marten pushed through the door and out into the rain. A metallic gray BMW was parked directly in front of the hotel; a lone man sat at the wheel. Double-parked across the street was a dark blue Jaguar sedan. Its parking lights were on and he could just make out two figures in the front seat. Both were looking in his direction. Immediately he turned right and walked quickly off. Back down Rua Garrett, toward the Baixa district. Seconds later he heard the hotel's door open behind him. A rush of feet followed. Beard, turned-up collar, pulled-down hat, or not, he'd been recognized.

He took off on the dead run.

10:57 P.M.

89

Marten turned off Rua Garrett and ran hard down steep, rain-slicked, white-cobblestoned steps that ran alongside whatever narrow side street he had taken.

"Marten!"

Someone shouted behind him. Conor White? Maybe.

"Marten!" it came again.

He looked back and saw two men crest the top of hill on foot. Just then the gray BMW came into view. It slid to a stop beside them. They jumped in and the car screeched off, coming after him.

He turned back and kept running, looking for a way out. Then he saw a darkened alley to his right and turned down it, moving, he thought, into the Baixa quarter. At the end he turned left and ran on. Seconds later he saw the dark blue Jaguar flash under streetlights as it cut in from a side street. He turned left again, ran up a hill, then cut right at the next street and started down it. For a moment there was silence. Then he heard a wild scream of tires behind him and saw the Jaguar slide around the corner, nearly hit a parked car, then regain control and race toward him. Where the BMW had gone he didn't know.

Suddenly he remembered Kovalenko's Glock automatic in his waistband. He slid it out and kept running. A hundred yards farther down was the bottom of the hill. There, it flattened out and went straight into the heart of the Baixa. If he could reach it, with its traffic and its myriad of streets and cross streets, he might still have a chance.

Then the Jaguar was alongside him. It flew past, then abruptly slid to a stop. The passenger door was wrenched open and a man stepped out, a machine pistol in his hand.

"Freeze right there!" he commanded in English.

"Freeze this!" Marten yelled and raised the Glock.

Boom! Boom!

He fired two quick shots. The man was blown backward, bounced off the passenger door, and dropped to the pavement like concrete. In the next instant the driver's door slammed open. Marten dove behind a parked car as a salvo of machine-pistol fire cut across it, showering him with pieces of metal and windshield glass. For a seemingly endless moment there was quiet. Then, the machine pistol up, the driver came forward in the rain and dark looking for him.

Marten let him come. Thirty steps, then twenty. He could see him now in the glow of the streetlights.

Short hair, medium height, slim build. Thirty, thirty-five. The rain continued to fall. Ten steps away. Then five. Then two.

Marten calmly stood up. Almost in his face.

"Right here," he said. The driver cried out in surprise and swung the machine pistol.

Boom!

Marten's lone shot caught him between the eyes. His head snapped back, taking his body with it. He tottered for a moment, defying gravity, and then his legs gave out and he collapsed on the pavement.

Instantly Marten shifted his stance and looked past him for the gray BMW. He didn't see it. Suddenly lights in the apartments on either side of the street were coming on and he could hear voices. He debated whether to chance retrieving the driver's machine pistol, then decided against it and quickly walked away. Down the hill. In the rain. And into the heart of the Baixa.

11:11 P.M.

90

• 11:17 P.M.

Irish Jack opened the left rear door of the gray BMW and climbed in next to Conor White. Carlos Branco was at the wheel, Patrice beside him.

"We're not dealing with your everyday landscape

architect." Irish Jack was rain-soaked, his hair and suit jacket especially. Branco had parked the car at the top of the hill, and the Irishman had gone down to the stopped Jaguar to see what had happened even as residents began coming out of their apartments and the singsong of approaching sirens echoed in the distance.

"My guess is he took three shots and they all hit their mark. Got the driver smack-fuck between the eyes. He knows what the hell he's doing."

Carlos Branco's eyes went to the mirror, and he looked at Conor White.

"Who is he?"

White stared back at him. He wasn't happy. "The question is, who are you, Mr. Freelance Accomplished Resource? We knew where Anne was and she got away. We had Marten and he got away. Two of your people are dead. Coincidentally, if I'm not mistaken, he got a good look at you in the hotel. You're supposed to be part of Congressman Ryder's RSO team that sets all three of them up tomorrow. What are you going to do about that?"

"What I look like tomorrow. He'll never make the connection."

"You fucked up everything. You tell me why should I keep you on."

The scream of sirens drew closer.

"Because it would be a mistake not to."

Just then two police cars, their light bars flashing, turned the corner at the bottom of the hill, started up, then came to an abrupt stop in front of the Jaguar.

White looked at his watch: 11:22 P.M.

"What time does the Ritz bar close?" he asked quietly.

"One," Branco replied.

"Good."

• Four Seasons Hotel Ritz, the Ritz Bar. 11:52 P.M.
Sy Wirth came in and looked around. The bar area where he'd been earlier was nearly as busy as before, but the fashionable seating area back from it where small round tables with plush chairs or couches were nestled intimately close, was not. A man sitting at a corner table raised his hand. Wirth went over and sat down. He was dressed in a dark suit coat over a hastily thrown-on white dress shirt and jeans.

"You're Patrice," he said tersely.

"Yes."

"Where's Conor White?"

"He's been delayed. He apologizes. He should be here shortly," Patrice said easily.

"That's what he said when he called and asked me to meet you. Where the fuck is he? What happened with Anne Tidrow?"

Patrice signaled for a waitress. "Ms. Tidrow had apparently been in the hotel for a short time and then left without being seen. Nicholas Marten showed up about the same time we did."

"Marten?"

"He saw us and ran. We went after him. He killed two of our people."

"What?"

"Afterward he got away." Patrice looked up as

the waitress arrived. "Mineral water for me." He looked at Wirth. "You?"

"Nothing."

"Please, Mr. Wirth." Patrice smiled. "It's been a long day, it may get longer. What do you drink?"

"Walker Blue," Wirth said irritably.

The waitress left, and Wirth leaned in close. "What the good fuck is going on?"

"There's been a new development. It has to do with Ms. Tidrow. Carlos Branco, you know him?"

"What about him?"

"He's been in touch with Conor. It's why the delay, why Conor asked me to see you and fill you in on what happened before he got here."

"Your drinks, gentlemen." The waitress smiled, put down cocktail napkins and then set each man's drink in front of him.

"Cheers." Patrice lifted his glass. Wirth took his and downed the whisky in one swallow.

Patrice looked to the waitress and grinned. "I think he might want another."

"Yes, sir," she said and left.

Wirth glared at him. "Get on your cell phone and call Conor White. Tell him I want him here. I want him here, now."

"He doesn't have to, Mr. Wirth." Conor White slid into a chair next to him.

12:08 A.M. Now Monday, June 7.

91

Banco Espirito Santo. Marten passed the bank building for the second time in the last twenty minutes and realized he was getting nowhere. He'd walked up and down the Baixa—Rua do Áurea, Rua Augusta, Rua dos Correeiros, Rua dos Fanqueiros, with others in between—to no avail. All he'd seen were several taxis, here and there a pedestrian, and darkened shops. Wherever Anne had gone after she'd left the Hotel Lisboa Chiado only she knew. The few other hotels he'd passed, the only public buildings still open and that she might have gone into, he'd ruled out because of the credit card situation and the risk of being seen himself.

Moreover, the police presence was heavy, which he knew it would be following the shootings. More than once he'd ducked into a doorway or around a corner as a patrol car passed. Luckily the rain kept the motorcycle units to a minimum, and there had been no foot patrol at all, at least that he'd seen. Meaning so far he'd been lucky, but how long that fortune would hold was, he knew, mostly up to him.

Finally he decided there was nothing more he could do about Anne. Her fate, like his, was in her own hands. The thing now was to try to get back to Raisa's apartment and wait for Joe Ryder's call. That meant a thirty-minute walk—through the Baixa, then up into the Chiado, and finally the Bairro Alto. A thirty-minute walk if he didn't get lost. A lot more if he did. The longer he was out, the greater the chance of being stopped and questioned by the police. If that happened he was done, especially since he was still carrying the Glock automatic that had killed Haupt-kommissar Franck and the two men in the Jaguar. A gun he could throw into any sewer opening or storm drain but didn't dare in the event Conor White and his men showed up.

The rain came down steadily, and he pulled the umbrella close overhead. He turned right at the next corner and kept going. Now he realized he was walk-ing toward the area where the shootings had taken place. There should be a way to circumvent it, but he didn't know how. So he kept on, staying as much in shadows as he could.

He was wet and exhausted. The thought of the long walk back to the Bairro Alto was numbing, but he had no choice. So he kept on. Another block, then two. Somewhere along the way he began to think of the shootings themselves. Before, in the apartment in Berlin, he'd been nearly crushed by the fear of approaching police sirens. The next morning, he'd seen the television reports of the murders of Marita and her students and had a panic attack, losing con-trol and physically assaulting Anne, blaming her for the killings. He nearly lost it again at the Bordeaux-Mérignac Airport when he'd been certain he had lost his edge and was no longer capable of surviving in a world of bloodshed and sudden death. But then had come the men in the Jaguar. Whatever security mechanisms that had been hounded into his psyche those years ago in the LAPD were still there. The gunmen had stepped from the car, and he'd done what he'd been trained to do. Shoot to kill in self-defense. Calmly, accurately. Then he'd walked away. There'd been no rapid heartbeat, no trembling hands, no indecision. Just swift, deadly action. And afterward no remorse at all. It was a thought that troubled him more than if he'd simply lost his nerve and run. What had Marita told him at the airport in Paris? *I think you're one of those people trouble follows around.*

As much as he tried to escape it, blood and violent death seemed to hover over him like some predestined curse. How long before it reached critical mass and took him over completely, making him wholly mad and coldly murderous, the way he had been with the men in the Jaguar? How much longer before it finally finished the job and swallowed him up for good?

Six minutes later he started up Rua do Carmo toward Rua Garrett. Somewhere in front of him he heard the sound of an accordion. It grew louder as he approached. Finally, in the spill of a streetlight, he saw the man playing it. He was alone, sitting out of the rain on a small folding chair inside a doorway. He wore an old overcoat and a beret that was too small for his head and seemed completely unaware of the world around him. There was no way to guess his age or even his race. But none of it

mattered. His soul was somewhere else, on a different plane and on a different journey than the world
around him. Whatever song he was playing was unbearably sad but at the same time hauntingly beautiful. Marten wished he could pull up a chair beside
him and sit there listening forever.

But he couldn't.

So he passed him by in the rain and dark.

And walked on.

12:25 A.M.

92

• 12:30 A.M.

The gray BMW sped along Avenida Álvares Ca-
bral, rounded the city park Jardim da Estrela, the
Garden of the Star, and raced off down Avenida Infante Santo toward the harbor. With little or no traffic to slow them, Irish Jack kept the accelerator to
the floor and an eye on the mirror looking for police
coming up from behind. Patrice rode silently beside
him, little more than a passenger himself. Conor
White and Sy Wirth sat side by side in the seat behind them with Wirth staring silently into space.

"Carlos Branco's found Anne." White had brought
the news when he'd joined them in the Ritz Bar.

"Where?" Wirth had been exuberant.

"A cheap hotel in Almada, across the 25th of April Bridge on the far side of the Tagus River. Branco thinks she's waiting to meet someone."

"Ryder?"

"Maybe. It's probably why she went to the hotel. To contact him."

"What about Marten?"

"He's not with her. After the shooting he vanished. She'll know where he is, or at least where they were staying before she went out on her own."

"Why would she leave Marten behind to meet with Ryder alone?"

"You know her better than I do," White said. "You tell me."

"There's only one way to find out."

With that Wirth had finished his drink and they'd left, crossing the Ritz's lobby and going out into the rain and dark, then walking up the block to meet Irish Jack waiting in the BMW.

Streetlights and the occasional passing car alternated the shadows inside the BMW. Black to bright to white to silhouette to something in between. Wirth glanced at Conor White as if in an angry dream, then stared off as he had before.

"What are you thinking?" White asked quietly.

Wirth kept his eyes straight ahead. "I'm trying not to."

• 12:35 A.M.

Irish Jack turned off Avenida Infante Santo and onto the freeway just above the Port of Lisbon docks. Seconds later he swung the car onto Rua Vieira da Silva, a shortcut to the cloverleaf that would take them onto Avenida da Ponte and then onto the 25th of April Bridge and across the Tagus River to Almada and the hotel where Anne was. Wirth was alert, excited. Conor White could see his mind working, his thoughts dancing all over.

A few seconds later White looked up to see Irish Jack watching him in the mirror; he nodded imperceptibly. For no apparent reason, the BMW slowed. Irish Jack pulled it to the curb and stopped. The area was a darkened neighborhood, a mix of apartment and commercial buildings and closed shops.

"What's this?" Sy Wirth snapped.

"We need to set some ground rules before we get to Anne," White said quietly.

"Rules? What rules? What the hell are you talking about?"

"You sent us after the Spanish doctor and her charges, Mr. Wirth. It was an unforgivable mistake. They didn't know a thing about the photographs. Worse, much worse, you brought the Russians into this."

"What are you getting at?"

"We have one last chance to get the pictures. I don't want you involved in any way."

Wirth was outraged. "Who are you to talk to me like that? I gave you an enormous contract. Gave you power and prestige and visibility you would never have gotten on your own in a million fucking years." He jabbed an angry finger at Conor White. "And you know what, I can just as quickly take it all away. All of it. So fuck your ground rules and get going. Get to Anne."

"Have a drink, Mr. Wirth. You're going to need it." Conor White lifted a bottle of Johnnie Walker Blue from a pocket in the back of the front seat and opened it.

"I don't want a drink."

"Yes you do." Patrice turned in the front seat to look at him. "Mr. Wirth."

A chill crept down Wirth's spine. Slowly he looked to Conor White. "What do you want?"

"I want you to have a drink and calm down and listen to what I have to say." White held out the bottle.

Wirth looked at it. "I need a glass."

"I'm afraid you don't."

Wirth stared at him, then suddenly and reached for the door handle.

"It's locked, Mr. Wirth." Conor White showed no emotion at all. "Just have the drink."

Wirth's eyes went to Patrice. Then to the mirror, where Irish Jack was staring at him. Again White offered the bottle. Finally Wirth took it and took a strong pull. Then he looked back to White. "I'll ask you again—what do you want?"

"Maybe you could explain these." White reached into the inner breast pocket of his jacket pocket and brought out two number 2 Ticonderoga 1388 pencils.

"They're yours. I believe they go with this." White slid several folded pages of a yellow legal pad from the same pocket, unfolded them, and laid them out on the seat between them. "Maybe this will help." He clicked on a vanity light over the seat. "Your handwriting, Mr. Wirth,"

Wirth hesitated, then looked down to see the notes he'd made in the Gulfstream while he was flying over northern Spain in pursuit of Marten. Notes intended for a dialogue later that day with Arnold Moss.

> *1: Prepare to quickly and publicly disavow any connection to Conor White, Marten, and Anne once the photos are recovered. Whatever happens, White acted wholly on his own, or— (check with Arnie) as previously discussed re: separate clandestine Hadrian/SimCo relationship—with no involvement by Striker whatsoever. White should immediately and very publicly be terminated (he will go to jail anyway) and SimCo reorganized for continued operation in E.G. (Side note: SimCo's a good operation with personnel already in place in E.G. No need to completely dismantle it.)*
> *2: As above, prepare quick, smart, well-placed public relations spin, esp. in D.C.—*

There was no need for Wirth to read more. He looked over at White. Rage devouring him, his eyes little more than tiny, furious dots. "You were in my room at the Ritz while I was talking to your man in the bar."

"I'm pleased to know SimCo is a good operation,

Mr. Wirth. Perhaps you'd like to make a call and tell me personally." He held out his left hand. In it was Wirth's blue-tape BlackBerry. "You must have left it in your room knowing you were going to see me in person and therefore would not have to call."

"I don't know what you mean."

"You have two BlackBerrys, Mr. Wirth. One to call me and one to call everyone else. You put the blue tape on mine so you wouldn't get them mixed up. Calls from the blue tape get routed through Hadrian headquarters in Manassas so it appears that they come from there and not you. I do my homework, Mr. Wirth. Even when it's necessarily rushed."

Wirth stared at him for a long moment. "How much do you want?" he said finally.

"Have another drink, Mr. Wirth."

12:47 A.M.

93

• 12:52 A.M.

The BMW moved south across the six-lane 25th of April Bridge at cruising speed, its windshield wipers slowly beating against what was now little more than a drizzle. One car passed them coming north. Another going south overtook them and went by, and then that was all; the roadway was dark in either direction. Behind, the lights of Lisbon glowed against the night sky. In front were the city lights of Almada on the southern shore. Beneath was the dark ribbon of the Tagus River two hundred and thirty feet below.

The only sounds inside the car were the hum of the tires and the steady beat of the windshield wipers. Josiah Wirth looked from Irish Jack to Patrice and then to Conor White. Each man was silent, looking straight ahead, nothing more than a passenger in a moving vehicle. "Where are we going?" he asked finally, fearfully.

"To a funeral," Conor White said softly.

Wirth saw Irish Jack glance in the mirror. Abruptly he swung the wheel, and the BMW crossed into the far right lane. A glance in the mirror and he stepped on the brakes. A heartbeat later the car slid to a stop, and Irish Jack and Patrice got out.

"What's going on?" Wirth yelled at Conor White.

"As you said, Mr. Wirth. We'll get out of this yet. We'll look back and laugh."

Suddenly Wirth realized. "No! No! No, please! No!"

"Don't beg, Mr. Wirth. It's beneath you."

Abruptly the door beside the Striker chairman was thrown open, and the strongest hands he'd ever felt in his life dragged him from the car. He glimpsed the face of Irish Jack and then Patrice. Each carried the stone-cold, passionless expression of a professional killer.

"No!" Wirth screamed. "No! No! No!"

There was a wild scuffling of feet as he was wrestled toward the rail. He tried to kick, bite, fight back.

Anything to get free. Nothing worked. He felt himself hoisted up and saw Conor White step out of the car and come toward him. Then he was standing next to him, the number 2 Ticonderoga 1138 pencils in his hand. He held them in front of his face and snapped them in half.

"Watch," he said and let the pieces fall away. They drifted down as if in some kind of super-slow motion to vanish in the darkness below.

"You won't hear them hit. You won't hear anything, Mr. Wirth."

"No, no—please! Don't do this. Please don't! Help! Help! God please help me! Please!" Wirth beseeched any man, god, or spirit for the first time in his life.

None answered.

"I asked you not to beg, Mr. Wirth."

Suddenly he was hoisted over the rail. The hands that held him let go. There was a rush of cool air and the sensation of falling from a great height. He heard himself scream. Then he glimpsed the lights of the city. For a long moment he felt as if he were flying. A majestic bird in a world he'd never known. Then the blackness below rose up around him and he plunged headlong into it.

12:57 A.M.

94

Nicholas Marten turned the key in the lock and let himself into the apartment. Save for a small lamp still on in the entryway, the place was dark. He set the umbrella on the floor, locked the door behind him, then went into the kitchen. A big red 0 glowed on the answering machine. Ryder had not called.

He was bone tired, his feet rubbed raw from shoes and socks soaked through by the rain. His walk had not taken the thirty minutes he'd imagined but closer to fifty, as twice he'd had to take cover to avoid patrolling police and twice more had to find other routes because of heavily manned roadblocks. Whatever had happened to Anne, wherever she was or had gone, he no longer let concern him. He'd done all he could to find her and bring her back. It hadn't worked, so there was nothing else. All he wanted now was a warm shower and sleep.

He walked down the hallway and past the darkened bedroom toward the bathroom as if in a dream, taking off his clothes as he went. The only thing he kept with him, and it was almost an afterthought, was the Glock.

He went into the bathroom and turned on the overhead lights. They were tiny, dim halogen fixtures, maybe fifty of them mounted in the ceiling. Some kind of special effect designed to warm the hard polished marble of the walls, bath, shower stall, and countertops. A tasteful, if overly conscious, effort to exude sex from every pore in the room.

The shower stall was directly in front of him. To the right was a large Jacuzzi tub, an extension phone on the wall beside it. It was then he decided to abandon the shower idea and instead soak in a steaming tub, maybe even fall asleep there. If Ryder called, the phone was in reach. The same for Anne, in the event she called, too, which he doubted. Still, she did have the number. She'd told him so when she'd left.

He turned on the water, adjusted the temperature, and let it fill the tub.

• 1:07 A.M.

Marten set the Glock on a marble ledge just above the tub, then took a hand towel and slid into the water. It was warmer than he'd expected, and it took a moment before he felt comfortable. Then he lay back and let out a sigh. A moment later he closed his eyes and put the towel across them, blotting out the world. One deep breath and then another. Where was he? How had he come to be here? Why had he come to be here? Sleep was all he wanted.

"I've been waiting for you. I was worried."

Anne's voice rocked him. He pulled the towel from his face and sat up, thinking it was a dream. It wasn't. She stood next to the tub beside him, one of

Raisa's expensive bathrobes pulled around her. "I fell asleep waiting. I didn't hear you come in. Then I heard water running and saw the light on. Where have you been? What about Joe Ryder?"

He stared at her in amazement. The fact that he was naked never entered his mind. "How long have you been here?"

"An hour or so."

He sat up angrily. "Yeah, well, fuck. Conor White and your Patrice found out you were at the hotel. They went there looking for you."

"How do you know?"

"I was there. White had the others waiting outside, for Chrissake. I killed two of them."

"What?"

"Kovalenko's Glock. They came after me. So I shot them. One right after the other on a street near the hotel. Then I walked off still looking for you. I've been dodging the Lisbon police ever since." Suddenly his anger deepened. "I'm out there in the rain with the police and you're in here fucking sleeping." He picked the hand towel up again, put it over his eyes, and leaned back in the water.

"I'm tired. Go back to sleep or whatever the hell you were doing. I need to think and try to put this all together, if that's even possible. Maybe at some point you'll do me the courtesy of telling me what was so damn important that you had to go out and get all this started. It might help, but I doubt it."

"I want to have sex with you."

He took the towel from his eyes and looked up at her. "What?"

"I said I want to have sex with you," she said again and slipped out of the robe. Without a word she slid naked into the water, opening her legs around him and fitting into the confines of the tub.

"Hey." He looked her in the eyes. "I'm mad at you. You did a hugely stupid thing going out like that. I nearly got killed because of it. You think I'm just going to forget about it and have sex with you?"

"I'm still mad at you for nearly strangling me in Berlin, but that has nothing to do with now." She ran a hand along his thigh under the water, then leaned forward. "Kiss me," she whispered. "Like you did in Berlin. In the middle of the street with the police watching. I liked it."

"You're nuts."

"Kiss me."

"Aw, Jesus, Anne."

The bedroom was dark, the bed wet from their bodies come straight from the bath. Marten made a sound as her lips encircled his penis. Slowly she began to move her head up and down the length of him; in time she let her hand join in, using it as well as her lips. He watched her for a moment, then leaned back and looked up at the ceiling. Lights from a passing car on the street below moved across it and then were gone, the ceiling dark again. Fire was rising inside him.

"Jesus, Anne," he murmured.

She kept going, slowly. Her tongue circling the top of his erection, then bringing her mouth back over the top of it and taking it far down into her throat. He was going to explode and knew it. He tried to push her head away. He didn't want to come now, not yet. She fought him off and kept on, hunching up a little as his hips began to rise, her breasts sliding across his thighs, her nipples as hard and erect as he was. He heard her moan. An animal sound. Then everything rose up at once. He tried to hold back. It didn't work and he erupted. Still she didn't stop. Soon pain overrode pleasure and he had to forcefully move her head away.

"It hurts," he breathed.

She stopped and looked up and smiled seductively. "But it hurts good, doesn't it?"

He saw her get up and go into the bathroom. There was a toilet flush and then running water, and then she came back with a warm towel to clean him. Afterward she moved up into his arms in the dark and kissed him. They lay that way for a long time, the only sound their breathing, which seemed to rise and fall in unison. Finally she slid her hand down and made him hard again, then looked into his eyes.

"It's your turn," she whispered. "Go down on me and then fuck me. Fuck me hard. And for a long time."

95

How long had they been at it? Marten didn't remember the last time he'd had sex like this. How many times had he come? How many times had she? And there had been something more. When he'd been on top she'd reached up and run her hands through his hair and held him, her eyes watching him as he watched her. Even in the dim light he'd seen pleasure, and escape, and maybe even love pass through her. Not just passed through but shared with him. He had never had any woman do that before. Not even his adored Caroline. He wondered how she could convey those exceedingly simple yet terribly deep emotions all at the same time without abandoning herself to any one of them.

"Let's go to sleep," he said finally. "Tomorrow—" He looked at his watch: 2:32 A.M. "No, today is going to be long and, I think, very dangerous."

"I want more," she whispered.

"You're kidding."

"No."

"I'm not sure I—"

"I know you can."

She reached down and stroked him until his erection filled her hand. Then she rolled over and got on top. She was still wet and slid him into her as if they'd never stopped. Then she began. The rhythmic sliding up and down, the smooth, steady pump of her hips. He tried to move with her, but she wouldn't let him. This time it was all her. Her movements, her timing, everything. His rod, little more than her own personal tool.

Slowly her pace increased, the movements more intense, her breasts sliding up and down over his chest as she worked. The moans that had come from her before were now longer and louder, but somehow different, as if rising from some place neither of them knew existed. What had Raisa told him?

"Something troubles her a great deal. It's why she left, to try and resolve it. When she does, or even if she fails, she will come back completely drained by whatever has happened and be looking for a release of the most profound kind. In my experience nothing does that better than a good fuck, especially when it's done with someone you like and trust. Be gentle with her. But not too gentle. For a little while at least she will want to forget everything."

Suddenly Anne picked up the tempo; with it came a series of powerful cries, nearly shouts. One after the other after the other. She was coming to orgasm in a way he'd never seen or heard or been part of, even with what they'd gone through in the last hours. She rode up and down the full length of him, again and again and again. Her breathing grew deeper, her cries unworldly. Then, with one final storm of thrusts, she let go a resounding wail and collapsed on top of him. To lie there in the dark, gasping and soaked with sweat.

For a long time he did nothing but lie beneath her, his arms around her, letting her recover. "Are you alright?" he whispered finally.

She gave no reply. Seconds passed, and he wondered if she had exhausted herself and fallen asleep. Then suddenly she let out a muffled sob, rolled off him, and got up, moving back away from the bed in the dark.

"What is it?" he said in concern and surprise.

Silence.

He sat up. "What is it?" he said again.

"Don't!"

He could just see the wild starkness of her eyes as she shook her head and moved farther back, climbing into an overstuffed chair in the corner and cowering there, still naked, like some fearful animal. Then the crying began. Tears and quiet sobs at first, followed by a torrent of both, louder and far more pronounced.

He got out of bed and came toward her. "What's wrong?" he asked tenderly. Her only response was a continuing rain of tears that were interspersed with wrenching sobs.

Marten was as much dismayed as he was concerned. This was something he never would have imagined, let alone expected—a strong, vibrant woman like she was suddenly coming apart in front of him.

"What is it? What's going on?" he pressed gently. "Tell me. Let me help."

"Fuck you!"

The crying and sobbing kept on. She was about as close to hysteria as anyone could get.

He crossed the room and found her robe, then came back and put it over her as best he could. She didn't seem to notice. He went to the closet, found a robe for himself, and pulled it on. Then he took a straight-backed chair, turned it around, and sat down close to her, watching her. He wanted to intercede, to help, but he knew it would do no good. Ten minutes passed. Nothing changed. He wanted to turn on a light but was afraid of how she might react.

Ten minutes more, then twenty. A car went by outside, its lights momentarily reflecting off the ceiling and letting him see her. She was still hunched in the chair, the robe over her, crying inconsolably.

"It has to do with why you went out, doesn't it?" he said. "What was it? What happened?"

There was no reply. Just tears and wrenching emotion.

"If you didn't want me to know, you wouldn't have come back."

Still there was no response.

A few minutes more and the crying slowed and then stopped. "My purse," she murmured softly. "It's on the chair by the bed."

"I can't see what I'm doing. I need to turn on a light. Is that alright?"

"Yes."

Marten got up, crossed to a lamp next to the bed, and switched it on. The room filled with a dim, warm glow. Then he found the purse.

"Open it," she said. "There's a zipper pocket just inside, near the top."

"What's in it?"

"You'll see."

Marten opened the purse and found the zipper,

then pulled it open. Inside the pocket was a single item. A drugstore-type film processing envelope.

"This?"

"Yes."

He opened it. Inside were several strips of processed 35 mm film. He looked at her, puzzled. Her eyes were red. What little makeup she wore had been streaked by rivulets of tears.

"In the bottom of the purse . . ." she said hesitantly, "is something I've . . . kept with me . . . ever since I . . . left the Agency. It was habit . . . The old . . . spymaster special. A 35 mm Minox camera. When . . . we . . . crossed . . . the city, the shops I . . . kept going into . . . I was . . . looking for a place that had . . . photo-developing service. I found one in the . . . Baixa district. One hour or less . . . just like . . . at home . . . Open till midnight . . . seven days a . . . week."

"I don't understand."

"You will." Deliberately she reached up and wiped her eyes with the palms of her hands. "Go into the . . . bathroom . . . turn on the light over the sink and . . . and hold the strips up to . . . it. Don't look . . . for pictures. There are . . . none . . . Only . . . words."

96

Marten entered the bathroom. The Glock was still on the marble ledge just above the Jacuzzi tub where he'd left it. He crossed to the sink and turned on the light above it, then opened the envelope and carefully held the first strip up to it. It was hard to see what had been photographed. It looked like the page of a document, but he couldn't read it without some kind of magnification.

"It's page one of three." Anne stood in the doorway, the robe pulled around her. In the brighter light she was pale and seemed wholly spent.

"Come over here and sit down, please," he said gently and touched the edge of the tub.

" 'Top Secret—XARAK Protocol' is the first line." She stayed in the doorway where she was. "The next follows beneath it. 'Central Intelligence Agency, Washington, D.C. Subject: Memorandum of Understanding or MOU. For: President/CEO and General Counsel for AG Striker Oil and Energy Company; and for Chairman, President, and General Counsel for Hadrian Worldwide. From: Deputy Director, Central Intelligence Agency. Via: Director, National Clandestine Service. The General Counsel—CIA Office of General Counsel. Reference: NSCID-19470; EO-13318; CIA Operational Targeting Authority 1A.'

"It's all there, Nicholas. Everything that happened in Equatorial Guinea since the Bioko Find was orchestrated by the Agency. I'll give you more. I memorized most of it as I photographed the pages. Memorization. I was trained in it. The way you memorized poems or the Gettysburg Address or the Preamble to the Constitution when you were in school.

"One," she continued. "Based on direct, as well as implied, National Security tasking authorities stipulated in REFs, and in accordance with the Letter of Instruction (LOI) submitted separately from the Deputy Director of the CIA (DD/CIA), the General Counsel has prepared a Memorandum of Understanding (MOU) among the so-named trilateral participants in paragraph three. This MOU describes an ambitious plan to secure unimpeded drilling access and petroleum exploitation rights for the USA in the West African country of Equatorial Guinea. This initiative is part of a broader national imperative to achieve energy independence from other global sources of crude oil.

"Two: This document, upon affixation of signatures of the principals (named by position below) and courier-delivery to CIA Headquarters by Agency Security Officers, does constitute an active and legally binding accord for the two corporate entities under penalties heretofore separately specified by the Office of the Attorney General, the Internal Revenue Service, and other ancillary judicial instruments employable at the Agency's discretion." Anne stopped. "That's just the first part. The rest is the same, all concise and neatly spelled out. Congressman Ryder will love it."

Marten put the strips back into the envelope. "How did you get it?" He was incredulous.

"It's why I needed an Internet connection and a large-screen TV. It was something I asked about at the hotel on our way here when I told you I had to use the loo. The hotel you were smart enough to go back to. The one where Conor White tracked me, because of my credit card, I'm sure. I knew they would be watching everything but it's all I had.

"I couldn't very well have photographed the screen on my BlackBerry, it's too small. Nor could I download the document or make an electronic copy of it because they would know immediately that the site had been accessed and a copy had been made. Immediately they would attempt to trace the intruder. But by photographing it the old-fashioned way, bringing the pages up one by one, and clicking off each with the Minox, then, at the end, simply turning off the television, you see?" For a moment her voice drifted off and she seemed to forget what she was talking about; then she came back. "They would probably know the site had been accessed, but there would be no evidence it had been compromised and nowhere to look for the hacker."

Marten was astounded. "That site has to be highly classified. How did you get into it? You would need a myriad of codes and passwords."

"I was in the Agency for a long time, Nicholas. I know a few procedures. I also sit on Striker's board of directors. Not long ago I sat on Hadrian's board as well."

"Hadrian's?"

"Yes. I know both companies intimately. Codes, passwords. Some I had to work my way around, but in the end I had a basis for it all."

"Since when do boards of directors have access to a company's classified codes and passwords?"

Anne smiled faintly and ran a hand through her hair. "I told you before I had been married twice. I didn't say to who. My first husband was Loyal Truex, founder and president of Hadrian. My second was Sy Wirth, chairman of Striker. We shared a lot of things for a lot of reasons. Like most couples do."

"Jesus, Anne." Marten felt the air go out of him.

"I knew when Erlanger warned me on the airstrip, and then with Franck and the other CIA people getting involved, there had to be more to it than just the photographs . . . So I looked for it . . . and . . . found it." Suddenly the tears welled up again. "What I've done . . . is . . . betray the Agency, my country, my father, and myself. Striker Oil is . . . finished. Probably I am, too . . ."

Again she used the palms of her hands to wipe away the tears. "The thing is . . . that contract, that memorandum, belongs in the hands of Joe Ryder. He has the right to know about it and should know about it. When he has it he will act accordingly through the proper channels. Whatever else it does, the CIA cannot have its own foreign policy. Especially when the result is the horrifying deaths of all those people." Her eyes found Marten's and for a long moment held there. "I did it because it was the right thing to do . . . I didn't mean to hurt you or frighten you or use you . . . . Now . . . . I'm . . . very . . .

tired. I would like to . . . no, I need to . . . sleep . . .
Please . . . excuse me."

Marten found a piece of paper and made a note for
himself, then folded it and put it in his pocket. He
waited several minutes more, giving Anne the time
and privacy to settle herself. Finally he picked up
the Glock and the envelope with the 35 mm negatives and went into the bedroom.

The lamp was still on, and he could see her on
the far side of the bed, under the covers with her
back to him. He glanced at the clock: 3:32 A.M.

Immediately he went to the closet, punched in
the combination to the safe, waited as the electronic
locks slid back, then opened the door and put the envelope inside next to the photographs and the camera's memory card. For the briefest moment he
studied them all, then closed the door, listening as
the electronic locks engaged. Seconds later, he set
the Glock on the bedside table and turned off the
light, then took off his robe and slid into bed next to
her. Ever so gently he leaned over and kissed her
lightly, then pulled the covers up around her and lay
back in the dark, wholly drained by one of the lon-
gest days of his life. All he wanted was sleep.

Instead thoughts crept in, one overlapping another
as he tried to understand what had happened. Anne's
sudden fragility, her tears and runaway emotion, reminded him of the tragic breakdown of his sister,
Rebecca, years earlier when, as a child, she had seen
their adoptive parents shot to death by intruders in

their California home. By the time neighbors and the police found her she was on the edge of complete hysteria. Shortly afterward she had gone into deep shock, retreating into a heartbreaking world of silence where she could neither speak nor hear. Institutionalized, she had remained that way for years until another monstrously traumatic incident brought her out of it.

The stark memories of her ordeal made him recall what Anne had told him in Berlin. *"My mother got very sick when I was three. She was in the hospital for a month. She didn't recognize me or my father. Nobody knew what was wrong. Finally she came out of it. The experience scared the hell out of me. It did the same to my father. I was very young, but I could see it. I wanted so much to help him, but I couldn't."*

Then: *"My mother died when I was thirteen. It was brain cancer. She didn't live long, but it was awful for her and my dad. Like the first time, he tried to protect me from it while he was falling apart himself. How he kept everything together—me, himself, the company—I don't know."*

Marten's experience with Rebecca had brought him into close contact with any number of mental health professionals. Transposing what he had learned then to Anne's behavior tonight made him think that the seeds of it might well have been planted when she was a child. With no siblings to comfort her, her only escape would have been to hide her own emotions and focus on concern for her father. The same thing played out years later when he lay dying after a series of strokes. Again she would have put her own feelings aside in favor of his. By then it would have become a way of life; the outwardly strong, confident woman, routinely dealing with profoundly troubling issues by not dealing with them at all and instead burying them deep inside her. Shift that behavior to the present, where she faced a colossal runaway train: the Bioko field, the Striker/Hadrian corruption situation in Iraq, the Ryder Commission's probe into it, Conor White and the creation of SimCo—involving both of her ex-husbands, no less; the photographs; the CIA video; Erlanger's warning; the growing suspicion that the CIA was involved with Striker and Hadrian in fueling the civil war; all but confirming it, the arrival of Franck and Kovalenko in Praia da Rocha in search of the pictures and the realization that Franck was a CIA operative.

She'd been a professional, so suspicion alone wasn't enough. She left him and went to the hotel and did what she'd been trained to do, obtain proof. Once she'd hacked into the Agency files and discovered the memorandum, she would have suddenly realized she was standing on a moral precipice. Either turn away and forget she ever saw it or risk losing her father's company, the Bioko field, and maybe her life by photographing it, then having the film developed and giving it to Joe Ryder. Boldly, she'd chosen the latter and returned to the apartment to hand the negatives over to Marten for safekeeping alongside the photographs.

Then she'd had second thoughts. Maybe even

third, fourth, and fifth thoughts. Physically exhausted, emotionally overwhelmed, she robotically reverted to the old ways, burying her feelings and focusing on something else. In this case a wild orgy of sex with him, thinking, hoping, maybe even praying it would give her sufficient release to make her clear-headed enough to destroy the negatives and perhaps the photographs, too. But it hadn't worked; roaring and retching, a hurricane of long-buried emotions flooded out, and she came apart. Finally she was spent enough and raw enough to find the courage to do what she thought was right and give him the negatives, telling him nearly word for word what the memorandum contained. After that the only thing left was sleep.

Whether any or all of his analysis was right, there was no way to know, but putting things together the way he had along with memories of what his sister experienced, what had happened made sense. All they could do now was stay where they were and wait until Joe Ryder arrived in Lisbon and contacted them. Then they would go from there.

Again Marten looked at the clock: 3:51 A.M.

He closed his eyes and finally, mercifully, fell asleep.

• 3:53 A.M.

They spoke in Portuguese.

"Which floor?"

"The top one, I think. I walked around to the back. There was only one light on in the building, and it was up there. It went out about twenty minutes ago. The woman entered around midnight, the man about an hour later."

"You're certain it was them." Carlos Branco stood in the darkened park across the street from the building at 17 Rua do Almada, a fisherman's cap on his head, his jacket collar turned up against the lightly falling drizzle. The woman with him was maybe twenty. Her dark, short-cropped hair, light pullover jacket, and jeans were soaked through. She'd been outside for a long time.

"I'm certain it's her," she said. "I followed her from the Baixa. The man—I'm not positive it was him. I only saw him from the park, but he pretty much fit the description I was given."

"You did well."

"I know."

Branco took her hand and put five one-hundred-euro bills into it. "Go home and go to bed. You were never here."

He watched her walk off in the dark, then pass under a streetlamp and then fade again into the night. He looked back, then slid a night-vision scope from his jacket and trained it on the top floor. Even in its green glow, he saw only darkness.

3:58 A.M.

97

Its headlights out, the gray BMW rolled to a stop on the far side of the park across from Rua do Almada. Seconds later a figure moved out of the dark, opened the rear door, and slid in beside Conor White.

"Number 17, top floor," Carlos Branco said.

"You're certain it's them?"

"The woman, yes. The man, not positive, but I would bet it's Marten. There's a narrow alley at the back and a rear entrance. I have a man there watching. No one's come out. My guess is they're sleeping. The door lock's easy to crack. You want to go in, now is the time."

White looked to Irish Jack at the wheel and Patrice beside him. "Jack, take us around back and down the alley, lights out."

"Colonel," Branco warned. "This needs to be done very quickly. Afterward go directly to your plane and get out of the country. Right then, right away."

"What do you mean, right away?"

"The police are everywhere looking for the shooter of my men."

"What does that have to do with me?"

"They are also looking for you and"—he nodded toward Patrice and Irish Jack—"them."

"Why? What the hell do they want us for?"

"The murder of a Spanish doctor and her medical students in the countryside near Madrid."

"What?" Conor White was stunned. "How do you know this?"

"I have many lines of contact within the police organizations. Whether you did what they say is not my affair. You were seen earlier tonight in the lobby of the Hotel Lisboa Chiado and a short time later in the bar of the Hotel Ritz. At the moment the police are sweeping the area between the Baixa where my men were killed and the Chiado, working this way in a grid pattern. So if you are going in after Nicholas Marten and Anne Tidrow, do it now, very quietly and quickly, and get out. Enter the airport using the same gate I brought you through when you came here. The police don't know the manner in which you arrived in Lisbon, so for now they are watching the main terminals, not civil aviation." Branco smiled thinly and reached for the door. "Good luck, my friend, I have to trust you will pay me when you can."

"Get down," Irish Jack spat suddenly.

In reflex action the four instantly slipped below window level. They were just out of sight when a Lisbon police car moved slowly by, its headlights sweeping over the car as it went. They gave it ten seconds, then sat up.

Branco stared after it. "So now they are here in Bairro Alto." He looked at White. "Take it as God's blessing they came when they did and not five minutes later when you were parked in the alley and going upstairs. Get out of here and go to your plane while you still can."

"No," White snapped. "Not when we're this close. Not after everything."

"Colonel." Patrice turned to look at him. "It's not worth it."

White looked to Patrice, his eyes filled with contempt. "What do you know about worth?" He looked back to Branco. "Your people will stay here. At some point Marten and Anne will leave to meet the congressman. When they do your men will follow. At the same time, you will be at Ryder's side as a member of his embassy RSO detail."

"You mean you intend to go back to the old plan. Even after this."

"That's exactly what I mean."

"I held up my end of the bargain."

"Yes. And you will be paid."

"You can't stay out on the streets."

"You say the police were working the Baixa and the Chiado, now they're here. If they knew we were at the Ritz they would already have swept the area between there and the Baixa. Correct?"

"Yes."

"Then they would have been satisfied we were no longer there, which is why they've moved their search this way. They will still have patrols, but patrols can be avoided, especially when one knows he is being hunted. This is a game of cat and mouse. All three of us have played it in far more dangerous situations and in considerably more horrifying places than the quaint streets of Lisbon. I assume your men doing surveillance are wearing team radio units."

"Of course."

"I need the frequency."

Branco nodded. "171.925."

"Good, we'll be listening. Now, we are going back to our apartment. When Marten and Ms. Tidrow make their move, alert us and follow them. We will meet you wherever it is they have gone. In the meantime, treat Congressman Ryder well. We don't want him to suspect he has a mole at his elbow."

Branco smiled admiringly. "I see why you carry the Victoria Cross." With that he opened the door and slipped out into the darkness.

4:37 A.M.

98

• 6:50 A.M.

Marten woke with a start. Anne was still asleep, looking as if she hadn't moved since she'd put her head down. Immediately he got up, pulled on the shirt and jeans he'd been wearing since Berlin, then found his jacket and took the dark blue throwaway cell phone from it. Another glance at Anne and he picked up the Glock from the bedside table and left, carefully closing the door behind him.

He was crossing the front room on his way to the

kitchen when something made him stop and go to the window. It was just dawn, and the morning light was beginning to expose the shadows in the park across from them. A truck rumbled past on the street below; seconds later someone went by on a bicycle. The park itself was empty.

Or was it?

He could just make out the figure of a man on the far side of the benches where he and Anne had been yesterday afternoon. He was alone and standing back under a tree. Marten's first thought was that he was watching the building. Immediately he wondered if either he or Anne had somehow been seen and followed back to the apartment, and if whoever had done it had been ordered to wait and watch and follow in the event either of them left.

Ordinarily he would have dismissed it, telling himself that maybe he was overdoing it. That there was no reason to be alarmed by a lone man standing in a public park, a lone man who might well be waiting to meet someone, say, for a ride to work. But he had to remember that only hours earlier he had been all but face-to-face with Conor White and Patrice. Had to remember that Anne had been very quickly traced to the Hotel Chiado Lisboa. Had to remember the men in the blue Jaguar. Meaning White or someone else, quite possibly the CIA, would have immediately put assets on the streets looking for them.

One last glance at the man in the park and he left the window and went into the kitchen.

It was now almost seven o'clock in Lisbon,

approaching two in the morning in Washington, and President Harris would be sleeping. It made no difference; it was imperative he know what was going on. Moreover, Marten needed him to get in touch with Joe Ryder right then. Whoever the man in the park was or wasn't, White knew they were in the city and probably somewhere in the vicinity of the hotel. The minute Ryder landed he would be under heavy surveillance. Wherever he went someone would be right on top of him. And if White's people were here watching the apartment, there was no way he and Anne and Ryder could go anywhere without being followed. Moreover, if they were going to meet with Ryder they would be physically carrying the evidence with them—Anne's copy of the memorandum and the photographs in her purse, the camera's memory card tucked unseen into his jeans. If they were caught, all of it would be gone in an instant.

He lifted the phone, started to punch in the number of the president's throwaway cell phone, then stopped. If White's men or CIA assets were watching the apartment, they might very well have listening devices that would pick up any phone conversation coming into or going out of the building. Not only would his conversation be heard, it wouldn't take long for them to analyze the voices and realize who he was talking to. Still, the president needed to know what was happening, and he needed to know now. What he had to do was assume the people outside were indeed White's men or CIA and take the chance they had only recently come on-scene and as yet hadn't received the kind of complex electronic gear they would need to monitor calls.

He punched in the number of the president's phone. It rang once, then twice, then—

"What is it? Something wrong? Have you spoken with Ryder?" the president said quickly, almost as if he'd been waiting for the call.

"The CIA," Marten said. "Anne Tidrow hacked into a secure Web site and pulled up a memo from the deputy director. He made a deal with Striker Oil and Hadrian to provide backing for the insurrection in Equatorial Guinea as a way to help gain favor with the rebels and drive out President Tiombe, chiefly as a means to secure Striker's leases for years to come." Marten took the note he'd scribbled earlier from his pocket. "I wrote down part of it, what I could remember, something like—'a plan to secure unimpeded drilling access and petroleum rights for the U.S. in Equatorial Guinea,'" he read. "'This initiative is part of a bigger national obligation to achieve energy independence from other world sources of crude oil.'"

"Are you absolutely certain what you have is authentic?"

"Anne photographed the entire memorandum off a hotel room TV screen. It's film, 35 mm negative. The quality may not be great, but it's all there, every page of it. You worried that the attorney general would have little to work with. Add the memorandum to the photographs and Anne's testimony and you'll have enough for a major firestorm.

"But that's putting tomorrow ahead of today. I haven't yet heard from Joe Ryder and have no way to reach him, but I have to talk to him, and soon. Conor White and his soldiers know we're here. They saw me and came after me. I had to kill two of them. White is very well connected. He may be CIA himself or closely tied to them, I don't know. There's a very good chance they know where we are and are watching the building right now."

"They *are* watching the building."

Marten looked up. Anne stood in the doorway, her hair twisted up in a bun, her robe pulled around her.

"Two men. Across the street in the park."

"Two?" Marten said. "A few minutes ago there was only one."

"Well, now there are two." Anne was calm and very matter-of-fact. "Ryder needs to know where to meet us before he lands. We won't be able to communicate once he enters the Lisbon cell phone grid. They'll have every one of his lines monitored. If he tries to use a landline, they'll have that covered, too."

Marten turned back to the phone. "Could you hear that?"

"I assume it was Ms. Tidrow."

"Hopefully Ryder's left Rome and is en route here now. See if you can reach him and ask him to delay his landing until I can find a place and time where we can meet unseen. The best would be somewhere at the airport itself."

"That won't work. His itinerary has been laid out

by the embassy. It means he's got to at least start to play the game and go to his hotel. After that he can try to make his move. But you can't just meet. You've got to get back to the airport, onto his plane, and out of Lisbon. We have to have Ms. Tidrow and every piece of evidence you've got in our custody and safely back in the States. Where you land and where she goes after that, I'll take care of. Your job is to get you, her, and Ryder onto his plane and airborne as fast as possible."

"We can't do this alone. I'm going to need Raisa Amaro's help. You said to trust her completely. I want to hear it from you again, just to be sure I didn't get it wrong. Right now everything is going to depend on her."

"You can trust her with anything, cousin. As I said, she is very smart and very gifted, and also very efficient. She and I go back a long way."

"I'll talk to her and get back to you, hopefully with a time and meeting place for Ryder. Then you can pass that information on to him before he lands. If Raisa can't help, we'll just have to figure out something else. With luck you'll hear from me soon." With that Marten clicked off.

"The old girlfriend," Anne said with the faint hint of a smile.

"Yes." Immediately he brushed past her and went to the front window to stand beside it and look out. The man he had seen earlier had moved closer to the edge of the park. Another was a little farther back standing by a decorative fountain, his eyes on the building. Several seconds passed, and he reached up and touched his ear as if he were listening to something. Abruptly he put his hand to his mouth.

"He's talking to someone." Anne moved in beside Marten. "If there are two there, there will be others watching the back."

"You don't think they're police," he said flatly.

"No, I don't think they're police."

Marten crossed to the room phone, picked it up, and dialed 11, the extension Raisa had given him. She answered on the second ring.

"Good morning, Mr. Marten."

"Good morning, Raisa. I know it's early, but I wonder if you could come up here right away. Yes, now. It's important. Thank you." Marten glanced at Anne and hung up.

7:15 A.M.

99

• The Apartment On Rua De São Filipe Néri. 7:17 A.M.

An hour and forty minutes of sleep had been enough. Conor White was up at six forty-five. By seven he'd showered and shaved, and then he woke the others. Barefoot and wearing nothing but a bath towel around his waist, he'd plugged a team radio unit headset into his right ear, tuned to the 171.925 frequency Branco had given him, and listened to the intermittent chatter of Branco's men watching the apartment at 17 Rua do Almada. Afterward he'd gone into the kitchen and made a pot of coffee. By seven ten he was at the kitchen table making notes on his laptop. Six minutes later he opened a map of Lisbon and pinpointed the U.S. Embassy on Avenida das Forças Armadas, a location that looked to be no more than a five to ten minute drive from where they were.

• 7:20 A.M.

White lifted his BlackBerry and punched in Carlos Branco's number.

"*Yes,*" Branco's voice came back.

"Where are you?"

"*Just leaving the Ritz. Congressman Ryder's suite is ready for him. We are on our way to the airport to meet his flight.*"

"I need a car and one of your men for a driver, a guy who knows his way around the city and knows what's going on with Marten and the congressman."

"*When and what?*"

"A limousine of some kind with UN plates, parked outside the U.S. Embassy. I need it fast. How soon can you have it?"

"*Not so simple a request. It will take a few calls.*"

"How soon, Branco?"

"*Within the hour.*"

Conor White glanced at his watch. "We'll leave here at eight twenty and arrive at the embassy by eight thirty. If there is a problem, let me know before that."

"There will be no problem."

"Good."

With that White clicked off and went into the bedroom Irish Jack and Patrice had shared. The covers on the twin beds were thrown back. Irish Jack was just out of the shower, towel-drying his hair. Patrice walked in from the bathroom doing the same. Both were in undershorts and nothing else. Despite their physical differences, both men were built like stone and carried the tattoos and body scars of the longtime combat veterans they were.

"You look like fucking lovers," White said impassively.

Irish Jack grinned broadly. "That towel does wonders for you, too, Colonel. Standing here with us pretty boys makes you look like some kind of chap who wants to join the party but hasn't been invited."

For a moment a boyish sparkle came into White's eyes. "My dick's too big for you pussies, you couldn't handle it." Immediately the playfulness vanished and his eyes narrowed. "Business garb today. Suits, shirts, and ties. Ready to move out at oh-eight-twenty."

White headed into the other room to get dressed himself. As he did, his BlackBerry signaled a text message. He looked at it and saw it was from Loyal Truex, still in Baghdad, and went into the kitchen to take it.

He read it once, then again.

This arrived five minutes ago from Washington with copies to Arnold Moss in Houston and Jeremy

Moyer, COS/Lisbon. I forwarded it to you and to Anne, in the event she can, and would want to, read it. As you know, Washington can be purposely terse and ambiguous, so I'm not sure if it's a reprimand, a compliment, or if they just want us to know. It reads like a newspaper brief tied to a world geography narrative.

"The 585-mile-long Tagus River rises in the mountains east of Madrid, then flows northwest through the mountains and across central Spain to form part of the Spanish-Portuguese border. Afterward it runs southwest into the Atlantic Ocean at Lisbon. It is here, between the cities of Paço de Arcos and Carcavelos, where the river meets the sea, that the body of Striker Oil chairman Josiah Wirth was discovered by fishermen just after dawn this morning floating in a tangle of debris and seaweed."

I forward, too, a second message. It was encrypted and sent to me and Moss only. Use your laptop to read it. It's self-explanatory. You will find it extremely disturbing. Know you will take immediate and appropriate action upon reading. Am returning to Washington within the hour.

White sat down at the table and pulled his laptop around, then booted it up and pressed the pound sign on the keyboard. Immediately a marker popped up asking for his personal code. He typed it in. A second marker called for a password, which he entered as well. The screen registered a number of symbols and, beside them, a time and date code. He moved the cursor to the most recent

entry—barely twelve minutes earlier. The message
was brief.

XARAK Protocol, file accessed, 4 June, 1717 EDT.
Access ceased 1720 EDT. Access code AZ101P-22-
0LX5-8.*.8.*.2.

Instantly White signed off and shut down the laptop. The access code belonged to Loyal Truex. The
time 1717 through 1720 EDT was 2217 through
2220, Lisbon time. The exact same time Anne Tidrow had been in her room at the Hotel Lisboa Chiado. The file had been accessed only, not copied or
downloaded. If an attempt had been made to do either, the program would have shut down immediately, a security breach would have been sounded,
and there would be an electronic record of the time
and location where the attempt had been made. All
things Anne would have known. It meant she had
read the document and most likely either hand-
copied it or photographed it off the screen.

"Fuck," he swore under his breath. Anne and
the photographs were trouble enough; now they
had to deal with this. In the hands of Joe Ryder the
first two would be crushing, but this last—the text
of the document Truex, Sy Wirth, Arnold Moss,
and himself had all referred to as *The Hadrian
Memorandum*—would be hard evidence of Agency
involvement in the civil war in Equatorial Guinea on
behalf of the Striker Oil company, an operation authorized by the deputy director himself. Having it
become public was not something that could be

tolerated under any circumstance. Meaning the line in Truex's text message *Know you will take immediate and appropriate action upon reading* had not been a directive but an explicit order: Retrieve the outstanding materials and eliminate Marten, Anne, and Congressman Ryder as quickly as possible. Before it had just been Marten and Anne, and Ryder if necessary. Now all three had been given a death sentence. One that was to be executed immediately and in any way most expedient.

Suddenly he wondered what he was doing. His entire adult life had been given to the single purpose of gaining his father's recognition. In the process, he had become a highly educated national, even international, warrior-hero. But all that had ended with the photographs. Since then he had done everything in his power to recover them for the sole intent of protecting his own image. In doing so he had become a murderer—of young women and men, of a despotic oil executive, and now he was hours, maybe minutes, away from killing three more, among them a United States congressman. Why? So that the man who had never acknowledged him would not be aghast at what he saw if the photos were made public. What kind of a reason was that?

The trouble was, Anne's interference had snowballed the whole thing into a gargantuan geopolitical complication, with a huge, far-reaching cost if things continued to go wrong. It meant the game was no longer his alone. At stake now was the heart and soul of The Hadrian Memorandum itself, the protection of a vast sea of oil for the West. It was a twist he could never have imagined. In a strange way it eased his mind and raised his spirits because it meant the deadly actions still to come would not be those of a common murderer but of a front-line soldier, a patriot-warrior.

7:48 A.M.

100

• Portela International Airport. 8:42 A.M.

Carlos Branco waited at the bottom of the steps as Congressman Joe Ryder and his personal RSO detail, agents Chuck Birns and Tim Grant, came down the steps of their Gulfstream 200 and stepped onto Lisbon soil. Grant and Birns, Branco knew, had been assigned to Ryder for the past fifteen months as his sworn protectors when he traveled outside of the United States, and he trusted them completely. That meant they had a long-standing, interlocking loyalty and made them people he might well have trouble wresting away from the congressman when the time came and he tried to pull the entire RSO detail back in order to give Conor White and his gunmen singular access to their targets.

"RSO Special Agent Anibal Da Costa, Congressman," Branco said smartly as he introduced himself. "Welcome to Lisbon, sir. This way, gentlemen, please."

Immediately he turned and led them toward a black Chevy Suburban SUV parked on the tarmac twenty feet away where two more RSO agents waited, the rest of the Lisbon embassy detail.

Moments later they were driving past security gates and heading into the city, taking the same route Branco had used barely twelve hours earlier when he'd brought Conor White and his men in from the same airport.

He'd been right when he told White that Marten would not recognize him the next time they met. The clean-shaven, dark-haired man in the Hawaiian shirt and blue jeans he'd seen last night in the Hotel Lisboa Chiado now wore a tailored black suit, white shirt, and tie, and had gray hair and a neatly trimmed full beard of the same color. Moreover, his natural hazel-green eyes were now covered by deep blue contact lenses, a further safeguard in the event Marten had been paying that much attention; which he might well have been, considering what he had done to the men in the blue Jaguar.

That thought, coupled with the presence of Congressman Ryder sitting in the seat behind him now, reminded him of the realpolitik of the situation, the cold truth of why he had been brought aboard as a "painter" to set things up for White. Anne Tidrow, Ryder, and Marten, each in his or her own way, and for reasons unknown to him and possibly even COS Moyer, had become exceedingly dangerous to the CIA and had to be treated as such. Ryder's personal RSO detail had to be looked at that way, too. It was why he had recruited the people he had: five former

members of the Portuguese army Batalhão de Comandos, counterguerrilla special forces commandos
who would shadow Anne and Marten the moment
they left the building on Rua do Almada to wherever he and his RSO detail brought Ryder to meet
them. Meaning they would have both parties covered from start to finish with neither aware of it and
giving them little or no chance for escape. And if, at
the crucial moment, Birns and Grant, Ryder's RSO
people, attempted to interfere with his pullback of
the entire RSO detail, his commandos would cut
them to pieces—dedicated State Department employees regrettably caught in a crossfire between his
own RSO detail and assailants unknown—in the
process leaving Anne and Marten and Joe Ryder to
the mercy of Conor White and the men he had
brought with him.

• Four Seasons Hotel Ritz. 9:30 A.M.
Branco opened the door to Ryder's seventh-floor
suite, and the entourage entered. Birns and Grant
went in first, giving the elegantly appointed quarters careful inspection. They would find nothing out
of the ordinary. The suite had been electronically
swept and cleared by the Lisbon RSO detail more
than two hours earlier. Everything was clean. Perfect. Everything except for the tiny listening devices Branco had installed himself when he'd come
there alone at six fifteen, bugging the landline telephones and Internet connections, devices he'd deliberately kept the Lisbon RSO people from finding

then and kept Birns and Grant from discovering now. Ryder's personal cell phone activity and that of Birns and Grant had been meticulously monitored by a private communications contractor CIA COS Moyer had employed from the moment the congressman's plane entered the Lisbon cell phone grid.

Their inspection completed, Birns nodded to Ryder, who in turn looked to Branco.

"Thank you. I want you to know we appreciate the special attention."

"We enjoy our work, sir." Branco smiled.

"I know you do. Now, I'm going to work out some travel fatigue with a quick swim in the hotel pool, then come back to the room and attend to some business. I'll need a car about eleven thirty. I'm having lunch with an old friend."

"Where, sir?"

"Café Hitchcock. In the Alfama district. You know it?"

"Yes, sir. It's less than a ten-minute drive from here."

"Thank you, Agent Da Costa."

"The pleasure is ours, sir."

With that Branco left, taking his two Lisbon RSO agents with him.

Ryder watched the door close behind them, then looked to Grant and Birns, who were booked into the connecting room. "I'm going down to the pool. Get yourselves settled, then come down to meet me."

"Best you wait for us, sir," Grant said. "We'll escort you."

"This is the Ritz, fellas, not a bunker in Iraq. But thanks, I'll wait."

"Give us a couple of minutes."

With that they opened the door and went into the adjoining room.

Ryder took a breath and walked over to the window to look out over the city's Eduardo VII Park, and the Marquês de Pombal roundabout at the top of the Avenida da Liberdade at the edge of it. Every tree and blade of grass sparkled joyfully in the morning sun, making the city itself, despite the circumstances at hand, seem clean and wonderfully refreshed from the rain of the night before.

President Harris had reached him just before his plane entered Lisbon airspace. The first thing he'd asked was if Ryder completely trusted his own RSO detail, to which he'd answered in the affirmative. The second was not a question but a warning: Trust no one from the Lisbon embassy. Assume your movements are being watched, that your room is bugged and all of your phones monitored, cells included. Then:

"Do not try to contact Marten. You'll have to take your own RSO people into your confidence and just hope to hell they're not professionally, psychologically, or in any other way beholden to the RSO/ Lisbon people. You will need to get out of your hotel quickly and unseen. Your people should be able to help you do it. Now," he said, *"write this down,"* and Ryder had.

"You are to meet Marten and Anne Tidrow at the Hospital da Universidade, University Hospital, 25

Rua Serpa Pinto at eleven local time. Come in the rear entrance. A large, balding man named Mário Gama, the hospital's director of security, will be behind the desk. Introduce yourself as John Ferguson of the American Insurance Company and say you are there to meet Catarina Silva, the accounts receivable director. He'll take you to where Marten and Anne are. At eleven fifteen a laundry truck will meet the three of you and your RSO detail outside the same entrance you came in. Go directly to the airport, get on your plane, and get the hell out of there." The president had been emphatic, the tenor of his voice emphasizing both the danger and the significance of what they were attempting.

"Anne and Marten will be carrying very important information, so the whole thing, once you meet them, has to be bang, bang, bang. If you run into trouble and can't make it on time, Marten will wait until eleven thirty. If you don't show up, if it doesn't work at all, then repeat everything at the exact same time tomorrow. Lastly, tell the embassy RSO people you're meeting an old friend for lunch and that you will need a car at eleven thirty. The place is the Café Hitchcock in the Alfama district. It's well away from the area where the hospital is. That will have them thinking you're staying in your room until then, and they'll stand down, for a little while anyway, which hopefully will be long enough for you to get out of the hotel and to Marten."

With that he'd wished him well and signed off quickly. He'd sounded like he felt he'd already spoken too long and was worried—calling as he had at nearly three o'clock in the morning Washington time—that someone from his Secret Service detail would come into his room to make certain he was alright and then set a wave of gossip rolling with speculation about who he had been talking to and why.

"Ready to go down to the pool, sir?" Agent Grant stood in the doorway to the adjoining room.

"You bet. Right now."

9:37 A.M.

101

• 9:40 A.M.

Hunched over, flashlight beam focused in front of them, the Glock automatic in his waistband, Marten led Anne down a dark, narrow, low-ceilinged, cobweb-filled brick-and-mortar passageway that led from the basement of the building at 17 Rua do Almada to that of the building next door. It was a corridor that, theoretically at least, would continue on to the building after that and the one after that, ending finally in the basement at number 9, the last edifice on the block, which was at the far end of the park and a good fifty yards down from where the lookouts were stationed.

These long-unused connecting passageways had been built during World War II, when a neutral Portugal became a temporary haven for Jewish refugees fleeing Central Europe and Lisbon was a major transit point for exit to the United States. Sections of the Baixa, Chiado, and Bairro Alto districts with their close proximity to the harbor were favorites not only of the refugees but of Nazi spies commanded to report their movements and the names and destinations of the ships they boarded. As a result, the owners of many buildings like those on Rua do Almada built secret, interconnecting subterranean corridors through, and sometimes under, the buildings' cellars in order to help smuggle people unnoticed to waiting ships in the attempt to keep the transit lines open and create as little political turbulence for Portugal as possible.

Anne and Marten were attempting much the same thing now. Only their destination was not a ship on the waterfront but an electrician's van parked at the end of the block. With luck, and if the passageways were still navigable after nearly seventy years of nonuse, and if they left the building at number 9 and climbed unseen into the van Raisa had waiting, they should arrive at Hospital da Universidade on Rua Serpa Pinto after a reasonably short ride and pretty much on time.

That Raisa had been able to put the entire rescue plan together so quickly was a marvel in itself. She had taken Marten's call at seven fifteen. At seven eighteen she was in the top-floor apartment dressed in the rose-colored bathrobe and slippers she'd worn

the night before and listening carefully to what
Marten had to say, knowing all the while that with
Anne present he would have to find a way to let her
know what was happening and what needed to be
done without referring to President Harris by name
or office.

And he had, telling her that an American politician had just flown in by private plane from Iraq,
and they needed to meet with him as soon as possible and in a place that was private and out of the
public eye. Further, there were people outside her
building now waiting to follow them to wherever
that place was. What they hoped she could do was
provide them with that meeting place and a way that
they could get to it, quickly and without being seen
by those outside. Further, wherever that place was,
they would all have to leave it soon afterward unde-
tected for a trip to the airport and the politician's
plane. Complicating things even more was the fact
that they had no way to contact their man without
the people outside knowing. It was a big order, Marten understood, and made on very short notice. He
ended his plea with a simple sentence. "I think you
appreciate where this is coming from."

"I appreciate very well where this is coming
from," Raisa said with a smile. "Old lovers die hard."

If Anne had been caught up in the game of "what
the hell's going on?" she didn't show it. Instead she
gave Raisa a warning. "The people out there watching will have very sophisticated electronic listening equipment. Any conversation coming into or
going out of the building will be heard, traced, and

recorded, and that includes the line in this apartment that transfers out through your laundry company."

"Then we'll have to find another means." Raisa walked off, lifting a BlackBerry from the pocket of her robe as she did. They saw her scan a list of names and numbers programmed into it. Immediately she put it away, turned, and came back.

"My laundry is called A Melhor Lavanderia, Lisboa, or Best Laundry of Lisbon. It's not far from here. I go to my office there every morning, as I will do now. When I have something to tell you I will send a messenger. A teenage boy named Otavio. He will give you a slip of paper with instructions. Follow them exactly."

"Raisa," Marten said, "we can't just walk out through the front door, or the back, either."

It was then she'd told them about the network of passageways, warning of their age and probable condition but saying she thought they were still passable. "Look for a blue electrician's van with white and gold lettering, Serviço Elétrico de Sete Dias—Seven Day Electrical Service. It will be parked at the end of the last house on the block. Go out the basement door and to it quickly. The driver will take you where you need to go. A truck from my laundry will get you to the airport."

"You realize our man will have to know where to meet us and when," Marten said quietly.

Raisa smiled again. "I will take care of it myself." She looked at Anne. "Dirty little secrets, my dear. I'm sure you understand."

"Of course," Anne matched Raisa's smile. "Old lovers, like old girlfriends, die hard." Her eyes went to Marten. He didn't respond.

• 9:45 A.M.

Marten moved the beam of his flashlight across an old, rough-hewn wooden barricade that closed off the passageway in front of them. He studied it for the briefest second, then looked over his shoulder at Anne.

"I don't know what this is. Hold the light," he said and handed the flashlight to her. They'd been less than twenty minutes in the underground corridors, passing from Raisa's building and then through the next and the next. The smell of must and mold permeated the air, and the going had been frustratingly slow. Rubble from partially crumbled walls, pieces of old furniture, and plumbing and electrical fixtures stored for years and forgotten had had to be moved, climbed over, or squeezed around. At one point there had been what was left of the carcass of a long-dead dog.

Now the way into the last building at 9 Rua do Almada was completely blocked off and the clock was counting down. Marten had no idea how long it would take to break through the obstruction. Or if it was even possible. And then there were the other questions. How long could an electrician's truck wait outside without drawing notice from the men watching number 17? And what about Ryder? Was he on his way to Rua Serpa Pinto and the Hospital

da Universidade? Had he even received the directive of where to go and when to meet? Even if he
had, had he been able to slip away from the main
RSO detail? What if he reached the hospital and
found they weren't there? What if they got there and
he never showed up? What if they had to revert to
the backup plans, retrace their steps, and do the
same thing all over again tomorrow? And if he still
wasn't there? What then? And what about the here
and now? What if they couldn't move the barricade
and had to go back to the apartment?

"Christ," he swore out loud, then put his shoulder against the heavy wood and pushed. Nothing
happened. He shoved at it again. Still nothing. He
looked at Anne. She, like himself, was coated with
more than a half century of brick and mortar dust. It
covered their clothes, was in their hair, smeared on
their faces, inhaled into their lungs. The only thing
that helped her even a little was the bucket hat that
he'd worn the night before and had asked her to wear
when they left, hopefully making her less recogniz-
able to anyone watching outside when they made
their break for the electrician's van.

Marten hit the barricade again. There was a sudden rain of dirt and dust from above and the obstruction gave just a little.

"Okay!" he said and hit it again. More dust and
rubble came down. One more time and it moved. Not
much but more than before. Once again. And then
again. Finally he had enough room for them to squir-
rel through.

"Give me the light," he said. Anne did, and Marten

inched his head and shoulders into the opening. As he did a rat the size of a small cat dropped down from above. It landed on his head and clung there.

He cried out and tried to shake it free. Instead the terrified animal dug its claws into his scalp and held on. "Get the fuck off me!" he yelled and managed to bring his arm up to swat at it. Finally the rodent let go, jumped to the floor, and scampered off into the darkness. Marten swung the light in time to see a dozen more rats scurry off after it.

He took a breath and turned the light back at Anne, then helped her past the barricade and into the passageway beside him, his eyes close on her purse that she'd slung crossways over her chest. The purse that carried the prized contraband—the photographs and the 35 mm film strips of the Memorandum.

He took a moment to look at her before moving on in an attempt to judge her psychological state. Her eyes were clear and intent, as they had been ever since she'd found him on the phone with the president. Hopefully, with sleep, the episode she'd suffered the night before had passed and the most he had to concern himself with now was the ticking clock of the present. She'd had a few changes of underwear, but she still wore the jean outfit she'd had on since Erlanger's house in Potsdam. It was worn and dirty and in desperate need of washing, but under the circumstances it didn't matter. That he was in the same clothes he'd worn since Berlin didn't matter, either. At the moment they might well have been thrust back in time, as much refugees as anyone who had passed that way those many years before.

The only difference now was the enemy. They were fleeing the agents not of Hitler's death machine but of their own country.

"What are you looking at?" she said finally.

"Trying to make sure you weren't afraid of rats."

"Only the human kind."

"Me, too." He swung the light into the passageway ahead.

"Nicholas."

"What?" He looked back.

"Thank you for last night. I kind of lost it."

He smiled gently. "I cried in Berlin. You cried in Lisbon. Now we're even, so forget it."

"I won't forget it."

"We have a congressman to meet."

"I know."

He watched her for a heartbeat longer. "Let's get to it," he said finally, then turned the light and they moved on.

9:52 A.M.

102

- Four Seasons Hotel Ritz. Same time.

Joe Ryder and his RSO special agents, Tim Grant and Chuck Birns, sat alone wrapped in towels in the men's sauna in the hotel's spa. Grant and Birns had stood by as Ryder spent several minutes in the lap pool; then the three retired to the men's changing room area and afterward into the sauna, where Ryder took the men into his confidence, telling them what was happening and what needed to be done.

By nothing more than coincidence, Special Agent Grant's physical build was almost the same as Joe Ryder's. Months ago and at the suggestion of a friend in the Secret Service, he had dyed his hair the color of Ryder's and had it styled in the same manner, then bought a pair of the same kind of rimless glasses the congressman wore. When he put them on, he was very nearly Ryder's double, and unless a person knew each man well, it would be hard to tell them apart, especially from a distance. It was a game Grant had no trouble in playing, and he had done it more than once in Iraq getting Ryder safely through potentially dangerous situations.

The plan was to act it out again here. Grant, wearing Ryder's clothes, would leave the spa and take the elevator to the lobby, very publicly pick up a copy of the *International Herald Tribune* from a table near the concierge desk, then take the elevator up to Ryder's suite. In the meantime, Ryder, dressed in Grant's clothes, and Agent Birns would return to the pool area and exit through glass doors that opened onto a small formal garden. Crossing it, they would go down a short flight of steps, climb a low fence, and enter Eduardo VII Park. Afterward they would walk to the nearest street, hail a taxi, and ask the driver to take them to the Café Hitchcock in the Alfama district, the restaurant where Ryder had told Lisbon/RSO detail leader Anibal Da Costa he had planned to go for lunch.

Partway there they would tell the driver that they'd decided to do a little shopping before lunch and ask him to pull over. When he did, they would get out, wait for him to drive off, then immediately take another cab to Rua Serpa Pinto, getting out several blocks from the Hospital da Universidade and walking the rest of the way. In the meantime Agent Grant would have changed from Ryder's clothes into jeans and a light jacket, gone down the back stairs and crossed into the park himself, then flagged down a cab and gone directly to the area where the hospital was. But he would use it only as a reference point for the driver, saying he was going to visit a friend on a street nearby where he had been before but whose exact name he couldn't remember. When they reached the area he would arbitrarily choose a street, tell the driver to stop, and then get out, saying he would know the building when he saw it. Like the others, he would wait for the driver to leave, then find his way to the hospital on foot, meeting Ryder and Birns just inside the rear entrance. Hopefully close to the appointed 11:00 A.M.

• 9:59 A.M.

Ryder and Birns came out through the pool area doors, crossed the formal garden, went down the steps to the low fence, and climbed over it. Two minutes later they were in Eduardo VII Park walking under an umbrella of palm and conifer trees. Ryder wore Grant's beige slacks, blue dress shirt, and light blue blazer. Birns wore a summer-weight tan business suit with a white shirt open at the collar. In his right hand was a briefcase. Inside it was a Heckler & Koch MP5K 9mm compact submachine gun with a thirty-round clip and fitted with a laser sight. In the event of an attack all he needed to do was point the briefcase at his target; a red laser dot would spot on the subject. After that it was easy. Simply pull the trigger in the briefcase's grip and let the weapon do its work.

• 10:02 A.M.
The two stepped out of the park where it met Rua Marguês de Fronteira. Less than thirty seconds later they saw a taxi coming toward them through traffic. Birns cautioned Ryder back, then stepped into the street to flag it down. The taxi sped past, then twenty yards later suddenly pulled over and stopped.

"Let's go," Ryder commanded.

• 10:04 A.M.
"You speak English?" Ryder asked as they climbed in.

The driver looked at them in the mirror and gave a cheery "Yes, senhor."

"Good. Café Hitchcock. In the Alfama district."

"Of course, sir," the driver said, and they drove off.

103

The car was a black Mercedes S600 sedan with smoked glass windows and, as Conor White had asked, United Nations license plates. Their driver was a handsome young black man called Moses, from Algeria, he said. He had a 9 mm automatic pistol mounted in a clip under the dashboard. The car itself had a 510 horsepower V12 engine. It could go from 0 to 60 in 4.5 seconds. Its top speed through narrow city streets was unknown.

Irish Jack had parked the gray BMW on a side street a block from the U.S. Embassy. Less than a minute later, at eight thirty-seven, Moses met them with the Mercedes. Conor White was dressed in a tailored pin-striped navy suit with a light blue French-cuffed shirt and a striped maroon tie fastened with a Windsor knot. Patrice and Irish Jack wore conservative blue suits, white shirts, and ties. Each man carried a hard-shell briefcase holding his primary weapon of choice. For Patrice and Irish Jack, highly modified 45 mm M-4 Colt Commando submachine guns with sound and flame suppressors. For Conor White, two modified MP5 submachine guns, also with sound and flame suppressors. Each man, too, carried a concealed sidearm beneath his suit coat. Burst-firing 9 mm Beretta automatic pistols for Patrice and Irish Jack. The

short-barrel 9 mm SIG SAUER semiautomatic for
Conor White.

All three wore team ratio units and constantly
monitored the on-and-off banter between Carlos
Branco's men watching the building at number 17
Rua do Almada. So far their communication had
been little more than idle chatter; nothing seemed to
be happening. That fact alone made White increasingly nervous. What were Anne and Marten—by
now he was convinced it was indeed Marten who
had been seen entering the building at close to one
in the morning—doing? Waiting for communication
from Ryder? Planning something else? So far he had
no sense of any of it. Ryder was under Branco's personal observation. His electronic surveillance team
monitoring communications to and from the apartment building had reported no transmittals or recep-
tions they could attribute to either Anne or Marten.

By nine fifty Moses had made two passes down
Rua do Almada. There had been no sign of police,
just a few pedestrians, several people in the park,
two of which had to be Branco's men, and normal
everyday traffic. The quiet had made White bold
enough to want to go in right then and take care of
business. The Mercedes sedan, the UN plates, the
men inside dressed like diplomats. Even if the police came by on patrol, it would be easy enough to
simply let them pass, then go inside, do what had to
be done, and quietly leave. But doing so might somehow alert Joe Ryder and would put Branco in the
situation of having to kill him himself. That, in
turn, risked a firefight with Ryder's personal RSO

bodyguards. Something like that would be loud and messy, and who knew how it would turn out? So going in after Anne and Marten was not a reasonable option. All he could do was wait until they made their move and Ryder made his in an attempt to join them. What he had to do was have patience, something every soldier in every war ever fought had had to have. Hurry up and wait. It was the unwritten heart of *les règles de guerre*, the rules of war.

• 10:09 A.M.

They had just taken seats at a small outdoor café on Rua Garrett and were ordering coffee to wait it out when they heard the alarm. One of Branco's lookouts was extremely concerned about two people who had suddenly appeared from the basement entrance of the building at the end of the block and climbed into an electrician's van that had been parked there for nearly a half hour. Seconds later the vehicle pulled away.

"Couldn't tell if it was two men or a man and a woman. One of them wore a pulled-down hat," a male voice spat in Portuguese. *"Blue van, Serviço Elétrico de Sete Dias, with white and gold lettering. Moving north toward Travessa do Sequeiro."*

Immediately they heard Branco cut in. *"Bernardo. Pick it up! Pick it up! Pick it up!"*

"Excuse me," Conor White said politely and left the table. He walked past several customers and crossed to where Moses waited in the parked Mercedes. Safely out of earshot, he lifted his right arm, pressed the KEY TO TALK button on the small microphone in the sleeve of his jacket, and spoke into it. "Branco," he said quietly. "Can you talk?"

"Yes."

"Was it them?"

"Don't know. Sit tight. We'll find out."

"Don't lose that van."

"I have a man on a motorcycle right behind it."

"Where is Ryder?"

"Went for a swim, then back to his room. Wants a car at eleven thirty to go to a café in the Alfama district."

"Where the hell is that?"

"Across the Baixa quarter from where you are."

"Which way did the van go?"

"I— Wait, what?" Branco paused, as if he were listening to some other transmission, then came back on. *"It just turned onto Calçada de Combro."*

"What's that mean?"

"It's not heading toward the Alfama district."

"Stay on it to wherever it stops. Then just watch, don't do anything. See who gets out and where they go afterward. If it is Marten and Anne I want immediate confirmation."

Conor White clicked off the microphone, went back to the table, and sat down next to Patrice and Irish Jack. "You heard?"

Patrice nodded.

"What do you think?"

"They know we're here and watching," he said in his distinct French-Canadian accent, "and have found a way around us."

"That's what I think, too." White glanced around, then lifted the microphone. Again he spoke quietly. "Where is the van now?"

"Rua António Maria Cardoso."

"Which way is it going?"

"Just city streets. No way to tell. As I said, sit tight. My guy's a good rider."

10:13 A.M.

104

• 10:14 A.M.

"**S**enhor, a motorcycle has been following us for the last minutes," the heavyset, middle-aged electrician said over his shoulder as he guided the blue van down a series of narrow cobblestone streets. He wore white coveralls and a Serviço Elétrico de Sete Dias baseball cap and was clearly nervous.

Quickly Marten moved forward from where he and Anne had been crouching among the electrical supplies to look into the van's side mirror. The motorcycle was two hundred feet back with a small car in between. It looked like a Japanese street racer, a Suzuki maybe. Very fast, with tremendous acceleration. Its rider was a man, or so it appeared. He wore jeans, a dark jacket, and a full helmet and visor, making it impossible to see his features.

"How close are we to the hospital?"

"About five minutes."

"If he's still with us after the next turn, pull over and stop and let him pass. We'll see what happens then."

The driver started to look back at Marten.

"Don't," Marten warned. "I don't want him to think you're talking to someone."

The driver looked back to the road, his anxiety growing. "I'm just an electrician, senhor. Doing a favor for Raisa. I have three school-age children."

"What's your name?"

"Tomás."

Marten smiled. "Don't worry, Tomás. You'll be fine. So will your children."

• 10:15 P.M.

Moses had pulled from the curb and was heading the Mercedes toward Rua António Maria Cardoso, the street where the van was last seen, when Branco's voice crackled through their headsets.

"Congressman Ryder's not in his hotel room," he said firmly. *"He came back from the pool and went up to his room. Then he vanished. The same with his RSO detail."*

"What?" White snapped, giving a quick glance to Patrice beside him. Irish Jack had turned and was looking at him from the shotgun seat.

"They're nowhere in the hotel. Not that we can determine, anyway."

"They're moving all at once," Patrice said. "Some-

THE HADRIAN MEMORANDUM   [507]

how they've communicated. It means they have an agreed-upon time and destination."

White looked off, staring at nothing. Five seconds later he turned back. "Branco," he said softly into the microphone, "you're an accomplished resource who would have done his homework before he moved his surveillance team in. Who owns or manages the building on Rua do Almada?"

"A Raisa Amaro. Lives on the first floor. She's French. Been in Lisbon for fifteen years. She also owns a commercial laundry close to the waterfront. She went there about seven thirty this morning."

"The name and address of the laundry."

"Give me a minute."

White's eyes were locked on nothing. He was thinking, planning the next step. This was like a fast-moving combat situation where every possible situation had to be considered, sorted out, and then acted upon.

Branco clicked back on. *"A Melhor Lavanderia, Lisboa. Avenida de Brasilia, 22, at Cais do Sodré. As I said, it's close to the waterfront."*

"Thank you."

• 10:16 A.M.
"He's still coming."

Tomás turned the van left onto Largo da Academia Nacional de Belas Artes. The motorcycle rider followed at a distance.

"Pull over," Marten said.

"Alright, senhor." Tomás slowed, then pulled the van to the side of the street and stopped beside a row of parked cars. The motorcycle rider slowed as well as he approached, then suddenly sped up and passed, turning at the far end of the street to disappear from view.

"Maybe he's waiting up there for us to continue. Get out and put up the hood as if you're having engine trouble." Marten reached down and touched the Glock in his waistband.

Tomás did. Quickly and nervously.

Marten slid up to look in the van's side mirror. They had stopped on a narrow cobblestone street in what appeared to be a relatively fashionable neighborhood. For a moment there was no movement at all, and then a car followed by a taxi turned the corner and approached, the bright midmorning sun flashing off their windshields. In seconds they had passed and the street was quiet again. Maybe there'd been no threat at all, Marten thought. Maybe the motorcycle rider had been doing nothing more than simply going his own way.

He was about to tell Tomás to get back in the van when the motorcyclist slid into view at the far end of the street. Seemingly he'd circled the block and come back. He slowed as he came toward them, then stopped at the side of the roadway.

"Dammit," Marten breathed and looked to Anne. "He's back. Stopped at the end of the street behind us."

Anne slid up beside him and looked in the mirror. "He thinks we're in the van but he's not sure. He's waiting for us to move. The minute we do, he'll follow. In the meantime he'll call for backup, probably is now."

Marten looked out at Tomás, his head poked under the hood. "Tomás," he said, loud enough to be heard. "Close the hood and get back behind the wheel."

Tomás hesitated, then stood upright and closed the hood. As he did, he hesitated, looking back down the street toward the motorcycle rider.

"Tomás, get in!"

"He's scared to death," Anne whispered.

"I don't blame him, but we can't sit here waiting to see what happens next." Marten slid the Glock free of his waistband. "Give me your professional opinion. Is our pal one of White's men or does he work for the Agency?"

"Take your choice."

"Not just somebody curious."

"No."

Tomás opened the door and got in behind the wheel. Immediately Marten climbed into the seat beside him. "How do I get to Rua Serpa Pinto from here? You said it was close."

"I don't understand."

"Just tell me how to get there."

"Up this street, past the fancy restaurant on the left. Then turn down Rua Capelo. At the end is the street you want. Number 25 is right there."

"Thank you." Marten looked over his shoulder at Anne. "Go with Tomás. I'll meet you at the hospital. If I'm late, if something happens, follow up with Ryder yourself. Give him everything you have and go with him. His people will protect you."

"What the hell are you going to do?"

Marten smiled. "Not quite sure."

With that he opened the passenger door and stepped onto the street. "Get out of here, Tomás. Now!"

Marten slammed the door and stepped into the shadows between parked cars. Tomás glanced at him and then drove off. Marten looked back down the street. The motorcycle rider was watching either him or the van, it was hard to tell which. Suddenly he moved his head animatedly, as if he were either receiving orders or replying to them over a radio-microphone in his helmet. A split second later he set himself and revved the machine. There was a vicious scream of engine and the street racer shot toward him. Its speed alone told Marten all he needed to know. The rider had been ordered to ignore him and follow the van.

By his estimation a bike like that would accelerate from 0 to 150 miles per hour in about ten seconds. Meaning it would be going close to a hundred by the time it reached him. He counted, one, two; then stepped into the middle of the street and directly into its path. He waited a half second, then raised the Glock with both hands, pointing it at the rider's chest and giving him three choices to make in less than a heartbeat. Swerve out of the way, hit him at full speed, or get shot. The distance between them was closing at warp speed. The machine and rider were little more than a blur. A bullet coming straight at him. Marten stood his ground, his finger closing on the trigger. Then it was right there. Marten saw the rider touch his brakes and veer sharply to the left in an attempt to go around him. Instantly the laws of physics took over. The machine slid out from under him and he was airborne. A split second later he slammed headfirst into the windshield of a parked car. His head snapped back and he bounced off it, his body twisting high in the air and then disappearing from sight on the far side of the car with a sickening thud. In the next instant the riderless motorcycle hit another car and exploded in an enormous fireball.

Marten watched for a moment, then slipped the Glock back into his waistband and turned and walked off toward Rua Capelo, the way Tomás had told him to go. Behind him traffic came to a standstill as flames and black smoke bellowed skyward.

10:21 A.M.

105

• 10:22 A.M.

"Stop here, please," Joe Ryder said abruptly as the cabdriver took them along a large tree-lined plaza called the Rossio. One of the city's main squares, it was alive with tourists peopling the shops and cafés surrounding it.

"We are not yet close to the Alfama district, senhor."

"I just realized this is my wedding anniversary. I want to get my wife a present."

"You're American, yes?" The driver slowed, then pulled to the curb near a large flower stand.

"Yes."

The driver grinned. "Then you mean you *have* to get your wife a present."

Ryder smiled in return. "That's one way to put it."

"I will wait for you, senhor."

"Not necessary, thank you. We'll find another cab when we've finished shopping."

Agent Birns got out first, briefcase in hand, his eyes sweeping the area. Ryder paid the driver, then followed Birns, and the cab drove off. Immediately they turned down a side street and went into a store selling brightly colored ceramics. Thirty seconds later they exited, walked to the end of the next block, and hailed another taxi.

"Rua Serpa Pinto," Ryder said as they got in.

The driver nodded, put his cab in gear, and pulled into traffic.

10:24 A.M.

• 10:25 A.M.

Conor White left Moses and the others in the Mercedes, then crossed a dusty parking area, climbed a short flight of stairs, and entered the side door of the large, one-story white stucco building that was A Melhor Lavanderia, Lisboa, Avenida de Brasilia, 22. In the distance was the 25th of April Bridge. Behind him, as Carlos Branco had said, was a large stretch of Lisbon's waterfront where vessels from hand-rowed dories to ferries to cruise ships plied the midmorning waters of the Tagus River. A world within a world chugging innocently on, a heartbeat away.

The door closed behind White, and he entered a loading dock area with space for two good-sized laundry trucks. One was there. The other, assuming there was another, would be out making pickups or deliveries. Across the way was a battered work desk where a dark-haired man in white trousers and white T-shirt talked on the phone. To the left was a large room filled with industrial-sized washers and dryers, tended by two men in white. If there were other employees he didn't see them.

White approached the desk. "Are you the super-.visor?" he said politely.

The man nodded, then finished his phone conversation and hung up. "I am," he said, his English thickly colored with Portuguese. "What can I do for you?"

"Raisa Amaro, please. I have an appointment."

The supervisor studied him. "I am afraid she's not here, sir. If you would leave your name and a number where you could be reached, I—"

"You don't understand," White cut him off. "I have an appointment."

"I'm sorry, but—"

"I spoke to her on the phone not five minutes ago."

Again the man studied him. Finally he reached for the phone on his desk. "I'll have to check."

Abruptly White put his hand on the man's hand, stopping him. "Just take me to her." Gone was the politeness. In its stead was a cold, deadly resolve. "It would be in your best interests."

The man stared at him unafraid; then his eyes abruptly shifted as the outside door opened and two men in business suits came in. Patrice and Irish Jack. In the distance came the deep-throated blast of a boat whistle, a tugboat, or maybe a ferry.

Conor White stared at the supervisor. "Raisa Amaro, please," he said quietly.

10:30 A.M.

• 10:31 A.M.
Marten walked quickly along Rua Capelo, the sirens of emergency vehicles hanging in the air behind him, black smoke from the still-burning motorcycle clearly visible as it drifted upward.

Fifty feet ahead the street ended at Rua Serpa Pinto. He kept on, stepping around a woman pushing an elderly man in a wheelchair, then dodging two young teenage boys running to investigate the smoke and sirens. Finally he reached the corner and stopped. To the left, partway down the block and across the street, was Hospital da Universidade. In appearance, a small, all-purpose hospital.

The building itself was tasteful and well kept, if unimpressive. Four stories tall, concrete and plaster covering its facade, it was connected, like almost every other structure in the city, to its neighboring buildings. Like the adjoining buildings wrought-iron balconies decorated the second-floor windows. To the right of its doorway was a simple call box.

He crossed to it, studied it for a moment, then walked on. At the end of the block he turned right and then right again into a narrow service alley. Somewhere farther down was the hospital's rear entrance. There was no sign of Tomás's truck, or of any other vehicle for that matter. Whether Anne was there and safely inside there was no way for him to know. Nor was there any way to know if Raisa had even reached the president with the details of what Joe Ryder should do.

Once more he felt as he had in the passageways with Anne, like a wartime refugee in an uncertain state with spies and lookouts everywhere, with everything they'd counted on falling apart around them, and with no way to know it until it was too late. Absently he touched the Glock under his jacket. Then, with a glance over his shoulder, he started down the alley in search of the hospital's rear entrance.

10:34 A.M.

106

Raisa Amaro looked at Conor White, then again at the identification he had given her. His name was Jonathan Cape, and he was a special investigator for Interpol. A man and woman had stayed in the top-floor apartment of her building the night before but were no longer there. They were wanted for questioning in the murders of the German novelist Theo Haas and the Berlin police Hauptkommissar Emil Franck. She had helped them escape and he knew it. She could avoid many years in prison if she told him where they had gone.

Raisa looked around her large, utilitarian office. The man with the British accent calling himself Jonathan Cape sat in a wooden chair opposite her desk. The two well-dressed men who had come in with him waited outside, visible through the large window that overlooked most of her laundry operation.

"I'm sorry, I don't know who or what you are referring to," she said quietly. "It's true I own the building, but I live alone and have little contact with the other residents. Except, of course"—she smiled a little—"when they are late with the rent."

"These fugitives remain at large, Ms. Amaro. People are in danger." White's manner was quiet but at the same time utterly intense. "I don't have time for lies."

Raisa looked at him directly. "If you think I'm involved with anything illegal, I suggest you call Chief Inspector Gonçalo Fonseca of the Lisbon police. He's a personal friend."

"Ms. Amaro, you are impeding an international investigation. I want to know where the man and the woman went when they left your building and how they managed to avoid surveillance. Who provided the electrician's truck and driver is a separate matter that will be taken up later. I want to know where they are now."

"Mr. Cape. I have no idea what you are talking about."

"I see."

Conor White turned in his chair to look at Patrice on the far side of the glass, then nodded. Ten seconds later Irish Jack ushered Raisa Amaro's supervisor and the two men who had been tending the washers and dryers into her office.

White sat back. "I will repeat my question. Where are the man and the woman now? Where are Nicholas Marten and Anne Tidrow?"

Raisa looked at her workers and then back to Conor White. "I simply don't know."

There was no need for White to give the order. Irish Jack already knew what to do. The same as Patrice had known what to do in the farmhouse outside Madrid. In a single move the Irishman slid the Beretta burst-fire automatic from under his suit coat, put it to the head of the nearest laundry worker—a dark-skinned young man no more than twenty-five—and squeezed the trigger. The stacco three-shot burst resonated across the room. A large portion of the man's skull and brains splattered across his two co-workers standing beside him. His body dropped to the floor with a sickening thud.

The other men shrieked in horror. Raisa's face froze to stone.

"Marten and Anne Tidrow. Where are they now?" Conor White repeated calmly as if the action behind him had never taken place. He could see Raisa fight through her shock and terror. Finally her eyes found his.

"The electrical truck took them to the Cais da Alfândega ferry terminal," she said quietly. "They were to cross the river to Cacilhas. Whether they reached it or not I—"

"They went nowhere near the ferry terminal." White cut her off angrily. "The shortest distance between two points is a straight line. I ask a question, I want the correct answer. That's how I operate. Do you understand? Now, where are they?"

Raisa just stared, saying nothing.

White lifted a hand. "Jack—"

"No, please!" White heard the supervisor cry out behind him. He saw Raisa turn in that direction.

"Don't!" she screamed.

Then came the second three-shot burst from Irish Jack's machine pistol. There was no need for her to look at what had happened.

"It's your card to play, Ms. Amaro," White said calmly. "One way or another I will find the people I am looking for. Whether you or your last employee is still alive when I do is in your hands."

Raisa gaped at him. Any sense of who she was, or had been even minutes earlier, was gone. "Hospital da Universidade," she murmured. "Hospital da Universidade."

"Thank you." Conor White stood and turned toward the door. As he did Patrice stepped behind the last man, slid his own Beretta from inside his jacket, and shot him the head.

White reached the door, then turned back. Raisa had managed to stand. She used the edge of her desk for balance. Numbed beyond reason, her eyes still managed to find his.

"You are a criminal of the worst order. May your seed roast in hell for eternity."

White smiled gently. "This is one day you should have stayed home." He nodded at Irish Jack, then walked out the door.

Behind him he heard a three-shot burst. There was a dull thump as Raisa's body hit the floor. For a moment there was silence. Then he heard the distant, thunderous bellow of a ship's whistle, and Irish Jack and Patrice followed him across the laundry, past the A Melhor Lavanderia, Lisboa delivery truck in the loading dock and out into the Lisbon sunshine.

10:41 A.M.

107

RSO Special Agent Tim Grant, the near-spitting-image of Congressman Joe Ryder, stepped out of a taxi on Rua Ivens, paid the driver, and watched the cab drive away. At the far end of the street he could see the flashing lights of emergency vehicles. A wisp of black smoke rose skyward just past them. Immediately he turned and walked off in the direction of Rua Serpa Pinto. By his estimation, it was a block, two at most, to the Hospital da Universidade. He wore jeans and a light, baggy jacket and had a small backpack slung casually over his shoulder. Inside it were his wallet and diplomatic passport, a map of Lisbon, and an MP5K submachine gun with two fully loaded magazines. For all intents, he looked like a tourist.

• 10:43 A.M.

Carlos Branco sat waiting in a five-year-old Fiat on Rua da Vitória. He'd made the call at ten fourteen, seconds before he notified Conor White that Ryder and his RSO detail had vanished from the Ritz.

"You asked me to inform you when I might have an apartment available for lease for your daughter," he'd said. "I have one now, but it's being shown this afternoon to another interested party. Perhaps you could come right away. I will meet you at Rua da Vitória just back from where it meets Rua dos Fanqueiros in the Baixa. The sooner you see it and make up your mind the better."

• 10:45 A.M.

A gray Ford with a fading paint job pulled up next to the Fiat and stopped. Branco glanced briefly around, then got out and climbed into the Ford's front passenger seat.

"What is it?" Jeremy Moyer asked without emotion as he pulled the Ford into traffic.

"The wheels are starting to come off," Branco said, telling the CIA/Lisbon station chief what he couldn't tell him over the phone. "Ryder and his RSO detail are gone from the hotel. Somehow they got out without being seen. The same thing happened with Marten and Anne Tidrow. They got help and slipped out of the apartment building using the cover of an electrician's van. I had an asset follow them on a motorcycle. He's dead. Maybe an accident. Probably not."

Moyer flared. "You're telling me with the all the talent under your control, you lost—"

"White found out where Marten and Anne Tidrow are headed." Branco cut him off. "Hospital da Universidade on Rua Serpa Pinto. It's either a stopping point for them or a place for them to meet Ryder. White's on his way there now. So far there's been no communication from Ryder or his RSO detail at all, so somebody on the outside has to be coordinating all this. Who it is, or where it's coming from, we don't know. What we do know is where they're going. If we have to take them down in the hospital it will be messy. But the longer we hold off, the greater the chance something will go wrong and we'll lose them altogether. What do you want to do? The call is yours."

Moyer ground his teeth and looked at the traffic in front of him. Suddenly he was riding a whirlwind. In the next seconds a thousand thoughts crisscrossed his mind. CIA Deputy Director Newhan Black had personally given him the order to put a trusted free-lancer like Branco in charge of the operation in order to set up a terminal action by Conor White. For a moment it appeared those best-laid plans were coming apart. But then, in a sudden turn, they began to come together again, never mind that the venue was a hospital. His choices were simple: either go back to the embassy, try to get Black on a secure phone, and ask him for a further directive; or take charge himself and do what Black had intended he do from the beginning—let White put the matter to rest. Careerwise, the second choice was extremely risky, especially if it ended in disaster. But considering the time constraints, and how long it might take to make a secure contact with Black, it seemed best that he act now and on his own. Besides, if it came out as it should, it would greatly improve his standing within the organization.

"Take your assets and back up White at the hospital," he said to Branco, then swung the Ford around and headed back into the Baixa.

"The rest of the embassy RSO detail is waiting at the Ritz for further instructions. What about them?"

"I'll take care of it." Moyer slowed for traffic, then abruptly pulled to the curb and stopped. He looked at the freelancer. "Compreenda?"

Branco nodded, "Sim." Yes. Then opened the door and got out. Moyer drove off, and he walked back toward his car in a gaggle of tourists knowing he'd just been given carte blanche to do whatever was necessary to bring the entire episode to a suitable end.

10:50 A.M.

108

• Hospital Da Universidade. 10:52 A.M.

Marten reached the rear entrance and hesitated. He had no idea what to expect when he went in. A Lisbon police car had come down the alley from the opposite direction just as he'd started toward the entrance, and he'd had to draw back and wait. It had stopped at the door, and a uniformed officer had gone inside. It was a full ten minutes before he came out again and drove away past Marten. Why the police had stopped there, what had happened inside that had taken so long, he had no way of knowing. Conor White and the others aside, he'd had to remember that he was still wanted for the murder of

Theo Haas. And, as the president had told him, both he and Anne were the prime suspects in the murder of Hauptkommissar Franck. The Portuguese police knew they had been in the Algarve the day before and might well suspect they were in Lisbon now. For all he knew the police visit to the hospital was one of many, giving the staff their description and instructions on what to do in the event either of them showed up. Still, he had little choice but to go ahead as planned, hoping that he was wrong about the police and that Anne was safely there and that Ryder and his RSO detail were either with her or on their way for the eleven o'clock encounter. With great trepidation he took a deep breath, then pulled open the door and went inside.

What he saw was a relatively small city hospital with corridors leading this way and that and people coming and going in any number of directions. A sign guided him toward the front of the building and to a waiting area where about a dozen people occupied its twenty-odd chairs. On the far side was a walk-up booth with two people behind it. One was a balding man, who fit Raisa's description of Mário Gama, the hospital's director of security. He was maybe fifty, wore a white shirt and a tie, gray slacks, and a dark green blazer, and was working at a computer terminal. Marten approached him.

"Excuse me, I'm looking for a Mário Gama."

The man looked up. "You found him, sir."

"My name is Marten. Has a Ms. Tidrow or a Mr. Ferguson arrived? I'm from the American Insurance Company. We are to meet with Catarina Silva, the accounts receivable director."

"Ms. Tidrow is here, sir. Mr. Ferguson has not yet arrived. Please come with me."

"Thank you," Marten said gratefully and followed him across the room and down a side hallway.

• 10:54 A.M.

Gama opened the door to a small examination room and ushered Marten in. Anne stood there, alone and waiting. He was surprised at the way her face lit up when he came in, as if she had been more than a little worried about his well-being.

"Please excuse me," Mário said and then left.

"What happened?" Anne asked as the door closed behind him.

"There was an accident. The motorcycle rider chased after you and Tomás in the truck. He was going very fast when he suddenly swerved to avoid something in the street."

"What?"

"I don't know."

She raised an eyebrow. "You don't?"

"No."

"But he's dead."

"I didn't hang around long enough to find out." Marten changed the subject. "No sign of Ryder."

"Not yet." Anne looked at him uncertainly, as if she wanted to tell him something but didn't quite know how.

"What is it?"

"I—"

"Go on."

"Earlier, I got a text message from Loyal Truex at Hadrian. I didn't tell you because we were on the run and there was no reason. But you should know. Sy Wirth is dead. They found his body floating in the Tagus River, downstream, where it meets the Atlantic."

"So he was here."

"Apparently."

"And with Conor White."

"Probably."

"White kill him?"

"I don't think he slipped and fell. Put the pieces together. Sy made a stupid deal with the CIA to protect the Bioko field. Then he and Loyal brought in White and created SimCo. Things were fine until the pictures showed up. Then everything started to come apart. At some point Sy probably pushed too hard like he always did and stepped all over Conor in the process."

"And that jeopardized the whole operation, and White, maybe at the Agency's request, got rid of him."

"I don't know. I doubt if we'll ever know. What's clear is that they—Conor, Loyal, Sy, and the Agency—wanted to recover the pictures from the beginning. Now, they want more."

"What does that mean?"

"I knew when I hacked in and found the memorandum that at some point they would learn about it. Not who did it, or from where, but that the site had been accessed and on what day and at what time. They know that on that day and at that time I was at the Hotel Lisboa Chiado, where the rooms have Internet access. They may not know I made a copy but will assume I'd tell you and Ryder what I found.

"The pictures were bad enough because they implicate Striker in the war. The memorandum implicates, even criminalizes, the CIA. And not just the Agency but the deputy director personally. Conor White has enough to lose as it is. Now he has this. If he is Agency, or even if he's not, he's got to protect it. He can't go down as the soldier who was supposed to guard something as massive as the Bioko field but lost it and at the same time disgraced the CIA.

"If he was fired up before, it's double that now. He'll come after us with everything he has, and there are few better than he is. He knows what he's doing and how to do it, and he has his people with him. There may well be others, too, like those doing surveillance outside Raisa's building. High or low, Conor pays people well. But bottom line, he's the one running things. And if he is CIA, they're letting him do whatever he wants because it benefits them most of all. What he wants is us dead and every piece of evidence we have recovered and destroyed. He can, and probably will, be very, very violent and won't shy away from any means necessary to achieve his ends. That's his training and the reason for all those medals. If he learns where we are he'll kill everyone in this hospital if has to just to get to us. I—"

Suddenly there was a noise at the door. Immediately Marten's hand went to the Glock in his waistband. Then the door opened and a man in a tan business suit and carrying a briefcase entered.

"Please don't, Mr. Marten." He turned the briefcase toward him. "It's not necessary. I'm Special Agent Birns, Congressman Ryder's RSO detail, half of it anyway." He glanced at Anne and then around the room, then stepped back. "It's alright, Congressman."

A half second later Joe Ryder walked into the room; his look-alike, Tim Grant, followed.

11:00 A.M.

109

• Avenida Das Forças Armadas. Same time.

Jeremy Moyer had spent the moments since he'd given Carlos Branco the green light to back up Conor White at the hospital taking a roundabout return drive to the embassy, trying to think of the best way to respond to the disaster that was only moments from making world headlines. At the same time, he had to find a reasonable excuse for pulling the remaining RSO detail out of the Ritz so that their ongoing presence wouldn't raise questions later, especially in the follow-up investigation by the FBI or the State Department about Congressman Ryder's killing. He mulled over a number of possibilities, then settled on the simplest: call Debra Wynn, chief of RSO/Lisbon, and tell her that a member of Congressman Ryder's personal RSO detail—Special Agent Birns, he distinctly remembered the name from State Department paperwork alerting him to Ryder's visit—had phoned him a short time ago to say the congressman had abruptly changed his plans and was on his way to the airport, preparing to leave Lisbon immediately. That had been the entire message. Whether Ryder had informed the ambassador or not, he didn't know. Nor did he know why Birns had called him instead of her. At any rate, would she please pull her people out of the Ritz and reassign them.

Which was precisely what he did, calling her as he approached the embassy, explaining it all and closing with "If there was a sudden security threat, he didn't mention it. My office has received nothing to raise the alert level any higher than it already was for his visit. Maybe it's political. Maybe it has to do with Ryder's commission. Maybe he's going back to Iraq. I don't know. It's one of those things. Maybe one day we'll find out."

With that he clicked off, took a deep breath, and tried not to think of what was about to happen.

• **Hospital Da Universidade. 11:08** A.M.
Special agents Grant and Birns stood guard in the hallway outside the examination room while Ryder, Marten, and Anne went over Father Willy

Dorhn's Bioko photographs one by one. Ryder had
already been told about the CIA briefing video and
seen the 35 mm negatives of the memorandum. Since
the document pages were too small to read without
magnification, he could only listen to Anne's detailed explanation of what was on them and accept
her assurance that once full-sized prints were
made everything would quite legible. In his mind
there was no doubt of the veracity of what she was
saying. Her tone of voice, her facial expression,
the way she held herself, the involuntary clenching
and unclenching of her hands told him, as much as
the document itself, the personal hurt she was going through in revealing it. Not to mention the legal jeopardy she was putting herself in; she had,
after all, stolen a top secret government document,
and she sat on the board of directors of what very
likely would become a federally indicted company,
with its leaders quite possibly brought before an
international court charged with crimes against
humanity.

The photographs were self-explanatory, as was
Marten's description of other photos on the camera's memory card that had been lost to the Russian
agent Kovalenko. Those showing Conor White with
the Chilean war criminal Mariano had been of particular interest, especially when tied to the CIA
briefing video that he knew could be subpoenaed.
That Kovalenko had killed the German policeman,
Franck, and taken the memory card posed another
concern because it raised the specter of Russian
political interference in Equatorial Guinea, even

THE HADRIAN MEMORANDUM   [531]

high-stakes blackmail if Moscow threatened to make the photographs public.

Marten had still not told anyone but President Harris that the real memory card was in his possession and that the one he'd given to Kovalenko was harmless. They were far from being out of the woods yet, and he wasn't about to give up the last piece of evidence when it was neither safe nor necessary. To that end he would keep custody of it until they were out of the country and the other evidence was secure and protected. Even then there was only one person he would give it to, the president himself.

• 11:10 A.M.

There was a knock on the door, it opened, and Birns stepped into the room. Mário Gama was with him.

"There is a man wearing the white jacket of Raisa Amaro's laundry in the reception room," Gama said. "He told the receptionist he was to ask for Ms. Tidrow or Mr. Marten and tell them he has a truck waiting. She referred him to me."

"He asked for us by name?" Marten said flatly.

"Yes, sir."

"He was to have waited until we came out. I'm not sure he even knew our names."

"Maybe he did know and simply forgot his instructions. He came in to make sure nothing went wrong."

"Maybe." Marten looked at his watch. "He's early. He was to have been here at eleven fifteen."

"Doesn't matter," Ryder said. "Put the photographs back together. Let's get out of here."

Anne felt her danger antenna come up. She looked at Marten.

He was already moving, nodding to Agent Grant in the hallway and closing the door. Now he looked to Gama. "Do you know the laundry's telephone number?"

"Yes, sir."

"Would you please call and ask for Raisa. When you get her, hand the phone to me."

Gama's eyes darted cautiously around the room. Then he lifted a BlackBerry from his pocket and punched in a number. They could hear it ring through; then someone picked up and a male voice answered in Portuguese.

"Yes."

"Raisa Amaro, please."

There was a pause and then, *"Who's calling, please?"*

Gama looked to Marten and covered the mouthpiece. "He wants to know who's calling."

"Tell him a personal friend."

Gama nodded and did as Marten asked.

"Just a minute."

Twenty seconds passed, then thirty. Gama looked to the others and shrugged. "He must have gone to get her."

Marten and Anne exchanged glances. Marten looked back to Gama. "Where is the laundry truck parked? Which door did the man come in through?"

"The front door. His truck is parked in front."

Marten felt the hairs stand up on his neck. Immediately he turned to Gama. "Click off."

He did, and Marten asked him another question. "Can you find out if an ambulance was called to the laundry in the last half hour?"

Concern spread over Gama's face. "Yes, sir."

"Please do it."

"Yes, sir." The security director said, with a nod, then turned away, punched a number into his Black-Berry, and waited.

Marten looked to the others. "Ten to one it was the police who answered the phone. If so, they were tracing the call. That was the reason for the delay. It also means that White found out about Raisa, learned where she worked, and went there. The driver out front is one of his men."

"Thank you," Gama said in Portuguese and then clicked off the phone, his expression grim. "Emergency medical vehicles were called there by the police. Four people were found shot to death. Three men and a woman."

"Raisa," Anne mouthed.

Marten looked at her and nodded faintly, then turned back to Gama. "What did you tell the driver when he asked about us?"

"That I didn't know anything and would see what I could find out. For some reason he didn't look like a laundry worker."

Immediately Marten's eyes went to Ryder. "I presume your men brought friends along."

"They're armed, if that's what you're asking."

Again Marten looked at Gama. "There are security

cameras covering the front and rear entries. I saw them when I came in. Are there more?"

"Yes."

"Where are the monitors?"

"In the Security Center. Down the hall the way we came in, just before you reach the lobby."

"Please take me there."

Gama hesitated, unsure of what was going on and more than a little concerned that the dead woman at the laundry was Raisa. Marten read his unease.

"I don't know how much Raisa told you, but the man you know as Mr. Ferguson"—he nodded at Ryder—"is United States Congressman Joseph Ryder, in Lisbon on a highly classified operation. The men with him are United States government security officers. There are people trying to find us and do us harm. It's why Raisa called you to help. She knew you could be trusted. Please, take me to your office right away. The guy out front starts to wonder where you are, he's going to come looking, and he won't be alone."

11:14 A.M.

110

Conor White had no misgivings about the information Raisa Amaro had given him before she died. Terror had been in her eyes and soul, the same as it had been with the Spanish doctor and her students when his interrogation had suddenly turned from severe to murderous. People in that state didn't lie unless they were martyrs, and Raiso Amaro cared too much about the lives of her workers to be a martyr. Once she realized what was happening and would continue to happen, she would have done everything she could to save the last of them. As she had proven.

From the backseat of the Mercedes he could see the *A Melhor Lavanderia, Lisboa* laundry truck parked outside the hospital's front door a half block away. Red-and-white stanchions set in square concrete blocks kept the area clear of parked cars. The only vehicle there now was the truck, pulled in tight against the stanchions, its taillights blinking, signaling a business pickup or delivery.

His appraisal of the situation as they were leaving the laundry for the hospital had been quick. There was no doubt Marten and Anne had known they were being watched and had escaped Raisa Amaro's apartment building via some kind of interior passageway and after that in a simple electrician's truck, in all probability with Raisa's help. If she had done it once, why not twice, using the same type of everyday transportation to get them from the hospital to wherever they were going next, either to meet Ryder, or to the airport and Ryder's plane in the event the hospital was the meeting place for all three.

Every hospital needed clean laundry. Some had their own in-house laundries; others used an outside service. Either way, a laundry truck would not draw attention and made an ideal escape vehicle, and the one parked in the loading bay at Raisa's laundry was large enough to accommodate Anne, Marten, and Ryder as well as his two RSO bodyguards. White knew his thinking might be pure conjecture, but he'd had enough experience with covert operations to know that such a scenario was more than possible, maybe even likely. What he had to do was look at it from Anne and Marten's point of view—desperate fugitives who had escaped capture and thought they were free of surveillance—then take the necessary steps to make their thinking work to his advantage.

Marten had seen him and Patrice in the Hotel Lisboa Chiado the night before. It was probable he'd also seen Irish Jack waiting outside in the BMW, so they would need an unknown face to drive the truck. Moses, the Algerian driver and gunman Branco had supplied with the Mercedes, was quickly recruited. Provided with a crisp white A Melhor Lavanderia, Lisboa delivery jacket and a team radio unit, with its tiny earphone and microphone hidden in the jacket's sleeve, he was to drive the truck to the hospital entrance, then go in unarmed and ask for Anne or Marten as if he knew what was going on and was a strategic member of their team. What happened next would tell volumes. Either he would be turned away, with some staff member informing him there was no record of anyone under those names having been admitted to the facility, or he'd be taken to them, at which time he would make radio confirmation. If they were lucky they might even find Ryder and his RSO detail with them. If indeed all five were there and expecting him, Moses could then walk them out of the hospital and into the truck. Afterward he would take them to a deserted construction site off Avenida Infante Dom Henrique on the waterfront that Branco had pinpointed. Alternatively, if Anne and Marten were alone, he would drive them to wherever they were to meet Ryder, and they would close the trap there as originally planned. Lastly, if Moses was turned away, they would simply wait and watch until Anne and Marten arrived. Or, if they were there, attempted to leave.

Branco and four of his former Portuguese army commandos were already in place, waiting in dark-colored sedans, a Peugeot and an Alfa Romeo, at either end of the alley behind the hospital. Each man was acutely aware of the less-than-hour-old death of their group member sent to tail Marten and Anne by motorcycle. Each had been warned, too, of Marten's deadly marksmanship in the shooting of the two others of their circle who had gone after him in the blue Jaguar the night before. That they had no idea who he really was, or what his training had been, wouldn't matter; their blood was up for a proper response, and they were more than eager for it to begin.

For his part, he, Patrice, and Irish Jack would stay were they were, parked at the curb fifty yards up from the hospital entrance, weapons and black balaclavas at hand, ready to play the game as it unfolded.

No matter what happened, or where, the end would be the same. The five targets would be quickly cut off and isolated from the public. He, Patrice, and Irish Jack would do the work. Branco and his team would back them up. It would take thirty seconds, no more. As quickly, Branco's people would fade into the city, and they would be on their way to the airport and the Falcon 50, safe with the knowledge that there were probably no more than a handful of policemen anywhere on the planet who would stop a highly polished black Mercedes with UN plates and three well-dressed gentlemen inside, no matter how fast they were going.

That was Plan A.

Alternatively, if something happened and Moses was exposed and/or he came out empty-handed, they would immediately shift to the uglier but still very effective Plan B. Call in Branco's men, pull on the balaclavas, then go into the hospital, lock it down, and begin a forced search of their own. The hospital was small, and they'd done such things successfully before. In Bosnia, Afghanistan, and Iraq.

"What's taking Moses so fucking long?" Irish

Jack squirmed uncomfortably behind the wheel. "If they're there, he would know it. If they aren't, he should have reported it by now."

Patrice raised a pair of binoculars and studied the building's front entrance.

"Give the man time, Jack," White said quietly. "Give the man time."

Irish Jack turned to look over his shoulder. "Colonel, my balls tell me he's taking too fucking long."

"I never distrust a man's balls, Jack. Let's find out." White lifted his arm, pressed the KEY TO TALK button on the microphone inside his coat sleeve, and spoke into it. "3-3, this is Control. Do you have a rabbit for us? Copy."

11:18 A.M.

111

• 11:19 A.M.

Marten, Mário Gama, and Special Agent Grant stood inside a darkened inner chamber of the hospital's Security Center studying a bank of monitor screens tied to security cameras throughout the building.

"There." Gama indicated one of the screens as a man in a starched white laundryman's jacket stepped into view near the front entrance. "He's the one who asked for you."

They could see Moses standing in a shaft of daylight just back from the door, a hand to his ear,
seemingly intent on something.

"He's plugged into a radio unit. Someone's talking to him," Grant said quietly.

They could see Moses nod, then lift his left arm to
his mouth and apparently say something. He waited,
then nodded slightly. A second later he turned and
walked out of view. Another monitor picked him up
as he approached the front reception desk to speak
with a hospital employee behind it.

"Whoever he was talking to wants to know what's
taking so long, and he's trying to find out," Grant
continued.

Other monitors showed nothing more than normal hospital activity at the front and rear entries.
Another showed the emergency room entrance, with
a vanlike ambulance parked in the drive-in bay.
One angle from a remote camera over the front door
showed the sidewalk and street outside with the
laundry truck parked on the far side of the traffic
stanchions.

"I'm going to speak to Agent Grant for a moment,
Mário," Marten said. "Keep an eye on our man. If he
leaves the area we need to know where he's gone."
Marten took Grant to one side and lowered his voice.

"White is a smart, tactical thinker who has all
kinds of connections and puts things together fast.
By now he'll know Ryder and you people are missing. He went to Raisa's, found out where we were,
and took a gamble that you and Ryder would meet
us here. His man came in asking for us on the belief

that using the laundry truck was part of the getaway plan and that coming in is what the original driver would have been instructed to do. He figured that out pretty well except that he couldn't have known what time he was to have come in, or that he was to use the back entrance instead of the front. That his man had spoken to Gama and wasn't turned away would be interpreted as meaning that we were not only here but were expecting the truck. Because of that he's probably brought in more assets, meaning any escape route we might have planned will be blocked off." Marten glanced at Gama, then looked back to Grant.

"He'll think he's got us, and because we're taking time and haven't yet responded to his driver he'll assume we're just being cautious and thinking things through. He'll expect that we'll soon realize everything so far has gone as planned and before long will follow his man out and into the truck."

"We can't do that," Grant said emphatically.

"Yes, we can. At least some of us can."

• 11:22 A.M.

"Control, this is 3-3. Copy?" Moses's voice came through their headsets.

White pushed the KEY TO TALK button inside his sleeve. "This is Control, 3-3. What's the delay?"

"There was an emergency on one of the upper floors. The security director, the man I spoke to earlier, sent his apologies and asked if I would wait. Instructions?"

White took a breath, then looked out through the Mercedes's windshield to stare at the hospital entrance. Finally he looked to Patrice and Irish Jack. "What do you think, gentlemen?"

Patrice's cold green eyes came up to White's. "They're there. They know Moses is waiting and are thinking it through. One way or another, at some point they will have to come out of the building. He walks away now, they'll wonder what happened. I'd tell him to wait it out, see how they respond."

"Agreed." Irish Jack nodded.

Again White pushed the KEY TO TALK button. "6-4, this is Control. Did you read 3-3? Copy."

Carlos Branco's voice crackled through their earpieces. *"6-4, roger."*

"We're going to sit tight. Copy?"

"Roger."

"3-3. Stay where you are and wait them out. Copy?"

"Roger."

● 11:25 A.M.

Marten, Agent Grant, and Mário Gama joined Anne, Ryder, and Agent Birns in the small examination room where they had remained. In the next minute and a half Marten laid out his plan.

They would split into two groups, he told them. Anne, Ryder, and Birns in the first; himself and Grant in the other. At the same time, Gama would recruit a woman and two men from the hospital staff, people who, from a reasonable distance, would resemble

Anne, White's driver, and Agent Birns. The man playing White's driver would wear the white laundryman's jacket. The second man, who would resemble Agent Birns as closely as possible, would wear his jacket and sunglasses and carry a briefcase. The woman playing Anne would wear the bucket hat Anne had worn in the escape from Raisa's apartment and now had in her purse.

The idea was to have Anne, Ryder, and Agent Birns slip into the ambulance in the docking bay at the hospital's rear emergency entrance. Then, on a coordinated signal, Marten, Ryder's look-alike Agent Grant, and the hospital recruits would exit the front door, go quickly to the laundry truck, get in, and drive off. In the meantime, the ambulance, with Gama driving, would leave from the emergency entrance and go directly to the airport and Ryder's waiting plane. For their part, Marten and Grant would lead White's pursuers through city streets back toward the Baixa district then suddenly pull over, let the hospital people out, and drive away. For a moment White and his followers would be thrown off by what had happened, giving Marten and Grant a brief escape window when they could abandon the truck and disappear on foot into the crowded Baixa itself. After that they would find a taxi and take it to the airport and Ryder's jet.

That was Marten's plan, and he was reasonably certain it would work. The problem was, Agents Grant and Birns strenuously objected. Armed gunmen were waiting for them outside, and their job was to protect Congressman Ryder. They knew that under the circumstances they couldn't call in outside help, but they were dead set against splitting up and leaving only Birns to protect Ryder. Furthermore, the driver had asked for Anne and Marten. That meant there was every chance they had arrived *after* Ryder, Birns, and Grant had come in themselves. So there was no reason to believe that they knew any of them were there and that the driver was being used to see if they could get some definitive information. Why not just get into the ambulance now and leave, all five of them?

"What if you're wrong?" Marten answered. "We have no idea when they got to the laundry and learned that we were coming here. What if they've had people outside the whole time? What if they saw each of us arrive? They can count. What if they know we're all here? They won't want to come in after us. It would be too noisy an operation. So they'll be waiting for us to come out, using the truck to bait us as if it's our plan, not theirs. Moreover, I can guarantee you Conor White and his gunmen are not out there alone. There'll be at least one other team, maybe more. So yes, we could take a chance with the ambulance, and we might get away with it. But then again, we might not. What then? What if they follow us, then cut us off and box us in? That happens, we're dead, all of us. Afterward White will go back to Bioko and pick up his game where he left off, and no one will know anything about his involvement here or what was at stake to begin with. You might want to take that chance. I don't." He looked at Ryder. "And I don't think the congressman does, either."

"He's right, fellas," Ryder said in the calm, every-day conversational tone he used in almost any situation. "Our job is to get to the plane and get out of here as quickly and safely as possible. Mr. Marten's plan is as sound as it can be under the circumstances. The only problem is that it puts him and you"—he looked at Agent Grant—"and the hospital people in some serious jeopardy."

"Unless they suspect something, White and his people aren't likely to take action anywhere close by. The neighborhood is too dense and too upscale," Marten said evenly. "It would be almost the same as storming the hospital itself. It would draw too much attention. My sense is they will have given their driver instructions where to go. If he doesn't go where he's supposed to, they'll think he's playing along with orders we've given him, so they'll follow the truck, shifting tails with as many cars as they have. Then, at someplace out of the way, a park or abandoned lot or something, they'll make their move. That means the beginning of the ride should be relatively safe." Marten looked to Gama. "My main concern is you and your people, because it will be dangerous. This is our fight, not yours. There's nothing that says you or any of them have to do it. If you decide against it we'll do something else."

"Let me find them, and you can talk to them yourself."

"Fair enough," Marten said. "The thing is, it all has to be done fast, before they begin to think about coming in."

Mário Gama smiled. "I already have three people in mind who I am sure will be more than happy to help. Perhaps you don't know. Raisa Amaro is, or perhaps . . . was"—his voice caught in his throat; then he recovered and went on—"a leading member of the hospital's board of directors. She fought for and saved many jobs during economic hard times. She is a legend here. People love her. Give me five minutes and I will be back with the people you desire. If necessary you can then give your speech, but I don't think you'll have to." With that Gama nodded at the others and left.

Marten looked at his watch, then at Anne. "Ten minutes at best until we get out of here. How much longer is White going to sit still?"

"Not much," she said, then abruptly opened her purse and took a small notebook from it. "If something happens and we get crossed up—" She scribbled something on a page, tore it out, and handed it to him. "My cell number. I'd like yours if it's alright."

"Sure," he smiled and took the notebook from her, then wrote the number in it and handed it back. When he did, their eyes met and held there. It was an exceedingly private moment despite the fact that Ryder and his RSO protectors stood only feet away. In that instant everything they had been through together registered in gut-wrenching shorthand, one that left them wondering—fearing—if this was the last time they would see each other. If, in the next hour or minutes, one or the other would die.

Then it was over. It had been a moment, nothing

more. But it had been there nonetheless. Powerfully
felt by both, yet neither saying a word. Love? The
terrible fragility of life? A deep understanding between human beings of how much had been shared
in so brief a time? Something else? Who knew.

11:30 A.M.

112

• 11:39 A.M.

"*C*ontrol, this is 3-3. Copy?" Moses's voice resonated sharply through their headsets.

Immediately Irish Jack and Patrice perked up,
their hands going to their earphones.

Conor White clicked on his microphone. "Go
ahead, 3-3."

"*I've just been told our relatives have been located. The security director is coming to take me to
them now.*"

"Do you know how many there are?"

"*The person who told me said only that 'your
people are here after all' and that he was sorry for
the delay.*"

"Take the bait, 3-3. I repeat your instructions. You
are a driver sent by Raisa Amaro. You were to meet
them at the hospital and drive them to wherever they
want to go. That's all you know. Once you get them
in the truck, take them directly to the construction

site off Avenida Infante Dom Henrique. We'll be right behind you. And take the earpiece out. We don't want them wondering about it. Copy?"

"Roger. Copy."

"6-4, did you read that? Copy."

"Roger," Branco's voice came back. *"We're good to go."*

"6-2, did you read? Copy."

"Roger, Control." The gruff voice of the driver of Branco's second car came back.

"Copy, 6-2." White clicked off and glanced outside as the shadow of a cloud passed overhead. He studied it for a moment, mumbled something about rain, then reached down, opened his briefcase, and took out one of the two MP5 submachine guns. He checked its clip, then absently felt for the short-barrel SIG SAUER 9 mm semiautomatic tucked under his jacket at the small of his back. "Systems are go, gentlemen, load up," he said quietly to Patrice and Irish Jack. "Systems are go."

• 11:43 A.M.

Moses followed security director Gama down a hallway past a number of examination rooms. Two-thirds of the way down, Gama stopped and knocked on a door.

"Security," Mário Gama said. The door opened, and Moses saw the people Conor White had described. Nicholas Marten, Anne Tidrow, and Congressman Ryder. What he didn't see were the two RSO agents who were supposed to be guarding them.

Immediately he tensed. It was too late. Gama shoved him inside. The door slammed closed behind him, and he found himself in the iron grip of the men he was looking for.

"Relax," one of them said, and the other quickly frisked him for weapons. "Nothing."

"What are you doing?" he pleaded in English. "I'm only doing what I was—"

"Oh, yeah?" the first man said.

In the next instant his laundryman's jacket was stripped from him. They saw the wire on his left wrist running up to a small transmitter under his armpit. Instantly he jerked away, trying to push the KEY TO TALK button. Grant and Birns scrambled to get him. Marten got there first, grabbed his arm, and twisted it back. Moses cried out in pain.

"Get that damn thing off him!" Marten snapped.

Birns did, and then Grant shoved him back hard against the wall.

"Mário," Marten said, and Gama stepped in with a pair of handcuffs.

"You are being detained in accordance with the antiterrorist laws and statutes of Portugal," he said in English, then repeated in Portuguese. Immediately he raised a radio of his own and spoke into it. Within seconds the door opened, two uniformed hospital security guards came in, and Moses was taken from the room.

• 11:47 A.M.

Irish Jack shifted impatiently, his hands on the wheel, his eyes on the hospital's front door. Two men came out and walked off down the sidewalk. A moment later a taxi pulled up behind the laundry truck, and a woman and a young girl wearing an eye patch got out and went into the building. Seconds passed and the taxi drove off. Then there was only the parked laundry truck with its emergency lights flashing as they had been from the beginning.

"Don't like it, Colonel."

"Neither do I," White said.

"Control. This is 6-4. What's the delay? Copy." Branco's voice spat through their earpieces.

"Control, 6-4. I'm giving Moses two minutes more. Nothing happens, we go in. Copy."

"Roger, Control. We're ready."

"6-2, you copy?"

"6-2. Roger, Control."

• 11:48 A.M.

The two groups were gathered in a hallway just off the reception area. Anne, Ryder, Birns, and Mário Gama, now in the white smock of an ambulance driver, were in the first. The other was made up of Marten, with the Glock automatic in his belt, wearing the earpiece and microphone from Moses's team radio unit that would enable him to monitor White's communications; the Joe Ryder look-alike, Agent Grant; and the impersonators of Anne, Birns, and the just-apprehended laundry truck driver, Moses. A female bookkeeper wore Anne's bucket hat pulled down over her ears; an anesthesiologist who more or less resembled Birns wore his tan sport coat; and Santos Gama, Mário's brother, who was a real-life ambulance driver and to some degree resembled Moses physically, had on the laundryman's jacket. Moments earlier he had put on a deep-bronzing makeup, courtesy of a male nurse, that darkened his facial complexion enough so that, from a distance at least, his skin color took on something of the Algerian's. It was he who would drive the truck.

"Everyone ready?" Marten asked. There was a murmur and unanimous nod. Then he looked at Anne.

"Good luck," she said.

"You, too."

"Good luck to us all," Ryder added and looked to the people around him. "And a very indebted and heartfelt thank-you to Mário, to his brother Santos, and to his friends for helping us in what we all realize is a particularly dangerous situation." He looked at Marten and nodded.

"Let's go," Marten said, and they parted: Anne, Ryder, Birns, and Gama down the corridor to the left and the ambulance bay; Marten and his people to the right, toward the front door. As they went Marten saw a fire alarm box on the wall. Quickly he turned back. "Mário," he called, "is there an alarm box near the ambulance bay?"

"In the corridor just inside it, why?"

"Just a thought, it's nothing, sorry." He glanced at Anne, their eyes met, and he turned back to his group. "Out the door fast and into the truck!"

11:49 A.M.

113

The two minutes were up.

Conor White had come too far, been thwarted too often through no design of his own, not to complete the mission now. Not with the objective right there, yards from his grasp. He hit the KEY TO TALK button and lifted the microphone in his jacket sleeve to his hand.

"6-4, this is Control. We're going in. Lockdown rules, full balaclavas."

"Roger, Control."

"6-2, you copy?" White reached for the balaclava on the seat beside him.

"Roger, Control."

"They're coming out," Irish Jack said sharply.

"What?" White looked up.

They saw five people quickly exiting the hospital's front entrance and heading for the parked laundry truck. Moses led them. Marten was next. Then Joe Ryder carrying some kind of backpack, Anne, and lastly one of the RSO agents. Patrice lifted the binoculars.

"6-4, abort action," White snapped into his microphone. "Our relatives are here!"

"That's not Moses!" Patrice had the binoculars tight against his face, watching Marten's group as they climbed into the truck.."It's not Anne, either!"

"Christ!" White lifted the MP5. "Gun it, Jack, gun it!"

Irish Jack turned the ignition key. The Mercedes's 510 horsepower V12 roared to life. A split second later he fishtailed it out of the parking spot after the laundry truck that was accelerating away.

"6-4, 6-2," White said into the microphone at his sleeve. "Marten's using the truck as a decoy. Anne and Ryder will be coming out in some other vehicle. Watch for it. We're in pursuit of Marten! Copy."

"6-4. Roger, Control."

"6-2. Roger, Control."

Marten rode in the shotgun seat watching the truck's outside mirror. "Here they come. Black Mercedes." He clicked on the power to the team radio unit he had taken from Moses and pressed the earpiece into his left ear.

Agent Grant was right behind him. He looked to the bookkeeper playing Anne and the anesthesiologist who had the part of Agent Birns. "Get down, flat on the floor!" he ordered, then opened his backpack and slid the MP5K submachine gun from it.

"Santos." Marten looked to Mário's brother at the wheel. "Take us into the Baixa, the shortest route you know."

Twenty yards ahead, Rua Serpa Pinto ended at the bottom of the hill. Santos touched the brakes, then leaned on the horn and took a sharp left, the top-heavy truck leaning dangerously to one side as it went. Marten could see the Mercedes slide through the same turn seconds behind them. His hand went to the Glock in his belt. He looked at Santos.

"They're coming hard. What can you do?"

To his great surprise, Santos grinned, almost as if he were enjoying it. "I have been an ambulance driver for twenty-two years. This is no ambulance, but—" Abruptly he swung the wheel right and turned the laundry truck down a narrow cobblestone alley that was almost impossible to see from the street. Marten saw the Mercedes fly past, then slide to a stop, back up in a cloud of burning rubber, and come down the alley after them. Then Santos was taking another right, then a sharp left. The Mercedes disappeared from view.

"How far is the Baixa?" Marten pressed.

"Three minutes."

"Get me on a street where I can drive to it myself. Then pull over and stop. I want you people out of here."

Santos grinned again. "Out of here? This is fun!"

"Fun, hell, those guys will kill all of us!"

Suddenly a sharp communication came through Marten's earpiece. "*Control, this is 6-4.*"

The men in the Mercedes heard Carlos Branco as well. "*A fire alarm was pulled in the hospital seconds after you left. I'm monitoring Lisbon Fire. They've got five vehicles rolling now. They'll probably ring a second alarm and double that. Every street in the area will be filled with fire apparat— Christ!*" Branco blurted suddenly and then there was silence.

"Christ! What?" Conor White spat into his microphone as Irish Jack slid the Mercedes through a corner and accelerated off. "What the hell's going on?"

"Hospital ambulance just shot past us in the alley. RSO Special Agent Birns was in the shotgun seat! Go!" they heard him yell to his driver in Portuguese. *"We're in pursuit now! Am assuming Anne and Ryder are with him, maybe the other RSO, too, if he didn't decoy with Marten!"*

"Stay on him! Stay on him! 6-2, back up 6-4. Copy."

"6-4. Roger. 6-2, copy."

"6-2. Roger."

"I see him. I see him!" Irish Jack glimpsed the laundry truck. There was a massive whine as he touched the accelerator and the Mercedes shot forward. In seconds they were on top of a lumbering vintage streetcar. Irish Jack cut left, started to pass it, then found himself in the path of an oncoming bus. He swore out loud and dropped back, letting the bus go by. In the next instant he pulled left. There was a scream of engine and then they were around the streetcar and cutting back in front of it. Ahead they could see the laundry truck turn down a side street. At the same time, an aging white Opel pulled out of a parking space in front of them.

"Get out of the fucking way!" Irish Jack slammed on the brakes, then jumped on the accelerator and fishtailed around it, just missing an oncoming taxi, whose driver leaned on his horn and threw up a fist in rage.

Santos turned the laundry truck onto Rua Nova do Almada. As quickly he swung right, and they were into the heart of the Baxia.

Marten looked in the mirror. Two blocks back he saw the Mercedes round a corner and race after them.

"Santos, next block pull over. Tell me which way to go afterward."

"Right turn, then left," Santos told Marten, "then two streets and—"

"*Control, 6-4. We've got the ambulance. 6-2's on their tail.*" Marten heard the quick rasp of Branco's voice. "*We're right behind them. Copy.*"

"*Control. 6-4. Where are you? Can you take them down now?*" Marten felt a stabbing chill as Conor White's distinctive British accent spat through his earpiece.

"*We're on Calçada do Carmo heading toward Rossio Square.*" Branco said. "*Streets are too narrow to make any kind of takedown move.*"

Suddenly the piercing scream of a siren followed by the thundering blare of an air horn shot through Marten's earpiece. A split second later he heard what sounded like a horrendous crash.

For a moment there was absolute silence. Then—

"*6-4. Control. 6-4! Copy,*" he heard Conor White bark. There was no reply. Then, "*6-2. 6-2. Control. 6-2! Do you read me? Copy!*"

"*This is 6-4, Control. Fire truck went through*

an intersection. Hit the ambulance and the 6-2 car. Ambulance is on its side. 6-2 car not drivable."

"Control, 6-4. How bad is it? Anybody killed?"

"Can't tell. Firemen are on it. My guys seem banged up but okay, don't know the extent of it. Firemen have the ambulance's rear doors open. I can't— Wait. I see Ryder. He's being helped out. Looks stunned. Don't know about the others."

"Get your men out of the 6-2 car." White was calm but emphatic. *"If they can't walk, carry them. Then get the hell out of there. You'll have emergency personnel including police all over the place before you can piss. You don't want them talking to your guys. Copy."*

"6-4, roger, copy."

"Control, 6-4. Imperative we meet close to accident scene. Our vehicle has GPS. Give me street coordinates. Copy."

"Roger, Control. Ah, Calçada do Duque at Rua da Condessa. Copy."

"Calçada do Duque at Rua da Condessa. Five minutes tops. Copy."

"Roger, Control. Five minutes."

For an instant Marten sat stunned. It wasn't just the unexpectedness of the accident and the acute fear that Anne and Ryder might be seriously hurt or worse; what struck him was how quickly White had read the situation and decided on what action to take next. Whatever that was, whoever his 6-4 and

6-2 people were, clearly none of them were running away.

As quickly, real time caught up. He glanced in the mirror looking for the trailing black Mercedes. He saw it several cars behind just as the driver did an abrupt U-turn in traffic, then accelerated off in the opposite direction. Immediately he turned to Grant.

"Fire truck hit the ambulance. It's on its side. Ryder seems okay. That's the most we know. White had two cars tailing it. One of them got caught up in the accident. He's regrouping to meet near the scene." He looked to Santos. "Your brother may have been hurt, I don't know. Get us to Calçada do Carmo near Rossio Square. Fast as you can!"

"Yes, sir." Santos glanced in his mirror, waited for a man on a bicycle to pass, then took an abrupt left and stepped hard on the truck's accelerator.

12:02 P.M.

114

Anne was on her knees. A young fireman with red hair poking out from under his helmet was with her, trying to help her stand up on what was once a sidewall but was now the floor of the overturned ambulance. She was a little woozy from the impact and rollover, and blood oozed from a gash above her right eye, but other than that she seemed alright. At least that was what she told the fireman. In the distance she heard the singsong of approaching sirens. She shook her head, trying to clear it. Then she saw Ryder sitting on the sidewalk partway up a hill on the far side of the street. Two firemen were attending to him.

"Easy," the fireman helping her said calmly in English. "Can you put weight on your legs?"

She tried, then nodded.

"Good. There's a fuel leak. We have to get out and away from the vehicle now." He started to lead her toward the door that by now had been propped open. As he did, her mind cleared and she turned back, looking crazily around in the upside-down confusion. Nothing was where it should have been.

"What are you doing?"

"I need my bag."

"Senhora. Leave it. We have to get out!"

He took her by the arm and was moving her toward the door when she saw it, thrown into the corner by the force of the crash. Abruptly she pulled away to retrieve it. He swore out loud and scrambled after her.

"Senhora, the vehicle is going to explode. Leave your purse, it's not important!"

"That's what you think." She lunged and grabbed it just as he caught her. A second later they were out and under an increasingly cloudy sky, rushing back, away from the stricken ambulance. The smell of raw fuel was everywhere. Feet away was the wreckage of a dark blue Peugeot, its front end all but torn off. Two men in jeans and Windbreakers, one with a hand to his head, stood next to it talking with a fireman. Behind them, up the hill they had been coming down when the collision happened, she could see a gray Alfa Romeo sedan stopped in the middle of the roadway just opposite a narrow side street. A slim, bearded man in a black suit had gotten out of it and was walking quickly down the hill toward them. Now the memory came back. The Alfa and the Peugeot were the cars that had been following them just moments after they left the hospital. Ryder had remarked about them; so had Agent Birns.

"Over here." The redheaded fireman led her toward the area where Ryder was. The approaching sirens were closer. Everywhere she saw faces of onlookers. People gathered on the sidewalks. Faces peering from shops and apartment buildings. She looked toward Ryder and saw him get to his feet. To his left, two firefighters were lifting Mário onto some kind of gurney. Suddenly there was an ear-shattering blast of sirens. Immediately they shut down. Two fire trucks had arrived at the same time, adding to the chaos. Firemen jumped from them carrying large canisters and rushed toward the ambulance to lay a carpet of gray-white foam over the leaking fuel. A police car came in from a side street and stopped. Another followed. Uniformed officers got out and began herding the onlookers back. Then more police arrived. It was all happening in seconds. Then an ambulance came, and then one more. The sound and confusion magnified. She looked back and saw the bearded man in black gesture to the men who had been in the Peugeot. The fireman guiding her told her to watch her step and again asked if she was alright and after that asked what her name was and why she had been in the ambulance.

She told him her first name, then murmured something about not remembering where they were going or why. She stepped up on the curb near Ryder and looked around for Agent Birns. She didn't see him. She looked to Ryder. He understood and shook his head. Then she saw two ambulance attendants run forward with a gurney. A body lay on the far sidewalk, a white sheet covering it.

A firefighter walked up carrying Birns's briefcase and spoke with the ambulance people. There was a short conversation; then he turned and went over to a policeman. Another short conversation, and a gesture toward the wrecked ambulance. Inside the briefcase was Birns's MP5K. They were going to need it and Anne knew well how to use it. She was trying to think of some way to retrieve it when the policeman took the briefcase from the fireman, then put it in the trunk of his patrol car and closed it. That was the end of any hope she might have had for it.

115

Santos slowed the laundry truck long enough to let Marten change places with the anesthesiologist who had been impersonating Agent Birns and slide into the back alongside Agent Grant and the bookkeeper who had portrayed Anne. With Marten out of sight, Santos continued on toward the roadblock the Public Security Police, the Polícia de Segurança Pública, had set up to keep traffic from the accident site.

Reaching it, he stopped and leaned out, telling the police who he was and asking to be let through. His brother, he said, had been driving the ambulance involved in the crash, and he wanted to get to him right away. As a longtime ambulance driver, Santos was known by almost every uniform in the Security Police, and those at the barricade were no exception; the bronzing face makeup he'd used in his role as Moses, which at another time would have been food for scurrilous comment, they let pass, telling him to park the truck down the hill and walk in. "I have hospital personnel with me," he said strongly and received no argument about the others accompanying him. Less than two minutes later he had parked the truck, and the four followed him back up the hill and through the police line.

They were barely inside it when Santos and the hospital people suddenly rushed forward toward the wrecked ambulance. Marten glanced back at the police; then he and Grant followed, looking for Anne and Ryder and Birns.

The cross streets—Calçada do Duque at Rua da Condessa, where White was to meet with whoever had the radio designation 6-4—were, Santos told them, partway up the hill from the accident scene. Meaning White and his gunmen were in close proximity and could easily infiltrate the swarm of people around them. Marten touched the Glock under his jacket and glanced at Grant, who now had the backpack under his arm so that the barrel of the MP5K submachine gun was just visible in its opening, his finger pressed through a hole in the material encircling the trigger.

Forty seconds of pushing past onlookers, firemen, rescue teams, police, and just-arriving media crews and they saw Anne and Ryder. Wherever Birns was, he wasn't with them. They moved closer. With the exception of a small bandage over Anne's right eye, both seemed to be physically unharmed. Anne, bless her after everything, had her purse with the photographs and the copy of the memorandum thrown over her shoulder and clutched to her side.

A little closer still and they could hear Ryder telling a fire captain that he and Anne were fine and that all they needed was a taxi to take them back to their hotel. Since there was no flurry of activity around him, it was clear he had not yet identified himself. Marten saw it as an opportunity to get them out of there before he did and signaled Grant to cover him in the event White or his men made their move.

He was just starting toward them when he saw a ranking uniformed police officer, a lieutenant maybe, approach Ryder. Once he reached him there would be questions, a lot of them. Who he was, who Anne was, why they had been in the ambulance, where they had been going. At this point Anne's identity was unimportant because once Ryder's identity was established the U.S. Embassy would be informed, meaning the CIA would almost immediately know where he was—if White hadn't informed them already and/or if the 6-4 designate and those who had been in the 6-2 car weren't CIA themselves. Whatever the case, it was imperative Marten get their attention and get them away from there right then.

Anne saw him as he was coming toward her. He nodded toward the approaching policeman and shook his head. At the same time, he realized he had a far better card to play. The police themselves. White would have his hands fully tied if suddenly Ryder and Anne were put into a police car and driven from the scene.

"That cop." Marten pulled Grant close. "The lieutenant or whoever he is. Intercept him. Show him your ID and tell him who you and Ryder are and that Anne and I are with you. You are charged with the congressman's personal safety. There have been threats against his life. What happened here might have been an accident, it might not. Ask him to get us out of here right now. He'll have to request permission, but once he gets it White and his gunmen will have to pull up short, at least long enough for us to try to work out something else."

Grant nodded and moved off. Marten let his eyes sweep the crowd. If White, Patrice, or the bull-like Irish Jack were there, he didn't see them. He looked back. Grant was in conversation with Ryder and the policeman. A moment passed and he saw the cop lift his radio and turn away, talking into it. Again Marten scanned the crowd.

The "permission."

The bureaucracy through which police machinery everywhere worked. Radio messages back and forth would take time, and he had to assume White and/or his people would intercept the exchanges and know what was going on. So would people at the U.S. Embassy, principally the CIA's chief of station.

He felt a drop of rain and looked up at the darkening sky. There was another drop and then another. Suddenly he felt a hand tighten around his arm. He whirled. It was Anne. Ryder and Grant were with him.

"You were right, he had to get approval," Grant said. "He's calling for it now."

Suddenly Marten remembered Birns. Where was he? Anne read his expression.

"Agent Birns was killed in the accident," she said quietly. "Mário's hurt. I don't know how badly."

Marten looked at Grant. Birns had been his traveling companion-in-arms for years. They were pals, buddies, as close as you get without being brothers. Maybe even closer than brothers. He knew that awful gut-eating loss too well from his days on the

LAPD. He also knew there was nothing you could do about it but say a prayer for him and move on, as Grant was doing now.

"I'm sorry," he said, and Grant nodded a solemn thanks. Then Marten looked at Anne. She was pale and still a little shaky and she limped a little, as did Ryder. "You okay?"

"Yes."

He looked at her purse and grinned in admiration. "The lady seems to know how to hold on to the important things in life."

"Once in a while." She smiled softly. "Once in a while."

Just then the rain that been teasing began to come down harder. A moment later the lieutenant returned. Two uniforms were with him. None of them paid Marten or Anne the slightest attention. Ryder was their man. Permission for a police escort had been granted. A large unmarked SUV was being brought up as they spoke.

"The U.S. ambassador was informed," the lieutenant told Ryder. "He asked that we take you directly to the embassy. You'll be quite safe there."

"Thank you," Ryder said graciously and then looked at Grant and Marten. His expression reinforced what Marten had known all along. The embassy was the last place they would be safe. Somewhere along the way they would have to make an abrupt change of plan.

12:22 P.M.

116

Conor White knew what to look for—a black unmarked Toyota Land Cruiser coming down from the accident site followed by a white unmarked Ford. The driver and sergeant in the Toyota and the men in the tail car would be members of the Public Security Police Special Operations Group—Grupo de Operações Especiais, or GOE—highly trained counterterrorist police.

The GOE vehicles would follow the road down to Rossio Square, then circle it and drive up the verdant Avenida da Liberdade on the way to the U.S. Embassy. Carlos Branco had given him the information seconds after getting off the phone with the CIA/Lisbon station chief, Jeremy Moyer. The route had been laid out by the GOE and approved by the embassy.

The GOE plan gave them all they needed, a map to follow and a time frame in which to work. The entire trip from beginning to end would take no more than fifteen minutes. Somewhere in between they would strike. Where, when, and how was up to White. Branco was, and had always been, the "painter" here, both the setup man and the backup for White. Whatever else might be required he was wholly open to, as long as he got paid. A sum that in this case would be substantial. No matter what White had personally promised him on the side, his wages here, one hundred and fifty thousand euros, would be picked up by Moyer and paid out through a clandestine fund set up by the Agency.

Branco's final radio communication with White had come immediately after the accident involving the fire truck and the ambulance. By then both men had realized Marten would have taken Moses's radio unit and be monitoring their exchanges. White had set the location near the accident scene deliberately, betting Marten would rush there to protect Anne and Ryder, thereby bringing the three of them together in a very manageable line of fire. After that all radio contact with Branco ceased, their communication continuing by cell phone only.

That Marten had taken the bait was affirmed by the *A Melhor Lavanderia, Lisboa* laundry truck parked just up the hill from the street where White, Patrice, and Irish Jack now waited in the black UN-license-plated Mercedes. Branco and three of his former Portuguese army commandos were in the Alfa Romeo parked on the same street less than a hundred paces behind them. The plan was to wait for the Land Cruiser and Ford tail car to pass, then follow them in traffic around Rossio Square, past the Metro station, and up Avenida da Liberdade to where Rua Barata Salgueiro crossed it. It was there they would strike. Irish Jack would accelerate alongside the procession as if to pass it. At the last second he would abruptly turn in front of the Land Cruiser, cutting it off. In the meantime Branco's Alfa would pull in tight behind the tailing Ford. The GOE was a

highly respected antiterrorist SWAT-type organization whose members had been trained in the same
manner as the British SAS, White's primary regiment, which meant he knew their tactics and mind-
set. He also knew that the only way to defeat them
was by striking hard and fast, with Branco's gunmen
taking out the GOEs in the tail car while he, Patrice,
and Irish Jack attacked the Land Cruiser. That a
number of policemen would be killed meant little.
Lisbon was a war zone, no different than if it were a
city in Iraq or Afghanistan. As he had said—thirty
seconds and it would be done. Then Branco and his
men would be in the Alfa and gone, and they would
be disappearing in the city's myriad of narrow,
twisting streets, racing to the airport and the waiting
Falcon 50 for the flight back to Bioko.

"Colonel," Patrice said quietly, his eyes on the
street above them, his Quebecois accent as distinct
as ever, "here they come."

12:30 P.M.

117

The Land Cruiser came down the hill slowly, its
windshield wipers beating a steady rhythm against
the light rain. The white Ford was tight behind it.

The task of getting the congressman and his
people from the accident scene to the U.S. Embassy
was commanded by plainclothes GOE Sergeant

Clemente Barbosa, a raw-boned man in his midthirties who rode in the shotgun seat. His driver, Eduardo, was several years younger and fully intent on the roadway ahead and the traffic, streets, and buildings around them. His world, like Barbosa's, was in the moment, nowhere else. The same was true for the four armed, uniformed GOEs in the tail car.

Ryder and Grant rode in the seats directly behind Barbosa and Eduardo. Marten and Anne were in the third row. The passenger compartment where they all were was shielded from outside view by the Toyota's dark-tinted windows. In the few moments before the GOE arrived, Marten, Anne, Ryder, and Grant had examined the situation. The consensus was that none wanted to chance going to the embassy, if for no other reason than that at some point they would have to leave it and, no matter how well guarded they were, White would know when they would be leaving and where they would be going. The same as he undoubtedly did now. The difference was that if they moved soon, meaning in the next few minutes, they would have an element of surprise they wouldn't have once they were in the confines of the embassy.

The idea of disappearing into a large crowd—as Marten and Grant had planned before the accident when they would have abandoned the laundry truck and dashed into the heavily populated Baixa district to lose themselves in it—still seemed best. Even as the rain toyed with them, this was still the tourist season and crowds were everywhere, most especially where they were headed: Rossio Square, where

Ryder and Agent Birns had stopped earlier that morning to change cabs. It was a place, Ryder was certain, that would be filled not only with tourists but also with readily available taxis.

So Rossio was the site where they would make their move. Grant would ask Barbosa to pull over and stop, saying that Ryder wasn't feeling well and needed some air. Barbosa would be reluctant but have no choice except to do as he had been asked. At that point they would simply open the doors and get out, with Ryder saying he needed a few minutes to walk the sensation off and Grant reassuring Barbosa that he was armed and that the congressman was perfectly safe. Seconds later they would be in the crowd and quickly disappear into it, splitting up as they went—Grant staying with Ryder to guard him, Anne and Marten going off in a different direction altogether. After that each group would find a taxi, take it to the civil aviation terminal at Portela Airport, then go to directly Ryder's plane, where the pilots would be waiting and the aircraft cleared for takeoff.

Not a word was said as they reached the bottom of the hill and Eduardo turned the Land Cruiser onto Praça Dom Pedro IV, following the one-way streets around Rossio Square in a line of traffic. At that point the rain came down in earnest.

118

Irish Jack changed the speed of the Mercedes's windshield wipers to keep up with the downpour and at the same time kept them a neat three vehicles behind the Ford tail car. Directly behind them was a silver Opel and then Branco and his men in the Alfa. He glanced at Patrice in the shotgun seat, then in the mirror at Conor White. Both men had their automatic weapons out and ready. His own M-4 Colt Commando rested in his lap. He looked back at the road in front of him just as the Toyota and Ford reached the far end of the square and began the run along its far side heading toward Avenida da Liberdade.

Ryder glanced at Grant, then turned to look over his shoulder at Marten. "Now what?" he said quietly. Because of the rain, the crowds they were counting on for cover were gone. The big plaza was void of anything but pigeons.

Anne turned to look behind them. "Nicholas," she warned. "Gray Alfa Romeo, several cars back."

Marten looked. He saw the Alfa and the black Mercedes in front of it. "The Mercedes is Conor White's car." He turned back to Ryder and Grant. "They're right on our tail," he said sotto voce. "All due respect to the GOEs, we're not going to get anywhere near the embassy."

Immediately he looked at the barren square on his left, trying to decide what to do, find any avenue of escape. There was nothing but the open, rain-soaked plaza. He looked right, along the facade of shops and cafés they were passing, but nothing jumped out at him. If they told Barbosa and they sped off, White would realize they had been seen, drop back, change cars, and wait for later. The same would happen if they called in more police, because he was certain White or his people would be monitoring the GOE radio frequencies. Then, in the distance, he saw it. A big red *M* marking the entrance to a Metro station. He looked to Anne, then leaned forward to Ryder and Grant. "We're going underground," he said quietly, "now."

Conor White sat forward, his black balaclava and MP5 submachine gun in his lap, preparing himself for the action that was to come in less than two minutes as they left the Rossio and started up Avenida da Liberdade toward the strike point at Rua Barata Salgueiro.

Suddenly he felt a dark shadow descend from the car's ceiling and settle around him like some precursor of doom. What the hell is this? he said to himself. Never in his life had he experienced anything like it. He tried to shake it off, but the shadow remained. In the next instant he had a soul-chilling premonition that things were about to go horribly wrong. The way they had gone wrong ever since Nicholas Marten arrived in Bioko. Until then everything had gone smoothly. Then, and almost immediately, the trouble with the photographs had begun and everything started to come apart.

"Jesus Christ!" Irish Jack shouted.

Fifty yards in front of them the big Toyota suddenly pulled to the curb. The tail car came in right behind it. In a blink the Land Cruiser's passenger doors opened. Ryder and Grant got out, followed by Marten and Anne. The driver and front-seat passenger got out at the same time. Marten looked at them, pointed toward the Mercedes, and said something. Then he, Anne, Ryder, and Grant dashed into the Metro.

"Take down the GOEs," White said coolly. "We're going in after them."

"Stay with Anne and Ryder," Marten yelled at Grant as they came into the station and headed toward a long flight of stairs that led to the Metro trains below. Immediately he turned back, lifting the Glock from his jacket and holding it tight against his side. The Metro entrance framed everything. The Mercedes pulled up behind the tail car as the uniformed GOEs piled out of it, their weapons coming into full view. The next happened in a millisecond. Three men wearing black balaclavas and business suits jumped from the Mercedes, their flame-and-sound-suppressed automatic weapons already firing. Clemente Barbosa and Eduardo went down almost in silence. So did the four uniformed GOEs, their weapons never discharged. The horror didn't stop there.

In the next second the three came running into the Metro station.

Glock in hand, his heart pounding, Marten reached the stairs and started down. He could see Anne, Ryder, and Grant mixed in with other travelers as they neared the bottom. He looked back to see Conor White reach the top of the stairs and start down. The balaclava gone, his suit jacket open, he was concealing something beneath it. An instant later he saw Patrice and Irish Jack come in behind him and follow him down. Like White, their balaclavas were gone and their suit jackets were open, and each was holding something out of sight beneath it. In between them and himself were probably twenty or more travelers.

Marten shoved the Glock into his belt and pulled the dark blue cell phone from his jacket. He hit the speed dial and prayed he'd entered the right number and that it was still in service. It rang once, then again, then once more. Finally a familiar voice answered.

"*Ya*," Kovalenko said in Russian.

"You here? In Lisbon?" Marten demanded.

"Where the hell is my memory card?"

"I need your damn help. Are you here or not?"

"I'm your guardian angel, always around when you need me. We Russians have big ears and wide eyes. I was going to meet you where you are going, the U.S. Embassy. Your friend Mr. Logan, with the books and dogs. It was kind of you to include his business card in the envelope you gave me when you switched the memory cards. Even then you were thinking you might need my assistance."

"I was and I do." Marten kept on down the stairs. He glanced over his shoulder, then stepped around an attractive young woman and pushed past a large, overweight man, trying to put as many people between himself and Conor White and his killers as possible. "We're in the Rossio Metro. White and two of his mercenaries are coming after us. They just killed a half-dozen cops. We need help, and soon, or I'll be dead and your memory card will end up in White's trophy case."

Marten looked up. He saw Ryder, Anne, and Grant stop at a ticket kiosk. Grant bought tickets and motioned for him to join them. The backpack was tucked under his arm, the MP5K at the ready, and he was being very cool. No need to alarm the other people crowding the station. People they would keep between themselves and White and his men until they could board a train. He looked up at a large Metro station guide. The next station in one direction was Martim Moniz. Baixa/Chiado was in the other. That was the one he chose because he guessed it would be the most crowded.

"We're going to try to make the Baixa/Chiado station. "Look for us there." There was no reply. Only silence. "Kovalenko. Kovalenko! Jesus Christ, are you there?"

119

Carlos Branco had seen the Toyota and the tail car suddenly pull over and stop. Had seen Marten and the others jump out and point at White's Mercedes, then run with the others into the Metro. Had seen the GOEs react as the Mercedes slid to a stop behind them. He knew what was going to happen and got out of there fast, racing the Alfa Romeo past the Metro entrance just as White and the others jumped from the car.

At the top of Rossio Square he stopped and looked back, then called Moyer on his cell phone. There was no time for clandestine meetings or secure phones. Moyer needed to know what was going on right then.

"The wheels have completely come off," he said. "White has taken down six GOEs in front of the Rossio Metro station and chased Marten, Ryder, and the others into it. There will be more people killed before it's over. What do you want me to do?"

For the briefest moment Moyer said nothing. Then he spoke, calmly and quietly. "Complete the project."

There had been no need to reply. Branco simply clicked off and looked at his men. They probably had sixty seconds at best before a GOE SWAT team arrived and closed off everything. They had to get to the Rossio station and inside it before that happened.

Patrice and Irish Jack caught up with White at the bottom of the stairs. They could see Grant hand Marten a rail ticket, and then the two followed Anne and Ryder through the glass-paneled entry gates into the station proper. Beyond them were the trains, and once they reached those and got on, everything would be lost. Moreover, he knew the GOE would respond to the killing of its officers with extreme prejudice and very fast. There was no time to finesse anything.

They moved fast toward the entry gates to the train platforms. "RSO's got a backpack," White said quietly, his eyes locked on their targeted foursome. "Anne's got a big purse. Ryder and Marten are carrying nothing. The photographs and the rest will be with the RSO or Anne. Take them down first and recover the goods. Then take out Ryder. I'm guessing Marten's still armed with whatever he used to kill Branco's men. I'll take him. Whatever happens, don't let any one of them get on a train. When we're done, split up and take the next train out. Either direction. We'll meet at the plane."

Two steps more and they were at the entry gates. A woman in front of them slid her ticket into a receptacle and went through. White, Patrice and Irish Jack followed, shoved past her, and started after their prey.

"Hey! Você três! Batente!" Hey! You three! Stop! A voice called out in Portuguese.

Irish Jack looked to the side. A uniformed Metro guard was coming toward them. Irish Jack smiled, opened his jacket, and took out the M-4 Colt Commando. The guard's eyes went wide with fear.

"No!" he yelled and tried to turn away. It was too late. Irish Jack fired a short, silent burst. The guard's body slammed backward into a wall behind him and dropped to the floor, his blood flung everywhere.

"Go!" White commanded, and they started for the platform area. Somewhere a woman screamed. Commuters watched in horror and puzzlement as the three well-dressed men raced past them.

"Here they come!" Grant yelled and shoved Ryder ahead of him toward a Metro train just entering the station. "Everybody back, please!" he yelled at the crowd of commuters. "Everybody back!"

Marten caught a glimpse of Conor White, then saw Patrice rush forward, an M-4 in his hands, shoving people aside. "Look out!" he yelled and raised the Glock to fire. An elderly couple were right in his sights and he had to step away. By then Patrice was gone in the swell of people on the platform—people who were beginning to panic. They'd heard the woman's scream and there were men rushing through them with guns.

The train stopped and the doors opened. Travelers started to get off. Grant shoved Ryder through them, the backpack tight under his arm, his finger on the MP5K's trigger.

Now Marten caught sight of Patrice: He was rushing forward toward Grant and Ryder. Then he saw Irish Jack shoving in from the side. He pushed Anne forward after Grant and Ryder, then swung the Glock at Irish Jack. The mercenary saw him and ducked into the crowd. At the same time, Patrice pulled up, raising the M-4. People shrieked. Grant whirled and lifted the backpack. The MP5K's red laser dot fell on Patrice's chest a split second too late. There was a burst of silenced M-4 fire and Grant's head blew apart, his body twisting around wildly to collapse among horrified passengers.

People ran screaming in every direction, some using cell phones trying to call for help. Marten grabbed Anne and rushed her toward the train, stopping only to pick up Grant's backpack and press it into her arms. "There's a machine pistol in there. Stay with Ryder. Get him to the plane."

"No!" she yelled, her eyes locked on his. Love. Fear. Horror. Everything. Before, in the hospital, it had been a parting with hope and without an end. They both knew that if Marten stayed behind now there was every chance he would be dead within seconds.

"Fuck it, Anne! You know what to do! Get Ryder the hell out of here! Now!"

Their eyes locked for the briefest instant; then she bolted into the car, trying to find Ryder. She saw him in the crush just as the doors closed and the train began to pull out. Through the window she glimpsed Irish Jack rushing toward them through the crowd. Then she saw Marten twenty feet away, the Glock up ready to fire. People shrieked, racing to get out of the way. Then Irish Jack disappeared in the melee and Marten was shoving through people trying to find him.

The train picked up speed. Suddenly Patrice

stepped out of nowhere only feet from it, his finger closing on the M-4's trigger.

"Get down!" Anne yelled and shoved Ryder to the floor as a burst of silent automatic-weapon fire raked the windows, obliterating them. She grabbed the backpack and got up. Patrice was gone. A half-dozen or more people were on the floor. Some were dead, others moving. Ryder was trying to help a blood-splattered woman on the floor next to him. They were nearly to the tunnel. Outside she saw Marten looking for Patrice. He didn't see Irish Jack move in just feet behind him, his M-4 up, readying to fire. In one motion she turned the backpack and squeezed the MP5K's trigger. The 9 mm slugs ran across the Irishman's formidable chest; his body danced in a semicircle, then toppled onto the plat-form to the screams of the terrified people around him. She turned to look for Marten and saw him. Their eyes met. Then the train was in the tunnel and the station disappeared from view.

120

Marten saw the train's lights vanish as it gained speed inside the tunnel. Glock in hand, he looked back. Faces stared out from every possible hiding place. Under benches, behind decorative sculptures, inside the lone newspaper kiosk. Most of them frozen in some kind of unbearable silence. Every expression raw and filled with fear and unimaginable horror. Each person questioning how much longer he or she had to live. Suddenly two young women rose up and bolted across the platform, dropping down onto the tracks and running into the tunnel after the train.

"Don't!" Marten yelled. They ignored him. Never mind the trains, there was a live electric third rail there. God only knew how many volts. Touch it with one foot on the ground and you were fried. He looked back. Where the hell was Patrice? Where was Conor White?

In the next second the lights went out.

A universal cry of alarm went up, then everything went deathly silent. Here and there were the sounds of crying or mumbled prayers, but that was all. The only illumination came from battery-powered emergency lights. They lit the stairways, dimly washed the station walls, touched the newspaper kiosk and the entrances to the tunnels at either end of the station.

"THIS IS THE POLICE!" an amplified male voice echoed through the chamber, first in Portuguese, then in English. "EVERYONE FACE DOWN ON THE FLOOR, HANDS SPREAD OUT IN FRONT OF YOU. ANYONE WHO TRIES TO STAND UP WILL BE SHOT!"

Marten could just make out the SWAT team as they fanned out from the stairs to form a line in front of it, a black-armor-suited, helmeted, visor-wearing assault force of about twenty to thirty men. Six of their own had been surprised and cut down only moments before. Those who had done it were somewhere here, among the terrified commuters. There was little chance any of them would walk out alive.

Marten had seen no sign of either Conor White or Patrice since the train had left the station. Things had happened with lightning speed, and there were probably forty or fifty people crowded on the platform, so they could easily be among them.

SWAT would have no idea how many gunmen had been involved in killing their men. Marten was wanted for murder. If they found him with the Glock, they might very well shoot him on the spot. On the other hand, he wasn't about to get rid of the pistol and then have Conor White and Patrice find him before the police did. Third rail or not, orders to lie facedown or not, he crept to the edge of the platform in the semidarkness and eased over the side and onto the tracks.

Conor White was just inside the mouth of the tunnel with Patrice directly across. What should have been an easy takedown of the principals and recovery of the photographs and other evidence—most importantly whatever sort of copy of The Memorandum Anne might have made in those few minutes when she was alone in the hotel room—had been anything but. In reality it should have been they who were on the train that left the station, not Anne and Ryder. White thought of the dark shadow in the car.

Everything that could have gone wrong had. It was Murphy's Law personified. He had never been superstitious in his life, but he was now, and Marten was at the core of it, the bearer of some kind of demon curse meant to destroy him. In that same moment he realized something else—that no matter how much he had convinced himself that his mission to protect the massive Bioko oil field for the West was singularly patriotic, in truth it was the same as it had been from the beginning, to recover the photographs and preserve his dignified place in British military history. And by doing so keep alive the soul-wrenching hope that one day Sir Edward Raines, the father who had refused to recognize him for so long, that he so hated and so desperately loved at the same time, might yet step forth and acknowledge him.

He looked back into the dark of the station, a cavernous space lit here and there by the beam and wash of the emergency lights as if it were the set of an abstract play. The police were there in mass, hidden among the terrified, trapped commuters waiting for them to make their move. Marten was somewhere there, too. Destroy him and the shadow, he knew, would disappear and the curse would be lifted. Afterward he and Patrice would retreat into the Metro tunnels to hide and wait for as long as it took—an hour, a day, a month—until the police finally left and they walked out free and alive. They had done it before.

They could do it again.

121

Carlos Branco and the three who had been with him in the Alfa Romeo, the best of his freelance former members of the Batalhão de Comandos, moved quickly down the darkened stairs toward the train platform where the GOE SWAT team had the area sealed off. Branco still wore the tailored black suit he'd begun the day in. The other three were dressed in loose-fitting, lightweight jackets over blue jeans with 9 mm Uzi submachine guns held out of sight under the jackets.

They'd arrived at the Rossio station less than a minute before the GOE force, immediately gone inside, then waited for them to come in. When they did Branco raised his hands and went to meet them. He identified himself and said he knew why they were there and who they were after, and asked to see the brigade commander. Seconds later the man was at his side.

Branco was well known to the GOE command. He'd worked Lisbon's underground for years and had been instrumental in collecting and passing on information about organized crime, terrorist cells, the African drug trade and more frequently following up with what was required—the dirty, illegal things that had to be done and that law enforcement agencies couldn't become involved with for fear of political or social blowback. In other words, he did what was viewed in higher circles as "necessary business." Consequently, when he showed up in instances like these, more often than not he was deferred to.

"His name is Conor White. Former SAS colonel. Victoria Cross," Branco told the brigade commander directly. "Now a professional mercenary working out of Equatorial Guinea and involved with the civil war there. He's the one you're looking for in the murders outside of Madrid. He followed a U.S. congressman here in an attempt to kill him, the man your people were escorting to the U.S. Embassy when they were shot down. If you kill him it will raise all sorts of questions as to why he was here and what he was doing. The inquiry will be public and potentially embarrassing to a number of countries. If we do it, the government can say he was caught by unknown gunmen who shadowed him to Lisbon, then killed him and disappeared, apparently an act of reprisal that had to do with the situation in Equatorial Guinea. Then it becomes an incident having to do with the war in that country and not Portugal, Spain, or the U.S."

The commander said he understood but that there were many citizens in harm's way and he couldn't stand by while more were killed.

Branco shared his concern then said the public might be better served by a four-man plainclothes team than an overwhelming force of uniformed GOE. "Cut off the power and secure the area," he said. "Then let me contact White and let us go in."

"You can get in touch with him now?"

"Yes."

The commander had studied him and walked off. Branco saw him speak into a microphone at his collar. Thirty seconds later he came back.

"Alright" had been the commander's one-word response.

"One thing more," Branco said. "You're going to have more media crowded outside this station than you've ever seen. Clear two stations down the line. Then I want an automated Metro car brought in. White has two men with him. We're going to take them out in that car. At the end we'll hand them over to you. No media. No gang of police. Just a handful of your men and a couple of waiting ambulances."

The commander stared at him, then finally nodded. "Done," he said.

Conor White was pushed back in the darkness against the tunnel wall, his eyes, his senses, trying to feel out where Marten was, when he felt his cell phone vibrate. That the phone system worked this far underground startled him, and for a moment he did nothing. Finally he slid it from his belt and looked at it. In an instant he knew who was calling and clicked on.

"Yes," he said quietly.

"*I'm with GOE*," Branco said. "*Where are the rabbits?*"

"Anne and Ryder got away on the last train out. The RSO is dead. So is Irish Jack. Patrice is with me."

"*Where is Marten?*"

"Somewhere here in the dark."

"I've made a deal with the police. I'm going to get you out. But I can't do that with all the people there. I want you to let them go."

"Branco, they're our protection. Hostages if we need them."

"The police know we're in touch. Once the people are out, they'll send in an automated Metro car. They're clearing two stations. They're expecting I'll bring you out at the second. We'll go out at the first. I want to tell them you've agreed to let the people go. Once they see they are out they'll pull back. We'll come in and they'll send the rail car."

"Just you."

"Yes. Altogether there are four of us."

"What about the lights?"

"What do you want?"

"Marten's here. I want him myself. You understand? *I* want him. Not you, not your men. Not even Patrice. Turn the lights on, get the people out, then turn them back off. "

"I understand."

"No! Not just understand. I want your word on it."

"You have it."

"Tell the GOE they can have their citizens."

122

Marten was crouched by the rails near the platform when the lights suddenly came back on. The unexpected brightness startled him, the same as it startled the others. A wave of nervous cries swept through the station. He stepped carefully over the third rail and slipped under the platform overhang, hopefully out of sight from above. Suddenly came the sound of a bullhorn.

"THIS IS THE POLICE." The amplified male voice echoed again through the cavernous station, the same as it had before, first in Portuguese and then English. "EVERYONE WILL STAND UP AND RAISE YOUR HANDS ABOVE YOUR HEAD, THEN WALK SLOWLY TOWARD THE EXIT AT THE FAR END OF THE STATION. LEAVE ANY PERSONAL BELONGINGS BEHIND. DO IT NOW!"

Marten was stunned. What tactic was this? What was going on? They couldn't have captured White and Patrice without his hearing. And neither man was about to walk out with his hands over his head. Instead they would take hostages, and the GOE would know that. His hand slid over the Glock and he crouched further down. The best he could do was stay where he was and wait. He could hear people starting to move and assumed they were doing as they had been told, the GOE screening them as they came out.

Maybe White and Patrice were already gone and

the police knew it. Escaped through the tunnels and out through a maintenance shaft. They knew Anne and Ryder had made it onto the train and assumed they would be going to Ryder's plane, which was exactly where White and Patrice would go. And there would be nothing he could do about it because he would be trapped there when the GOE swept the area the moment the people had gone. He took a deep breath and waited, wholly unsure what to do.

Suddenly the station went dark again and the emergency lights came back on.

Christ, he thought. *Now what?*

"It's just us now, Mr. Marten." Conor White's British-accented voice suddenly came through the radio earpiece he had forgotten he still wore. His manner was calm, even gentle. *"I'd like to know who you are. Complex chap, I think. English landscape architect with an American accent. Quite the expert with a handgun. Killing people is relatively easy, but far different when they are trying to kill you first, like Branco's men in the Jaguar."*

Marten came alert. Who was Branco? Then he thought of the man in the Hotel Lisboa Chiado who'd been playing Anne's brother just before White came in. Clearly, he was one of his team.

"Carlos Branco. The bearded fellow driving the Alfa Romeo. One of two cars pursuing your ambulance before the incident with the fire truck."

Marten took out the earpiece and listened in the dark, hoping he could hear White speaking and get some sense of where he was.

"You arranged for the fire alarm to be pulled just

after you left the hospital. You nearly had Anne and Congressman Ryder killed in the process. Clever but foolish. You are not perfect."

Marten could hear White's voice through the earpiece but that was all. There was nothing else to suggest he was close by. Nevertheless, he was here somewhere. The business with the lights and letting the people go free meant he'd made some sort of deal with the police. Though it was hard to believe after he had just killed six of their men. On the other hand, he had to remember there was a strong possibility White was CIA. Meaning a dark political hand might well be maneuvering behind the scenes. There was something else he dared not forget. White hadn't received the Victoria Cross and his string of combat medals because he was timid. There was every reason to believe he had gotten out of worse situations than this on guile and guts alone. And then there was Patrice, who would be every bit as dangerous as White himself.

"Marten, why don't you come out and we can have a little chat about all this."

Marten put the earpiece back in, then eased up and peered over the top of the platform. The people were gone; so were the police. What was left was at once eerie and gruesome.

A long empty platform with the bodies of four dead bystanders sprawled across it, and with the corpses of Irish Jack near the tunnel entrance and Agent Grant not far away. All of it lit by a wash of emergency lights with the newspaper kiosk near the center and the entrances/exits at either end.

"Coming out, Marten?"

He checked the clip in the Glock, then felt in his pocket for the backup. The magazines held fifteen shots. Four had already been fired from the clip in the gun—one by Kovalenko when he'd killed Hauptkommissar Franck, the other three by himself as he fought against the men in the Jaguar. That meant he had eleven shots left before changing magazines.

"I'm waiting, Marten."

He pulled up his sleeve, touched the KEY TO TALK button on the radio unit, and spoke into its tiny microphone.

"You first."

123

Marten saw the four step into the light just inside the platform entrances. Two at either end. One of them wore a stylish black suit, had gray hair and a neatly trimmed beard, and was clearly the leader. There was little doubt he was Carlos Branco. The others, his compatriots, were armed with submachine guns, Uzis it looked like, and were clearly cut in the mold of the gunmen he had encountered in the Jaguar the night before. Curiously they did nothing but stand there. Maybe that was their intent, simply to block the exits and make certain he didn't get away. The fact that they were there and armed meant they had the blessing of the GOE. Something that, in turn, suggested that they, too, were somehow connected to the CIA.

Suddenly he realized something else: White knew Anne and Ryder had gotten out on the last train. That Branco was here meant he and White had communicated. In the process Branco would have learned that Anne and Ryder were gone.

"*Marten* . . ." White's voice rattled through his earpiece.

Marten stuck the Glock in his belt and took out the cell phone. He prayed that it would work in here and that Anne was somewhere where she could take a call. Fearfully he punched in the number she'd given him. He let out a breath as he heard it ring through. An instant later she clicked on.

"*Where are you? Are you alright? We've just left Baixa/Chiado station and are in a taxi to the airport.*"

"Don't go near Ryder's plane," he said with an emphatic whisper.

"*Why?*"

"White's people are here. The police let them in. It means the Agency knows you and Ryder are out and is assuming you're on your way to his plane. Can you arrange for another aircraft? You, not Ryder. They'll have his phone bugged. Maybe yours, too. Use a pay phone. Call somebody you know in the oil business or some other deep-pockets people you travel with. Can you do that?"

"Yes, I think."

"Then do it. Go somewhere, a park or something, and stay there until it's ready. When it is, get the hell to it and out of Lisbon."

"What about you?"

"I don't know about me. It doesn't matter." Marten glanced around. Branco and his men hadn't moved.

"Marten." Conor White was beginning to sound impatient. *"If we have to come get you we will."*

"Anne, do as I told you." Marten was resolute. "We had a lot of fun together. Maybe sometime we will again." With that he clicked off and slid the phone into his jacket. Then he lifted the Glock, hit the KEY TO TALK button and spoke into the microphone.

"Like I said, Colonel, you first."

Conor White glanced across the tunnel entrance at Patrice, or what little he could see of him in the dark. Suddenly there was the glint of a light on the rails behind them. Two pinpoints of light were coming down the tunnel in their direction. The automated Metro car Branco had promised. White looked at Patrice, then back down the tunnel. Something didn't feel right, but he didn't know what it was. Again came the feeling of impending doom. The otherworldly sense of Marten as a demon come to destroy him came flooding back. He had to be crushed and crushed now. A foot put on his neck and a bullet through his brain.

Marten saw the approaching lights too, then heard White's voice.

"I'm coming out, Marten. A big fat target for you. Come get me."

Marten could hear the icy confidence in his voice, the professional soldier anxious to do his murderous work once again. At the same time, he saw the faces of Marita and her medical students. Saw Raisa in her red hair and pink robe. Next came Bioko and the bodies of the native woman and her children, their throats cut, floating in the branches of the dead tree; Father Willy and the young boys clubbed to death by Tiombe's soldiers; the grotesque photographs of White and Patrice and Irish Jack lunching with General Mariano in the jungle; the soldiers with the flamethrowers and the naked man as he was burned alive. Then the Rossio Metro station and the GOEs as the balaclava-hooded White and his killers ambushed them outside. Agent Grant as he was gunned down on the platform scant moments earlier. Never in his life had he felt such contempt for a human being as he did now for Conor White.

"Make your move, you son of a bitch!" he spat into the microphone as the rail car neared, its approaching headlamps far too bright and garish for the scene. Suddenly a shadow dashed from the tunnel in front of it, jumped up on the platform, and ran across it. He raised the Glock and fired once, then a second time. Both shots missed, his rounds

ricocheting off the concrete walls. The train came
closer. Suddenly its lights revealed someone
crouched in the tunnel entrance. Patrice. An instant
later the same lights fell on him. Patrice swung the
M-4. Marten hit the ground between the tracks as a
burst from the M-4 chewed up the base of the concrete platform where he'd been. Once again he raised
the Glock and squeezed the trigger.

Boom! Boom! Boom!

The gunshots were ear shattering. Patrice was
caught square in the face and chest and toppled
backward into the tunnel. A blue arc of electricity
sparked as he fell across the third rail. A split second later a burst of 9 mm slugs from White's MP5
danced over his head, spraying off the tunnel
walls. Then the train was on top of him. He pushed
down, hugging the ground between the rails. With
a nearly silent whoosh the car went over him,
inches above his head. In a second he was up and at
the edge of the platform. He pulled himself up,
then rolled to one side and into deep shadow. Glock
at the ready, he got to one knee and looked around.
Where the hell was White? Where had his shots
come from?

There was a screech of brakes and the train
stopped. One man stood inside it, a machine pistol
in his hand. The doors slid open and he stepped out.

Kovalenko.

"Get the hell out of the light," Marten yelled.
"You're going to get killed!"

"Fuck you! Where's my memory card?"

"I don't have it!" Marten's eyes darted over the

area. Where was White? Where had he gone? He shifted the Glock to his left hand and raised his right, pushed the KEY TO TALK button, and spoke into the microphone in his sleeve.

"White," he said softly. "I'm here, near the tunnel. Come get me." Quickly he shifted the Glock back, holding it in a two-hand grip and slowly moving it back and forth over the area, his eyes alert, looking for any movement at all. He saw nothing but a faintly lit empty station with the bodies of Irish Jack and Agent Grant sprawled barely twenty feet apart and close at hand.

"Tovarich," Kovalenko said quietly and nodded toward the newspaper kiosk.

Marten moved forward. If White was there, he couldn't see him. Kovalenko came in from the side, the machine pistol up, his finger on the trigger. Suddenly Marten stopped.

There he was.

Inside the kiosk, his body in a sharp contrast of black and white, apparently sitting on a stool or something like it, staring blankly into the dark of the station.

Marten raised the Glock, unsure what was happening. Kovalenko eased closer. Slowly White turned his head toward Marten.

"He's dead," he said quietly. "He's dead," he repeated, then looked off once again.

Marten inched forward. What was going on? Was White playing some kind of trick?

"Careful, tovarich," Kovalenko warned.

"Throw the gun out!" Marten barked.

White didn't react.

"Throw the gun out! Now!"

Kovalenko looked to the left and saw Carlos Branco coming toward them in the dim light, a Beretta automatic in his hand. His men moved in from either side. All three carried Uzis.

Marten glanced at them, the Glock still trained on Conor White. "Stay back or I'll shoot him right now!" he ordered.

Branco stopped. So did his men.

White sat motionless, staring into the distance.

Marten glanced at Kovalenko. "Cover me."

Kovalenko nodded. Marten waited a half beat, then rushed the kiosk, fully expecting White to make a sudden move. But he didn't. Then Marten was in the kiosk and on top of him. All he saw was a tableau—White sitting in the center of the kiosk, half his face in light, the rest in deep shadow, a newspaper in his hands, the MP5 and a 9 mm SIG SAUER semiautomatic resting on a stack of magazines next to him. It might as well have been a still photograph.

Marten pushed the Glock against White's head, then eased over and carefully slid the weapons out of reach. He was still expecting a trick, a sudden move. None came. White just sat there staring at nothing, his chest rising and falling as he breathed. In a heartbeat the fight, the life, everything, seemed to have gone out of him. Marten lowered the Glock.

Kovalenko stepped in beside him. "What the hell happened?"

Marten shook his head. "Don't know."

" 'He's dead.' What was he talking about? The guy you shot in the tunnel?"

"Maybe."

Marten looked to the newspaper in White's hand, as if that might have had something to with it. It was a copy of that morning's copy of the *International Herald Tribune*. He could see part of a headline about a suicide bombing in the Middle East, a column about the ongoing global financial crisis, and a few more everyday items. Nothing that would bring a man like Conor White to his knees. Whatever had happened had to have been something else. Something physical. A small stroke. Some kind of mild heart attack. Who knew?

Kovalenko glanced at Carlos Branco. "One of White's men is dead inside the tunnel. The bodies on the platform. Several appear to be people caught in the crossfire. Another is from White's team. The last is Ryder's RSO guy."

"I know," Branco said.

"Marten and I are taking the train car out. When we get to where we're going, I'll send it back." He looked to Marten. "Give me the pistol."

Marten's eyes came up to Kovalenko's. "Why? What the hell are you going to do?"

"Just give it to me."

Marten glanced at Branco and then at his men. Finally and reluctantly he did as Kovalenko asked. The Russian took it, pulled out a handkerchief, then wiped off Marten's fingerprints and put the gun down next to White. Still the Englishman didn't move. Didn't even acknowledge their presence.

"Get on the train, tovarich." Kovalenko gestured with the machine pistol. "I want to talk about my memory card."

Marten looked at White once more, then walked off toward the train car. Kovalenko followed him inside and pressed a button. The doors closed and the car started back up the track the way it had come. Then they heard the boom of a single gunshot.

Marten looked at Kovalenko. "White. Branco shot him."

The Russian nodded. "White was CIA. Branco was freelancing for them."

"Then why did he kill him?"

"The chapter had to be ended, tovarich. They would be afraid of what might come out if he was put on trial."

"The police think I killed Franck and Theo Haas. They're going to have the same problem with me if I get caught. Branco would have known that. Why didn't he take care of me, too?"

"Because I paid him not to. He makes a lot of money not doing things."

"Anne got away, Ryder got away. And then he lets me go. What happens to him now?"

"He goes to his handler and says, 'We took care of White. His shooters are dead, too. Sorry, the rest didn't quite work out the way it was supposed to, but call me the next time you need me.' And they will. It's a dirty business all around."

Marten let out a sigh of disbelief, then looked back down the track toward the Rossio station. A tiny iris of bright at the end of a dark tunnel.

"Take off your clothes," Kovalenko said behind him.

"What?" Marten whirled around. The machine pistol was pointed at his chest.

"Strip search, tovarich. Take off your clothes! Socks, skivvies included. Turn everything inside out!"

"I don't have the memory card."

"Ms. Tidrow, no doubt, had the photographs, which would now be in the possession of Congressman Ryder. And very soon put into a diplomatic pouch. But you wouldn't have given her the memory card because you didn't really trust her. I saw that in Praia da Rocha. It means you kept it yourself."

"You're right, Yuri. I did have it. But I lost it. I'm not sure where."

Anger flashed across Kovalenko's face. "You plotted nicely to leave a trail I could follow, and you knew I would come once I realized you had made the switch. You counted on me helping you because you knew things were going to get tough. In doing that you would have also known such help would come with a price. I cannot go back to Moscow empty-handed, tovarich. If I do I will soon be out of a job. Maybe worse."

"You're not going empty-handed. You have a memory card. It shows any number of lovely young women sunbathing. Is it your fault Theo Haas had such a hobby?"

Suddenly Kovalenko stepped into the driver's cubicle and punched a button. Immediately the car slowed, then stopped midtunnel. He turned back and gestured with the machine pistol. "Take off your fucking clothes, tovarich. If I have to I will even check your asshole!"

124

They came out of the Martim Moniz Metro station in bright sunshine, damp sidewalks and puddles the only suggestion that a rainstorm had passed. A silver Peugeot was parked at the curb across the street, and Kovalenko nodded toward it.

Marten looked at him in surprise, if not admiration. "The train could have been sent in from the other direction. How did you know which way it would come?"

"It's my business to know."

Five minutes later Kovalenko was driving them past the Intendente Metro station and away from the city center. Two ambulances were parked outside it with two police cars behind them.

"Waiting for Branco's delivery," Marten said quietly. "I feel bad about Ryder's RSO detail. They were good men, both of them."

"Like I said, it's a dirty business." Kovalenko kept his eyes on the road. Thirty seconds went by, and then he looked at Marten. "I want you to know I'm very upset about the memory card. You did something with it. And don't tell me again you lost it. Where the hell is it?"

"What if I were to promise you the pictures will never be made public, nor will the CIA have them. None of them. 'The photographs and memory card you were after were either destroyed or never existed.' That's how the official record will read. The memory card you recovered is the only one there was. Knowing that, you can take it back to Moscow with a clear conscience and let your people examine it themselves. Soon everyone will smile and make jokes about what an awful job you're paid to do, but you'll be off the hook."

Kovalenko glared at him. "You design gardens in England. The photographs and most probably the memory card are now in the hands of a United States congressman. That means every security agency in Washington will know about them. So how can you promise such a thing?"

"Because I can. From me to you, Yuri."

"Bullshit."

"It's true."

Kovalenko looked off in disgust and then back at the road. They were traveling up a long tree-lined boulevard. Traffic was moving normally; people were chatting on street corners, going in and out of shops and offices, as if nothing out of the ordinary had happened. The way life usually is in cities, people getting on with their own lives and for the most part wholly unaware of what murderous intrigues may be going on around them, or in the subways beneath their feet.

Suddenly Marten grew wary. "Where the hell are we going?"

"To the airport. I'm sending you home and hope you stay there for many years. As I said to you a long time ago, tovarich, your English gardens are where you belong. This other kind of life does not suit you." Abruptly he looked at him. "I trust you haven't lost your passport."

"Yuri." Marten was more than apprehensive. "I can't go to an airport, not to a commercial airline anyway. I try to check in, the police will have me in handcuffs before I can turn around."

"Why, for the murders of Franck and Theo Haas?"

"Yes."

Kovalenko smiled. "As much as I'd like to see you in jail for stealing my memory card, don't worry about the police. It's why we left the Glock with Conor White. It's the gun that killed the Hauptkommissar. The authorities know he was in Praia da Rocha that same day. It also happens to be the gun that killed two of Branco's gunmen here in Lisbon. Last night, I believe." He looked at Marten accusatively. "Correct?"

"What was I supposed to do, let them kill me? It's why you gave me the thing in the first place. *Correct*?"

Kovalenko grinned. "If the police miss connecting the dots, Branco will help them, and rather quickly, I imagine, because he knows where I'm taking you. As for Theo Haas, his murderer was captured before Franck and I left Berlin."

"What?" Marten was stunned.

"The killer was a young man."

"With curly hair. I know, I chased him."

"When he was caught he confessed right away. Franck ordered it kept quiet. He wanted the photographs. You knew where they were. At least that's what we thought, so better to keep the pressure on. With luck some police agency would spot you and follow you until we got there. Which is exactly what happened and how we found you."

"Did you ever think that maybe I could have been shot dead in the process?"

"Sure, that could have happened."

"Christ!" Marten looked off, burning. Almost immediately he looked back. "Why?"

"Why what?"

"Why did the kid murder Theo Haas? He give a reason?"

"Yes." Kovalenko nodded. "He hated his writing."

125

• New Hampshire. Thursday, June 10. 8:03 P.M.

Nicholas Marten watched the newly leafed-out trees fly past in the summer twilight. Sugar maples, he thought, with some conifers in between and here and there oaks. The driver slowed and turned the Lincoln Town Car down a gravel road and through a thick stand of birch. The evening was gray, and a chill hung in the air. There were puddles in the roadway, and the surrounding forest was soggy from rain. More was promised.

Three days had passed since Kovalenko put him on a British Airways flight out of Lisbon for Manchester. As he had been promised, there had been no interference from the police, at least none that he knew of. He'd boarded the flight without incident and six hours later was back in his top-floor loft on Water Street that overlooked the River Irwell.

Physically and mentally exhausted; the reality that he was finally home barely registering, he'd immediately picked up the phone to call Anne after having failed to reach her from London during the layover for his connecting flight to Manchester. Each of his half-dozen calls had been answered by her voice mail. The same had happened again here. Finally he'd left a message giving her his home number and saying he'd returned there safely. Frustrated and increasingly anxious about her fate and Ryder's, he'd taken a shower, had a sandwich and a cold beer, then tried her once again with the same result. Afterward he'd gone to bed and slept without moving for ten hours.

The call had come early the following morning. Not from Anne but from President Harris. Ms. Tidrow and Congressman Ryder had, he'd said, arrived safely back in the country courtesy of a private jet she had arranged through an investment banker in Zurich. She was currently in the protective custody

of federal marshals and being held at an undis-
closed location. Congressman Ryder was in protective seclusion as well. Neither his family, his
office, nor the media knew he was back in the country. Both were to be secretly debriefed by a special
assistant appointed by U.S. Attorney General Julian
Kotteras. Kotteras wanted Marten's testimony as
well, as did Harris. Was he prepared to come to the
States to give it? His answer was "of course," and
he was asked to stand by for further directives. The
president's demeanor had been matter-of-fact, if
not distant, and Marten hadn't known why, because
they'd never had anything but a warm, even broth-
erly relationship. The reason, he thought, was either the pressure of something else altogether, or
because of what had happened to Raisa. He brought
it up.

"You know about Raisa."

"Yes."

"I'm sorry."

"So am I, thank you. We'll talk about it later."

And that had been the extent of it. Then the president had hung up, after saying he would get back to
him when he had more information.

After that he'd gone back to work at Fitzsimmons
and Justice, still exceedingly troubled by what had
taken place in Portugal and by the ongoing war in
Equatorial Guinea that seemed to have no end as
Tiombe's forces pushed hard against Abba's one day
with Abba's people countering the next. He was dis-
turbed as well—perplexed was more the word—by
what had happened to Conor White. That a man like

White had simply given up without a fight and let himself be killed made no sense. Still, troubled as he was, he knew there was nothing he could do about any of it so he tried to shift his life back into everyday mode. Twenty-four hours later President Harris called instructing him to fly to Portland, Maine, the following morning. A Secret Service agent would pick him up at the airport and drive him to a place where they would meet. He should be prepared to spend several days.

The driver eased the Town Car over a wooden bridge and then up a heavily forested hill. Here and there Marten glimpsed armed men among the trees, a periphery guard of Secret Service agents. At the top of the hill the road evened out and the thick woods gave way to cleared meadow. At the end was a large Victorian farmhouse set in a grove of conifers. Several black SUVs were parked in front. As they neared, he saw a sniper, and then a second, take up positions on the building's rooftop. Then they were there and two men in Windbreakers and blue jeans stepped out from between the SUVs. One of them opened the door.

"Good evening, Mr. Marten," he said. "The president is waiting for you."

They were sitting around a large conference table in the home's living room as he was ushered in. President Harris, Congressman Ryder, a man he recognized as Attorney General Kotteras, several others he didn't know, lawyers, he assumed, and Anne. Most were dressed casually. Anne wasn't. She wore a conservative business suit, her dark hair cut a little shorter than he remembered, expensive makeup done to perfection. Her eyes followed him as he crossed the room. He could almost read her thoughts. "*So this is your 'old girlfriend,' darling. You've been using me the whole fucking time, you cocksucker.*" On the other hand, there was the slightest hint of a sparkle in her eyes, as if beneath everything, she appreciated it all, even admired him for doing it.

"Mr. President, Congressman, Anne," he said formally.

"Please sit down," the president said as formally, then introduced the attorney general. The distance was still there, more so in person, Marten thought, than when Harris had called him in Manchester. "Would you like something to eat or drink?"

"No, thank you, sir."

The president looked at him. "The people here are aware that I asked you to go to Bioko to meet with Father Dorhn because of his brother's concern for him and for what he feared might be going on between the Striker Oil and Hadrian companies in Equatorial Guinea. In that regard you should know that President Tiombe resigned his office early this morning and has left the country. Abba and his people have taken over. The announcement will be made public tomorrow. We, the United Nations relief services, and a number of other countries are sending in humanitarian aid as we speak. The politics of it we will address after we see how Abba sets up his new government and determine if he is a man we want to trust and support, a consideration which, at the moment, seems to be running in his favor.

"I'm aware that you and Ms. Tidrow are greatly concerned about the welfare of the tribal people. As you know, I saw the CIA briefing video. Congressman Ryder and Mr. Kotteras have seen it, too. We've also looked over the photographs and have examined eight-by-ten prints made from the 35 mm negatives of the document known as The Hadrian Memorandum. The only thing missing seems to be the camera's original memory card, which I believe at one point you told me contained even more controversial pictures and which you had in your possession."

Suddenly Anne was looking at him. What was this? He'd given it to Kovalenko in Praia da Rocha. She'd seen him do it. He looked at her and smiled gently.

"I switched cards at the last minute," he confessed gently, then looked back to the president. "Mr. President, if I may."

The president nodded.

"Seeing you and Attorney General Kotteras here personally, and knowing the way Ms. Tidrow and Congressman Ryder have been kept in protective seclusion, I think it's safe to assume you've kept this whole thing very compartmented, an extremely close-to-the-vest, eyes-only investigation with just the people here and a few select others included on a need-to-know basis. With the exception of certain people in the Secret Service and the Marshals Service, neither the CIA nor any other agency has knowledge that this is taking place. Is that right?"

"The attorney general and I are old friends. We're here on a brief fishing trip. This house belongs to his family. That's all anyone knows."

"Then"—Marten stood up—"I imagine we're reasonably secure." He reached into his jacket pocket, lifted out a handkerchief, and unwrapped a small square object from it, then handed it to the president. "The memory card from Father Willy's camera. On it are at least two hundred more photographs of what was going on in Bioko, some of them, as I told you previously, far more damaging than those you've already seen."

Anne glared at him.

"Insurance." He smiled. "I kept it in case anything happened to the photographs, or to you. I put it in an envelope and addressed it to myself in Raisa's apartment. I forgot I had until we were in the hospital, then I asked Mário to mail it for me. I was afraid maybe he hadn't. It showed up in my mail a couple of days ago."

"And Kovalenko got the card with the indecent pictures of sunbathing nubiles," she said flatly.

A smile tugged at the corners of his mouth. "I don't know that they were all that indecent."

"Mr. Marten," the president cut in firmly. "You should know that Ms. Tidrow has agreed to tell us what she knows about the Striker/Hadrian arrangement in Iraq and the Striker/Hadrian/SimCo conspiracy to arm the rebels in Equatorial Guinea. You should also know that, aside from Mr. Ryder's investigation into possible violations of State Department contracts, the heads of all three companies may be charged in the World Court with sponsoring war crimes and crimes against humanity. Of particular interest will be the photographs of Conor White with General Mariano in the Bioko jungle that Ms. Tidrow has described and that I trust are on the memory card."

"Yes, they are."

"Mariano has already been convicted in absentia by that same judicial body for war crimes committed while he was a commander in the Chilean army under Augusto Pinochet. Attorney General Kotteras and Congressman Ryder believe members of the boards of directors of both Striker and Hadrian may be subject to prosecution as well, dependent on the depth of their involvement with company operations. Ms. Tidrow's testimony, while extremely helpful, will not shield her from prosecution if evidence of her complicity should be found. It's something she's been made aware of."

"Mr. President." Marten looked around the room. "I respectfully suggest that all of it was done in accord and agreement with in this Hadrian Memorandum that was drawn up by the deputy director of the Central Intelligence Agency. I don't think you would want that to come out in The Hague. And it would have to come out if Ms. Tidrow or myself, for that matter, were subpoenaed to appear, simply because we are both aware of the memorandum and what it contains. Also, Ms. Tidrow was at one time a CIA operative and would have knowledge of how these things work. Legally, I don't know how that would affect you or Congressman Ryder or Mr. Kotteras or the deputy director. Or if any or all of you might be called upon to publicly testify. The other principals—aside from Loyal Truex, headman at Hadrian, and probably one or two others at Striker—are dead, Conor White and Sy Wirth." Again Marten looked around the room; then his eyes came back to the president. "Could I see you alone for a few moments, Mr. President?"

They entered a large, wood-paneled library at the back of the house. The president closed the door, then went to a small bar and poured them each three solid fingers of Scotch. He handed a glass to Marten and they both sat down in worn leather chairs in front of a crackling fire that lessened the chill and dampness caused by the summer rain.

Marten took a sip of the Scotch and then looked to the president. "You're on edge, and I don't blame you."

"Yes, and I apologize." President Harris took a drink, then let his eyes find Marten's. "This has all gotten to me in a way it probably shouldn't have but did anyway. I should be thanking you, both as a close friend and as president, for what you did and had to go through. And I do thank you. But Raisa's death, how she was killed, made it deeply personal, maybe even more so than my concern for you. I set you up with her, I know. I apologize to you both. One day we'll get properly drunk and I'll tell you about her. But there's more to it than my own feelings. I'm going to tell you something you probably don't want to hear, but I sit in a chair that you don't, nor does anyone else, the attorney general and Congressman Ryder included."

The president got up and crossed the room to stare out at the damp, forested land surrounding them, as if just being in its presence gave him a moment of peace away from the overwhelming weight of the presidency. He watched for a few seconds more and then turned back to Marten. "At the risk of sounding parochial or corny—that comes with the job, too." He smiled a little. "It's my responsibility and sworn oath to protect the people and the Constitution of United States of America to the best of my ability and at the same time, and to one degree or another, keep a clear eye on what else is going on in the world. That said, what the deputy director authorized in the memorandum, I would very likely have done myself, but with, God help me, God help us all, a much softer touch. Having that much oil under our control is a guarantee we can't be blackmailed over petroleum for decades even as we work toward finding other sources of energy. It's insurance against something going catastrophically wrong, like having our entire oil supply shut down overnight by some cabal or unforeseen circumstance. The deputy director learned about the Bioko field and that the leases were owned by an American company and recognized how strategically important it was for us to control it. That the company and its partner were having legal problems in Iraq was beside the point. There was a very unstable political climate and it was his job to see that the oil was protected. He did it the way he thought it should be done, by support- ing the side most likely to prevail without overtly involving the United States government."

The president came back to his chair, picked up his glass, and sat down.

"As you know, the position of the director of the Central Intelligence Agency is a political appoint- ment. The deputy director's chair is a career posi- tion, and the person occupying it is the one who in fact runs the Agency. He or she is where they are because they've worked their way up through the ranks and know how things work and where the all the skeletons are, and the skeletons behind them. I can tell the director what I want done and he can pass it on to the deputy director, but that directive doesn't stop that person from covertly doing what they think is right or see fit. The trouble is, I can't have that person making our foreign policy and in effect hiring gunslingers where the result is the kind of human ruin we've seen in Equatorial Guinea. It's one thing to quietly back an insurrection that has merit and benefits, especially against a dictator like Tiombe, but you can't bring in mass murderers like Mariano and give them carte blanche to pump up the music and burn people alive. There's something terribly wrong in that kind of thinking. It's got to change, and it will change, I assure you. It's one of the reasons the attorney general is here, to get as much firsthand information as he can to help us find a way to bring the situation under control."

Marten looked at him directly. "That was pretty much what Anne said when she gave me the film of the Memorandum and why she did what she did to find it and photograph it in the first place. I seriously doubt that even as a member of the Striker board of directors she had any idea that the company was involved in the war. She did know she was violating the law and at the same time betraying the Agency, her country, her company, and herself when she hacked in and copied the document. Believe me when I tell you the whole process devastated her. But she was looking for anything she could find that might slow down the war and stop the slaughter. Any one of us would have done the same thing, you included."

"I understand that, Nick, and fully appreciate what she did. But what happens to her is not up to me."

"You can put in a good word."

"Yes, and I will."

Marten took another drink, put the glass down, then stood and crossed to the fireplace to stare into it. "CIA practices aside, right now you need Abba's unconditional trust and support more than ever, but you can't let it appear that, other than leading the cause for humanitarian aid, the U.S. is soliciting it. Correct?"

Harris nodded.

"May I offer a suggestion?"

"Of course."

"First, I would like you to promise me something."

"What?"

"It has to do with a personal pledge I made in Lisbon."

EPILOGUE

PART ONE

• Manchester, England.
Wednesday, September 22. 10:35 A.M.

Marten stood with a three-man survey team as they mapped the landscape of a forty-acre parcel of forest and meadow a private organization wished to turn into a park as a gift to the city. The day was sunny and warm with big puffy clouds overhead. The surveyors moved off and down a long grade, carrying their transits, tripods, bipods, levels, and other equipment, giving him a moment alone. As he watched them he realized there was really no need for him to be there at all. They were measuring raw land, nothing more. They certainly didn't need a landscape architect looking over their shoulder; his work would come after theirs was completed and he had their drawings. It made him realize, too, that he had been pretty much doing this kind of thing since he'd come back from New Hampshire. Keeping inordinately busy. Working, then going home to work some more, meticulously poring over everything he had done that day and planning for the next, and on top of it sketching out ways the firm might expand into other areas of the new "greening" world.

He saw women from time to time and enjoyed their company, but with no real enthusiasm for a lasting relationship. One time Lady Clementine Simpson had come up from London to visit old friends from her days there as a university professor. She'd abruptly awakened him in the middle of the night with a sharp knock on the door, the same as she had several years before when she'd suddenly arrived to announce that her marriage was over and ask if she could spend the night. Two days later she went back to London; then she and her husband reconciled and they returned to Japan where he was still the British ambassador. This time she not only woke him but brought the proud news that she was pregnant. Discussion of that and its consequences lasted until five in the morning, when she'd suddenly stood up, kissed him, and told him she still loved him and probably should have married him, then abruptly left to catch the early train back to London.

Now, as he watched the surveyors set up near the bottom of the hill, he let his thoughts drift back to his conversation with President Harris in the private library at the heavily guarded farmhouse in New Hampshire.

"I guaranteed the Russian agent, Yuri Kovalenko, that the Bioko photographs would never be released, especially not to Washington's security agencies, where, for any number of reasons, they might be leaked. If they were, he would be put in a very compromising position that could cost him his life. The only reason I'm not ashes in an urn somewhere is because of him. I gave him my word because I trusted you would back me up, not just because of our relationship but because I knew you were concerned the Russians might circulate the CIA video and wouldn't want the photographs released, either. Without them there's no evidence that Striker or Hadrian or SimCo was involved in the war, meaning the video alone would be nothing more than a clandestine record of the atrocities Tiombe practiced against his own people and of little use for either propaganda or blackmail."

He remembered President Harris listening carefully and then telling him that he would do everything he could to see that Kovalenko's life and reputation were not put in jeopardy but that he could not guarantee the photographs would not be brought forth if the matter went to trial. Marten told the president he was aware of that and in the pause that followed offered his suggestion.

"Mr. President," he'd said, "you want the backing of Abba and his people. This other stuff comes out, General Mariano, the memorandum—all or part of it—and suddenly Abba's not a friend but an enemy. World opinion of you and the U.S. will be ugly, maybe even provoke violence, and you'll have the Russians and probably the Chinese stepping all over themselves to secure the Bioko leases. All the things you worried about when I told you about the photographs in the first place. Yes, you can go to trial against Striker and Hadrian and SimCo or—"

"Or what? Just forget about it? Is that your idea?"

"Hear me out."

"Go ahead."

"Somebody takes Hadrian's Loyal Truex aside and strongly recommends that he get out of the protective security business. Maybe announce that the company made mistakes in Iraq and has decided to change its name and go in a different direction. As for Striker, the real heavy there was Sy Wirth, and he's dead. Anne's father built the business from the ground up, and she wants to shed its tarnished image with Hadrian. She's been in and around the oil business her entire life. Give her the reins. Let her run the company."

"And do what?"

"Equatorial Guinea is a tiny, impoverished country that's been stomped into the ground by Tiombe and dictators before him. Abba appears to be some kind of democratic savior, but he has nothing to work with, so the best he can do is try to heal the misery the war has left behind, something that can take years to achieve, if it can ever be done at all. So let Striker stay there and exploit the Bioko field with Anne as boss and with the caveat the company give Abba's government eighty percent of the gross oil revenue after costs are realized. And with a caveat to Abba that the money be used for infrastructure— clean water systems, sewage treatment plants, schools, hospitals, paved roads, things like that, and with a chunk of it put into the development of new businesses. Maybe even arrange for a third party to oversee the transfer and allocation of funds to make sure they go where they're supposed to. You and I both know that sooner or later the idea of oil as a major energy source is going to slide into history, and you can't have an entire country lifted up from nothing to something approaching a decent life that is wholly dependent on something that is going to vanish and leave them with nothing.

"I may sound like a dreamer, but what I'm suggesting can work. I was there. I saw those people and the conditions they live under. Poverty and abuse by Tiombe and his regime is the reason why Abba came to power and why all the disparate tribes united behind him. He gave them hope and they followed, but now Tiombe is gone and the war is over. As well-intentioned as Abba might be, he's got to deliver on that hope or he'll have a tribal backlash on his hands with people wondering what they did all this for and looking for a new leader.

"The size of the country makes it manageable. The oil is there. Striker has its equipment and people in place. Everything's ready to go. Unless Abba's a fool, and you don't seem to think he is, he'll be more than happy to accept his eighty percent, caveats and all, because it gives him the chance to prove he was the right man all along and the opportunity to make his country look like a model for other emerging nations. More than that, if it's done right, and Anne can certainly do it, Striker Oil will be seen as a company that cares with its checkbook about the people and places where it operates, and the image of a greedy American corporation elbowing its way into the riches of third world countries like Equatorial Guinea will slowly begin to fade. Geopolitical suspicions about other motives can be left to the pundits."

Marten remembered sitting in that little den of a

library waiting for the president to dismiss everything he'd said. But he didn't. Instead he smiled, finished his drink, and stood up. "Cousin," he said, "I think you have the makings of a true politician." With that he crossed to the door and was gone.

"Mr. Marten, we need you for a few moments." Marten's musings were suddenly broken by one of the survey crew coming up the hill toward him.

"Sure," he said and followed the man back down the hill to where the others waited. He looked out over the land as he went—the rolling meadows, the great copses of wood, the clouds rolling overhead. Autumn was in the air. Fresh and sweet. This was where he wanted to be. This was what gave him life. He'd had enough blood and violence to last a dozen lifetimes. He'd killed three men in Lisbon, four if you counted the motorcycle rider, and, much to his horror, had done it well and without remorse.

"I think you're one of those people trouble follows around," Marita had said. Well, maybe so, but now it was resolutely in the past and he vowed it would remain that way for the rest of his life.

PART TWO

• The Squire Cross Pub, Oxford Street. 7:30 P.M.

Marten ordered a pint of Banks & Taylor Golden Fox ale and his favorite chicken curry with balsamic rice, naan bread, and mango chutney. The food had come, but he hadn't touched it. Instead he was working on his third Banks & Taylor.

He'd read the letter three times when he'd gotten home and twice more here. Now he picked it up again. It was a copy of a correspondence that had arrived in the day's mail and been sent to him from Moscow with no return address. A scrawled note had accompanied it.

See International Herald Tribune, *dated Monday, June 7, bottom of page one.*

That had been all. Just the copy of the letter and the note. There was no need to wonder who'd sent it. Kovalenko.

The letter itself was brief and hugely personal and, to Marten at least, very moving. It had been sent, most ironically, in the form of a memo and dated a day before the incident at the Rossio Metro station in Lisbon.

TO: *Colin Conor White*
FROM: *EKR*
Dated: *4 June*

Dear Son,

I began this note many times over the years, and each time I crumbled it up and threw it away out of shame and embarrassment and perhaps the fear that my wife and children would find out.

Finally I came to realize that the matter was my own, not theirs, and that I am getting on. I would not want to leave this life without having reached out to you to tell you how very proud I am of your accomplishments and how sorry I am not to have accepted your kind invitation to stand alongside you when you received the VC.

I know that you have tried numerous times to contact me in one way or another. That I did not respond is nothing more than a sad showing of personal weakness. If you would still be open to it, I would very much like us to meet, if to do nothing more than shake hands and perhaps share a pint and get to know each other as best we might. Since I have no idea where you are or where your current travels have taken you, I have sent this on to your old SAS regiment with the request that it be forwarded to you. I have also left word with my private secretary to immediately put us in touch, should you respond. You would, of course, know the phone number. By mail: House of Commons, London, SW1A 0AA.

I very much look forward to your response and,
of course, to seeing you.

Your loving father,
EKR

Following Kovalenko's directive that he see the
Monday, June 7, edition of the *International Herald
Tribune*, bottom of page one. Marten had accessed
the paper's Web site and brought up the edition of the
day in question, then quickly scrolled to the bottom
of the first page, where he saw the photograph of a
distinguished, silver-haired man. Above it was the
caption

SIR EDWARD KERCHER RAINES, DECORATED
BRITISH WAR HERO, LONGTIME MEMBER
OF PARLIAMENT, DEAD AT 75.

There was no need to read the story; the caption
told it all, its tragic revelation made all the more
chilling when one knew it had been the paper
clutched in Conor White's hand as he sat motionless
in the dim light of the subway kiosk. It was what he
was referring to when he'd looked to Marten and
said *"He's dead."*

Clearly, Raines was a father he'd never met but
very much wanted to. In that moment when he'd
slipped into the kiosk, prepared to use it as a blind
from which to ambush Marten, he must have inadvertently seen the newspaper and been instantly shat-
tered. There was little doubt it was the reason he had
acted as he had.

Marten left the Squire Cross Pub and walked slowly back to his apartment. The night was crisp and clear, the moon nearly full. People were out, the traffic heavy, the air filled with the sounds of the city. He paid little attention to any of it. His thoughts were on Conor White, and he wondered if he'd invested his entire life, physically and emotionally, in trying to gain his father's recognition; if he had chosen the career he had for no other reason than to prove himself worthy. Then, like that—a photograph and a caption in a newspaper—any possibility of it ever happening had been stripped away. The emotional blow would have been staggering, his life suddenly become meaningless. The grand heartbreak of it was that he had died never knowing his father's note of reconciliation was in the mail.

Walking on he thought how important a figure Anne's father had been in her life. The difference was, they had been able to share it. Some of the journey, especially that surrounding her mother's illness and death and later her father's, had been rough. Still, some big portion of their lives had been rich and filled with adventure and joy and love.

For the first time in years, Marten thought of his own father. Not the caring, loving adoptive father he and Rebecca had grown up with in California but his birth father. He wondered if he was still alive and, if so, where. Who he was. What he had done for a living. How old he would be. His birth mother, he knew, had died from a heart ailment only weeks after he'd been born. But his birth father, even with open public records, he'd been able to find nothing about. The name he'd given when he put him up for adoption, James Bergen, turned out to have been false, as was the address where he said he lived. Why he had lied about those things and why he had given him up were questions that would haunt him forever.

Marten turned down Liverpool Road. His apartment was nearby, but he chose instead to take the long way to it and walk along the river. The lights and life of the city reflected off its surface, the rising moon giving it an almost magical silver shimmer. For a moment he thought of the young curly-haired man who had murdered Theo Haas. His gut feeling, as he'd chased him toward the Brandenburg Gate, had been right—that he was not a professional killer but a madman. Or, in retrospect, an overzealous critic. Disliking a book or play or film is one thing. Murdering the writer because of it, quite another.

A boat moved slowly past, its wake breaking the smoothness of the river's surface and sending ribbons of moonglow rippling across it. He thought now of Anne and their last moments together in New Hampshire. They had left the farmhouse and gone to walk in the woods to be alone. President Harris and Congressman Ryder had left hours before, and Attorney General Kotteras was preparing to leave then, as they would within the hour. His suggestion to the president, that in lieu of prosecution Anne be allowed to take over the company and continue to develop the Bioko field with the bulk of the profits going to the people of Equatorial Guinea, had been received with merit and discussed at length between the parties. But no final decision had been made. Nor had the topic been brought up on their walk.

She could have asked him about his shooting to death of the men in Lisbon and his rather remarkable ability with firearms. Or about his warning to the drug pusher in Berlin that he was an L.A. cop. Or how he had come to be so close a confidant of the president of the United States. But she hadn't. In fact, little had been said at all. They simply walked under gray skies through the still-damp woods, glad to be alive and in each other's company. More than once they stopped and hugged and looked into each other's eyes. "I love you," one or the other might have said, but neither did. That she was a few years older than he made no difference. Their worlds were far removed and wholly different, yet they had shared more in a few short days than most people would in a lifetime. Nonetheless it was time to move on and, in doing so, best to leave some things unsaid.

It was just after nine when he climbed the stairs to his apartment on Water Street. The phone was ringing as he came in the door and he picked up.

"Mr. Nicholas Marten?" a female voice with a Manchester accent asked.

"Yes."

"This is the H&H Delivery Service. We have a

parcel for you that is perishable. Will you be home in the next hour?"

"I will, yes. Thank you," he said without thinking and hung up.

He glanced once more at the letter from Conor White's father, then put it away. As he did, the thought suddenly struck—what was the H&H Delivery Service? He'd never heard of it. Furthermore who delivered something "perishable" after nine o'clock at night?

In the next moment his doorbell rang.

"Christ!" he breathed. The image of Carlos Branco flashed across his mind. Maybe the CIA had told him to go back and finish the job. Whoever it was had probably been outside watching, waiting for him to return, then, when he did, rang him up to make sure he had gone to his apartment and not someone else's. The doorbell chimed again. He wished to hell he still had the Glock. In its stead he picked up a baseball bat he'd bought in New Hampshire as a kind of nostalgic souvenir of the American life that still resonated in his soul, turned out the light and went to the door. He waited a moment then carefully opened it and peered out. There was no one there. The stairs were directly across, and he could hear someone rushing down them. Immediately he went to the balustrade and looked over the side. He glimpsed a hand on the lower railing, and then the front door opened and whoever it was went out. Just then he heard a sharp cry behind him. He whirled.

What he saw was a big wicker basket padded with a dark green blanket. In the center of it, its face poking over the side, eyes brown as the richest soil, its coat as black as shining coal, was a Newfoundland puppy. Eight, nine weeks old at most.

It was love at first sight for both, and they stared at each other unmoving and unblinking for a long time. Then Marten put down the bat and picked up the dog, holding it above his head, all the while grinning from ear to ear. The pup was a male, and he could feel its strength as it struggled in his grip. He brought it close and got a big, wet, sloppy doggy kiss for his trouble. Then he saw the tag around its neck and dropped to one knee to read it.

Bruno wanted you to have the pick of his first litter. He knew you'd make a great dad.

Suddenly an immense feeling of sadness and vulnerability swept over him. With Bruno Junior cradled in one arm, Marten eased into the worn leather chair he used for reading. For all the joy and purity of the little fellow nestled in his lap; for all the warmth and thoughtfulness of Anne; for however hugely thankful he was to be safely home and back doing the work he loved, what he had seen and experienced on the journey that began those long months ago in Bioko weighed on him more deeply than he ever could have imagined. The words President Harris used when they were alone in the library in New Hampshire—"This has all gotten to me in a way it probably shouldn't have but did anyway"—cut into him like a scalpel.

He took a deep breath and then another. Finally

he looked down and saw the puppy watching him the way his father, Bruno the Elder, had in the VW bus as Stump Logan drove them toward Lisbon—as if he understood everything that was going on inside him. It was then he realized he had tears in his eyes. They were tears for what people did to one another. For the victims of the violence and injustice he had witnessed every day of his life on the LAPD, and later seen again in France and Russia and Spain, then, much too recently and horribly, in Equatorial Guinea, and on his voyage from there until his return home. But tears could not change the past nor correct the future. All he could do now was breathe in the sweet innocence of the puppy in his arms and try with everything he had not to think of the horrors embedded in his heart.

ACKNOWLEDGMENTS

For technical information and advice I am particularly indebted to my friend and fellow writer Chase Brandon, retired CIA operations officer, clandestine services, who provided immeasurable counsel regarding the politics, mind-set, and inner workings of the CIA, and who was instrumental in preparing the formal text for the "Memorandum" itself; and to Anthony Chapa, assistant director (retired), United States Secret Service; Paul Tippin, former homicide investigator, Los Angeles Police Department; noted German mystery writer Hartmann Schmige was particularly helpful in providing information about Berlin and the Berlin police; Norton F. Kristy, Ph.D., gave me valuable insight into the psychological motivations of the characters.

For suggestions and corrections to the manuscript I particularly grateful to Eric Raab, with a very special thank-you to India Cooper. I am also indebted to my agent, Robert Gottlieb; and to Tom Doherty, Linda Quinton, and Robert Gleason for their continued enthusiasm and support of my work.

Finally, I want to thank Jeffrey Weber, M.D., and Thomas Woliver, M.D., whose caring and expertise made the writing of this book possible.

THE HADRIAN MEMORANDUM

was not the beginning—read more
from *New York Times* bestselling author

ALLAN FOLSOM

THE
EXILE

978-0-7653-4835-7 • Paperback

THE
MACHIAVELLI
COVENANT

978-0-7653-5158-6 • Paperback

If you want to know more of the adventures of Nicholas
Marten; his past with the LAPD; how and why he was forced
to change his name and relocate to England; about his sister
Rebecca and the enigmatic Lady Clementine Simpson; how
he came to know the Russian agent Yuri Kovalenko; and how
he became such close friends with John Henry Harris, the
president of the United States; those stories are told at length
in *The Exile* and *The Machiavelli Covenant*.

tor-forge.com